Blue Water & Me

Tall Tales of Adventures With My Father

Pendelton C. Wallace

Julie,
Smooth Sailing

Aberdeen Bay

Harbin - Washington, D.C. - San Diego

Aberdeen Bay
Published by Aberdeen Bay, an imprint of Champion Writers.
www.aberdeenbay.com

Copyright © Pendelton C. Wallace, 2011

International Standard Book Number
ISBN-13: 978-1-60830-072-3
ISBN-10: 1-60830-072-2

Printed in the United States of America.

Foreword

Papa was in his thirties an Chips was and old man when they met in the depths of the Depression. Chips followed the sea all of his life, starting out in square-rigged sailing ships. He took Papa under his arm, taught him to sail, filled his head with visions of far away ports, exotic women and the lore of the sea.

Chips was long dead before I came into the picture, yet he lives as a vivid character in my mind. Papa shared Chips' stories with me. I was enthralled by the excitement and adventure of the sea-going life. By the time we shared that magical summer in 1962, Papa was pushing sixty. He was the old man and I was the novice.

Papa is gone now and I am the old man. I sit here at my keyboard reflecting on the cycle of life. Some old sea-dog taught Chips about the sea. Chips passed his knowledge to Papa. Papa taught me. Now, to close the circle, it's my turn to pass on that legacy.

Readers ask "Is this story true? Could all these things really have happened to one person?"

These stories are true to the best of my memory. It has been half a century since these events took place. Time has a way of messing with memory. Many of these tales were told to me by Papa and his friends. What can I say? They were fisherman. Everyone knows that fishermen never lie.

There are a couple of places where I tell the stories out of sequence, to make the flow of the book smoother. And I borrowed two stories, one that happened to Santos and one that happened to Mama. But they actually happened.

I sit here writing this introduction at the mess table of my sailboat, the *Victory*, on a cold, wet Northwest July morning. It may take a year or so to get ready, but I will set sail again. I'm headed for the warm blue waters of Baja, to have one last chance to relive the adventures in this story. Come to think of it, that's just what Papa did in the summer of '62.

Penn Wallace
On board the *Victory*
7/16/2011

Acknowledgements

I want to thank my mother first. When she first read the manuscript for *Blue Water & Me* she was mad at me for three weeks. A very private person, she did not want the intimate details of her life paraded in public. But like all good mothers, she wanted me to succeed. Eventually she gave me her blessings and permissions to write anything I wanted about Papa and her.

Many thanks to the members of my first book group, Karen Heines, Gordon Steward and Dave Gross. They suffered with Papa and me through revision after revision, helping to polish the book down to something readable.

I must also thank the members of my second writers group, Jaricia Jaycox Nirula, Steve White, Doniella Boaz and Leslie Adkins. They didn't struggle through the labor pains on *Blue Water & Me*, but they taught me so much about writing and became such close friends that I would be remiss in not acknowledging them.

Next, a big thank you to Barbara Sjoholm, my developmental editor. She took a wildly scattered manuscript and helped me hone it into a coherent story. In her wake she left hundreds of pages on the cutting room floor.

Of course I must thank Jill Cline and Ross Murphy from Aberdeen Bay Press. Jill first recognized the merit in my manuscript. After she was forced to leave Aberdeen Bay Press because of a family emergency, Ross picked up and carried the project to conclusion.

I must thank my late wife Connie and daughters, Katie and Libby. Without their support and understanding, this book would never have been written. My heart breaks that Connie never got to see the final copy. She always told me that "I'll wait until its printed before I read it." I hope you can read it from where ever you are now.

Now, I save the best for last. Susan Aaron Moller is my best friend and confidant. She has read and re-read this manuscript so many times that she could probably recite it in her sleep. Many of the improvements in the story are Susie's.

For over twenty years she has selflessly edited everything I've written from college term papers to suspense novels.

And to all of you, who are reading this book, I say thank you. Without a reading public, there is no point to writing in the first place. Keep reading. I don't care what you read or what format you read it in. The written word is our most powerful tool for passing on and preserving knowledge. I salute you.

I hope you enjoy this little tale. As for me, I think it's time to go sailing.

Penn Wallace
Lynnwood, Washington
July 16, 2011

Part 1

Chapter 1

I Go To Sea

"*Pescado*," Papa yells as he tosses a fish over his shoulder. He turns and reaches back, grabbing the jig and wiggling the hook free. He tosses the line back into the warm tropical water, as soon as it hits the water another fish takes it, stretching the line out bar taut. Excitement ripples though his body like electricity.

I dream about Papa often. I'm a grown man with a family of my own now, but in my dreams he is always young and vital, the way I remember him from our days fishing, not a wizened old man in a wheelchair. I sit in my office in a Seattle high-rise and look out the window. I stare past the Space Needle to the clear, blue water of Elliot Bay and remember Papa.

We're on the *Marine View*, standing in the cockpit, side by side, pulling albacore. The *Marine View* seems alive as she climbs the face of a swell, then surfs down its back side, occasionally bucking like a bronco. The steady rhythm of her little Ford diesel is her heart-beat.

It's a good school. They're biting as fast as we can pull them in. The jig poles bend back with the weight of a couple hundred pounds of tuna on each pole. Salt air tickles my nose. I feel the briny taste on my tongue and the warm breeze caresses my skin. We have a following sea. The boat's stern drops into the trough and the sea rises behind us. I look up and see the rainbow colored fish streaking towards us over my head; then the wave passes under us, lifting the boat until Papa and I are standing on the edge of a watery cliff, looking down into the blue abyss beneath our feet.

The tuna is a fierce fighter. The line tears at my fingers as I haul it in hand over hand. When the fish is up to the boat Papa reaches down with a long handled gaff and hooks the fish in the gills. The sea passes beneath the boat, giving us a lift, and he heaves on the handle, flipping the heavy fish over his shoulders onto the deck. Time after time the torpedo-shaped fish strain against my muscles. I hear the hum of the line as the albacore fight against it, the slap of the fishes' tails as they hit the deck.

Then I awaken. Lying in my cozy bed on a cold, dark winter morning, the wind howls through the trees outside my window. I luxuriate in the warmth of the dream. Having the chance to see Papa again, to spend a few precious moments at his side fills me with an inner glow. Over the years and distance, the bond that we built that summer still pulls me towards him. I feel him every time I pick up one of his tools, plot a course on a chart or take the helm of my boat. He is always walking beside me.

Tall and thin, Papa had pale blue eyes that could cut through you like a saber or twinkle with mischief. In my mind's eye I see him in an open collared work shirt, light blue dungarees, his sea boots rolled down. He wears his ever-present sailor's cap at what he called a "go to hell" angle, covering the neatly trimmed ring of white hair that encircles his bald head. One foot up on the bulwark, his fists on his hips he tosses his head back in a laugh. The memory reminds me of Errol Flynn playing Robin Hood, where he says "Welcome to Sherwood Forrest." I will always see Papa treading across the planet in his seven league boots.

Papa was a big strong Scotsman, I looked up to him like some Olympic god, throwing lightning bolts down at the mere mortals, laughing in the face of adversity. Everything he did was of heroic proportions.

I first went to sea with Papa in 1959, shortly after my eighth birthday.

"You're getting old enough to go fishing now, *Mijo,*" he told me. "When you get out of school this summer, you can come along on a fishing trip."

Papa moored the *Marine View* on a float out in the middle of the harbor at Newport Beach, California, rather than at a dock or marina. It was much less expensive. To get to her, we had to put our skiff, which we named *Corky,* into the water and row out. I worried about the *Marine View* being moored out in the harbor. I was afraid she'd be lonely, away from the other boats.

During that winter we built *Corky,* an eight foot pram, to use as our shore boat. She was built mostly out of marine plywood. We worked in the carport of our house in Costa Mesa.

"Hold the sheet of plywood for me, *Mijo,* and watch your hands." Papa and I lifted the clean, sweet-smelling sheet of half inch marine plywood onto two saw horses. Using full-sized plans printed on tissue paper, he traced the shapes onto the plywood. I held the sheet steady while he cut the pieces out with his saber-saw. It was loud and noisy and I ended up covered in sawdust, but I loved it. I was working with my father and I could see the boat take shape, come to life.

"OK, now you can start sanding," Papa told me when we had the major components cut out. "Start with a medium grit and when you get it good and smooth, switch to a fine grit." I spent hours with a sheet of sandpaper wrapped around a block of wood smoothing the plywood until it was like a baby's bottom. In the meantime, Papa cut out the frames. It was ready to be assembled.

"We're going to glue the pieces together with Weldwood Glue." Papa carefully measured the powdered glue out of the little orange can and mixed it with the prescribed amount of water, stirring it with a little stick.

"Why can't we just nail it together? It'll be faster."

"We want this boat to last. You have to be patient and do it right."

So we clamped the sides and the ends onto the skiff with Papa's long bar clamps, adding one piece at a time. I just wanted to be done and go play with it.

After what seemed like a lifetime of sanding, shaping, and gluing we added the final touch: a coat of paint. The hull was buff like the masts on an old sailing ship, the gunnels and seats bright white. Brass oar locks completed her traditional look.

Putting the back seat down on the 1953 Ford station wagon we slid *Corky* into the back. She stuck out the rear, so we tied her down and put on a red flag. When we got to the beach, we carried the skiff from the parking lot to the water. It was about one hundred yards, but carrying a boat through beach sand, it seemed like miles.

Even though I was only eight years old, I always held up my end of the skiff. I was big and strong for my age and it was a matter of pride that I never dropped her no matter how much I thought my arms were going to come out of their sockets, I couldn't let Papa down.

Once we got the skiff to the water, we made trips back and forth to the car to bring our tools, supplies and other assorted items that we needed to ferry out to the boat. When the skiff was loaded, I climbed onto the center seat and Papa shoved us off into the water.

He taught me to row a boat. He sat in the back seat and held out his hand vertically in front of him.

"Don't look over your shoulder, you don't need to see where you're going. Look at my hand, I'll tell you where to go." If he pointed his hand to my left, I needed to steer the skiff to the left; if he pointed it to my right, I steered to the right.

I got really good at rowing the skiff. I learned to row

with both oars and steer by rowing with only one oar at a time, to rotate the oars with one oar in the water at a time, to row backwards and forwards. I learned to pick out a mark on shore directly behind the boat to keep my course straight.

As spring approached I was in a whirl of excitement. I didn't even pay attention to baseball and spring training that year; I was so worked up about going fishing.

May came, and Papa spent all of his spare time working on the *Marine View*. I helped him on weekends, but missed most of the work because I was in school.

The *Marine View* was a working boat. She wasn't one of those racy young things that dashed about the harbor, but a solid, beamy old girl designed to last a lifetime of hard work. Papa used to tell me that when he was growing up, his mother told him, "Son, when you get ready to get married, you find yourself a Texas girl. No matter how bad things get, she's already seen worse." The *Marine View* was a Texas girl.

Thirty-six feet long, her hull and deck house were painted white, her decks and trim were buff colored. Her bulwarks were tan with dark brown cap rails. She had a tall buff colored mast, painted white at the top, with jig poles on either side. Her foredeck was raised and aft of the small deck house her fish hold hatch cover sat forward of, the engine room hatch cover.

Papa moved the *Marine View* to the public dock to prepare for the upcoming tuna season. He realized that he needed a deck hand because he wasn't planning on my being much help. As usual, he didn't want to have to pay full shares. At eight years old, I did not understand how hard the times were, but while Papa was working on the boat, getting ready to go fishing, a steady stream of fishermen walked up and hailed him from the dock. It seemed like everyone was looking for a berth (job).

"Say, Cap, you goin' after albacore?"

"Yep, they should be off of *Cedros* Island in a couple of weeks."

"You need a deck hand?"

"You have any experience?"

"Yeah, I been two seasons on the *Lucky Strike* with Portagee John and three seasons with Bob on the *Sea King*."

"You need a full share then. I don't have any positions for a full share man."

In the fishing fleet when the catch was brought into port and sold it was divided by the time-honored share system. Half the income went to the boat. Two shares went to the captain because he ran the boat and found the fish. The cook got a share and a half because, in addition to working as a fish puller, he had the additional responsibilities of getting up before everyone else and fixing breakfast, cooking all meals and keeping the galley clean (or as close to clean as you can get on a fishing boat). If the boat had an engineer, he would get a share and a half. That left the deck hands with one share a piece. If it was a large boat and there were rookies on board, they might get a half share or a third share since they were learning their trade.

The proceeds of the catch would be divided by however many shares there were on the boat and paid out in cash. A large boat with a big crew had more shares to pay out, but because it could hold a larger catch, it could mean a bigger payday for each man.

June arrived and Papa was ready to go fishing, but I was still in school. He started getting reports of albacore off of Baja California and couldn't wait. As was his usual habit, he hired an inexperienced deck hand who knew nothing about fishing. They made a couple of trips with mediocre results.

Then school was out. I was free to go fishing at last. On my first trip Papa took Tom, the green deck hand, with us. Papa had one berth, Tom had the other and I slept on a shelf at the bow of the boat with a cut-down mattress. I was in heaven.

"You read the compass here," Papa told me as he pointed to the little arrow on the box compass. I wasn't tall enough to see over the dash board so Papa found a milk crate for me to stand on. "I'll give you a course, say two hundred seventy degrees, and you need to keep the boat going that way. If you start to swing to port, give her a little starboard rudder. If you start to swing to starboard, give her a little port rudder." He stood beside me with his hand on my shoulder. I stood on the old wooden milk crate staring intently at the compass, paying no attention to the world outside. At first, I cut a zigzag course across the ocean as I made big corrections, then went off course the other way. Eventually, I cut down my corrections and learned to anticipate the boat coming back on her heading. I was holding my course, but could have been running into anything. Finally, as I learned to steer the boat. Papa told me that I took to the sea like I was born to it. I guess, in a way, I was.

Tying knots was imperative. Many times a seaman's life and those of his shipmates might depend upon his ability to tie a knot that would hold or one that could just as easily be untied.

"This is a square knot," Papa instructed. "It's one of the most useful knots. You use it to tie two pieces of line together. You have to be careful though. If you don't get it right, you'll have a granny knot. It looks a lot like a square knot, but won't hold worth a damn. Now look at this, you go right over left, then left over right." He slowly patiently taught me the fine art of knot tying. I soon mastered the square knot, then the bowline, used to attach lines to some fixed object, and the clove hitch, used to tie the boat to a bollard.

Next he taught me how to splice and seize lines. Splicing two lines together was a much more permanent solution than tying them with a knot. Splicing involves unraveling a length of the line, then braiding the unraveled length back into the line to form a loop or intertwining it with another line. Sometimes you needed to join two lines together, sometimes you needed to put a permanent loop in the end of the line or maybe fasten the line around a thimble. Everything was new and exciting for me.

Seizing was used to protect the ends of the line from unraveling. Papa showed me how to take small twine and wrap it around the end of a line or over a splice and pass it back through itself so that it wouldn't come lose. When we were done seizing the line, he dipped it into a can of varnish to make the end hard.

As the boat left the protection of the Newport Beach jetty, we encountered a large swell. The boat rode up over the top of the wave, then slid down into the trough. This was repeated time after time, hundreds of times an hour, day after day. It became as normal as the floor of the house being fixed and unmoving.

"You know, I'd never have a thirty-eight foot boat," Tom told us as we ran south.

"Why not, Tom?" Papa asked.

"Because the seas are exactly thirty-eight feet apart. A thirty-eight footer will get hung up with the bow on one wave and the stern on another. That's how they break their backs."

"Where the hell did you hear that cock-and-bull story?" Papa asked.

"I was listening to a couple of old fishermen in the tavern just before we left."

Papa roared in laughter.

"Did you ever go snipe hunting when you were a kid?"

"Yeah, we were on a camping trip and my uncle told us we were going snipe hunting. He gave each of us a gunny sack, a flash light and a stick. He told us we were supposed to catch the snipes sleeping on the ground and beat them over the head with the stick."

"Did you catch any?"

"Of course not. There's no such thing as snipes. He was just hazing us on our first camping trip. Oh . . ." Tom's mouth hung open, his face flushed red. "I guess they got me, huh?"

While Papa and Tom were busy fishing or handling the boat, much of my time was spent playing pretend games. The companion way ladder between the deck house and the fo'c'sle (the living quarters in the front part of the boat) was the perfect place for me to make a desperate last stand against boarding pirates. I could climb the rat lines to the top of the mast and look out for new lands to discover. I would stand in the bow, holding on to the forestay and be on the forepeak of a Viking long ship. We had seen the Tony Curtis movie *The Vikings* the year before and I was fascinated with Vikings.

The sump in the fish hold was the lowest point on the boat. Papa poured a ton of concrete into the bottom of the boat for ballast when he built her. He left a square box about eighteen inches across at the aft end of the fish hold to collect any water that accumulated in the boat. In the sump a powerful bilge pump sucked the water up and sent it overboard.

I listened to Papa and his fishing friends talking about the tides since I was little. I hadn't figured out what was so important about tides yet, but I knew they were important. Why else would they be such a frequent topic of discussion?

Often, when I didn't have anything else to do, I slid the fish hold hatch cover open, climbed down into the hold and checked the sump. I convinced myself that I could tell the state of the tides by the amount of water in the sump. If the sump was empty, we would be on an ebb tide (low tide), if the sump was full, it was a floodtide (high tide) and if it was really full, then it must be a spring tide (the highest tides of all). Of course, when hundreds of miles out to sea, the tides had no impact on our boat or our fishing.

"Shark!" Tom yelled.

Looking in the direction he was pointing I saw a dark gray fin cutting through the water parallel to our course. "It's a big one."

"He's pacing us, waiting to steal our fish." Papa appeared from out of nowhere with his old British Enfield rifle in hand. The rifle was war surplus, from World War I.

After spending his boyhood in frontier Texas and eight years in the Army, Papa was an expert with firearms. The ancient Enfield had an adjustable rear sight. When you were shooting at a close-up target, you left the sight down and lined up the bead on the front of the barrel with the notch on the rear of the rifle. But the Enfield had a range of almost three miles. To aim at a distant target, you had to take the pull of gravity into account. To solve this problem, the sight assembly flipped up for a distant target. It was calibrated on the left side by the hundreds of yards. On the right side of the assembly there was a little dial that you used to move the notch up and down until you had it at the appropriate distance marker. This caused the barrel to be tilted up when you sighted it in and compensated for the effect of gravity as the bullet traveled through the air.

Papa quickly, efficiently, raised the rear sight and dialed it in for the estimated distance, chambered a round and put the heavy rifle to his shoulder.

A loud explosion rent the air. The recoil from the huge rifle was so strong that Papa's shoulder was kicked back a good six inches.

A white spout of water erupted just this side of the fin. The shark arched in the air, a red trail behind it, pieces of flesh flying in the air. The great beast rolled over in the water.

"Watch this," Papa said.

In a matter of minutes we spotted another shark fin, then another, then another. Soon the surface of the sea was covered with them. The water boiled, arriving sharks swirled around the dead beast, grabbing great chunks out of its flesh, fighting and biting at each other in their frenzy to get at the food.

"That'll take care of the bastards," Papa told me. "The sharks'll be so busy eating the one I shot that they'll fall behind our school. Sharks can smell blood in the water. They have one of the most highly developed senses of smell of all fish. When they smell the blood, they get excited and go crazy."

Among Papa's many talents was predicting the weather. He could look at the sky, the moon, the stars and tell what the weather was going to be tomorrow. He looked at the swell on the ocean and battened down the hatches.

"We're in for a blow," he'd say, or "Gonna have a nice day tomorrow."

I never understood what he saw or how he knew it, but he was never wrong.

When the fish were biting, it was my job to operate the boat and Papa and Tom pulled the fish. At night Papa cooked dinner, but I always cleaned up the galley. I was used to washing the dishes at home with my sister, Quita, so it was no big deal.

One of my favorite jobs was stacking and icing down the big fish. I probably weighed eighty or ninety pounds. The fish averaged from twenty to thirty pounds so it was a struggle, but I always managed to wrestle them to the right bins. Then I got to ice them down. We had a big, flat shovel, much like a snow shovel, that I used to shovel ice over them. It was so hot on deck that it felt good to be working in the freezing fish hold, besides it was more fun than scrubbing down the decks to get rid of all the fish scales and blood.

We didn't get rich that trip, but we caught enough fish

to pay our expenses. At the end of the trip Papa paid Tom off and told him he wasn't needed anymore.

I swelled with pride when Papa told me "You were a lot more use to me than Tom. From now on it will just be the two of us." I felt like I had just passed into manhood.

Chapter 2

The *Munashima Maru*

We spent the next couple of days ashore tending to loose ends, making small repairs, getting ready for my first big trip as a full-fledged deck hand. Late in the afternoon the *Marine View* took us over to the Standard Oil fuel dock. We filled her tanks with diesel oil and fresh water, then iced down her fish hold. The *Marine* View felt like she just had Thanksgiving dinner. While we were alongside the dock, we took the opportunity to load our stores.

It took endless trips back and forth between the boat and our old Ford station wagon to get ready for the trip. Boxes of food, frozen goods, cases of beer and root beer, bags of bread, eggs and canned goods all had to be ferried aboard, as well as our sea bags and personal luggage. It seemed like an endless night. When everything was stowed, Mama took the Ford home so she could use it while we were gone.

In the early hours of the morning Papa made us a big breakfast and we got ready to shove off. He wanted to sail with the tide. Around five thirty in the morning the tide began to ebb and we headed out on our great adventure.

It was still dark when we cast off, but as we cleared the jetty, the sun broke clear of the land. The sky behind us, over the land, turned a brilliant red. Before long the summer sun marched across the clear sky.

The day was perfect, the sea relatively calm. A gentle breeze tickled our hair (at least my hair), the sun provided a delicious warmth. At first we were alone on the sea, then we started seeing other working boats. Later in the morning we started to see sailboats and big motor yachts. Everyone was out on a day like this.

The *Marine* View was happy to be back to sea. She frolicked through the endless waves like a colt through a pasture. The day dragged on and we got further and further from shore. Finally, late in the morning we were alone on the vast Pacific Ocean.

"PC, I want you to take a wheel watch. I'm bushed. I'm going below to catch a quick nap."

"I'm tired too, why can't I have a nap?"

"You can go next. I need to get an hour or so's sleep so that I can run the boat." And that was that. You didn't argue with Papa.

Since I couldn't see out the windows, I jumped up on the galley counter; it was much more comfortable than standing on my milk crate. Sitting on the counter, I could see out of all the deck house windows. The boat was steered by our somewhat problematic Hill-Cunningham automatic pilot.

Papa went below and crawled into his bunk. I was miffed.

"Why can't I have the first nap?" I asked the *Marine View*. "I worked just as hard as he did and I deserve it."

The sun beat in through the glass windows and raised the cabin temperature. The *Marine View's* smooth motion rocked me like I was in a cradle. She knew I was tired and wanted to help me get some rest. Before I knew it, I was having a problem keeping my eyes open.

Scanning the ocean in all directions, there was nothing to see. No land, no boats, no fish, no nothing.

"I'm gonna just close my eyes for a few minutes." I told her.

What seemed like an instant later I awoke to an ear splitting blast. To this day I still hear the loud, low

OOOOOOOOH, OOOOH, OOOOH in my nightmares.

There was a massive green wall in front of us. I blinked, looked up and couldn't see the top of the barrier. My heart seemed to run wild, I could feel it pounding in my throat. *Where had they come from? How could a giant ship just materialize out of thin air?* Jumping down from the counter, I flipped the auto-pilot off and grabbed the tiller bar as Papa came clawing his way up the companionway ladder.

"Jesus Christ," Papa yelled as he looked out the window. I was more surprised to hear him cussing than I was to see the giant ship in our path. Time seemed to freeze.

Papa grabbed the tiller bar from me and spun it around but we couldn't turn in time. I darted from the deckhouse to the side deck, I don't know what I was planning on doing on the deck, but I had to get closer to the action. The *Marine* View climbed the enormous bow wave put out by the giant ship, surfed down the backside and smashed into the green wall. She shrieked in pain. I heard the sound of wood splintering. For an instant, she seemed to stand on her head, her bow hidden in a wave of white water, then she righted herself and the water cascaded back over the foredeck. Papa clung to the tiller, but I was thrown off my feet. As I tumbled through the air I saw the short plank over the bow shatter and the brass roller we used to pull up the anchor line hang in mid-air for what seemed like hours, then disappear into the water. Knowing that the roller had cost us five dollars, I was more concerned with losing it than I was with losing our lives.

We hit the wall so hard that we bounced off. Our momentum pushed us forward again; so we rammed the ship a second time. As I crawled back into the deckhouse I saw water rushing into the fo'c's'le. We were sinking.

"Should I get *Corky* off of the deck house roof?" I yelled. My voice cracked in panic.

Papa looked down into the fo'c's'le and saw the water

flooding in. Loose articles swirled around in the maelstrom. I fought down the fear, but Papa had faith in the *Marine* View's ability to withstand the disaster.

"No, we're better off staying with the boat." His reply was short and clipped as he reached for the radio transmitter, switched on the set and sent out an SOS.

"Mayday, Mayday, Mayday, this is the fishing vessel *Marine View* calling the ship that we just rammed, over." There was dead silence on the radio. When we hit the ship, our radio antenna, which was attached to the top of the mast, snapped off. We couldn't receive and we couldn't broadcast.

My anger swelled as the ship continued on its course. They must have known that we hit them and were in big trouble, but they just kept on going.

"Why don't they stop? They must know that we hit them." I whined. I could feel the heat rising in my face.

"A ship that big is difficult to maneuver." Papa responded. "It takes about three miles to come to a complete stop. A turn could take more than a mile."

All we could do was follow the ship. Far from land, they were our only life-line. Papa stood at the helm and fell in behind them. The water stopped rising in the fo'c'sle, but the *Marine View* was bow down. She wallowed like a wounded pig as each sea passed underneath. Her rudder and propeller were out of the water, she was virtually out of control. When a wave moved under our stern, the propeller caught and moved us forward, as the wave continued further aft, the stern came out of the water and the propeller whirled in the air. The rudder couldn't get a grip in the water either and we were unable to alter course.

My heart raced and it was hard to get air. My breaths came short and fast. For the first time in my life, I experienced the rush of adrenaline that comes with the fight or flight response. I wanted to escape but there was no place to run. Papa, after his first emotional response, was as calm as Sunday morning.

Somewhere deep inside of me I knew that if he wasn't scared, then I was going to be all right.

After an eternity, the ship came to a full stop. We limped up to her, but the *Marine View* was out of control, she couldn't stop when we came along side, so we rammed them for a third time. Once again I heard her cry out in pain with crunch of splintering wood as we struggled to get her under control.

From high up on deck, the freighter's crew dropped us a massive two inch line. Papa made this fast to the tow bit on the bow. Then they dropped a second line that he made fast to a cleat on the stern. Now that we were securely tied to the freighter I felt a sense of relief, at least now we wouldn't sink.

"What ship are you and where are you bound?" Papa yelled up at them. The tiny figures in white uniforms on deck looked at each other and spoke in some unintelligible tongue. They shouted back down to us, but we couldn't understand them.

"Doesn't anyone speak English?" Papa shouted.

"Ah, so, Engrish," they replied, but no one started speaking to us. We hung off of the side of the ship forever. Finally, the young second engineering officer came up out of their engine room.

"Yes, yes," he said. "We are *Munashima Maru*. We out of San Pedro."

"Where are you bound?"

"Yokohama." There was a long silence. "We pickie you up and set you on deck." This was a perfectly logical solution to the problem. After all, at thirty-six feet long, we were the same size as the ship's lifeboats. "We drop lines to pickie you up."

"No, you call the Coast Guard. They'll come get us."

"No, no, we have to keep schedule. Can't wait for Coast Guard. We pickie you up."

With that they dropped lines from their davits as if they were retrieving one of their life boats. Papa refused to allow them to pick us up.

"Can you imagine Mama's face when I call her and tell her we're in Japan?"

"You come up on deck where you be safer," instructed the officer.

"No, I'll stay here."

"You send boy up." The young officer was plainly frustrated and concerned for our safety. "He be safer on deck." With that they dropped a rope ladder down the side of the ship.

"PC, you go ahead. Climb on up the ladder."

"No, I want to stay with you." Despite the fright and fear of the last hour, I felt that my place was at Papa's side. What if he needed me? I couldn't help him from the deck of the ship.

"You'll be a lot safer on their deck than on our boat. I'll come along when I can."

It was a long climb on the swinging rope ladder. Half the time I was swaying away from the ships side, hanging over open water, and half the time I was banging against the steel hull. Pausing half way up, I looked down on our mast. Suddenly I realized the peril that I was in, suspended high over the tossing sea. Fighting down the rising tide of panic, I caught my breath and continued climbing. Finally, I reached the bulwark and they lifted me over it and set me down on the steel deck. Blood dripped from my knuckles where they bashed against the ship's side.

The *Marine View* looked like a toy far below us.

We were tied up to the Japanese freighter for what seemed like hours. At around noon the engineering officer invited me to lunch. Never one to miss a meal, I readily accepted I was amazed as the young officer led me into their deck house. The officers' mess hall was a long room, paneled with dark wood, the floor was covered in a deep green carpet. There were tables with white table cloths, crystal glassware and fine silver tableware. Each table had a steward in a white uniform with white gloves assigned to it. We wanted for nothing. The engineering officer had some sort of soup with noodles and all kinds of vegetables in it. They graciously prepared a hamburger for me.

"You like Coca-Cora?" the second engineer asked.

"No, do you have root beer?"

I was fascinated by the luxury of the big freighter. In addition to carrying thirty thousand of tons of cargo, they had passenger quarters in the deck house. There were accommodations for forty or fifty first class passengers.

After lunch the engineer took me to the bridge deck to see how the ship ran. The sheer size of everything overwhelmed me. There was a huge teak wheel, just like the ones in the pirate movies. We were far, far above the water. The *Marine View* looked like a bath tub toy.

Papa refused to climb the ladder up to the ship. He knew that if he left the boat, they would hoist her on board and we would be off for Japan. He would have no leverage standing on their deck. The size and luxury of the ship so captivated me that I didn't think going to Japan would be such a bad idea, it would be a grand adventure.

Finally the ship's captain relented and called the Coast Guard. The Coast Guard dispatched a ninety foot cutter to pick us up and tow us in. We stayed tied to the ship's side for hours before the cutter finally got there.

When the cutter arrived, they tied up to our other side. Sandwiched between the *Munashima Maru* and the big cutter I thought we'd be crushed. The ship acted like a sea wall and we felt like we were on a perfectly calm sea. With the cutter along side of us, I climbed back down the ladder, disappointed to leave this fantasy ship. A young Coast Guard officer came aboard to talk with Papa and assess the damage. He decided that we would float long enough to make it back to Newport

Beach.

The huge freighter cast off their lines and continued on their way. We had a bow line and a stern line attached to the cutter as she lay on our lee side. As the ship moved away, the seas started to buffet us and the *Marine View* bucked against the side of the big cutter. The captain gave the order to get underway and we took a terrible beating.

"C'mon," the Coastie said under his breath. "Gi'me the order to cast off." The cutter needed to cast off the stern line and allow us to follow behind them on the line attached to the tow bit on our bow.

"Why doesn't he cast off, Papa?" I asked.

"Because he has to follow orders. The skipper hasn't given him the order to cast off yet."

"But we're getting smashed against their side. He should just cast off." Anger was rising in my throat.

"He can't. He'll get into a lot of trouble if he does something without an order."

It seemed to me to be a silly way to live. If you knew what needed to be done, then you should just go ahead and do it. It was stupid to have to wait for someone else to tell you to do what you already knew needed to be done.

While we were being towed in, the captain of the cutter invited me aboard for a tour of his ship, my second tour that day. Although much smaller than the big freighter, it was still an enormous vessel, three times the size of our boat. It had a large crew. The engines were taller than a man. The machinery was huge. It had a cannon on the foredeck and machine guns on each side of the bridge. I liked the cutter much more than the big freighter, because it was lean and fast and had cannons.

Unlike the Japanese freighter, the Coast Guard cutter didn't have a teak wheel. Instead, it had a big polished stainless steel wheel that reminded me of the war movies where the helmsman on a destroyer spins the wheel to quickly change course. I pictured John Wayne giving the order "left full rudder, all ahead flank."

The telegraph on the bridge that the captain used to communicate with the engine room intrigued me. The captain didn't have direct control of the engines from the bridge like on smaller boats. He pushed the lever on the telegraph forward until a bell rang. This told the engineers that a new command was coming. Then he set the lever in the position representing the speed he wanted to travel. The engineers saw this on their version of the telegraph and adjusted the engines accordingly. There was also a speaking tube that captain yelled in to talk to the engineers two decks below.

Our run-in with the *Munashima Maru* was a disaster for Papa, but a great adventure for me.

The Coast Guardsmen were very good to us. They towed us back in to Newport Beach and all the way to Hans Dickman's Boat Yard where we put the boat on the ways.

The ways are marine railways. They are rail road tracks that extend down into the water and a flat car that runs up and down the rails, powered by a big old gasoline engine turning a winch with a huge steel cable on it. The cable is let out, the car is lowered into the water and the boat is brought over the car and secured. Then the cable is pulled in, bringing the car out of the water and the boat is high and dry.

Water shot from the *Marine View's* bow like arterial bleeding when we hauled her out. The planks split where they joined the stem post and hundreds of gallons of water flooded in. Because of the watertight bulkheads, the water flooded the fo'c'sle, but did not invade the rest of the boat. The other two water tight compartments kept the boat afloat. This same technology was invented for and first deployed on a large ocean liner named the *SS Titanic*.

Papa called Mama to come pick us up and take us home but there was no answer. He called again and again and got no answer. Finally we resigned ourselves to spending the night on the boat as it set on the ways. We cooked dinner in the galley and slept in our bunks. Because the bunks were high above the water line, they remained dry.

The next morning, Mama, my big sister, Quita, and my two little brothers showed up at the boat yard. They heard on the radio about a boat accident and knew it was us. The reason they had not answered the phone the night before was because Aunt Gussie took them out to a Chinese dinner to celebrate all the money we were going to make fishing.

That was the end of our fishing season. I didn't understand the financial implications at the time, but the accident was a disaster for our family. Papa not only lost the money he spent outfitting the boat for the fishing season, but he could not afford to take the time off from work to repair the boat. To make matters worse, he couldn't afford to just let the boat sit in the boatyard because Hans Dickman charged him by the day for using his space.

As usual, we managed to get by somehow on the dimes and quarters Mama brought home from her tips at the restaurant every night. I could feel the tension between Mama and Papa.

"Tell your father to pass the potatoes," Mama told me at dinner on Sunday night.

"Tell your mother we need more milk," Papa replied. This went on for three weeks, with neither of them willing to speak directly to the other. Somehow or other I was always selected as the intermediary.

The rest of the summer was spent repairing the boat. Every morning Papa got me up early and we were out of the house before Mama awoke. By the time that Mama got home in the evening we were already in bed. We repaired, replaced and refastened every plank in the forward section of the *Marine*

View. By the time she was back in the water, the albacore disappeared and I had to go back to school.

Papa had a sadness about him. He no longer was in the jovial mood that we shared when we were building the boat. He no longer talked about the adventures we would have or the money we would make. He never said a word of condemnation to me. I was too naive to even realize the predicament into which I had put the family.

When the repairs were complete, Papa moored the boat for the winter and went back to the Carpenters Union Hall to put his name on the hiring list. As usual, I worried about the *Marine View* being lonely, moored in the harbor far from the other boats. I also wondered if she had healed and felt as good as new or if she would show the effects of her injuries. Soon Papa was back at work building tract houses.

"I'm looking for Pendelton C. Wallace." The deputy sheriff stood in the doorway of our little green house in Costa Mesa.

"What do you want with Penny?" Papa asked. He was not pleased with the idea of the police knocking at our door. I couldn't imagine what kind of trouble I was in.

"I can only discuss that with Mr. Wallace. Are you Pendelton Wallace?"

"No, that's my son." He pointed at me. "What you have to say to him, you can say to me."

"I have a subpoena for him."

With the excitement of a new school year I quickly forgot about the accident, but the collision between the *Marine View* and the *Munashima Maru* had become an international incident. A tribunal was called to establish blame and assess damages. The Japanese shipping company had subpoenaed me as a witness.

Mama, Papa and I drove up to San Pedro for the hearing. This was a serious matter for Mama and Papa. We didn't have two nickels to rub together, we couldn't afford to hire a lawyer and if damages were assessed against us, we had no way to pay them.

For me it was an exciting excuse to miss a day of school.

We arrived at the typical cold gray government building in the morning. Since I was being called as a witness, I was not allowed sit in the court room while the other witnesses testified. They needed to keep witnesses separate so that it didn't contaminate our testimony. Each witness was assigned to a different waiting room.

"I might have scraped two bits worth of paint off of their hull," I heard Papa tell the Coast Guard captain who chaired the hearing as I was led out of the courtroom. "I'll be happy to go down and repaint the scratch." The captain wasn't amused.

The morning dragged on. Mama went out and bought me an Uncle Scrooge comic book to keep me occupied. It was OK, but I preferred Batman or the Green Lantern. Finally, the hearing broke for lunch.

Mama, Papa and I walked down the street to a little diner where we had hamburgers for lunch. This was a rare treat for me; missing school, getting a comic book, eating in a restaurant.

After lunch, a bailiff called me to the witness stand. Mama brought me into the court room. She never looked prettier. Dressed in a soft, fuzzy, pink sweater, a full skirt and high heels, she had a little pink pill-box hat on her long, soft black hair and carried a pink purse. With her head erect, her eyes straight forward and her heels clicking on the tile floors, she led me into the Valley of Death.

The room looked like the one in the Perry Mason TV show. There were dark wooden benches for the spectators and a wooden rail separating the benches from the attorney's tables. At the front of the room was a large, wooden table raised on a sort of dais. Behind the table were several older men in immaculate white Coast Guard uniforms. To the right of the table was a jury box. To the left of the dais was another table at floor level that was occupied by several younger people in the same white uniforms. Everybody took themselves very seriously.

At the attorney's table, on the left side of the courtroom, several older Japanese men in business suits and the captain of the *Munashima Maru,* in his dress whites, sat with an American man. He was an older gentleman, tall but somewhat stooped. He had a bushy white mustache, a full head of white hair and was immaculately dressed with a handkerchief in his suit coat pocket that matched his tie.

At the table on the right Papa sat by himself. He was dressed in his Balboa Blues, deck shoes and a white dress shirt buttoned at the collar. He looked very out of place, out-numbered and out-gunned.

A pretty young woman in a white uniform led me to the witness stand. I stood behind the little railing in front of a big wooden chair.

"Place your left hand on the Bible and raise your right hand, please," she instructed me. "Do you swear to tell the truth, the whole truth and nothing but the truth, so help you God?"

What a ridiculous question. Mama and Papa raised me to tell the truth, all the time, even when I knew it was going to get me in trouble. I wanted to defend my honor, how dare they ask me if I was honest? But I had watched enough Perry Mason TV shows to know that the proper answer was "I do."

The American man at the other table got up and slowly walked over to the witness stand. He stood for a minute, just looking at me. I fidgeted in the hard wooden chair. I couldn't get comfortable and my hair kept falling into my eyes.

"Hello Penny, I'm Mr. Anderson."

"Hi."

"Penny, I understand that you were on watch when this accident occurred."

"Yes, sir." He turned and smirked at the officers behind the table.

"Why were you on watch at this time, Penny," Mr. Anderson asked.

"Papa was tired and wanted to get some sleep." I had the feeling I was telling something I shouldn't, but I had to tell the truth. "We'd been up all night getting the boat ready for our trip."

"I see. And you were up all night with him?"

"Yes sir." I fidgeted in my chair.

"And were you tired too?"

"Yes sir. I wanted to take the first nap."

"I see. And why didn't you get the first nap. Why did your father take a nap instead?"

"He said that he needed to be rested enough to run the boat."

"There were just the two of you on the boat?"

"Yes sir." I had a vaguely uneasy feeling about the questions he was asking.

"Did it ever occur to him that an eight year old boy might not be competent to stand a wheel watch?" He was addressing the officers of the court more than he was asking me a question.

"No sir." I sat up proudly in the hard chair. "The last trip we had a deck hand with us, but Papa said that I was a bigger help to him than Tom, so he let him go."

"Hmm. . . " Mr. Anderson turned from me and walked over to an easel. "There is a magnetic diagram of the ships on this easel. Could you please position each vessel in the position it was in when you first saw the *Munashima Maru*."

I got up, went over to the easel and moved the vessels into the proper positions. Mr. Anderson raised an eyebrow as I put the large magnet that represented the *Munashima Maru* in the center of the diagram, then put the smaller magnet that represented the *Marine View* on its right side and returned to the witness stand.

"Now, Penny, how come you didn't change your course to avoid the collision?"

I dropped my head and answered softly. "I fell asleep. I didn't see the ship until we were too close to it to change course."

"If you were asleep, how could your boat continue on its course?"

"We have a Hill and Cunningham automatic pilot. You set the course, then pull out the knob and it keeps the boat on that same heading."

"Well, I am amazed at the level of technical knowledge our young witness has," he said to the court. I rankled at the sarcasm in his voice, but didn't know what to do, so I just sat there.

Finally, he was done.

"Captain Wallace, do you have any questions for this witness?" asked the captain who served as President of the Court.

"No, sir."

Since I was done testifying, I was allowed to sit in the spectator section and watch the rest of the hearing. It was boring. The American lawyer called witness after witness from the Japanese ship's crew. Through an interpreter, they all told the same story.

They saw our boat, but were sure that we would change course to avoid them. We were smaller and much more maneuverable. By the time they realized that we were not going to change course, it was too late for them to change course and avoid the collision.

I read my comic book and dozed off. Finally, Mama woke me up and said it was time to go home.

"How did we do?" I asked, "Did we win?" I was too young to understand how the world worked, but it was like David against Goliath. I had unending faith in my father's ability to come out on top of any situation.

"We won't know their decision for a couple of weeks." There was a sadness in Papa's voice.

Several weeks later, when I had all but forgotten about the hearing, Papa received a letter from the US Coast Guard. They found in our favor. The *Munashima Maru* violated the international rules of the road when they failed to yield the right of way to us. The court ordered them to pay restitution. Papa received a check for seven hundred and fifty dollars to pay for the repairs to the boat. That seemed like all the money in the world. We were amazed. The repairs, that Papa and I had done ourselves, cost less than one hundred dollars.

Papa never scolded me about the accident. Never a word of condemnation or any punishment was meted out to me. Papa felt that he was responsible for the collision. The tension between Mama and Papa continued.

Quita and I shared a room across the hall from Mama and Papa. I lay awake at night listening to them fight in the next room.

"Charles, this has to stop. You can't keep running off and leaving us. You can't keep sinking money into that boat."

"It was an accident, Vicki. I didn't plan to hit the damned Jap steamer. If not for that, we could have made good money this summer."

"It's always if. If this and if that. When are you going to settle down and start supporting the family? We have four children now. I can't be mother AND father to them AND support the family at the same time."

"It's over. The boat's tied up for the winter. Just leave it alone."

"How could you have just gone to sleep and left Penny running the boat?" Mama continued.

"It was my fault, Mama. I should never have left Penny on watch. He isn't old enough yet to be responsible."

I was crushed. I wanted to get up and run in their room shouting "Of course I'm responsible." How could Papa think that? There was nothing in the world worse than Papa's disapproval. I had failed him once, but I vowed that I would never let him down again. Tears rolled down my cheeks as I sobbed quietly and eventually slipped off to sleep.

The accident sealed the end of Papa's fishing career. He tied the boat up to a mooring buoy in Newport Harbor and went back to work as a carpenter. The day that we unloaded all of our gear from her, there were rust stains running down her bow from her running lights. It looked for all the world like the *Marine View* was crying. If she wasn't, I was. I cried all the way home and long into the night.

That winter Mama and Papa made plans to leave California. The following summer we went on a camping trip to Oregon to find a new home. On Saint Patrick's Day in 1961 we left our old life behind us and embarked on a new adventure.

Chapter 3

My Magical Summer Begins

My legal name is Pendelton Carroll Wallace. I was named after my great-grandfather, a Civil War hero. Over the years, Papa called me by many names. When I was little, everyone called me Penny, but by the time I was in the fourth grade I chafed at the diminutive name. Shortly after we moved to Oregon in 1961 we decided that I should be called Pen, with one "N." On the first day at my new school the teacher introduced me to her other students.

"Listen up, everyone," Mrs. MacVicker said, "we have a new student in class today. His name is Penn Wallace." With that she wrote my name, P-e-n-n, with two "N's" on the blackboard. I was terribly embarrassed that I had misspelled my own name. Penn, with two "N's" stuck.

When Papa was feeling intimate with me, he called me *mijo* which is a contraction for *mi hijo*, "my son," in Spanish. In his later years he reverted to calling me *mijo* almost exclusively.

Papa was the only one who ever called me PC. It is funny, but even now, three decades after he last called me PC, I still call myself PC when I talk to myself.

Papa had something on his mind as we sat down to dinner that wet Sunday evening. We always had our big family discussions at Sunday dinner.

Our family meetings could go one of two ways. Either Mama and Papa could lay down new laws and restrictions for us or we could discuss plans for some exciting future adventure.

***

Mama and Papa always worked out their differences in private, then laid down the law for us. It was very unusual for Papa to bring an issue to Mama at Sunday dinner.

"Mama, I've been thinking about the *Marine View*." Papa's soft drawn out vowel tones gave just a hint of his Southern upbringing.

Mama gave him a cold stare. The mashed potatoes froze in her hand as she just looked at him. She had made it very clear that she could have lived the rest of her life without ever hearing that name again. On the other hand, I was excited by just hearing the words. I knew right away that Papa was planning a new adventure.

"We have a lot of money tied up in that boat. It's not doing us any good sitting down there in Newport Beach." Papa reached across the table to spear a chicken breast. Southern fried chicken with mashed potatoes and gravy, green peas and fresh baked biscuits was his favorite dinner.

"We're just getting settled in on our new life, Charles. Can't you leave it alone?" Mama had not put a morsel on her plate.

"You know, I'm not getting any younger." Papa would turn fifty-nine in May. "It's getting harder for me to get a job swinging a hammer."

"You're not going fishing again. We've already decided that, you promised me."

A long silence followed. Papa filled his glass from a gallon jug of dago red. Playing with my peas, I glanced around the huge old farm kitchen. Oak floors, chrome edged table with a yellow Formica top and chrome chairs with matching Naugahyde covering, white painted cabinets. It was all so different from our previous life in California. I did not believe that Papa would never go to sea again, that's who he was.

"I've been thinking that we should sell the boat," Papa said.

He stabbed a dagger into my heart. I lay awake in bed at night dreaming about bringing the *Marine View* up to Oregon; about the adventures we would have. I would rather have sold my sister, well at least maybe my two little brothers. Jon and Jim were four and five years younger than me and not worth very much as playmates.

"We could use the money to open that restaurant that we've always talked about." Mama gasped. She had dreamt of opening her own Mexican restaurant for as long as I could remember.

"Sell the boat?" she whispered. "You would sell the boat?"

I held my breath. This was an adult conversation. I didn't dare open my mouth. We were privileged to be listening. I wanted to intervene, to yell "You can't sell the boat!" but I knew that if I opened my mouth, I'd be sent away from the table.

"It's not doing us any good down there. We could make enough money to set ourselves up in business."

Mama got up to take empty dishes to the kitchen. This was very unusual. My sister Quita and I were responsible for clearing the table and washing the dishes. Mama needed time to think.

Looking across the table at my big sister we exchanged glances. We had a way of communicating without using words, we always knew what the other was thinking. Her look told me that I would get no help from her.

***

I thought that the sun rose and set on Quita. She had always been my barometer; she told me what to think and when to think it. I couldn't believe that she could just sit there calmly while we were discussing selling our boat. My brothers were playing with their mashed potatoes and oblivious to the conversation.

"How much do you think we could get for the boat?" Mama asked.

"Well, in her present condition, probably about four or five thousand dollars, but if PC and I went down there this summer and cleaned her up, put her in top shape, maybe eight or nine thousand." At the mention of my name, my heart raced. There was nothing I would rather do than to spend time on the boat with Papa.

"Do you think you can you sell it? Is there a market for tuna boats anymore? Remember how hard it was to get rid of the *Aventura* and the *Amy D*?" Mama asked.

"I've been watching albacore prices. They're still at about two fifty a ton, but the West Coast canneries are buying again. In the *National Fisherman* they're predicting they'll buy three hundred thousand tons this summer. That should be enough to interest somebody."

Papa must have been reading the *National Fisherman* on the sly. Mama would sooner have let him bring *Playboy* into the house. Papa apparently had been hatching this plan for some time.

"Hmmm," she was non-committal.

"You know though," Papa said as he buttered a biscuit, then heaped on home-made blackberry jam, "our best bet might be some rich sucker that just wants a boat to play with. If we could find someone like a lawyer or accountant who makes ten thousand a year, they could afford a toy. Anyway, it's costing us money sitting down there. We have to pay for moorage every month, whether we use her or not."

Over the course of the winter Papa continued to work on Mama. He first convinced her that he should sell the boat, then he persuaded her that he needed to go south and clean up the boat. Finally, he talked his way into one last grand adventure. He and I would go to California to pick up the boat and fish our way north. Then, in the fall, he would sell the boat and invest the money in a business. I was going to join him on his last great adventure in the eleventh summer of my life.

That was the summer I forgot about baseball. Somehow, leaving an exciting pennant chase was a small price to pay for a summer on the high seas. All of my life spring and summer revolved around baseball. I idolized a young pitcher named Sandy Koufax. The Los Angeles Dodgers were rolling. Having spent my formative years in Southern California, I was a die-hard Dodgers fan. The Yankees of Mickey Mantle and company were the hated, evil dynasty.

During the winter and spring I could hardly think of anything else but our coming fishing trip.

"We'll cruise down the coast of Mexico," Papa told me as we sheet rocked the attic in our old farmhouse. "We can go ashore on *Cedros* Island and go back to *Magdalena* Bay, maybe work our way around the southern tip of Baja and up to La Paz. Don't tell Mama about this. She thinks we're just going to go down and bring the boat back up here."

My friends talked about going hunting or fishing with their fathers for a weekend, but this was a whole summer. We would spend it on the high seas, working our way down the coast of Mexico and back up the California coast to Oregon.

I was the center of attention at the lunch table at school. My friends were full of questions.

"What's an albacore look like?"

"How big are they?"

"Where do you sleep at night?"

"How far out to sea can you go?"

"Where do you go to the bathroom?"

I, of course, was the resident expert. They were dying with envy by the time that school let out in the first week of June.

On Friday, Papa picked up the last check from his job. Mama watched silently while we packed our old Ford station wagon that night.

"Come on, Penny, wake up," Mama said as she gently shook me early Saturday morning." Papa is ready to get started on your trip." I smelled her clean, sweet smell before I opened my eyes. Mama was wrapped in a blue terry cloth bath robe. Her long black hair tickled my face as she leaned over me.

She had breakfast ready when I came down the stairs. Papa was already sitting at the table eating his bacon and fried eggs. He was chatting eagerly as he dipped a piece of toast in his egg yolk. While I pulled up a chair Mama sat quietly at her end of the table and played with a cup of coffee.

"*Vaya con Dios, Mijo,*" Mama said with tears in her eyes as we said goodbye to the family and took off. Neither Papa nor I even thought to look back.

The Ford was a burgundy 1953 Estate Wagon with "wood" trim. We tied our skiff, *Corky*, to the luggage rack on the roof and lowered the back seats to fill the old wagon to the gills with the tools, materials, clothes and supplies we needed to get the boat ready for a summer of fishing.

Leaving Eugene, we headed south on the brand new freeway, Interstate 5. Mama packed sandwiches made from home-canned tuna for us to eat on the trip. At Medford, we stopped for lunch at a pretty park alongside the river. Before getting back on the road, we filled the gas tank.

"Twenty-five cents a gallon? This is highway robbery. Those damned pirates think that they can soak the turistas just because they're next to the highway," Papa said as he sighted a fruit stand across the street.

Medford is an orchard rich area and the stand brimmed with ripe red cherries. Papa bought a bag full to munch on as we drove. An eleven year-old boy is an appetite with a hide wrapped around it. We had no sooner gotten back on the road than I tore into the bag of cherries.

From Medford to Ashland is about thirty miles, then it's another twenty or thirty miles to the California state line. That gave me about an hour to work on the cherries.

"Have you finished those cherries yet?" Papa asked as we neared the border.

"No, I still have most of a bag-full."

"Well you better eat them fast. There's a produce check station at the border where they check to make sure you aren't bringing any prohibited fruit into California. They'll take them away from you there." I could picture the border crossing from Mexico into the United States just south of San Diego. When we returned from trips into Mexico Papa always teased us that they wouldn't let us back into the United States. I thought that California must be protected from all sides, they couldn't be too careful about who they allowed to enter the "Golden State."

Not wanting to lose a single cherry, I ate as fast as I could. It was a warm late spring day and we were driving with the windows open. I popped a cherry into my mouth, quickly ate off the meat and spit the seed out the window. Too soon we came to the border check station.

"Good afternoon, folks," the bored border guard said as he scratched his nose. "Do you have any tomatoes, oranges or other citrus fruit with you? Any other fruit?"

"Well, officer, we have a bag of cherries we bought in Medford. The boy's been trying to eat them all up before we got here." I hated it when he called me "the boy." I wanted to spit a cherry seed at Papa, but knew better.

"I'm afraid I'm going to have to confiscate them, sir."

With that, Papa gave the guard my depleted bag of cherries and we drove on.

All was normal for a few minutes, then I had a strong desire for another cherry. I popped one in my mouth and spit the seed out the window. A few minutes later, I had another cherry. Before long I was rapidly popping the cherries into my mouth and spitting seeds out of the window.

All of a sudden, Papa realized what I was doing.

"Whoa. Where did you get those cherries?"

"From my pockets." As we neared the border, I feared that I was going to lose my cherries so I filled all my pockets with them. I had more cherries in my pockets than were in the bag we had given to the guard. Papa laughed and we drove on.

The Ford had dark brown vinyl seats with light tan colored trim. There were no seat belts in those days; I sat in the front bench seat next to Papa or curled up on my side when I got tired. The changing landscape flashed past the hard metal dashboard.

We climbed up the pass through the Siskiyou Mountains and emerged into a volcanic moonscape. Little craters and cinder cones dotted the valley.

As we drove we talked. Papa told me about the books he was reading. Currently, he was reading Gibbon's *Decline and Fall of the Roman Empire*. Absorbing every word he spoke, I thought that all eleven year old boys discussed the Roman Empire and Shakespeare with their fathers.

We drove through the night. Papa planned it so that we would miss most of the heat of the Central Valley. Dawn found us rolling south towards Fresno and Bakersfield. Before long, it felt like we were in an oven.

"It's too hot," I complained. We didn't dare stop the car because our only air conditioning was the air flowing through the open windows. If we stopped, we would have withered from the heat.

"We'll be out of it soon. By noon, we should be up to the Grape Vine."

The Grape Vine is the road that leads up from the Central Valley into the mountains that surround Los Angeles. In those days, it was a two lane road with pullouts for runaway trucks. All along the road there were watering stations for you to fill up your radiator when your car boiled over. The road was littered with cars that overheated trying to climb the steep slope that had to stop and cool off. Many cars had their engines permanently damaged making this torturous climb.

"Fortunately for us, I planned for this." Papa had a canvas bag filled with water hanging in front of the grill. His theory was that the air passed through the canvas bag and cooled down the radiator. When we eventually boiled over, he had the water in the bag to refill the radiator.

Our heavily loaded Ford slowed as we made the climb. A funny looking little car zoomed up the hill past us. It looked like an old car, but was shiny new.

Sure enough, steam started rising from under the hood. Our temperature gauge was in the red. Papa found a wide spot to pull over, behind a big De Soto sedan.

"Damn it." The canvas bag with our extra water hung too low. It dragged on the pavement and wore a hole in the bottom. Our spare water was gone. We had to sit and wait for the car to cool in the hundred degree heat.

"That's the fifth one of those funny little cars that's passed us," I said while we sat alongside the road waiting for the engine to cool down. "How come they never overheat?"

"That's because they're air cooled and there's no water to boil over," They had a funny German name too: Volkswagen.

"I guess we're going to get a ticket," Papa said after we got back on the road and passed a sign that said the speed limit was fifty miles per hour. "We can't go that fast." If we couldn't drive a fancy new car, at least we could laugh about the beat up old one.

Finally, we crested the mountains and there below us lay the city of Los Angeles.

Chapter 4

We Arrive

When Papa was silent for a long time I knew he was thinking about his book. He had been writing a novel about his fishing adventures for as long as I could remember. When he was carpentering, he went out to our 1953 Hudson sedan in the evenings with his pad and paper, pulled down the arm rest in the back seat and wrote. He filled dozens of writing pads with ideas, character sketches, plots and chapters. He still didn't have the story quite right.

His story was about a widowed fisherman and his daughter on their big steel boat. He populated his world with a fantastic cast of characters drawn from his real life cronies and acquaintances.

"I've been thinking about Elizabeth," he finally said. "She's a real beauty. I've been thinking that she should meet this rich yachtie. He's a Hollywood movie producer type. He tries to seduce her by offering to get her into the movies. That can be my main conflict, her struggle with leaving her father alone and going off with this rich guy."

It all sounded great to me. He had been talking about his book and its characters for so long that I felt like I knew them. They were as real to me as some of the fishing buddies he talked about whom I had never met. Elizabeth became as much a sister to me as Quita.

A sea of smog enveloped us as we descended into the LA basin. After two years in Oregon, I forgot about the smog in

Southern California. It was a bad day and visibility was only a few blocks. In a matter of minutes my eyes burned.

We drove through LA and on to Santa Ana where we planned to spend the night at Abuelita's house. Papa, the Southern Gentleman, always mindful of manners, did not want to drop in at dinner time expecting to be fed a meal. We stopped at Russ's Hamburger Stand for burgers, fries and a milk shake before going on to Abuelita's. The only time we ever ate out as a family was Chinese food, and that was only because Mama didn't know how to cook it. I couldn't remember the last time we had gone out for a hamburger.

Mama's parents emigrated from Mexico in the early part of the Twentieth Century and settled on a tomato farm of about twenty or so acres on Goat Hill in Southern California. Goat Hill was on the bluffs above Newport Beach. About an hour drive in *Don Teodoro's* ancient flat-bed Ford truck from Santa Ana, it was a collection of small farms. Most of the Mexicans owned truck farms producing vegetables for the local market. The big, commercial fields were owned by the Japanese.

Don Teodoro, my grandfather, died when I was two, but *Abuelita* (Grandmother) still lived on the farm when I was little. In the late Fifties there were five houses on the farm. As Mama's brothers and sisters grew up and got married, they built their homes close to *Abuelita's*.

By early 1960, not long before we moved to Oregon, Goat Hill was all grown up. It was now the city of Costa Mesa. A factory that built fiberglass boats bought the land across Placentia Street from *Abuelita* and that farm disappeared. To the left of her farm a paint factory was built; to her right a factory that built radio equipment. Behind her a pump factory sprang up. Her neighborhood became an industrial area and the rich land paved over, except for her little farm.

Abuelita mourned the loss of her old neighborhood.

Her friends were all gone. The older generation died off and their children sold the farms. She hated being surrounded by factories.

My uncle Kenneth, Mama's oldest brother, was in construction. He was ambitious and studied for and got a real estate license. The housing market exploded in California and he saw that there was a fortune to be made. He convinced *Abuelita* to sell the farm and retire to a nice little house.

Kenny found a buyer and got a premium price. With the proceeds from the sale, he found a new housing tract in Santa Ana where he bought all of the houses on a dead end street. The whole family moved into these houses and the neighborhood instantly became Mexican.

When we lived in California, Mama worked nights at a restaurant called *La Fonda*. She dropped my little brothers, Jon and Jim, off at *Abuelita's* on her way to work. Quita and I rode the bus to *Abuelita's* after school. Papa picked us up on his way home.

Abuelita was the neighborhood grandmother. All of the kids in the neighborhood hung out at her house. The parents in the neighborhood, even the Anglos, asked her to take care of their kids after school. On any day there might be twenty or thirty kids playing around her house.

When the kids got home from school she always had a snack waiting for us. It might be *frijoles* and *tortillas, sopapillas, sopa, enchiladas, empanadas, quesadillas, tortas,* etc. But it was never a peanut butter sandwich. *Abuelita* never learned to speak English. All of the kids in the neighborhood, even the Anglos, learned to speak Spanish to communicate with her.

After eating at Russ's, we drove the short distance to the Pantoja enclave in Santa Ana. My cousin Virgie greeted us at the door.

"Charles, Penny, what are you doing here?"

"We came down to pick up the boat. *Abuelita* knew we were coming,"

"Oh, she must have forgotten. She's so excited about Santos coming home that she hasn't thought of anything else for a week."

Santos is Mama's youngest brother. She and Papa took him fishing with them when he was a little boy. At age thirteen, he ran away from home and hitch hiked all the way to San Juan Island in Washington State to live with Mama and Papa and finish school. After high school, he won a scholarship to Central Washington College in Ellensburg, then joined the Air Force. He was now Captain Pantoja and just completed a tour of duty in Guam. *Abuelita* was throwing a welcome home party for him after two years out of the country.

All the family was there, plus distant relations who didn't live in the little enclave. All the neighbors and anyone who walked in off the street were welcome.

"There must be a hundred people here," Papa said.

Friends and family wandered all over *Abuelita's* back yard, her house, her front yard and all up and down the street. It was a fiesta. We heard the strains of music coming from the back yard

Santos and my cousin Tony played their guitars. Soon Uncle Leonard arrived with a full Mariachi band. Everyone sang and danced.

Tables covered with food lined the patio behind her house. Everybody brought their favorite dish. The ubiquitous *frijoles* and *tortillas, chiles rellenos, enchiladas, tamales, taquitos, carnitas, chile, tortas, arroz,* a turkey in *mole,* and *carne asada* packed the table.

Papa and I were full of hamburgers, but this fiesta could not be ignored. Besides, it would be bad manners not to eat, so we pigged out. I never remember being so full in my life.

That night we stayed with *Abuelita;* the next day we

moved onto the boat. We awoke early to the smell of roasting chiles, *Abuelita* was already up. She had a pot of coffee brewed for Papa and was making breakfast. She always made the same thing.

When the chiles' skins were black, she wrapped them in a dishtowel to sweat and then peeled and diced potatoes and onions. As the potatoes and onions sautéed, she peeled the skins from the chiles. In her *molcajete* she ground the chiles, onions and tomatoes to make fresh salsa. Fried eggs were served with the potatoes and covered in fresh chile.

From the bedroom I heard a rhythmic slap, slap, slap. *Abuelita* was making *tortillas*. She made her masa out of wheat flour, then divided it into little balls. After sprinkling a little flour on the cutting board to keep the *tortillas* from sticking, she flattened a ball of masa with the palm of her hand, took a rolling pin and rolled them out into perfect circles. While she made the dough and rolled out the *tortillas*, her grill heated up.

She casually tossed a *tortilla* onto the grill while she rolled out another. In a few seconds, small bubbles began to form on the *tortilla*. She picked it up with her finger nails and flipped it over. A few more seconds on the other side and it was done. She put the *tortillas* into a large earthenware bowl lined with a dish towel.

Papa and I eagerly grabbed fresh *tortillas* and scooped up our potatoes and eggs.

Abuelita sent us out the door with happy stomachs.

By 1962 Newport Beach morphed from a sleepy little fishing village to a cosmopolitan beach town. Most of the canneries and working waterfront vanished, to be replaced by high-end restaurants with Cadillac and Lincoln convertibles, as well as the occasional Jaguar or Rolls Royce, in the parking lots. Beach clothing stores, surf shops, yacht brokers, apartments and beach houses lined the streets. The basin that once was a haven for small fishing boats now filled with expensive yachts.

Papa and I stood on the cannery dock and looked out across the Newport Channel to Lido Isle. Lido Isle was quickly becoming the most expensive real estate in Southern California, with large homes lining the beach. The next float over from us was overcrowded with charter fishing boats, what Papa called "cattle boats."

"They'll put fifty or sixty people aboard one of those barges and make them stand shoulder to shoulder with a rod and reel."

Beyond the charter boats, out in the basin, white steel buoys floated in neat rows. Attached to the buoys was an assortment of boats, from big old sailboats to run down cruisers to down on their luck fishing boats. This was the low rent district. This was where Mama exiled the *Marine View*.

The *Marine View* had laid sadly at her moorings abandoned and deteriorated for a couple of years. Everything needed to be cleaned, painted or repaired.

"The first thing we need to do, PC, " Papa told me as I rowed *Corky*, out to the boat. "Is to move her from the mooring buoy to the public dock. We need to be able to get on and off the boat easily so we can load and carry stuff."

"Up oars," Papa said as we pulled alongside. I pulled the oars in and he reached out and grasped the *Marine View's* rail. I grabbed the painter (the line attached to the front of the skiff) and clambered aboard. The *Marine View* had high wooden bulwarks, so I lifted a section out to make it easy for Papa to climb from the skiff up to the boat.

"What a mess." I was shocked. Papa told me that we would have a job cleaning up the boat, but I wasn't expecting this.

Everything was covered in a layer of dirt and seagull poop. There were clam and mussel shells shattered on the deck, one of the windows in the deck house was busted, the hasp on Papa's big tackle box broken, the lid pried off and all the contents gone. Rigging was stripped from her mast and all of the fishing lines had disappeared. It was disgusting. The *Marine View* seemed to be embarrassed to be caught in this condition.

"What happened to her?"

"Well, PC, the docks are full of seagulls," Papa replied without a hint of ire in his voice. "Anything that isn't tied down will disappear. When someone is working on their boat and needs a part, if they see it sitting on your boat, it's easier to grab yours than to go to the store and buy one. No one means any harm by it, but if you let your boat sit unused for a couple of years, they'll strip it."

"But she's been moored out in the harbor all this time; she hasn't been at a dock."

"The locals get to know which boats are being watched and which aren't. If they see that no one is taking care of a boat, they figure it's fair game."

"You mean they rowed all the way out here just to strip her?"

"I suppose so. Well, we'll have to make her livable again. You can start by cleaning up her deck house and fo'c'sle."

When we built the *Marine View* Papa raised her foredeck to create standing room in the forward section of the boat. Under the foredeck was the fo'c'sle. At first I thought Papa was saying "fox hole," then he explained to me what the fo'c'sle meant.

"Fo'c'sle is a contraction for forecastle. In medieval times ships of war were built with high towers on the bow and stern for archers to use to shoot arrows down at their enemies. The tower in the front of the ship was called the forecastle; the one in the back was the stern castle. Sailors, being the lazy buggers that they are, shortened forecastle to fo'c'sle." Even though no boat or ship has been built with a forecastle in more than five hundred years, the term endured and the forward living section of any boat is the fo'c'sle.

I pictured Prince Valiant, sailing away on adventures, sleeping in his forecastle.

The deck house was small but serviceable. It had big glass windows all around. A sliding door on the aft, starboard(right) side provided access to the deck. As you came into the deck house, there was a galley on the port (left) side with a two burner counter top propane stove, a sink, a counter with fiddle rails to keep things from sliding off when the boat rolled and cabinet space under the counter. Papa ran a coil of copper tubing from the cooling unit in the fish hold to provide refrigeration. We had a massive deep freeze in the fish hold, powered by our main engine, so there was never any shortage of frozen goods. At the end of a thirty day cruise we were still eating ice cream.

Across the front starboard side of the deck house was the steering station. There was a big box compass and engine instruments on the console. Papa couldn't afford to buy a real ship's wheel, so he fashioned a brass tiller bar with a wooden knob on one end. I always pined for a wooden ship's wheel like they had on pirate ships. The tiller bar was attached to a shaft that had a big gear on the other side of the cabinet with a bicycle chain that ran down to a sprocket on a long shaft over my bunk. The shaft ran to the back of the boat where a worm gear attached to the rudder steered the boat. I watched the gear turn while I was in bed.

There was no mess table on this boat. In good weather, we took our meals out on deck and sat on the hatch cover. In foul weather, we took our meals down to the fo'c'sle and sat on our bunks.

A wooden bulwark about two feet high came aft from the foredeck, all around the rear section of the boat. The bulwark gave me a great deal of comfort because it was designed to keep us from slipping off of the deck into the ocean. It was at the same level as the raised foredeck so it gave the *Marine View* a smooth sheer flowing aft. (The sheer is the line that runs from bow to the stern along the top of the hull. It's the view of a boat that you get when you look at her from the side.) About eighteen inches above the bulwark a steel pipe handrail gave us a place to grab onto when the seas were rough. The rail ran all the way forward to give some protection against slipping off of the foredeck, however the foredeck did not have a high bulwark.

The fish hold was aft of the fo'c'sle. The hold measured twenty feet long and twelve feet wide. Papa built water tight bulkheads at each end to keep the boat afloat should any of the three water tight compartments spring a leak. The hold itself was insulated and had ceiling planking on the inner side of the ribs. On the aft bulkhead of the hold a refrigeration plant powerful enough to bring the temperatures in the hold below freezing allowed us to stay out for extended trips. At the aft most end of the hold the sump was the lowest place on the boat. Any water that leaked or ice that melted would eventually end up in the sump where a powerful bilge pump waited to suck it up and spit it out over the side.

The engine room, the "glory hole" to old salts, filled the aft end of the boat. The engine room measured about six feet long and ten feet wide in the front narrowing to four or five feet wide at the rear. The boat got narrower as you moved aft.

Like the fish hold, the hatch cover to access the engine room stood about two feet above the deck. The purpose of the raised hatches was to keep water from entering the below deck compartments should the boat ship a sea (take a wave) over the rails. Sliding the hatch cover back revealed a ladder that led into the lower depths.

Papa reached in his pocket and produced a key for the padlock that secured the hasp on the cabin door. He unlocked the door and slid it open.

The scene inside was no better than the deck. Water entered through the broken window. The countertop and cabinets were warped and stained. Several inches of water sloshed around in the fo'c'sle.

Unlocking the engine room hatch, Papa climbed down the ladder and reached for the light switch.

"Hand me a flashlight, PC, the battery's dead."

He passed the beam of the flashlight over the engine and machinery, everything looked OK. He dropped to his knees and lifted the floor boards. Once again, several inches of water sloshed around in the bilge. He reached down with his cupped hand and brought a handful to his face. He sniffed it, then tasted it.

"Salt water. This is from the propeller shaft packing box."

That was to be expected. All boats leaked a little bit where the propeller shaft exited the hull.

Now he bent down and sniffed in the bilge.

"No propane fumes, no gas fumes. We're OK to start her up." We needed the engine running to move to the dock and to provide electricity. "Check the fuel tanks."

I reached in the engine room hatch cover and grabbed the bamboo pole strapped to the combing. The pole had black rings painted around it with numbers written above each ring. This was our fuel dip stick. I ran to the deck house and found the brass key to open the fuel filler fitting on the deck, then returned and removed the cover from the starboard tank. Dipping the bamboo stick into the opening, I tapped on the bottom of the tank.

"We have about half a tank of diesel oil," I said as I pulled the stick out of the tank and read it.

"That's good, now let's check to see if there's any water in it," Papa replied from the engine room. He opened a little valve on the bottom of the stainless steel fuel tank and drained off a half cup or so of fuel into a Mason jar. He stood and held it to the light. Water is heavier that diesel and settles in the bottom of the tank. You tell if there was any water in the tank by draining off a sample into the glass jar.

"No water."

Next, Papa checked the engine oil and the oil in the reduction gear. You don't fire up the engine without adequate lubrication.

"OK, let's start her up."

I knew my job. Papa removed a steel crank from the bulkhead and attached it to a fitting on the front end of the crankshaft as I climbed down the ladder into the engine room. He pushed a little lever on the top of each cylinder to release the compression and opened the throttle half way.

"OK, crank," he said.

Turning the crank was hard at first, but as the engine started turning over, it became easier.

"Now," he shouted and slammed the little levers on each cylinder shut. Pulling the crank free I jumped back. The engine sputtered, then fired roughly. In an instant, it settled down into a steady drone. Our little Ford diesel never failed us.

With the engine running, we had electricity. Our first task was to pump the water out of the bilge. After finding our dock lines in the forepeak of the fo'c'sle, we hung a couple of old automobile tires over the side for fenders, dropped our mooring buoy and motored over to the public dock.

My job when docking was to take the lines onto the dock. With the bow line in my left hand and the stern line in my right hand, I leapt from the center of the boat across to the dock when we got to within about three or four feet. Then I quickly wrapped the stern line around a cleat to arrest the forward motion of the boat and pulled on the bow line to bring her snug to the dock. Papa had long ago taught me how to tie off a line on a cleat or throw a clove hitch around a bollard.

A man in slacks, white canvas deck shoes, a button up sport shirt and an LA Dodgers baseball cap stood on the dock as we closed with it. Obviously a yachtie, he came running to help us tie up. Not wanting any help I leaped across to the dock with a line in each hand.

"Here, let me take it," the man said, grabbing the stern line out of my hand. He pulled in the slack and the line went taunt. The boat continued to move forward. He pulled on the line to stop the boat, but it pulled him with it. As Papa came along side the dock, the yachtie reached out with his hand to stop the boat. He was not strong enough to stop twenty tons of tuna boat in motion. The *Marine View* continued on forward and rammed the boat in front of it. I quickly dropped my bow line over the cleat and brought her to a stop while the stern swung wide into the channel.

"You're supposed to wrap the stern line around a cleat," I shouted at the man.

"Oh, I'm sorry," he muttered, "I didn't know."

"I know how to dock a boat, why did you grab my line?" I yelled. The man just turned and slunk away.

Secured to the dock, we set to work on the superficial stuff. Cleaning, sanding, scraping, painting and varnishing.

At eleven years old, I was very capable. I could use most of Papa's power tools. He took me to work with him every summer on his jobs. On weekends we did projects around the house.

I liked independence. He gave me the topsides jobs and the clean and paint jobs, then he left me alone. He took the machinery and equipment jobs below decks.

We spent our first day cleaning up the deck house and fo'c'sle so the boat was livable. We cleaned and scrubbed long into the night. While I was scouring out the refrigerator, Papa drove up to a hardware store and bought a replacement for the broken window. He also bought two tanks of propane to replace the tanks that disappeared in our absence. After hooking up the propane, he painted each of the joints in the tubing with soapy water, looking for leaks. If bubbles formed on the joints, the propane was leaking and that was deadly. After Papa determined that it was safe, we fired up our countertop two burner propane stove and warmed up a can of chili for dinner then dropped into our bunks exhausted.

"When are we going to get all this stuff done and go fishing?" The work seemed endless. I couldn't see far enough into the future to envision getting done and going to sea. It just went on day after day. Papa lured me with the promise of fishing and adventure, I hadn't signed up for all this work.

Living on the boat was problematic. We didn't have a head and we didn't have the refrigeration running. The next morning we trudged up to the restroom at the marina facility to use the bathroom and brush our teeth. They had showers and we showered about once a week, unless we worked on a particularly dirty job that day.

The next thing on our agenda was supplies. We made a trip to the grocery store where Papa did the shopping. I found the block ice so that we could keep our food cold. Milk, beer, root beer, etc. stayed cold for a couple of days. After that I had to walk up to the marina store every day or two and buy ice.

Papa did all of the cooking. We had bacon or sausage, fried potatoes and eggs for breakfasts most mornings. Lunch was usually sandwiches while we were working. For dinner we rarely had a salad, our vegetables were usually cooked into some kind of one-pan stove-top meal.

This was a life a boy could learn to love. I only had to shower once a week, I didn't have to eat vegetables and I got to drink root beer with dinner. I was a modern day Huck Finn. I wondered what Mama would think of this as I settled into my bunk at night. During the day I was too busy to be homesick, but at night, as I lay in my bunk listening to the gentle slap of the sea against the hull I missed her soft voice and sweet smell.

As Papa worked in the galley, I noticed an old couple setting up folding chairs on the end of our float. I moved closer to see what they were doing. They had short fishing poles and plastic buckets with them.

"What're you fishing for?"

The old woman turned to me.

"We're smelt fishing, honey."

"What's in the buckets?"

"They're full of bread heels to use for bait. We fill the bucket with water to let the bread get soggy, then we'll toss a handful of the bread in the water. The smelt come to the surface to eat it."

"Do you bait your hooks with bread?"

"No, no," the old man said. "We use treble hooks to snag the smelt."

"Treble hooks?"

"Yeah, they're fish hooks with three prongs, see?" He held up a hook for me to look at. "The shafts are back to back to back and the prongs stick out in three different directions."

"When the fish rise to the surface," the old woman said. "We drop our lines with half a dozen treble hooks on them in the water and jig trying to hook the fish."

"What's 'jig'?"

"That's pulling your line up and down, like this." She demonstrated with her short pole. "The fish don't bite the hook, it snags them in the body. Then we reel the fish in, drop the line again and repeat the process."

The old couple filled a bucket with smelt in a half hour. That was my kind of fishing, so I convinced them to teach me how. The next night, after I made a trip to the local tackle shop for gear. I brought a bucket of smelt home for dinner.

I cut off the heads, scraped off the scales and gutted them; Papa rolled them in corn meal and fried them in bacon grease in his cast iron skillet. He fried a pan full of potatoes with onions and warmed a can of corn to complete the dinner. We ate the smelt, bones and all. The bones were so small and delicate that we didn't even notice them. I was so proud of bringing home dinner that night that I didn't even think about the daunting task ahead of us.

Chapter 5

Getting the Boat Ready

Owning a fishing boat requires a Jack-of-all-trades. We had to be shipwrights, finish carpenters, engineers, diesel mechanics, refrigeration mechanics, electricians, painters and plumbers. And that was just for getting the boat ready. Once the dock lines were cast off, Papa was responsible for the lives and well being of the boat and its crew. He had to be a boatswain (pronounced bosun), a navigator, a fish-puller, a deck hand, a sea cook, a helmsman and a lookout. He also had to be a business man and make a profit.

"Hey boy, what here you doing?" said the short, stocky little man with traces of red still showing in his close cropped gray hair. This was my introduction to Hans Dickman. Hans, a grumpy old Dutchman, had owned the boat yard on the waterfront in Newport Beach since sometime in the Thirties. He ruled his domain with an iron fist, but had every conceivable part for building a new boat. Being from the Old Country, he slaughtered the English language. He was gruff and grumpy with everyone, but for some reason had taken an instant liking to Mama. Everyone fell in love with Mama.

Hans always called Mama "hey girl," he never used her name. This continued for years, until my sister Quita was born. The first time he saw Quita, Mama became "hey missus." Some of this fondness transferred over to me, from our first meeting he always called me "hey boy."

"Hans, you old son of a gun," Papa said.

"Charlie, you I have not seen in years."

"We moved to Oregon. The boy and I are here to fix up our boat and take her up the coast."

"What for you can I do?"

"Well, for starters, we need to haul her out."

That began what seemed like an endless list of tasks we had to complete to make the *Marine View* ready for sea. Late that afternoon, on the floodtide, we put the *Marine View* on the ways. She hadn't moved in a couple of years so she was coated with barnacles and seaweed.

"Wow, how are we going to get all that junk off her bottom?" I asked.

"With a lot of elbow grease." Papa handed me a broad, stiff putty knife. "I'll start at the water line and you can start at the keel, since you can crawl under her better."

I worked my way under the boat near the keel, lay on my back and began scraping. It was an ugly job. By the end of the day I was soaked to the bone with dirty, oily sea water and covered in pieces of shell and weed.

"This is disgusting," I mumbled as I spat pieces of barnacle and muscle shells from my mouth. I guess I should work with my mouth closed. As tough as the job was, we worked hard and by the end of the second day, we had her clean.

"We're going to need to do some re-caulking," Papa said as he pulled oakum from the seams between the planks.

The *Marine View* was a carvel planked boat. There are several ways to build a wooden boat. The carvel method is the most traditional in the United States. A carvel planked boat has a wooden keel running the length of the boat that acts as a "back bone." At the front of the keel is the stem post to which the planks are fastened to make the bow. At the rear of the keel there's a stern post to which the rudder is fastened. At regular intervals along the length of the keel the ribs are attached in pairs on either side. Each pair of ribs give the shape to the hull and strength to the boat. Planks are fastened over the ribs. These planks seal the hull against the water, add strength and give the boat its final shape.

The planks are carefully measured and cut, then shaped by hand to ensure a good fit with the plank above it and the plank below it. Inevitably, the seam between the planks leaks. For this reason, hundreds, maybe thousands, of years ago, ancient shipwrights invented caulking. Long balls of hemp, called oakum, are made from old rope and used to caulk the boat. The oakum, a very loose, thick course string, is forced into the seam between the planks. When the boat is put in the water, the planks absorb water and expand. The planks expanding on both sides of the seam put pressure on the oakum and it is evenly distributed throughout the seam to form a water tight seal.

"You have to do this just right," Papa told me patiently as he unwound a length of oakum. "You push it into the seam with an awl, twisting the oakum as you go. It's called paying the seam. If you make any mistakes, the boat leaks." When he had three or four feet of oakum in the seam, he took a tool called a caulking iron that looked like a putty knife on steroids and tapped on it with a wooden mallet with a long curved head to drive the oakum deep into the seam.

"Why do we use such a funny looking mallet?"

"That's to get the caulking iron to ring. You can tell if you've paid the seam properly by the sound of the mallet. Listen . . ."

He gently tapped on the caulking iron with his mallet. It made a dull thud.

"Now listen to this . . ."

He repeated the process, but this time took short, quick strokes. The caulking iron rang like a bell.

"You can tell if you've gotten the oakum seated properly by the sound of the iron. It needs to ring.

"The last seam on the deck, where the deck meets the hull is called the devil; it's the most difficult seam on the boat to caulk. In the old days, a seaman might be punished by being made to re-caulk that seam. That's where we get the term 'there'll be the devil to pay.' That's also where we got the phrase 'between the devil and the deep blue sea.'"

"I don't get it."

"The only thing between the devil and the sea is the width of the top plank on the boat's hull. If you're standing between the devil and the deep blue sea, you don't have much to stand on."

"C'mon, PC," Papa said as he worked above the water line. "You might as well learn to do some caulking." Under his watchful eye, I learned to caulk.

"No, that's not right." The first few times, he made me pull the oakum out of the seam and redo it until I got it right. Beaming with pride as the caulking iron finally rang, I met his standard and he went off to another part of the bottom to work.

After three days of cleaning, scraping and caulking, it was time to add the copper bottom paint. Any boat that sits in the water needs anti-fouling paint on its bottom. In fresh water, grass and weeds attach themselves to the bottom of the boat and foul the bottom. In salt water, barnacles, mussels, and kelp (seaweed) attach themselves to the bottom of the boat. The dirtier the bottom of the boat, the more drag. The more drag, the slower the boat goes, the more fuel it takes to push it. A clean bottom means a faster boat.

In salt water there are also torredo worms. The worms bore into the wooden planks on the boat's bottom and destroy the strength and integrity of the wood. Eventually, if left untreated, they will sink the boat.

"How come this paint is so thick?" I asked as I dipped my brush in the paint can.

"That's because it's full of copper and all sorts of other

noxious chemicals. In the days of old sailing ships, they covered the bottom of their ships and boats with sheets of copper to keep the worms from boring into the wood. Then some smart Yankee discovered that they could add the copper to paint and still keep the worms out. It's a lot cheaper and easier than covering the whole bottom with copper."

Picture painting the ceiling in your house with this heavy, sticky paint. Now imagine that the ceiling was curved upward, away from you. Finally, imagine that the room is about two feet tall in the center and six feet tall at the edges. This is something like the surface of the boat that must be painted. It's a nasty and tedious job. It took us all day to paint the bottom. By the time we were done, I had more red paint on me that we had on the bottom of the boat.

"Well, PC, it looks like it'll be safe to put you in the water this summer. No barnacle is going to attach itself to you."

We worked on the boat during day, then at night we climbed up the ladder and fixed our dinner in her galley before retiring to the fo'c'sle exhausted. On our fourth night on the ways, Papa cooked "boatman's goulash."

He started by chopping up a pound of bacon. When it was browned, he poured off the grease into a tin can to be used later and added a couple of diced potatoes, a diced onion and a diced green pepper. The smell of the bacon, mixing with the sweet aroma of the onion and peppers was enough to drive me to distraction. He added a can of cream style corn when the vegetables were cooked. Then he broke a couple of eggs into the pan and stirred them in. Once the eggs were cooked it was ready to eat, all we had to do was to add salsa.

"It's Hap," Papa practically danced as we returned from a trip to the grocery store, when he saw a dirty old gray wooden boat tied up a couple of floats away. It was the *Happy Days*. "Hap's one of my best friends. Somehow we lost touch. I haven't heard from Hap in years." A devilish grin crept across his face. His eyes twinkled mischievously.

"I want you to board that boat," he told me, "go down into her deck house and say 'Have another enchilada, Hap' to Hap."

I had never met Hap before, but Papa was so excited that I got caught up in the moment. Anyway, I've never been very inhibited.

I jumped across onto the *Happy Days*, entered the deck house and there he was sitting on a water keg. A fat old man with a ring of gray hair around his bald pate and a twinkle in his blue eyes, he clinched an old brown pipe between his teeth. A cloud of fragrant smoke clung near the ceiling. If he had a full beard and a red suit, you might have thought he was Santa Claus.

"Have another enchilada, Hap," I shouted out.

He jumped to his feet and grabbed the pipe from his mouth. "Why, you're Vicki's boy, goddamn it."

With that, Papa came aboard and the reunion commenced. They broke out a bottle of Canadian Club (I got root beer), and talked all through the day and late into the night. I came away feeling I had known Hap all of my life.

"You know where that 'Have another enchilada, Hap' comes from don't you?" Hap asked me.

"No, Papa just told me to say it."

"I served on destroyers in the Navy during the First War," Hap said. "After the Japs bombed Pearl Harbor, I was at the recruiting office the next day to sign up to go back in the Navy. I was still under the maximum age, but I failed the physical. I was too fat.

"I fussed and fumed about being left out of the war for three years. Finally, the tide of the war was turning and I knew it couldn't last much longer. I went on a crash diet. I cut my eating way down, knocked off liquor and began an exercise program. I needed to lose forty pounds to get down to the maximum weight for my height." As fat as Hap was, I couldn't imagine him losing enough weight to go into the Navy.

"I suffered for months and finally reached my goal. I rushed down to the recruiting station the next day; I wanted to get into the war before it was over. I didn't eat breakfast that morning because I didn't want to take a chance on weighing a pound more.

"I waited in line all morning. Finally, the recruiters knocked off for lunch. I held my place in line though; I didn't want to get bumped to the back of the line. After the lunch break, I was the next man in line.

"I went through all the talk and paperwork and finally it was time for the physical. You know that all scales are different? I was worried about what their scales would show, but I made it. I was one quarter pound under the maximum. They finished processing me and swore me in.

"By that time it was late afternoon and I hadn't had a bite to eat all day long. I was so famished that I made a bee-line for the little diner across the street from the recruiting office.

"In the diner they had a diet special, a hamburger patty, cottage cheese and tomato slices, that I ordered. The waitress brought it and I wolfed it down.

"When the waitress came by to offer me another cup of coffee she asked 'Would you like anything else.'

"'Yes, I'd like another diet plate,' I says.

"After the second diet plate, I ordered a third, then a fourth. By this time, the waitress must have thought that I was crazy."

"What does that have to do with enchiladas?" I asked.

"The first thing I did when I got back to Newport Beach was to tell your Daddy. He invited me over for dinner to celebrate. Your mother served enchiladas. I'd been starving for so long I could a eaten the hind end out of a skunk.

"'Would you like another enchilada, Hap?' your Mama asked.

"'Why yes, Vicki, I believe I would,' I says and she serves me another enchilada. When I finished that, she asked 'Would you like another enchilada, Hap?'

"'Why yes, Vicki, I believe I would. Could I have two more enchiladas this time?' I says.

"So she serves me two more enchiladas. I had eaten five enchiladas at that point. 'Have another enchilada, Hap,' she says as I cleaned my plate again.

"'Thank you Vicki, I believe I will,' I says."

"They kept going on like that," Papa broke in. "Mama had made a big tray of enchiladas so that we'd have left-overs. They were all gone. She fed Hap her last enchilada, but she didn't believe anyone could eat that much. She thought he couldn't eat another bite. He was sweating up a storm, his face was flushed and he was panting between bites. She figured he was done so she teased him a little bit, expecting him to throw in the towel."

"'Have another enchilada, Hap,' she says," said Hap, taking up the story again.

"'Why, Vicki, I'm so full I think I'm going to burst,' I says, 'but these here enchiladas are so good, that I believe I will.'

"She was stunned. She didn't have anything else to feed me. Your daddy roared with laughter. When he explained the joke to me, I roared too. Your Mama was just embarrassed.

"Charlie, I says, a friend of mine once was going on a trip to Mexico. He asked me for some tips on good behavior so that he didn't offend the Mexicans.

"I thought I'd pull a little trick on him. You see, when you're dining in a Mexican's home, you never refuse food. It'll insult 'em. So I told him that when he finished his dinner, to show how much he enjoyed it he should tell the hostess '*Quiero mas frijoles, por favor.*'

"Now, that means, 'I'd like more beans, please,' in Spanish but this poor dumb son of a bitch didn't know a word of Spanish and he said it. The hostess kept bringing out beans after beans and he kept eatin' 'em. I think he would have eaten until he died if she didn't run out of beans."

After this story, there was a long pause. Hap refilled their glasses. I slumped down on the forward berth, my eyes getting heavy.

"Charlie, I thought you'd given up fishin'. How come you're back here again?"

"Well, Hap, I had the opportunity to get in on this little thirty-six foot Navy launch. The first couple of seasons weren't too good. After a couple of accidents I had to promise Vicki that I'd go ashore."

"Then what are you doing back here?" Hap repeated.

"We made a deal. The boy and I are going to fish our way north. In the fall, we'll put the boat up for sale and use the money to open a little business. . . "

I melted into the berth. I had this vague sensation of flying. I was being lifted up, up into the air. I dreamed singing. I dreamed that I could smell the sweet odor of whiskey. I felt warm and safe. When I awoke the next morning, I was in my own bunk on the *Marine View*.

"*Mijo*, run up to Hans Dickman's and ask him for two sacrificial zincs," Papa told me as he collected our painting tools and started cleaning up.

"What are sacrificial zincs?"

"Zinc ingots that we attach to the bottom of the boat to protect against electrolysis. In salt water we have electrolysis. An electrical current passes through the water and causes a chemical reaction on all metal below the surface. The softer metals get eaten away and molecules are moved from the soft metal to the harder metals. For instance, if you have a brass propeller on a steel shaft, over time the propeller will melt away. Worse yet, you could have brass screws holding the planking to the bottom of the boat. If these get eaten away, the bottom of the boat falls off and you sink."

Long ago, sailors learned how to combat this problem. Zinc is the softest of metals. It will be dissolved and the molecules transferred to any other metal on the bottom of your boat. For this reason, most boats have sacrificial zincs. These are ingots of zinc attached to the bottom of the boat specifically for the purpose of getting eaten up instead of some other vital part of the boat. As these zincs get dissolved, they must be replaced to protect the other metal on the boat's bottom.

We spent the morning of our fifth day on the ways, wrapping up a bunch of little tasks.

"Let's take a look at the pintles and gudgeons while we have her out of the water." (Pintles and gudgeons are nautical talk for the hinges on the rudder.) "Then we need to true up the propeller shaft and make sure the propeller turns properly. Before we put her back in the water I want to check all the through-hulls to make sure that they don't leak."

I learned that all boats have some kind of through-hulls. You want to keep them to a minimum because they're a potential source of problems. A through-hull is a fitting that is essentially a hole in the bottom of the boat. It has a valve on the inboard side so that you can shut off the water. Through-hulls are used to bring water into the boat, such as for cooling the engine, and for taking water out of the boat, such as for draining your sink or head.

For safety's sake, wise boaters have oak cones with holes drilled in the big end tied to each through hull with a length of nylon line. The reason for these plugs is to put in the through-hull valve in case it fails. You can put the plug in the hole, drive it in with a hammer and stop the sea from invading the boat.

Needless to say, healthy through-hulls are critical to the

well being of a boat. We inspected each one, tested it to make sure it worked properly and made sure that it was properly caulked so that it didn't leak.

"*Mijo*, it's time to put her back in the water. Run up and tell Hans Dickman that we're ready to float her again."

"Mr. Dickman," I said when I found him behind the counter in his store, "my Papa says were ready to float the *Marine View* again."

"So, boy, you want into the water to lower her, huh?"

Hans ambled out to the boatyard in his stooped shuffle, wiping his hands on a rag. He fired up the gasoline engine that ran the ways. With the engine huffing and puffing, the marine railway car lowered into the water until the *Marine View*, with us aboard, floated.

"What did I teach you about putting the boat in the water?"

"The first thing we do is check for leaks. Then we sniff the bilge for fumes."

She was dry.

Papa was a good and careful teacher. Like with handling guns, he taught me to go through a careful checklist every time I set foot on the boat. The first thing I did was to check the sump in the bilge to see how much water had accumulated. All boats with inboard motors leak a little where the propeller shaft goes through the hull; it is just a question of how much. Once I had established that the boat wasn't sinking, I dropped into the engine room and checked for propane odors.

If a boat has a gasoline engine, the hazard is doubled because both gasoline fumes and propane are heavier than air and will settle in the bottom of the boat. When the engine is fired up, it is likely to create a spark that will ignite any fumes and cause an explosion.

"Several years after I sold the *Cuantos Pescados*," Papa told me, "her new owner blew her up at the fuel dock by not checking for gasoline vapor."

"I don't smell anything in the bilges."

"Good, I'll fire up the engine, then you cast off the lines." Since I had never smelled propane or gasoline odors in our bilge before, I wasn't one hundred percent sure what we were sniffing for, but if Papa thought it was OK, then it was OK with me.

I untied the lines securing her to the car and she was swimming again. We moved the boat over to Hans Dickman's dock.

"It's time to knock off for lunch. Let's walk up to the burger stand today," Papa said. I was always ready for a good burger.

We walked up the street towards the commercial part of the city. In a couple of blocks the boat yards and ship chandlers turned into clothing stores, an Ace Hardware store with a beautiful Schwinn racer that I lusted after all summer in the window, and finally the little cement block building painted blue and white with a walk up window where we bought lunch.

When we returned from lunch we motored back to our berth at the public float. The *Marine View* looked like a happy Easter chick in her new paint and clean bottom. Each task brought us closer to being ready to sail.

Now that the boat was sound, we still had a huge task to get her rigged to go fishing.

"We're going up to the marine salvage store in San Pedro this afternoon," Papa told me. It was about an hour's drive up the coast in our old Ford.

San Pedro, the port for Los Angeles, was a real working harbor. The bay was full of ships anchored waiting to be loaded and unloaded. There were long docks where the huge cargo ships tied up to be swarmed over by longshoremen (this was before the era of containerized cargos). Huge cranes swung cargo nets into the ships holds empty and raised them out full. On shore, there were ship's chandlers, supply stores, repair facilities, metal fabricating shops, canvas shops, woodworking shops; everything necessary to keep the ships and boats that called in San Pedro in good working condition. Mixed in with everything else there were restaurants, bars, taverns, tattoo parlors, cheap hotels, cheaper theaters and barber shops to cater to the needs of the sailors coming off the ships. Everything looked dirty and dingy; the smell of diesel oil and chemicals overwhelmed the sea air.

The surplus store sat a block or so off of the water front. For an eleven-year old boy, it was a nautical wonderland. Outside, there were stacks of buoys, anchor chain thicker than my legs, four inch thick rope that was used as mooring lines on big ships. Everything was jumbo sized.

"What kind of ships need anchors that big?" I asked looking at the huge Navy anchors that weighed tons.

"Those probably came off of a battleship or an aircraft carrier."

Inside the giant steel building were rows upon rows of shelves filled with the most minute parts. There were bins of needle valves, bushings, bearings, snap hooks, swivels, you name it. There were floats, life jackets, foul weather gear, life lines, rope, chain. It went on and on. Endless processions of all sorts of gear necessary to outfit a boat.

"What are we going to buy today?" I asked.

"We'll start with an Air Force parachute to rig as a sea anchor." He bought spools of monofilament line to use as leaders for his fishing lines. He bought hooks, swivels, rope. He bought a pair of galvanized steel stabilizers to hang from our jig poles to smooth out the motion of the boat.

Papa had a big plywood tackle box that he built just aft of the engine room hatch that was about eighteen inches deep and ran the entire width and height of the engine room hatch. He needed to fill the box with fishing lines, leaders, lead weights, jigs made from chrome and chicken feathers with red glass eyes, rubber squids, swivels and all the paraphernalia necessary to troll for tuna. Papa had to anticipate all of the tackle we would need to go on an extended fishing trip. We might be offshore for weeks and we couldn't end the trip for want of a line or a hook.

While we were in the marine surplus store he ran into several of his old fishing buddies. His demeanor changed when he was in their presence. He always preached perfect grammar to his children and corrected our mistakes, but now his language grew courser and he swore a whole lot more. He also called me "the boy." I hated this. I wasn't a little kid anymore. I was doing the same work that a hired deck hand would do. I had a name, why didn't he introduce me to his friends as he taught me was the polite thing to do?

"Yeah, me and the boy just came down from Oregon to take the boat back up," he said. "The trip's gonna be a son of a bitch, but the boy is smart and strong as a bull, so he should be a big help." What would Mama say if she could hear him swearing?

We loaded the back of the Ford wagon with fishing gear and returned to Newport Beach. By the time we unloaded all of our purchases it was late, so we grabbed a quick bite and hit our bunks. The next morning, we started to rig the boat for fishing.

Papa taught me the difference between rope and lines. On shore, you may call it a rope, but there is no rope on a boat. Once it comes aboard, it becomes a line.

A troller has a tall mast and two long, solid wooden poles called jig poles fastened to the bulwark with hinges. There are lines called halyards that run from the top of the jig poles to pulleys near the top of the mast. These lines run down the mast and allow the fisherman to lower the jig poles out over the water giving him a broad span over which to run his fishing lines. Each jig pole has from four to six lines on it, depending on the size of the boat and the length of the poles. On each line lures, or jigs, drag behind the boat in the water. They are designed to catch the fish's attention. Making erratic movements, like a wounded fish, they are supposed to trick the albacore into thinking that it is going to be an easy meal.

Papa lowered one of the jig poles over the dock. We rigged the lines, then turned the boat around and lowered the other jig pole. Each nylon fishing line had to be securely fastened to the pole so that it could take the hit of a thirty to sixty pound fish. Then we put a length of elastic parachute shock cord on the jig pole end of the line so that a loop of line hung down. When the fish hit the line, the shock cord stretched out, the loop of line straightened out and we knew we had a fish on. About six feet from the trailing end of the line we attached a lead weight to hold the line down in the water.

At the end of the line, Papa attached a leader. The nylon fishing line ended in a little brass swivel fitting. To the free end of the swivel, he attached a heavy monofilament line about six feet long. At the end of the line he attached the jig. This was a very precise, painstaking process. Each knot had to be tied just so, no loose ends were allowed because they alerted the fish that something was wrong.

After ten days of working dawn to dusk, the boat was now rigged and ready to go. It was mid-June by the time we were ready for sea, about two weeks behind the rest of the fleet.

"Hey, Mannie, you in fish?" came the voice over the two-way radio. Papa kept the radio on all the time we worked on the boat.

"Yeah, cousin, we been pullin' tuna since daybreak. We already over the hump." The hump was the magical one hundred fish mark.

"Damn, we've got to get done and get out there," Papa

muttered. It was driving him crazy. Other boats were out on the fishing grounds filling their holds with tuna. Every day we heard about someone making a big strike (of course, fisherman never lie about how big their catches are). The closer we got the boat to being ready, the more anxious he got.

"If the other boats bring in too many fish, it'll drive the price down." He told me. "They're all doing well, I hope that by the time we get out there the run won't be fished out."

Every night we talked about what was going on and how to find the fish. My anticipation grew.

Now that the *Marine View* was ready for sea again, we went about the tasks of provisioning her for a long trip. We carried enough fuel and water for thirty days, so we needed food and sundries to last the trip as well.

Papa took us to a wholesale grocer in Long Beach, just north of Newport Beach. My excitement grew as we entered the store and loaded cases of canned goods, pasta, beer, root beer, gallons of milk, piles of bread and boxes of meat into the carts. We needed enough food, toilet paper, paper towels, soap, tooth paste, etc. to last two people for a month. I made sure we had a healthy supply of ice cream, peanut butter and raspberry jam.

We stopped by the Pacific Seafood's cannery on the way back to the boat and caught up on the latest gossip. "You know, PC," Papa told me, "it's beginning to look like a good year. The *Cromale* and the *Sea King* both came in with full loads yesterday."

Part 2

Chapter 6

The Early Years

"We're going to Len Yi's for dinner tonight," Papa announced as we finished stowing the groceries. We had slaved over the *Marine View* day and night for ten days. "Anything we don't have done now, we'll finish underway."

"Len Yi's?"

"It's an old tradition, our last night ashore dinner."

"I hate Chinese food." When we went out to Chinese restaurants with Mama, she always let me order a hamburger. Papa said she was spoiling me.

"Well, you better start liking it, because that's what we do the night before we sail." I really didn't have much choice. The excitement and tradition of the occasion won me over. After cleaning up at the marina showers, we walked the several blocks to Len Yi's.

"Charlie, good to see you again," a tiny middle aged Chinese woman said as we entered. "Where you been all this time?"

"We moved to Oregon. We came down to take the boat up north."

"You only here a short time?"

"No, we'll be around all season. We'll be fishing our way north."

"Who the kid?"

"Oh, excuse me, Mama Lee, this is Penn, my oldest boy."

"Hi kid, how you doing?"

"Ah, just fine ma'am."

Mama Lee led us to a table by the window. We could see the parking lot and the boats in the marina across the street. A pretty young Chinese girl came to take our order.

"We'll have an order of prawns, pork fried rice, egg flower soup and an order of barbequed pork," Papa told the waitress.

The food arrived and I was more hungry than wary of the strange cuisine. I started by picking at the barbequed pork, before long I was devouring it.

"Be careful of the hot mustard," Papa told me. He was too late. I had a major sinus burn.

We found some silly straw hats with dried flowers on them that we wore to shade our heads. Actually, Papa needed his head shaded a lot more that I did. I had hair. We wore those silly hats to our big Chinese dinner and it made me feel pretty special.

After dinner we returned to the boat. We had a long walk to the restaurant and back, but the day was so exciting I would have flown if I could have flapped my arms fast enough.

"We need to get everything secured for sea, PC," Papa told me before we cast off our mooring lines. "We're going over to the Standard Oil dock for fuel, water and ice."

The fuel dock was like the fuel docks in most marinas. Isolated from the other floats due to the danger of explosion, a single float was at the end of the dock. A small wooden shed with a big neon Standard Oil chevron sign towering over it distinguished it from the other floats. Short, squat fuel pumps for gasoline and diesel lined up in front of the shack. An overhead pipeline snaked out the dock from an ice house and down to the float. Boats could tie up on three sides of the float to take on fuel, water and ice.

Diesel is much safer than gasoline, but Papa still took all precautions when fueling. He shut down the engine and checked to make sure all flames were out. The electrical system was turned off to make sure an errant spark wasn't generated by some malfunctioning piece of equipment. In the evening darkness we filled our fuel tanks and lashed two fifty gallon drums of diesel oil on our aft deck. We topped off the water tank, then were ready for the ice.

Icing down the fish hold was a fun operation. We put on our rubber sea boots, heavy pea coats, watch caps and rubber gloves despite the warm summer weather. A bored looking guy on the dock passed a big black rubber hose down to us. The hose, suspended from a heavy pipe over our heads, was about 6 inches in diameter. When Papa gave the signal, he turned on the ice and it came out with the kick of a fire hose.

Papa filled each bin in the fish hold with crushed ice. The flying ice made me think of Christmas. While he was blowing the ice in, I took the snow shovel and packed it neatly into the bins. When the bins were full he carefully filled the walkway down the middle. We needed lots of ice because we would bury the fish in it to keep them fresh.

When the icing was done we were ready to go. Papa paid the man and we settled down for a short night's sleep at the fuel dock before casting off in the morning to catch the ebb tide. Actually, Papa got a short night's sleep. I tossed and turned, my head full of dreams about our coming adventures, while I listened to his snoring. Finally, I managed to close my eyes. Seconds later I hear Papa's voice.

"Rise and shine, sunshine. It's time to get underway." I blinked my eyes open. Papa was at the sink doctoring up his coffee. It was still dark out, the engine was humming in the background, the *Marine View* had come to life.

I pulled on my jeans and climbed up to the deck house.

"We're ready to shove off. Go ahead and cast off the lines."

I staggered out into the dark and jumped across to the fuel dock float. Untying the stern mooring line from the cleat,

I coiled the line, tossed it onto the after deck and gave the
stern a shove with my foot to move it away from the dock. As
I untied the bow line, I coiled it down and tossed it up onto
the foredeck. I walked back to the break in the foredeck and
grabbed the handrail, put one foot up on the deck, with my
other foot shoved away from the dock and swung up onto the
boat. The routine now was for me to stow the mooring lines,
then pull in the old car tires that we used as fenders and stow
them under the anchor lines on the foredeck. We were finally
headed out to sea in late June. It was a two or three day run
down to the fishing grounds down off the coast of Mexico.
While we steamed south, we had plenty of time to talk. During
our run to the fishing grounds I pieced together Papa's story.

Papa was born in the shadow of Bald Knob Mountain
in Arkansas in May of 1903. His father, Jack Wallace, was a
farmer with eleven other mouths to feed. His mother, Leticia
was deeply religious.

When Papa was three years old, Jack decided to move
his family to Texas. Jack had the typical Scot-Irish restlessness
that led the pioneers west. When a neighbor moved in a half a
mile down the road, Jack decided it was time to move on.

"A man's gotta have some elbow room," he announced.

Texas was cotton country and cotton was still King in
the south. Jack thought that he could trade subsistence farming
for the opportunity to raise a cash crop. Cotton meant big
money.

Jack sold his farm, bought a couple of big covered
wagons and started out on a wagon train west with Leticia's
parents and a group of friends and relatives. Texas was still a
wild, untamed place when the Wallaces arrived there.

Papa hated the cotton farm. He couldn't get away soon
enough. Even though his grandfather had fought for the Union
during the Civil War, like every little boy in the South, his

lifelong ambition was to grow up to be Robert E. Lee.

Upon graduation from high school in 1921, Papa won an appointment to West Point. In every state each of the senators gets to make one appointment to the Army Academy. He applied for the appointment and out of all of Texas his grades and recommendations were in the top two. It was the first in a long series of disappointments in his life.

His Pa died when Papa was thirteen so his Ma took him to the train station in Wichita Falls.

"You be careful now son, write me every week and don't forget to say your prayers," Leticia said through her tears. The Great War was over, but she had fresh memories in her mind of all of her friends who had received telegrams from the War Department.

"I'll write you once I get to Brownsville," Papa cried out as he stood on the steps of the coach. He was excited beyond measure. This was the biggest adventure of his life.

The train arrived in Brownsville and a bus waited to take the recruits to the Army base.

"OK, Son, read the smallest line you can see," said the officer in a white lab coat.

"F, E, L, O, P, Z, D."

"Good, now cover your left eye and read the smallest line."

"F, E, L, O, P, Z, D."

"Excellent, now cover your right eye and read the smallest line."

"I can't see it sir."

"You what?"

"I can't see too good outta my left eye, sir."

Papa was born with a cataract on his left eye and was virtually blind in that eye. He failed the physical and was sent home.

Determined to make a career for himself in the Army,

Papa hung around the recruiting office in Wichita Falls shooting the breeze with the recruiting sergeants. He became such a fixture there that soon the recruiters failed to notice him. When no one was watching him, he memorized the eye chart.

"Hey Wallace," shouted the sergeant. "Ain't you ever gonna sign up?"

"Well, I don't know Sarge. I guess I could. Ain't got nothin' else to do today."

This time he passed the physical exam because he knew the order of the letters on the eye chart.

Papa worked his way up to sergeant in the field artillery and caught the eye of his colonel. The colonel called him into his office and offered him the opportunity to take the test for promotion into the officers' ranks.

"I'll give you a couple of weeks to get ready for the test," the colonel told him.

"I can take the test this afternoon if you like, sir," replied Sergeant Wallace.

"You cocky son of a bitch," snapped the colonel, "I'm calling your bluff. Report to my office at two p.m. for the test."

By dinner time, Papa was brevetted a lieutenant in the U. S. Army. A few weeks later he received a letter from the new President, Calvin Coolidge, officially making him an officer and a gentleman.

Army issue field glasses used for sighting the great guns had cross hairs on the left lens. Papa was blind in the left eye so he had a special pair of field glasses made with the cross hairs on the right lens. This way no one knew that he was covering up a handicap.

A couple of years later his company was on maneuvers when he discovered that he left his special binoculars in his quarters. He had to borrow a pair of Army issue field glasses. He was standing on a ridge, directing the fire of a battery of French 75's with the left lens over his right eye and the right lens poking out to the side of his head. A captain, who felt Papa was breathing down his neck, walked up behind him and saw how he was using the glasses.

"Mr. Wallace, am I to assume that you can't see out of your left eye?"

An eye test later and Papa was out on the street, facing civilian life for the first time in his adult life.

As soon as we cast off our lines and cleared the jetty, Papa went down to the fo'c'sle and took off his watch. He emptied his pockets of change and put it, along with his watch and wallet in a little wooden cigar box.

"We won't need any money out here," he told me. "And we don't need to answer to any man about being anywhere on time." He felt truly free when he was at sea.

The *Marine View* steamed southwest. By early afternoon we put the Coronado Islands behind us.

"That's our first sight of Mexico," Papa said. "From now on, we're in Mexican waters."

The three dry-looking islands rose out of the water to port, surrounded by numerous rocks that didn't quite qualify to be called islands. A gentle swell softly rolled the boat as she moved sedately across the surface. There was a constant grumble from the engine's exhaust stack. The boat seemed to hum with a life of her own. A salt smell filled the air and a gentle breeze teased our hair. Well, my hair anyway.

It didn't take long to get used to the motion of the boat. Soon I was compensating for the motion as I moved around without even thinking about it. As you walk, you wait for the deck to rise up and greet your foot, you are careful not to step on the down swell or you may go tumbling forward and lose your balance.

During the day, we were both up all the time, so we didn't set any watches, but at night Papa set a watch schedule for us. At night when we were underway, when one of us was asleep, the other had to be awake to make sure we didn't hit anything. Later in the summer, when we were fishing, we often shut down for the night and both slept without keeping watches because the boat wasn't under way.

As we steamed south I learned that Papa's love affair with the sea started in 1929 after he got out of the Army, when he moved to Oakland, California to be near his mother and sister, Jewel. They moved from Texas to live with his brother, Bob. From the start he was enamored of the busy sea port with the comings and goings of the great ships. This was during the last days of the Age of Sail and the graceful ships floated into the bay on wings of white. He spent hours on the docks just watching, fascinated with the romance of these ships, dreaming of sailing anywhere in the world

During the Great Depression, Papa took a job selling life insurance in San Francisco. One of his customers lost his job and was behind on his payments. In those days, the salesman called on the customer every week to collect the insurance payment. This man had been a good customer, so Papa made his payments for him until he could get back on his feet. Finally he was more than fifty dollars behind and that was some serious money. Papa was making thirty-six dollars a month in those days.

Papa met with his customer and told him he'd have to pay up or Papa would have to cut off his insurance. The man made him an offer.

"Listen, Mr. Wallace," the customer said, "I have a sail boat that I can't pay the moorage on either. I'm going to lose it too. How about I give you the boat to cover the insurance payments?"

Papa had never had a boat before, but he had always wanted to sail, so it sounded like a good idea. He couldn't wait to go down and look at his new pride and joy. She was the *Bonita*; a forty-two foot ketch. She had a cabin below decks that was big enough to live in.

He took possession of the *Bonita* at the Berkeley Yacht Harbor. The cost of moorage there was out of the question, so he motored her across the bay to the Aquatic Park and dropped his hook. He lowered her dingy and rowed ashore.

As Papa pulled up to the dock, an old sailor stood with his legs wide apart, hands on his hips, squinting at the *Bonita*. Papa looked him over and thought that here was a man who would have been at home on the quarterdeck of Henry Morgan or Sir Francis Drake.

He looked like an old salt with wavy, thinning gray hair and a trimmed white beard. He had tiny, dark, wicked-looking eyes and was constantly chewing the stem of an old pipe. There was a vaguely piratical look about him with a brass ring in his left ear, tattoos on both arms and skin like dried, crinkled leather.

The old timer stood looking at the *Bonita* for a long time, never giving Papa the slightest indication that he knew that he was there. Papa shuffled uncomfortably from one foot to the other, waiting for some great pronouncement from this ancient mariner. Finally he spoke with the voice of authority, a voice that brooked no questions.

"That's a fine ship you got there, mate," the old sailor said.

Papa felt a sense of overwhelming relief. He wasn't sure what he was expecting, but he was sure that it wasn't good.

"Thank you, sir," he replied.

"Yes sir, she's a fine ship; in spite of her sheer line ain't fair at her taff rail."

Papa was crushed. He didn't know what a sheer line was, or a taff rail for that matter, but it must have been awful. His little ship had a fatal flaw. He knew that he couldn't afford any major repairs.

"It'll be a big job to fair her up; but I can do it easy," the old sailor said.

Maybe the flaw wasn't fatal after all, Papa thought.

Papa managed to tear himself away from the old sailor and walk up town to take care of some errands. When he returned, his dingy was tied to the *Bonita's* side. Papa managed to bum a ride out to his boat with another yachtsman. There on the afterdeck stood Chips, the old sailor, gazing up at the mast head, sea bag at his feet.

"She's right fair enough, matey," Chips said. And with that, he moved aboard. He neither asked nor expected permission; it was just the right thing to do. Papa was so awed by the old sea dog that he never thought to object.

Chips was well into his seventies. He'd been a ship's carpenter in the days of wooden sailing ships. (All ship's carpenters were named "Chips," just like all radio men were named "Sparky" and all ship's doctors were named "Bones.") When he was thirteen years old he'd survived the wreck of the famous *Flying Cloud* clipper when she ran aground on the Beacon Island Bar near St. John's Nova Scotia. He'd sailed on every ocean in the world; he'd seen everything and done everything.

They became great friends. Chips had an endless supply of sea stories. Papa had never set foot on a boat before the *Bonita*; Chips taught him to be a sailor.

The first problem was to find an inexpensive place to moor Papa's new boat. He couldn't afford to pay the moorage fees at a marina. Finally, he found an old, run-down boat yard in Oakland that had mooring buoys off the beach. For a couple of dollars a month he could tie up to a mooring buoy.

A couple of weeks later Chips and Papa were out sailing near Oakland when they ran aground. There's an old saying that there are only two kinds of sailors in this world: Those that have run aground and those that are going to. Papa had just joined the former.

The mud bank that they ran into was off of a run-down, ramshackle group of boats and barges. There was a community of people living on these old derelicts, it was the Depression and this was a floating Hooverville. Papa saw the people and shouted over to see if one of them could come tow them off of the mud bank. He stood in the cockpit, waved his arms and yelled "Ahoy."

"My God, Charlie," Chips cried, "Sit down and shut up. If they hear you talking like that, they'll think you're some rich yachtie and charge a hundred dollars to tow you off. Watch this." With that Chips cupped his hands to his mouth and shouted in a quarter deck voice that could have been heard over the roar of a hurricane.

"Hey comrades."

Sure enough, someone responded and the *Bonita* was soon on her way.

Money was always an issue. Papa couldn't afford to keep up a fine sailing yacht and support his family on his income as an insurance agent. He had lots of friends though and soon he was taking them for Sunday sails on the bay, charging a fee for the ride. The first time they came for the excitement of sailing, but after the first trip they came to listen to Chips.

All day long Chips held court in the cockpit, telling his sea stories. He told of faraway places like Honolulu and Singapore, of bare breasted native women in the South Pacific, of being chased by pirates and running gun battles with German raiders. After the day's sailing was done and Papa was putting the boat away, the party moved down to the cabin. When Papa was done flaking lines and furling sails, he went below for a mug of beer or a glass of wine to find Chips in his glory.

"During the Great War (to Chips, the Great War was WWI), I was sailin' on the *Louisiana Belle*, one of the last sailin' oil tankers, outta Gavleston," Chips told his audience. "We'd taken on a full load of Texas crude and was headed into Dabrovnik when we was attacked."

"Were you torpedoed by a German U-boat?" asked one of Papa's friends.

"Hell no," Chips replied, "We was sunk by a British Cruiser. We was running crude oil to Kaiser Bill."

"What do you mean, you were running oil to the Germans, they were the enemy."

"Yep, they was, but they paid in greenbacks and ol!' John D, he didn't care who's side you was on as long as you paid cash money.

"Anyways, we'd cleared Gibraltar in the night and snuck between Malta and Sicily without seeing no limeys, then one mornin' as we was entering the Adriatic, this Brit cruiser was waitin' for us.

"They signals us to heave to, but the ol' man, he panics and tries to make a run for Dabrovnik. We set all sail, even the stun'sls, in a tops'l breeze; the old girl had never moved so fast. We could practically see the harbor by then.

"The limey opens fire on us with his big guns. Shells was falling all around us, geysers of water as high as the main mast gushed up when a shell exploded along side; the decks was running with water. One shell passed through the mizzen course, rippin' her wide open. Finally, on his fourth or fifth try, we takes a hit just abaft the deck house. I was on the foredeck at the time, securin' the halyards to the pin rail on the foremast. The explosion threw me offa th' deck and sets me afloat.

"'The old *Belle*, she settles by the stern and slips into the clear blue sea. The damned Limey never even stopped to look for survivors, he just steamed off leavin' me there in the water, clingin' onto a floatin' hatch cover."

"'Well, what happened next Chips?" a guest asked. "How did you survive?"

"That's a interestin' story. Ya see, I was picked up by this Slavic fisherman. Now let me tell you about his daughter . . . "

All of Chips stories ended with a fisherman's daughter or a bar maid. And he always shipped out the next day in the clothes on his back.

Things started breaking down on the *Bonita*. Papa and Chips found ways to make do. The *Bonita* had a four cylinder gasoline engine. Sure enough, the engine started giving them trouble. Finally, it died. Papa couldn't afford to have a mechanic come fix the engine and he couldn't afford the parts to try and fix it himself. That was no problem for Chips.

"Well, Charlie I sailed for most of my life without engines. I reckon we can sail without one now."

So Papa's education continued. Chips taught him how to sail the *Bonita* up to the mooring and pick up the mooring buoy without the engine. He taught him how to anchor and get under way under sail.

Papa had numerous lessons in sailing his craft in narrow, confined spaces. They sailed all over the San Francisco Bay and out through the Golden Gate without auxiliary power. Papa learned the power of the tides and how to use them in his favor. There is a heavy tidal current through the Golden Gate. When sailing out, they needed to go with an ebb tide because they couldn't buck the tidal current coming into the bay. When coming home, they needed to sail on a floodtide as the tide was flowing into the bay.

Papa, Chips and their passengers were returning from a sunny Sunday sail in the Pacific Ocean. They timed their entry into the Golden Gate to coincide with floodtide so that the strong tidal current pushed them along. There is a rush at seeing the land fly by as the boat is at hull speed, but a five or six knot current increases the speed to nearly fifteen knots.

They felt like they were flying.

What they hadn't counted on was the fickle wind. As they entered the Golden Gate, the wind died completely. That was unusual for San Francisco Bay. They were completely becalmed and at the mercy of the tide and current. Their sails hung limply from the masts and the boat drifted aimlessly on the water. They didn't even have enough forward motion to be able to steer the boat.

Time drifted by. Papa noticed that they were drifting down towards Alcatraz. It was still miles away and of no real concern. He figured the wind would return before they got anywhere near the prison island.

The afternoon faded into evening. The skies began to darken. The *Bonita* continued on her path towards Alcatraz. At this point, Papa was beginning to get concerned. It was well known that no boat was allowed within shouting distance of the island.

As the night set in, the light in the lighthouse on Alcatraz lit up. Suddenly a bright spot light fixed on the *Bonita*.

"Standoff," came a metallic voice through a loudspeaker. "Don't come any closer."

Papa stood in the cockpit and yelled back.

"Our engine is dead and we don't have any wind, we can't control where we go."

"Standoff or we'll open fire," replied the metallic voice.

At this point, Papa and Chips could see a group of uniformed guards taking up positions along the beach. All of them were armed, either with rifles or Tommy guns.

"Goddamn storm troopers," Chips sneered. "I ain't afraid of them. I been threatened by goddamn Barbary pirates, I been chased by U-boats, shot at by German raiders, them pikers can't scare me."

"This is your last warning. Standoff or we'll open fire."

"Well, you better open fire then," Papa shouted. "I can't

control the boat. We'll go where the tide takes us."

The leader of the guards on the shore pulled back the bolt on his Thompson sub-machine gun and aimed it over the bow. He pulled the trigger and let loose with a short burst of automatic fire. The muzzle flash from the gun lit up the night and the roar echoed off the rock walls of the Golden Gate. There was nothing Papa or Chips could do.

"This is your last warning. The next burst will be into your boat."

The winds gods are fickle. They chose that moment to fill the poor *Bonita's* sails. Suddenly, she heeled over and responded to the helm. Chips ran to sheet in the sails and Papa grabbed the wheel, steering quickly away from Alcatraz and sure death.

"I tol' you, them sons-a-bitches don't scare me. I been threatened by experts." Chips sneered, despite his pale face, shaking knees and shortness of breath.

"Well, Charlie," Chips started, "one of these days I'm gonna quit the sea. I reckon I'll be too old to be of any use to anyone anymore, so I'm gonna move ashore." Papa and Chips were sitting around the *Bonita's* cabin after a long day's sail, sipping homemade wine from Mason jars. "I'm gonna throw an anchor over my shoulder and start walking inland. When some dumb farmer stops me and says 'Hey mister, what's that funny looking hook you have over your shoulder,' that's where I'm gonnna drop my anchor and settle down."

Papa, told me this story as the *Marine View* steamed south. Years later, when I was in high school we read Homer's *The Odyssey.* I came upon a passage that set my heart skittering. I couldn't wait to get home to discuss it with Papa.

It seems that after thirty years of fighting to get home from the Trojan Wars, Odysseus finally made it. When he returned, his friends told him

*You must take a well-made oar and carry it on and on, 'til you
come to a country where the people have never heard of the sea . . . A
wayfarer will meet you and will say it must be a winnowing shovel
that you have got upon your shoulder; on this you must fix the oar in
the ground.*

I couldn't believe it. Chips told Papa the same story that
Homer told over two thousand years ago.

"Chips didn't make up that story himself, he stole it
from *The Odyssey*," I told Papa.

Papa thought about this for a minute and answered.

"No, I don't think so. Chips was practically illiterate.
He went to sea when he was nine years old. He never went to
school. He could write his own name, but not much else. I never
saw him reading anything in all the years I knew him. I don't
believe that he could have read *The Odyssey*. I think that he got
the story from some old sailor who got it from some other old
sailor. I bet that story has been around since men first went to
sea. Homer must have gotten the story the same way Chips did,
from some old salt who was sitting around yarning."

That story had been going around among sailors since
the time of the ancient Greeks. They probably got it from the
Phoenicians before them. Someday I thought to myself, when
I'm an old man, I'll tell the same story to some young buck that
is new to the sea.

"My last contact with Chips was on the day I sold the
Bonita," Papa told me. "Chips had been living on her for almost
five years at the time. When I sold the *Bonita* I sold Chips with
her. As the new owner took possession and sailed off, Chips
was there, standing on the foredeck, holding onto the forestay
looking forward to new adventures."

It was a typical Southern California morning with warm
sunshine and a gentle breeze. A placid swell was running and

the *Marine View* easily cut through the waves as she made eight knots. Papa loved telling stories and I was hypnotized by his tale.

After selling the *Bonita,* Papa bought a boat that he could afford. She was the *Seal,* a twenty-eight foot John Alden sloop. When he worked on her, he always dropped a crab pot over the side.

Papa finished work one day and got ready to go home. He pulled up a crab pot full of crabs.

"Hey, mister," a burly looking Italian guy standing on the dock shouted at Papa. "What ya going to do with all that crab?"

"I'll take them home and maybe make myself a crab Louis I guess," Papa said.

"No, no, no," the Italian man said. "You waste a the crab. You come home with me. I show you how to make a cioppino."

"'OK, bud, my name is Charles," Papa said offering him his hand. The barrel chested Italian had an iron grip.

"You can call me Dino."

On the way back to Dino's apartment house in Little Italy they stopped for supplies at a fish market and bought clams, mussels, prawns, halibut and cod. Then they stopped at an Italian grocery store and bought onions, peppers, tomatoes, Italian bread and a gallon of 'dago red,'

"Now wait a minute, Dino," Papa said. "What are you going to do with all that wine? Surely you don't need a whole gallon of wine to put in the cioppino?"

"No, no." he laughed, "We put half the wine in the cioppino. We put the other half in the cooks."

They got back to Dino's apartment and started cooking. Dino was true to his word. He opened the wine and poured each of them a glass. He never let the glasses get less than half empty.

"Hey Charlie, you like the opera?" Dino asked.

"Sure," Papa said, "I go whenever I have a chance. We have a great opera company here in San Francisco." Papa had a wonderful baritone voice and was always singing opera, along with millions of other songs.

Dino started singing. His voice shook walls. They drank the wine, ate the cioppino and sang opera late into the night.

"Dino," Papa finally said, "don't your neighbors ever complain?"

"Why should they complain?" Dino asked. "Most of them pay good money to go to the opera. Why would they complain when they can hear the same opera here at home for free?"

It turned out that Dino was Dino Borgioli, the lead tenor for the San Francisco Opera Company. Not only did he have a good voice, but he made a hell of a cioppino.

During the Depression Papa scratched to take any no-count job he could find. As he struggled to get by in an unjust world, he developed a sense of political consciousness and became first a union organizer and then a member of the Communist Party. He met and fell in love with a liberal rich girl at one of his party meetings.

Soon they married and had two daughters, but politics was his first priority. He scheduled his jobs around his political activities to the exclusion of his family. It wasn't long before the marriage broke up.

Finally, war broke out in Europe and President Roosevelt promised that America would be "the Arsenal of Democracy." The whole country geared up for the war effort. Suddenly there were jobs for everybody.

Papa worked with his brother, Bob, during the Thirties building houses and the Mare Island Naval Shipyard needed carpenters to build warehouses for their ship building materials, so he went to work there.

The Monday morning after Pearl Harbor, Papa was the first one in line at the Army recruiting office when it opened. He wanted to sign up that day to go fight for his country.

Unfortunately the Army didn't want him. The FBI thought he was a subversive and must have had a file on him two inches thick. When he reported to the induction center, they told him "Sorry, we don't need you."

Papa felt like he had been kicked in the teeth. When he was a boy in Texas, the only thing he ever wanted to be when he grew up was Robert E. Lee; he was going to be a great general. He had spent eight years in the Army preparing for this moment. Now here was a shooting war, he was a trained officer, and they were going to make him sit on the sidelines.

When the Army threw him out, Papa said. "To hell with 'em" and took his induction notice to his foreman at Mare Island. In those days jobs were frozen; if you worked in the war industry, you couldn't quit your job. He told his boss that he had to report to the Army.

"Well, Charlie," the boss said, "I guess the Army needs you worse than we do. Good luck."

So at age thirty-nine, Papa ran away to sea. He packed everything he owned into his car and headed south to Newport Beach. In Newport Beach he hung around the old fishermen and shipped out on other people's boats until he learned enough to go out on his own. Then he bought a beat up old stink pot called the *Cuantos Pescados* and went fishing.

Chapter 7

Papa Goes Fishing

When Papa built the *Marine View* he designed a Rube Goldberg line shaft that ran off of the Ford diesel to run all of the accessories like alternators and the refrigeration plant. Unfortunately, the drive shaft worked better in theory than in practice. It was always throwing V-belts and the equipment stopped working. We hadn't been at sea long before we lost our electrical system.

"Damn," Papa said from the glory hold as I kept a watch on the horizon. "We've thrown a V-belt and it's tangled in the alternator's pulley."

Papa knew that this was a potential source of trouble and always kept extra V-belts on hand, but this was very early in the trip to be having problems. He patiently fought the old, worn belt out of the alternator and installed a fresh belt. While he was working he told me the story of how he became a fisherman.

When he first moved to Southern California, Papa prowled the docks for weeks, looking for a berth. No one would hire him as a deck hand because he was green. He got a job in Hans Dickman's boatyard to hold him over while he looked for a berth. Eventually, the *Santa Maria* came in for some repairs.

Papa talked to the captain of every boat that came in, looking for work, so he asked around and found out the captain of the *Santa Maria* was named Big Manuel.

"Hey Cap," Papa said to him, "you have any openings for a deck hand?"

"No, we don't need no deck hand," Manuel said. "But I

need a cook. I just fire our last cook."

Papa knew his way around a kitchen. He wanted to go fishing so badly that he asked for the job on the *Santa Maria* as a sea cook.

"I don't know." Big Manuel says, "we never had a American cook before." Big Manuel was Portuguese and so were all of his crew.

"Listen Cap, I'm a good cook. Give me a try. I'll go out with you for one trip, if you don't like my cooking, you don't have to pay me and you can set me ashore when we get home." Money talked and Papa had a job.

All of the crew on the *Santa Maria* were named Manuel, every one of them. Most of the time they spoke Portuguese, but in the galley they spoke English so that Papa could understand. He joined the boat during the winter when they were long-lining. They had a crew of six. During the tuna season the *Santa Maria* had a crew of twenty.

"Pasquale," Big Manuel said when Papa first came aboard, "you show Charlie here where to dump his kit."

"I'm glad at least one other man on this boat isn't named Manuel," Papa told Pasquale.

"Oh, Charlie, my real name is Manuel too," Pasquale said. "On this boat, we have five fishermans, all name Manuel. Hafa the Portagee fishermans, they name Manuel, so we have names for each of them. Old Manuel, we call El Viego. Young Manuel we call Joven. Little Manuel we call Maurice. The capitán, we call Julio. And me, they call Pasquale, so you see nobody get mix up?"

Papa needed to win the crew over, so he went all out. He decided to fix a special breakfast on their first day at sea. He fried up bacon and ham, made hash browns and pancakes with real maple syrup, fried up eggs to order.

One by one the crew wandered into the galley. They each took a cup of coffee and sat silently around the table not eating. Papa crossed his arms and furled his brow, what was wrong with these people?

"Hey Mannie, fill up your plate," He said as he shoved a plate toward Maurice.

"Ugghh," was all Maurice said.

"Young Mannie, have something to eat," Papa said.

"Ugghh."

This went on for several minutes, with the crew unwilling to touch any of the food. Finally, Julio, the skipper, came into the galley and poured himself a cup of coffee. The others looked at him expectantly.

Julio settled himself down at the galley table, he reached over with his hand and grabbed a flapjack off of the platter. He reached up and opened the port hole over his shoulder and threw the pancake out the port hole. The whole crew ran to see. They gasped and there was a moment of hushed anticipation, then they all cheered.

Maurice was the first back to the table. He reached over and grabbed about a half a dozen pancakes, eggs, potatoes, bacon and started in. The rest of the crew was right behind him and in a few moments, the table looked like a plague of locus had passed over it. There wasn't a crumb left.

"Goddamn it Mannie," Papa said to Julio, "What's going on here? I put this breakfast on the table and no one takes a bite. Then you throw a pancake out the God damned window and everyone picks the table clean."

"Well, Charlie, the last cook we had on this boat, he made a pancakes that sink. We eat his pancakes, we sink. We throw him overboard and he sink. Your pancakes, they float. We eat your pancakes, we float."

The crew burst out laughing, but kept eating.

The *Santa Maria* was a big wooden tuna clipper. A hundred and three feet long, with a high raised bow and big deck house. She tapered down to a low freeboard at the stern so men could fish off of her. They had a huge bait tank on deck and her hold held over a hundred tons.

I remember seeing tuna clippers on *Seven League Boots* on TV. On these boats the men fished with poles.

For tuna they had a crew of twenty men on board. Iron baskets hung over the sides of the ship from which they fished. They fished for blue fin tuna, which are big fish. Usually two men had poles that met at a single leader. When they got a strike, both of men had to work together to bring the fish aboard. If they hit a school of big fish, then they put three men on each line.

The men stood in those baskets pulling fish all day. They drug them aboard hour after hour and the fish piled up on the deck so thick that the crew had to walk on them. The hold man's job was to clean the fish and stow them below in the ice.

Papa tried hard to win over the crew of the *Santa Maria*. He roasted a turkey, with all the trimmings. The crew picked at it and were polite, but they weren't enthusiastic. He cooked pot roast and Swiss steak. He made steaks and roast pork. The crew was polite, but Papa could tell they weren't enthusiastic about his cooking.

During a lull in the fishing, Young Mannie dropped a hand line over the side and caught a couple of sea bass that he brought to Papa to cook for dinner. Papa thought and thought about how to prepare them. Then he had an idea, *These Portagees aren't that different from the Italians, maybe I should make a cioppino.*

Papa cleaned the fish and cut them into little cubes. He peeled and chopped onions. The smell of the onions and garlic and peppers frying filled the galley. Pretty soon Maurice walked by the deckhouse and stopped dead in his tracks.

He stopped and sniffed the air. He took a huge breath and tried to locate the source. He sniffed around, then stuck his head in the port hole. He sniffed, then inhaled like he was going to blow out the candles on a birthday cake. A huge smile broke across his face.

He turned and cupped his hands to his mouth. "Chaaa -ping" he yelled to the crew. Everyman on the boat dropped what he was doing and rushed to the galley. They stood around sniffing and smelling, jumping up and down, slapping each other on their backs. "Chaping, Chaping" they shouted.

Papa won over the crew of the *Santa Maria*. Every second or third day the crew brought him bass or perch or crab or lobster or prawns or something from the sea. And every second or third day he cooked up a big pot of cioppino, or chaping as the Portuguese called it, and had them eating out of the palm of his hand. He never had a problem with the crew on the *Santa Maria*.

The *Santa Maria* was a good boat with a good crew. That first winter Julio (Big Mannie) took the *Santa Maria* all the way into the Sea of Cortez, on the east side of the Baja peninsula, looking for fish to wholesale to fish markets.

"Hey, Julio," Maurice, the engineer, yelled one evening as he climbed up from the engine room. "We got trouble."

"What's a matter?" the skipper asked.

"The cooling manifold, she is leaking. She got a goddamn crack, Julio. It no good. We gonna have a big problem if we don't replace her."

"Sheet, we twelve hundred miles from San Diego. Where we gonna get a goddamn cooling manifold?"

"La Paz"' chipped in Viego, old Mannie. "La Paz a big town. They got ever'thin' there."

Julio thought it over.

"No, it no make sense to run into La Paz. It two hundred miles out of our way. We don' even know if they got a damn GM dealer."

"They got ever'thin' there" Viego repeated. "I been to

La Paz lots a times. It a nice city. You can get anythin'."

The argument went on, but Julio really didn't have a choice. He could radio San Diego and have a part shipped to them, but God only knew how long that would take, if it ever got there. And he didn't know where they would be when the part finally arrived.

Without the new manifold, the big GM diesel would eventually overheat. Then they were out of business all together. No, Julio reasoned, they had to take a chance on La Paz. Julio charted a course and they steamed all day and all night.

"La Paz, she a beautiful city," Viego told the crew at dinner, in English for Papa's sake. "She on a big bay, with a long, narrow channel. You gotta be careful coming in or you run aground.

"In the evening there's a on-shore breeze that kill the heat of the day. The Mexicans call it the Coromuel."

Papa had heard of it. "It's named for an English pirate, Captain Cromwell, that used La Paz as his headquarters," he said.

"They were lots a pirates in La Paz," continued Viego. "French, Dutch, English, you name it. They was waiting for the Manila galleys that used ta bring treasure ever' year from the Philippines."

"I hear there's still buried pirate treasure around La Paz," chipped in Joven, young Mannie. "My ol' man says they dug up a chest full of silver and golda couple a years ago when they was puttin' up a new buildin'."

"The real treasure," Maurice chipped in "is the pearls. La Paz been the pearl capital of the worl' for four hundred years.

"I heard of the Cave of the Dead Beasts. It's a lost cave that the local injuns used to worship their gods. They's supposed to be tons a pearls adornin' their idols there."

"I don't give a good God damn about no pirate treasure or pearls," Julio said. "I just wanta find the GM dealer so's we can get back to fishin'."

Early the next morning, they sighted the harbor. It was easy to pick out the channel because the water over the shoals was a lighter blue than the channel. Julio brought the big tuna clipper up to the shore near *El Malécon*, the wide palm tree lined promenade that runs along the beach.

As soon as they had the *Santa Maria* safely anchored, the entire crew piled in to the big skiff and headed ashore. They landed on the beach with the flair and bravado of a boat load of pirates coming ashore.

"OK, Viego, where this GM dealer?" the skipper asked.

"You follow me," Viego said.

He led the crew up the dusty, cobble stone streets through the plaza. The plaza, with a big gazebo in its center, was a city block square and the only patch of green in the city. On one side sat the Catholic cathedral, the other three sides were lined with arcade-fronted buildings.

Papa was responsible for feeding the crew so he took a detour into the public market. There were stalls filled with every kind of fruit and produce imaginable. *Where, in the middle of this god-forsaken dessert,* Papa thought, *do the Mexicans grow this kind of produce?* In the *carnecería*, the butcher shop, beef, pork and chicken hung un-refrigerated. A small brown boy spent the day waving a fan to keep the flies off the meat. Pigs' heads and organs hung from metal hooks on the wall. Plucked chickens dangled beside them.

In a small stall, off to one side, a group of Mexican women patted out tortillas by hand and cooked them on a hot grill. Next to them was a *tamalería* where another group of women made tamales by hand and wrapped them in *hojas* (corn husks).

Further into the market were the fish stalls. Wahoo, tuna, dorado, swordfish, marlin, squid, octopus and dozens of other strange looking denizens of the deep filled the shelves.

Another table was stacked with lobsters, langostinos (small, clawless lobsters), clams, oysters, and mussels.

Papa worked his way through the stalls, picking out what he needed to keep his crew happy. At each stall he always asked "*Que Costa*?" (How much does it cost?) and always offered the vendor a lower price.

Viego led the rest of the crew through the winding streets of La Paz.

"Hey, Viego," Pasquale said, "How far is the GM dealer? This look like a residential neighborhood?"

"Not far, you stick with me," Viego replied.

They rounded a corner and came to a plain, white washed building with wrought iron shutters over the windows, a red clay tile roof and wrought iron gate leading to a central courtyard. Soft strains of guitar music and the tinkle of a fountain leaked from the courtyard.

"This is it"' Viego said.

"What, you nuts? What is this place?" Julio asked.

"This is *La Casa Isabella*, the best whorehouse in all of Mexico."

"Whorehouse? I thought you was takin' us to the GM dealer."

"GM dealer? What GM dealer? There ain't no GM dealer in La Paz."

On their next trip, the *Santa Maria* fished for blue fin tuna. They were rigged for live bait and had twenty men on board. When they hit a school of fish, they chummed with the live bait to attract the fish to the boat, then jigged for them with chicken feather jigs.

Viego, well into his seventies by then, was the hold man, the most important job on the boat. As the fish came aboard, Viego cleaned and gutted them, then iced them down in the hold. When they got back into port, the buyers looked at each fish as it was hoisted out of the hold, and if it had not been cleaned and iced right, they set it aside. Maybe it could be saved and the boat might get paid for it, but sometimes it couldn't and they sold it for cat food.

Viego was good at his job, he was an artist with a knife. He had a long thin bladed filleting knife. He made a cut on each side of the big fish, just behind the gills, and pulled the head free. Then he made a quick cut from the anus to the gills and opened up the fish's belly. With a quick swish of his hand, he pulled the guts free and tossed them, along with the head, in the bin, then flipped the huge fish into the fish hold. It didn't take him a full minute to clean and gut one of the fish.

When he had a pile of clean fish in the hold, he went below and iced them down. He filled the body cavity with ice, stacked them carefully in the bins, then covered them with a layer of ice. How such a small, old man could handle those big fish, Papa never understood, but he did a better job than any other man on the boat.

When they hit a school, of tuna, Viego got into the baskets like everyone else and pulled fish. When they had a good load on deck he left the bucket and started cleaning them.

Viego, Young Mannie, and Papa were a team. They always fished in the first basket on the starboard side. When the deck load built up, Viego left and Young Mannie and Papa pulled by themselves. Young Mannie was built like a bull, so between the two of them, they did the work of three men.

They hit a good school. These were big fish, all of them three pole fish. All morning long they pulled those giants. Papa kept asking Viego "you ready to head for the hold yet?" Viego, covered with sweat and laboring for breath, kept saying "Now Charlie, you need three men for these fishes. I clean them when the school she settles down."

Papa was the lead, so when he gave the shout, they pulled together and flipped the fish aboard. They had a big one on and Papa shouted "heave." The three men dragged the fish over the bulwarks and Viego shouted "Ughh, Ughh, Ughh." Papa turned to look at him and he was grabbing his chest and turning blue.

"Jesus Christ," Papa shouted. "Mannie, get the captain." Then he lifted Viego over his shoulder and climbed out of the basket back on deck. By that time, Julio was there. Papa felt Viego's throat for a pulse, but he was already gone.

"He's dead, skipper," Papa said.

"OK, back to work then."

"We can't just leave him here. We need to take care of his body." Papa said.

"There's nothing we can do for him now. We take care of him when the fish they stop biting. Leave him where he lies and get back to the baskets."

Like the captain said, they went back to the baskets and kept pulling fish. Viego just lay there in the fish bins and they covered him in blue fins.

"Charlie, you the hold man now," The captain said about an hour later. "You the cook, so you can handle a knife. You clean these sons-a-bitches and gets them iced down."

When the sun went down and the fish stopped biting, the crew cleaned and iced all the fish, then they had to figure out what to do with Viego.

"Shall we bury him at sea?" Papa asked the captain.

"No, he go home with us. Put him in the hold, his body'll keep. His wife, she will want to bury him in the church yard on consecrated soil. Does anyone want to say a few words before we put him away?"

Everyone looked around at each other and no one spoke up.

"Doesn't the captain read over his body?" Papa asked

"Not this captain,' Julio said. "I ain't got no Bible.'

"OK, I'll say something." Papa replied.

"He's deader 'n nails,' the fo'c'sle said, ''n' gone to his long sleep';

"'N' about his corp,' said Tom to Dan 'd'ye think his corp'll keep.

"Till the day's done, 'n' the work's through, 'n' the ebb's upon the neap?' (Salt Water Poems and Ballads, John Masefield, The Macmillan Company, 1912, pg 13)

With that they lowered him down into the hold and Papa put him in an empty bin.

It was a good trip and they filled the hold on that huge old barge. Papa spent the rest of the trip as the hold man. Every day he went to go down into the hold with old Viego's corpse. As the bins filled up, Papa stood the frozen corpse up and lashed it to a post. He spent so much time in the hold that he started talking to Viego, and after a while he swore that Viego answered him.

When he went down to the hold, Viego was there to greet him.

"Charlie, we have a good day today?" Viego asked.

"Si, good day," Papa answered. "Now, Viego, where am I going to put this big mother?"

"You put her in the second bin on the starboard side, Charlie,'" Viego told Papa.

When they pulled into San Diego, Julio radioed ahead and Viego's family waited for them at the dock. There was a black hearse with an undertaker in a dark suit, a priest to pray over him and all the women folk from his family. His wife was there and his daughters and daughters-in-law, his granddaughters and granddaughters-in-law and all the great grandchildren. There were no men. His sons, sons-in-law, grandsons and grandsons-in-law were all away fishing.

They pulled up to the cannery dock and the dockside crew lowered a sling. Papa started to untie Viego to lift him on deck.

"No, Charlie, Viego goes last," Julio shouted down, "The boat always comes first, then the fish, then the crew." They unloaded every fish in the hold before Julio let them bring Viego out. His family waited patiently and never said a word. He had spent his whole life following the sea and they knew the rules.

Papa's job on the *Santa Maria* lasted one season. At the end of the season Julio and Papa agreed to part ways as friends. One of Julio's old cooks became available again and Bill Bacchus on the *Albatross* offered Papa a berth as the sea cook.

"Newport Beach was a different town then," Papa told me as we steamed south. "There were three canneries on the west side of the bay and that whole area that's covered with expensive beach houses now was just an empty sand spit. Out past the canneries there was a marina where the movie stars kept their boats.

"The Duke had his boat there. The *Wild Goose* was an old Navy minesweeper that he converted into a yacht. When I first moved to Newport and was working in the boat yard, I did some work for him during the conversion."

"John Wayne? You met John Wayne? What was he like?"

"Just a regular guy. He came down, put on his dungarees and worked with the rest of us. He always took care of his crew and the people working on his boat. He had lunch brought for us and had a cooler of beer when we knocked off at night.

"I hit it off real good with the Duke. We were installing cabinets in the galley and got to talking. I told him that I had been a cowboy in Texas as a young man and things just took off from there."

"Wow, was there anybody else famous there?"

"Well, the Duke introduced me to Bogey. Bogey had

just bought a 58 foot schooner named the *Santana* and didn't
know how to sail. Cap'n Kidder and I taught Bogey to sail.

"We were coming back from a trip with Bogey when I
noticed an old hulk sitting on the beach south of the marina. I
wandered over to look at her. She was a thirty-six foot double-
ender that had been holed and her owner ran her up on the
beach to keep her from sinking. He stripped her of all of her
equipment and she was just laying there rotting away. I asked
around the docks and found out who owned her. They were
going to burn her to salvage the metal parts in her.

"I'd just come back from the trip on the *Albatross* and
had some money burning a hole in my pocket. I found the
owner and offered him two hundred and fifty dollars for her.
He jumped at the chance to get rid of her and I was back in the
boating business. I fixed her up there on the beach, patched the
hole and made her water tight, then I found an old Chrysler
gasoline engine for her.

"She was named the *Cuantos Pescados*."

***

I knew that meant "how many fish?" in English.

"The *Cuantos* was a cranky, leaky old thing; she was so
old that she still carried a sail on her mast. Her ancient gasoline
engine never ran when you needed it. She took on water, was
full of dry rot and wouldn't sail in a straight line without a
constant hand on the wheel, but she was mine."

I had seen enough old derelicts in the fleet that I knew
that fishermen sometimes took awful chances. They ventured
far out to sea in marginally seaworthy boats and every year,
one or two of them didn't come back.

"In the summer I took the *Cuantos* out after tuna," Papa
continued. "I'd usually pick up a kid off the beach for crew. In
the fall and winter I fished for mackerel or squid. In the spring

I'd go down the coast of Mexico after fresh market fish. After three seasons, I was an old hand."

Mackerel were caught in nets at night. They were attracted to the boat by chum, ground up pieces of fish, fins, guts and anything else that smells bad and attracts fish. Papa took the *Cuantos* out past the jetty and towards Catalina Island. After an hour or so, he slowed the boat down to where it just barely had headway.

Throwing handfuls of the chum in the water, he left a 'chum stream' behind the boat. He could leave a stream for up to half a mile.

The mackerel couldn't resist the tasty smell. First there were a few silver flashes at the stern of the boat, then Papa dropped more chum and the water began to boil with fish.

When he was in shallow water, he dropped the anchor. If the water was too deep, he put out a sea anchor to keep the boat over the school of fish. It was important to keep the boat pointing into the current, because the mackerel swim against the current. By keeping the boat headed the same way as the fish, the fish tend to swim along behind the boat, eating the chum. When he had a good school going, he hung a shaded electric light over the stern. The light brought the fish to the surface and let him see where he was working. When the sea boiled with fish, Papa stepped into the iron basket that hung on the rail off the stern of the boat with his sea boots just above water level, and sometimes underwater, and used a long handled net to scoop up the fish and drop them on deck.

Fishermen called this brailing because the net is called a brail. He scooped load after load of fish over his shoulder and onto the deck.

Sometimes he fished alone and sometimes with a partner. Mac was his favorite mackerel partner. They stood side by side in the iron baskets and brailed mackerel all night.

"Mac taught me the fine art of mackerel fishing," Papa

told me. "But Mac never left sight of land. I liked fishing for mackerel but they only brought home a small paycheck, I wanted a big payday. Everyone else fished for albacore in the summer and only fished mackerel after the tuna season."

"I hooked up with Jim Trammel who took me on a tuna cruise aboard his troller. The first time I pulled a big albacore over the gunwale, I was hooked. Mac was horrified that I wanted to take the *Cuantos* off-shore. The *Cuantos* didn't have refrigeration or carry enough fuel or water for a long trip and besides, he didn't think it was safe to go that far out in a leaky old stinkpot."

"Mac, the big money is in albacore," Papa told him. "And beside, I want to be a blue water fisherman."

"Well, Charlie," Mac said, "You might make it out there for a trip or two, but mark my words, if you keep it up they'll end up buryin' you in blue water."

After that Mac started calling Papa "Blue Water Charlie" and it didn't take long for the rest of the boys in the fleet to take it up.

Chapter 8

How Papa met Mama

As Papa learned his new trade, the war raged on. It was 1944 when Papa met Mama. Hitler was on the run. Ike had just landed on the beaches of Normandy. Here at home, everyone was involved in the war with a "home front" mentality. People tore up their lawns and planted Victory Gardens in their front yards, schools held recycling campaigns and war bond drives. Factories were converted to war use. Tanks rolled off of the automobile assembly lines in Detroit.

"There was a sign on Harbor Boulevard in downtown Santa Ana with a picture of a Sherman tank on it and the caption 'When Better Cars Are Built, Buick Will Build Them,'" Papa told me as we went about our chores.

With the men off at war, women flocked to the factories and shops to help the war effort. In California, for the Mexican women, this was nothing new. The majority of the Mexicans in California were poor. Just like in the Old Country, women and children worked to help support the family.

For the Mexicans, the war was an opportunity. The young men, like my Uncle Kenneth, rushed off to join the Army to show that they too could serve their country. When the Army rounded up the Japanese-Americans and sent them off to internment camps, the Mexicans were happy to step in and take their place in the economic food chain.

I remembered Mama's stories about how the tomato and strawberry fields that had been carefully developed by the Japanese farmers were taken over by the Mexicans during the War. In the strawberry fields where Mama worked, the Japanese field bosses gave each worker a metal police whistle to blow. The berry pickers had to blow on the whistles all day long. If they stopped whistling they were fired because the field boss knew that they were eating strawberries.

When the Mexicans took over the fields, the whistles went away. Instead, Mama said, a galvanized tub filled with ice and cold pop sat at the end of each row. At lunch and at the end of the day, the workers broke out their guitars. Life was good.

Mama had told me how, as the sun moved low over the nearby ocean, one of the men would stand and stretch and let out a "grito."

"*Aye, aye, aye.*" Then he would break into song. It was usually a fast paced ranchero.

"*Aya en el rancho grande, aya donde vivia.*" The whole work crew joined in. "*Aye una rancharita, que allegre me decia, que allegre me decia . . .*"

Soon the berry fields echoed with happy music. It was a fiesta every day.

Mama's father, *Don Teodoro.* believed that you became a man or a woman at age thirteen. He pulled each of his children out of school on their thirteenth birthday and took them out and got them jobs. Like the rest of her family, Mama never got the chance to finish high school. Papa had instilled the importance of an education in us so strongly that I couldn't imagine leaving school in two years to go to work.

Mama and her family worked in the berry fields every spring after the tomatoes had been planted in their own fields so they could to bring home cash for *Teodoro.* When the word came that the canneries were desperate for workers Mama, my Aunt Mellie and *Abuelita* all took jobs at the cannery in Newport Beach.

Papa was an important man in the fishing industry. He helped organize the Fisherman's Union and was its president at that time.

One of the biggest problems facing the fishermen was that they could catch more fish than the canneries could can. Boats were laid up at the cannery dock waiting to be unloaded. They couldn't go back to sea and were losing money every day they were tied up.

The problem wasn't the machinery. The canneries had taken every fish they could catch in the past. The problem was the labor pool. There weren't enough men to operate the machinery and keep the cannery going, so Papa came up with a solution to the problem. He got every fisherman to donate one day's work to the cannery each week to help keep them running.

Papa met with the cannery owner, Brad Owens, to set up the schedule.

"Everything is for the war effort you know," Brad said "Things are tough and I can't afford to pay you for your time."

"The bastard was getting top prices for his canned tuna from the War Department," Papa told me. "And he was using free labor from us."

I was indignant. I had read enough to know that this was called profiteering.

"Why did you do it then? Couldn't you just not work for him?"

"Well, PC, we were in a bind. If we didn't help him out, we couldn't sell our fish to him."

Papa worked the first shift at the cannery to set an example. His first job was unloading the boats. They used huge iron buckets to remove the fish. A crane lifted the buckets out of the boat, but the buckets needed to be manhandled into the fish holds and out of them without doing too much damage to the fish or the boat. The buckets held dozens of fish each and easily weighed a thousand pounds. This wasn't a job, the bosses thought, for a woman.

After the boats were all unloaded for the day, Papa wandered through the cannery. He wanted to get a feel for all of the jobs so that he would know where to put the fishermen. As he came to the line where the cans came out of the big pressure ovens and were checked before being put in boxes, this pretty young girl caught his eye.

She had long dark hair, a trim figure and deep brown eyes that could make a man's knees buckle.

"Hi, my name is Charles," Papa said as he sauntered over. "I'm working here one day a week now."

"Shh," the girl growled, "Go away, my mama is watching me. She will see you." Then she turned her back and ignored Papa.

Papa made it his business to watch her the rest of the day. He spotted her mother, a tiny middle-aged Mexican woman packing the cans in boxes. She kept an eagle eye on her daughter. When *Abuelita* was called off of the line, Papa approached the girl again.

"Can we start over?" he said. "My name is Charles."

"Sharles," she said in a delicious accent. "I'm sorry. I couldn't let my mama see me with you. My name is Vicki." When *Abuelita* wasn't around she was free to flirt.

"Is there some place where we can talk?' Papa asked her.

"Meet me at the pier," she said, "by the park benches where the gringos take their lunches, after the shift."

She told her mother some lie about why she couldn't walk home with Mellie and her and met Papa after the shift. She was wearing slacks and a white blouse with a bandana around her long black hair. She smelled of sweat and fish and lubricating oil. It was love at first sight. Papa knew right then that he was going to marry her.

They met a few times after that, on the sly. Then he asked her to go to dinner with him. She told her mother that she was going to a USO dance at the Navy base in Long Beach. *Abuelita* never let her out of her sight without a chaperone, but Mellie was going to the dance with her. Mellie was dating a Marine that she wanted to see too. Her mother had to let her go to a USO dance; it was part of the war effort.

To keep *Abuelita* from becoming suspicious, Mama ate a full dinner before she and Mellie left for the "USO dance." Papa picked her up at their meeting place on the pier. He had a fairly new Dodge automobile and never had any problem getting gasoline, despite the war-time rationing. He could get all the gasoline he needed for his boat and siphon it off into the car.

Papa took her to Santa Ana to a fancy steak house. He had a New York steak with the works. Mama ordered the petite sirloin and only picked at it. She wasn't hungry after a full meal of frijoles and tortillas at home.

While Papa told her stories about his adventures she just sat and listened. Papa was forty-one when he met her and she was only nineteen. Mama had told me that he was this big, strong, suave Anglo who swept her off her feet. He owned his own boat; he had money for a car and dinner. He was well read, spoke perfect English, and had the manners of a southern gentleman. She saw him as this big, strong Viking that could do anything.

Lost in her dreams when Papa stopped talking, she looked up at him and he was staring at her. Mama panicked, she didn't know what to say. Papa asked her a question and she hadn't answered. She was lost in her fantasies and could only think of one thing that he might have asked.

"But Sharles," she said, "I can't cook."

"I don't want a cook," he told her. "I can cook, I want a play mate. I want someone to share my adventures with. I want someone to come home to at night."

When he dropped her off at their place on the pier, they took a walk along the water front. It was a warm, romantic night with the city lights and the moon reflecting off the water.

Back in those days, the future seemed endless. They thought that the boom would go on forever.

"I want a new boat, a bigger boat," he told her. "I want a boat that can go anywhere in any weather. Then I can really make money. When I save enough, I'd like to buy a house with a marine view. I want to be able to sit in my living room and look out on the ocean. I want it to have a captain's walk so my wife can stand at the rail and look for me to return when I'm at sea."

The thought of a real house, with running water and electricity was more than Mama could hope for. She was raised in a shack without plumbing or electricity. She dreamed of a white house with a picket fence around a green lawn; in the driveway she wanted a shiny new car and a garden with fruit trees and flowers, lots of flowers.

At the end of the wharf, he tried to kiss her.

"Sharles,' she said, "I have to go. Mama will be waiting for me." With that, she pulled away from him and ran off up the road.

Mama is a very private person, she didn't share many details about her feelings with us, but, over the years, she told me her side of the story. She said it was a secret romance. She couldn't let her parents know that she was dating a gringo. Her Papa would beat her; her Mama would lock her up. It had always been assumed that she would marry Jose Gomez, the son of one of her mother's friends. She dated Mexican boys, but they were boys, she couldn't imagine herself settling down with any of them. Papa was a man. He offered safety and security.

Mama told *Abuelita* that she was going to spend the whole day sewing with Maria Juarez, helping her prepare for Maria's wedding. Of course, Maria, who loved a good romance, was sworn to silence. More and more of Mama's friends got in on the secret. A huge wave of excitement engulfed them. No one had ever dated a gringo before.

Papa took her out on his boat, the *Cuantos Pescados,* for a ride around the bay. At the end of the day, he gave her a present of fish, "To take home for dinner."

Abuelita hated fish because they smelled up the house. Mama graciously accepted them. When Papa dropped her off at the pier she waited for him to leave, then threw them into the bay.

"By the time I met your mother, I had pretty much figured women out," Papa told me. "I knew that if I told them what they wanted to hear and bought them little presents, I could have any woman I wanted, but there was something special about this little Mexican girl."

He wanted to take her home, to care for her and protect her. Finally, he asked Mama to marry him. She said yes. She couldn't wait to get away from her father. However, she was reluctant to tell her mother.

They got married by a justice of the peace at the Orange County court house. Mama put on her best dress and snuck out of the house to meet him. It was February eighth 1945, she had just turned twenty. After the ceremony, Papa took her back to her mother's house. She didn't get up the nerve to tell *Abuelita* that she was married until February twelfth.

"Victoria, what are you doing?" *Abuelita* asked as she walked into Mama's room with an arm full of laundry. Mama had a little brown cardboard-sided suitcase on her bed and her clothes spread all over the room.

"Mama," Mama hesitated. "I'm packing. . . I'm leaving today."

"Leaving? Leaving where? Where are you going?"

"Mama, I'm married. I got married Thursday."

"Married. . .? To who? Who did you marry?"

"His name is Carlos, Charles. He's an Anglo."

"No, you can't be married. He never asked your father, you never talked to us. You can't be, not to a gringo. It will kill your father."

Mama continued to pack her clothes, fighting back tears.

"You're too young. You're just a baby."

"Mama, you got married when you were sixteen."

"That's different. I had no family, no one to take care of me."

"How about Anna?" Mama's oldest sister had gotten married when she was sixteen too.

"We knew Antonio. He was from a good family. He was part of our race. He asked your father for Anna's hand." For a moment the two women were silent. Then Grandma took charge.

"This won't do. I will talk to Father Garcia. He can arrange for an annulment. You didn't get married in the Church anyway, it's not really a marriage."

Mama burst into tears, grabbed her suitcase and rushed past her mother in the doorway. Sobbing she ran down the road to her meeting place with Papa.

"Vicki, what's wrong?" Papa asked when he saw her.

"I just told Mama, I just left my family." Papa was reminded of the lyrics from the old song *Billy Boy*, "She's a young thing and cannot leave her mother." From then on, *Billy Boy* was their song.

Mama celebrated their anniversary on February eighth and Papa always celebrated it on the twelfth.

Even as an eleven year old, the Mexican half of my personality was hopelessly romantic. I loved hearing the story of my parents' romance, their triumph against all odds. I could picture it as a Hollywood movie. I could see Clark Gable and Kathryn Hepburn playing my parents.

Papa's family had a hard time accepting Mama. They had grown up in the South and were used to a rigid social hierarchy. At the bottom were the blacks and just above them were the Mexicans. They weren't ready to accept a Mexican as their equal.

Papa told me that Mama's family had a hard time accepting him. First of all, he was a gringo. Her father hated gringos. Secondly, he couldn't speak Spanish. Her father didn't allow English in his house.

This was confusing for me. I couldn't imagine the world any other way, but I always felt a little out of place. When I was with my mother's family, I struggled to keep up with the conversations in Spanish. I always felt just a little uncomfortable. When I was out in the world, I always felt ashamed to be this little Mexican kid. I got used to being called "wetback" and "lazy Mexican" at school. I always felt not quite good enough.

Papa said that he didn't give a damn what his siblings thought of his wife, but he wanted desperately to be accepted by her family. He tried to learn Spanish, but it just wouldn't click in his mind. For the next fifty years he tried, but never was able to form more than a rudimentary sentence or understand what was being said to him. He managed to memorize the words to some Mexican songs, but usually butchered them.

He was good to her brothers and sisters. *Abuelita* fell in love with this strong American and gradually *Don Teodoro* forgave him for marrying his daughter.

Mama tried to Americanize her family. As November approached that first year, she decided that they should put on a big American Thanksgiving dinner at *Abuelita's* house.

The family still lived on the tomato farm on Goat Hill. Her sister, Anna, had married Big Tony and built a little house on the other side of the driveway on *Abuelita's* farm. In those days her parents' house was a glorified shack. There was no indoor plumbing. A two-holer outhouse, complete with a Monkey Ward catalog for the paperwork, was behind the houses. The house had a large living room and a big kitchen with a wood-fired stove.

"Mama," Mama told *Abuelita*, "Sharles and I would like to make a Thanksgiving dinner for the family this year."

"What is this Thanksgiving?" *Abuelita* asked.

"It's a gringo holiday. The day that they thank the *indios* for helping them get settled in this country."

"Why would they thank the *Indios*?" *Abuelita* wanted to know. "They took their land and killed them off. What kind of thanks is that?"

"It's an American tradition, Mama," Mama said.

"They took our land." *Abuelita* told her. "All of this land used to be part of Mexico. Now we are beggars in our own country."

"But Mama, this is just a holiday. It doesn't really mean anything."

"If it doesn't mean anything, then why do we have to do it?"

"Our family has nothing to do with this Plymouth Rock, or Thanksgiving or Pilgrims," Don Teodoro said. "Our heritage is *Cinco de Mayo* and the 16th of September." But Mama persisted. All through her childhood she listened to the Anglo kids talk about roast turkeys and gravy and Pilgrims. Now it was her turn.

Finally, Teodoro wavered, if it meant a turkey dinner, he was willing to allow a celebration in his house.

There was a general sense of excitement in the air. With most Mexican families, any excuse for a party was always welcome. The kids ran though the house and around the yard all day. Vergie and Jenny brought home paper turkeys, pilgrims and Indians that they made in school. *Abuelita* was nervous having a stranger working in her kitchen. Mama was a wreck. Her feast had to be just like it had been for the Pilgrims and the Indians.

"Sharles," Mama asked, "have you basted the turkey yet?"

"Yes, Vicki. It's already done."

"How about the potatoes? Are they peeled yet?"

"They're already on the stove."

"The rolls, are the rolls rising yet?"

"Vicki, calm down. It's all under control."

"But Sharles, it all has to be perfect. My family has never had a Thanksgiving before."

"Don't worry about it, Vicki. Everything is just fine."

They made sage dressing, mashed potatoes and giblet gravy, cranberry sauce, green beans, fruit salad. Sitting on Abuelita's cabinet in the kitchen were five golden pumpkin pies.

Teodoro and Big Tony were in charge of setting up a table in the living room.

"*Oye, Antonio*," Teodoro said, "Get the old doors behind the cow shed that we use for a table; I'll get the saw horses."

Abuelita covered the doors with lace tablecloths to make a pretty table. Anna brought dishes and tableware from her own house. They had a Tower of Babel of china on the table.

"Tony, you and Santos run over to our house and get more chairs," ordered Big Tony.

The family began to file in and find their places. Mama and her sisters started bringing dish after dish to the table. Papa brought in the crowning touch, the turkey, golden brown and smelling wonderful.

He placed the turkey on the table and prepared to carve. As he sharpened the carving knife the room was silent. He sensed the discomfort and didn't know what was wrong. Instead of diving into the food, everybody just sat there, staring.

The adults picked at the food, the children just looked at their mothers with disappointment in their eyes. There was a long, tense silence.

"But Mama, where are the frijoles, the tortillas?" My cousin Jenny finally asked what everyone was thinking. The other children jumped in.

"No frijoles, no tortillas?"

Little Margarita, who could barely speak added "Joles? Tillas?"

Mama looked over to *Abuelita*. They exchanged a knowing glance, then *Abuelita* got up and walked into the kitchen. She came out with an earthenware pot filled with refried beans, another pot of salsa and a basket full of fresh, hot flour tortillas. Papa had no idea when she cooked them, but as they hit the table, the group exploded in conversation. Food began to be passed around enthusiastically. Little Jenny grabbed a tortilla, filled it with beans and added some turkey and dressing, then rolled it into a burrito.

At the head of the table *Teodoro* cried out "*Da me la mole Americano*"(Pass me the mole Americano). He wanted gravy for his potatoes. Even though everyone ate too much they were able to find room for pumpkin pie and whipped cream later that evening.

After dinner, Papa told and Mama translated the story of the first Thanksgiving. Everyone begrudgenly admitted it was a fine story, but not nearly as exciting as the stories of the Aztecs and Conquistadores or the stories of Grandpa's childhood in Mexico.

Mama's family learned to function in the American system, but they still had a lot of the Old Country in them. At Christmas, Mama and Papa were invited to a party at Anna's house where Papa learned a big lesson about their make-up. He didn't understand much of the Spanish so he sat around, drank beer and enjoyed the music.

Anna noticed that Papa was sitting by himself.

"Charlie, you come, sing for us."

"Do you know *Besa Me Mucho?*" Papa asked the band. He did OK for the first few lines, then he ran into trouble.

The song goes "Que tengo *miedo* perderte, perderte después" which means "For I am frightened to lose you." Instead, Papa sang "Que tengo *mierda* perderte, perderte después," that means "I am scared that I have to shit."

Mama's family never let him forget that mistake.

Joe came over and sat down next to Papa.

"Charlie, how you doin'? I'm Tony's cousin Joe," he said.

"Joe, you speak excellent English. Were you born in the Old Country?" Papa asked him.

"No, no, I am an Americano. I was born here, in Los Angeles. My older brother, Roberto, he was born in the Old Country. He was born in a shell hole at the battle of *Santa Rosalia.*"

"Born in a shell hole," Papa asked, "what in the hell are you talking about?"

"My Papa, he was a *soldado*, a soldier in the army of Pancho Villa," Joe explained. His chest expanded with pride as he spoke. "My mother, she was a *soldadera.*"

"A *soldadera*? What's a *soldadera*?"

"The Mexican woman, her place is at the side of her man. He works the fields; she works the fields with him. He goes to the army, she goes with him. Her job is to wash his clothes, cook his tortillas and load his rifle.

"My mama, she went with my father when he joined Pancho Villa. While they were fighting, she became pregnant with my brother. Then the *Federales* attacked.

"There was a great battle at *Santa Rosalia.* My mother was nine months pregnant and the *Federales* shelled them with cannon. The *Federale* infantry, they attacked and drove Villa's army back. They had to run. They took shelter in a shell hole. My father and his friends, they shot at the *Federales*, my mother and the other *soldaderas*, they loaded the rifles.

"They fought and they ran. And they ran and they ran. Then, my mama, she says 'The baby, it is coming.'

"My papa asks, 'Can you hold it?'

"Mama says, 'No, it is coming now.'

"My father calls the other men around him and says that they have to make a stand. They fell in a shell hole and my mother went into labor.

"The *Federales*, they set up a machine gun. The men in the shell hole fought on. The *Federales* charged; the men in the shell hole fought them off.

"The women, they loaded rifles. My mama screamed and sweat. One of the other women put down her rifle loading long enough to help my mother deliver the baby. Then my mother wrapped the baby in her *reboza* and they ran again. They were the lucky ones, they survived that battle."

Now Papa understood. For the rest of their lives, whenever Papa went off on some insane adventure Mama always followed. It was because, as Joe had said, "Her job is to wash his clothes, cook his tortillas and load his rifle."

Chapter 9

The *Cuantos Pescados*

"When I married your mother I was still fishing on the *Cuantos*" Papa told me as we continued to steam south. "Mama went with me and never uttered a word of complaint. When she first went to sea with me, she was a new face in the fleet. Most of the fishermen didn't know her, although they heard that I'd gotten married. On our first trip together, we headed down the coast of Baja after fresh market fish; our first stop was San Martin Island.

"When we pulled into the bay late in the day there were several other boats already at anchor. By morning there were more than a dozen fishing boats in the anchorage.

"As I was getting ready to start the day, the devil touched me," Papa was always quick to play a practical joke on someone. "I got up and grabbed stuff from Mama's sea bag and ran up on deck. I went to the mast and untied the signal halyard and attached Mama's bra and panties and ran them up the mast."

Mama was not happy.

Papa's troubles adjusting to married life didn't stop there. Mama told me her version of her first trip with Papa. Mama was twenty years old, a naïve kid who had never been outside of Goat Hill. Papa was an experienced man of the world.

It was winter, or what passes for winter in Southern California, and tuna were out of season. Papa decided to take a busman's holiday for their honeymoon. He rigged and prepped the *Cuantos* for a trip to Mexico to fish for fresh market fish.

When they fished for tuna or mackerel, they knew that their product was going to canned, so they weren't as concerned about the care of the fish as they were with fresh market fish. Whatever they brought home for the fresh market was going to be displayed on ice in a fish monger's stall for the city's housewives to select. It had to be in top shape and look fresh and pretty.

They also didn't know what they were going to catch. They caught wahoo, barracuda, perch, sea bass, bonita or any number of species. Fresh market fish took a whole different kind of fishing gear. Papa used long-lines. These were fishing lines with long leaders every six feet or so with baited hooks. These lines were over a mile long. Every few hundred feet they had a buoy with a pole and flag to tell other boats where the line was so that they didn't run over the lines and cut them. Even worse, if two boat's lines got tangled together it made a Gordian Knot that took all day to straighten out.

Papa kept his fishing lines coiled down in wooden tubs on the afterdeck. He instructed Mama, his new deck hand, to run the boat while he set his lines. He wanted Mama to keep the boat on a straight course and moving just fast enough to pay out the line as he baited each hook.

"Slow her down Vicki, you're going too fast," he shouted towards the deck house, making a downward patting motion with his hands. Then, "Starboard a point, no, no starboard, right, go to the right." He was getting more exasperated, his volume rising and his tone took on a hard edge.

Mama had never been on a boat before. She was just learning how to handle it. She didn't know the nautical terms; she had grown up in a house where she was required to speak Spanish and had never been exposed to seafaring.

"Five knots, Vicki, keep her at about five knots," Papa screamed.

What did he mean by "five knots?" Mama wondered. She couldn't see any rope to tie.

"Slower, Goddamn it. You're paying out too fast."

"DON'T YELL AT ME!" Mama snapped. She would not be yelled at that way. She pulled back on the throttle to take the boat out of gear, abandoned the helm station and retreated to the fo'c'sle and her bunk.

But she had not taken the boat out of gear. She put it into reverse.

"Vicki, what're you doing? Get back to the wheel. You're backing up. Goddamn it. Put her in forward again." The boat backed down over Papa's fishing lines.

By the time Papa made it to the deck house to take the *Cuantos* out of gear, it was too late. The fishing lines wrapped themselves around the propeller and rudder. It was a hopeless mess. The boat was dead in the water. She wouldn't go forward or back up with her propeller wrapped. With lines also enmeshed in the rudder Papa couldn't turn the wheel either.

After a few choice words of condemnation, Papa accepted the situation and went to work to fix it. He burned with rage as he lowered the skiff into the water and tied the painter to the bulwark. He jumped into the skiff and pulled himself around to the stern of the boat to work on the lines. He tried pulling the lines loose; it wouldn't work. Then he tried putting the engine in forward at a slow speed to unwrap the line. It didn't work either.

"I can't reach the propeller from here," he mumbled to himself. "Vicki, get up here, I'm going to have to go in the water." There was no reply from the fo'c'sle.

Well, what would I do if I was by myself? he thought. He stripped off his clothes and climbed down into the skiff with his sheath knife clenched between his teeth. I pictured him like an old-time pirate boarding a treasure ship.

From the skiff he tied a rope around his waist and

lowered himself into the blue Baja waters. It was a warm, clear day with a gentle sea running. The sea was warm on his skin. He took a deep breath and dived below the stern of the boat. He swam under her bottom to the rudder and propeller.

His first dive just gave him an idea of what he was up against. Soon he was out of air and had to return to the surface. Time after time he surfaced, took a deep breath and dove under the boat again. Under the boat he took his knife and cut away at the lines, then pulled them loose.

It was a mess. A good portion of the mile of fishing line wrapped around the propeller and entwined in the rudder. Papa worked for hours, diving, cutting, surfacing and diving again to get the propeller free. By the time he was done, he was exhausted.

He pulled himself back into the skiff and lay there naked, breathing hard. Finally he gathered enough strength to climb back aboard the *Cuantos* and pull the skiff back on board

During the entire debacle, Mama remained in the fo'c'sle reading a new Steinbeck novel.

"What are we having for dinner?" Papa asked as he dried himself off and got dressed.

"Whatever you're cooking."

It looks like I've got myself a little spitfire here, Papa thought. *She really has a temper.*

They lost their entire long-line rig. Mama said that it cost them over two hundred and fifty dollars to replace the rig in Newport Beach. Papa never learned how to handle Mama's temper.

Shortly after Mama married Papa, Papa had a problem with the compass on board the *Cuantos Pescados*.

"I don't know what's wrong," Papa said as the *Cuantos* cruised up the coast on a warm California evening. "Look, we're paralleling the coast and the compass says we're headed due west."

"Maybe the compass is just broken?"

"Compasses don't get broken. It was working just fine this morning, now look it's all haywire."

The problem seemed to be intermittent. Sometimes the compass was deadly accurate, sometimes it didn't work worth a tinker's damn.

"Well, Sharles, that compass is so old, maybe it's just worn out."

The compass was an old box compass. It had a black steel bowl gimbaled in a pine wood box. The old fashioned card in the box showed the points of the compass rather than degrees. When Papa rebuilt the *Cuantos Pescados* he found some kind of deal on the ancient instrument and reasoned that sailors used this kind of compass for over nine hundred years so he could get a few more years out of it.

"Compasses don't wear out. I don't know what could go wrong with a compass."

The compass works by magnetism. The card has a magnet in it and floats in bowl of alcohol. Because the earth is a giant magnet, the card always points towards the magnetic north pole. All courses are charted relative to magnetic north. With a compass, a watch and a chart fishermen cruised all over the Pacific Ocean.

"I'm going to have to call Cap'n Kidder to repair it when we get home." This was the ultimate indignity for Papa. He prided himself on being able to fix anything.

Cap'n Kidder was born late in the previous century. He followed the sea all of his life. As a young boy he worked in a shipyard in his native state. A card-carrying "Downeaster," as natives of Maine are called, he learned all about ships and the sea.

When I knew Cap'n Kidder, he was an old man. Although a large man with a full head of gray hair; he was stooped but had powerful legs and shoulders. His massive hands looked like they could crush a skull, but could work with the most delicate electronic equipment. Being hard of hearing, his voice was somewhere between a roar and a full hurricane. He was an independent old cuss and was totally self sufficient. He was already in his eighties when he built a little sloop, the *Compass Rose,* and sailed her single handed up the coast to Washington where he and Mrs. Kidder retired on Orcas Island in the San Juans.

Cap'n Kidder was an old hand at repairing compasses. In many installations, there are large amounts of magnetic metal near enough the compass to affect it. In these cases, the compass is "swung." The skipper lines the boat up on a course that he knows is true north, based on landmarks on shore. Then the compass repairman moves iron balls attached to the compass box either closer or farther from the compass to cause the card to swing until it lines up on the correct north.

"Mr. Kidder," Mama screamed in delight when she saw the tall, bent old man climbing over their gunwale.

"Victoria, what are you doing here?"

"I'm married now. This is my husband's boat."

"Well, congratulations."

"Let me start a pot of coffee."

Because of his great generosity, I knew Mr. Kidder as Mama's Santa Claus. When Mama was a little girl during the Depression, Mr. and Mrs. Kidder prowled the city dump looking for toys that the Anglo kids threw away. Mr. Kidder rescued them and took them home to his shop to recondition them. He salvaged parts from many toys to fix the broken toys that he recovered. Mrs. Kidder sewed new dresses for the dolls from scraps of cloth. Every December, the Kidder's children helped wrap the gifts.

On Christmas Eve, Mr. and Mrs. Kidder made the rounds of the poor Mexican families. Mama said that her brothers and sisters practically died each year waiting to hear Mr. Kidder's Model T putt-putting up the long driveway. They always had a gift for each boy and girl. These were the only toys the Mexican children received all year.

Mama and Mr. Kidder were lost in old times when Papa climbed aboard and joined them in the galley.

"Well, this is pleasant, but I suppose you want me to take a look at that compass," boomed Cap'n Kidder. He walked over to the helm station and set his tool box on the counter next to him. He looked at the compass and began laughing.

"What's so funny?" Papa asked

Cap'n Kidder reached into the compass box and started removing hands full of hairpins. Mama had long, beautiful black hair and found the compass box a convenient place to store her hairpins. The hairpins were made out of iron and affected the compass' orientation. As the boat rolled in the swells, the hairpins moved around, causing the compass to go totally crazy.

"Charlie, the next time you can remove your own damn hairpins," Cap'n Kidder said with a laugh as he handed Papa a handful of them.

The time seemed to fly. Papa's stories carried us past San Clemente Island and well out into the Pacific. Suddenly I realized that I was getting hungry.

"I'm going to make myself a fried bologna sandwich, you want one?" I asked Papa.

"Sure, go ahead."

I fired up a burner on the propane stove and warmed the cast iron skillet. Into the skillet I tossed four slices of bologna. While the bologna cooked, I grilled four slices of white bread on the round griddle. When the bread browned, I slid the bologna over onto it, then fried a couple of eggs over medium. The real trick with a fried bologna sandwich is to cook the eggs enough so that the yolk doesn't run all over your hands, but is still soft enough to make the bread good and soggy.

I handed Papa his sandwich and a bottle of beer.

"Now this is high living," Papa laughed as he took a bite. He stopped to wipe his lips with the back of his hand, then he wiped his hand on his pants. I guess I made his egg a little too runny.

There were still innumerable tasks to be completed. With the boat on automatic pilot, Papa went to work splicing lines and I replaced the broken hinges on the tackle box.

"I think I'll go ahead and put the weights on the lines now," Papa said. Choosing the weight was a real art. "I want the outer lines to lie near the surface, but the inner ones to run deeper." If the weight was too heavy, the line sank straight down in the water and the fish wouldn't take the bait. If it was too light, the jig bounced around on the surface of the water as the boat trolled and the fish wouldn't bite. After you got used to the boat, you just knew what size weight to use. Papa kept several different sizes in his big tackle box, because the weather and sea conditions could affect how much weight to use. While Papa worked, he sat on the engine room hatch cover near me.

To Papa, a summer fishing for albacore was an on-going vacation. When he was fishing with Mama, they took days off and went ashore to explore deserted islands or meet the local people. With Mama on board the language barrier ceased to exist. Papa could meet all the Mexicans he wanted and with Mama acting as his interpreter, learn all he could about their lives. He had an insatiable curiosity and an unending desire to talk with new people. Long after Mama's patience had worn out, Papa went on and on.

Papa told me that *Cedros* Island caught his imagination, and they decided to take the day off to explore it.

"I'd never been ashore there before and it looked interesting, I'd heard that the *Ceilo de Cedros* mountain was worth the climb."

Cedros Island is about forty miles off the coast of Baja and about twelve miles north of Punta Eugenia. Like all of the islands along this coast, it's dry and covered in scrub brush, the kind of place where you could imagine being ship wrecked for years before someone found you.

They ran in to Cedros at night and dropped anchor. In the morning Papa launched the skiff to take Mama ashore. I remembered seeing a picture of Papa in the skiff. Unlike Corky it had a pointed bow and was longer than our skiff. As far as I knew, it never had a name.

"Mama climbed down into the skiff like a monkey with our lunch and a bucket of cold beers. I grabbed the oars and started to row us ashore" Papa said

"There was a surf breaking on the beach but that wasn't really a problem. When you're beaching a small boat, you time your approach so that the boat will surf in on top of one of the breakers and be flung up on the beach." He used his hands to illustrate the point. "Then you need to jump out of the skiff and pull it above the water line so that it won't wash out to sea on the next wave.

"I rowed us ashore, keeping an eye on the breakers. I had to time it just right, but I didn't. I missed the breaker and we fell into the trough. The next wave broke above us and flooded the skiff. The boat capsized and Mama and I and all of our possessions were tossed into the ocean. I went down, then stroked to the surface." Papa was a good swimmer. I knew that Mama was not a swimmer at all, she hated the water.

"When I came up I took a quick look around and saw that Mama hadn't come back up. I took a deep breath and dove under again to find her. She wasn't too far away, sinking to the bottom with her cheeks puffed out, bubbles escaping from her lips and a dazed look in her eyes. I swam over to her and got a good grip on her shirt. Then I pulled her to the surface, where she exhaled loudly and passed out. I put an arm around her and swam ashore.

"When I touched bottom, I stood up and picked Mama up in my arms. I carried her up on the beach and stretched her out in the sun. I did artificial respiration on her by compressing her diaphragm and pulling on her arms.

She spit water out of her mouth, opened her eyes and yelled, ' You hit me with the skiff.'"

I pictured Mama's anger as she came to. She had willingly followed Papa, assuming that it was safe. She never thought to thank Papa for saving her life; she always blamed him for getting her into the pickle to begin with. To Papa this was a little adventure, to Mama it was a life threatening situation.

The afternoon melted away as we worked on little chores. The block for the starboard stabilizer halyard was jamming. Papa had built rungs like a ladder between the shrouds supporting the mast. He called these rat lines. Now he climbed up the rat lines to the top of the mast to repair the block.

Working at the top of the mast with the boat rolling to the swell was a demanding physical task. As the boat rolled, the mast swung in a wide arc through the sky. Papa had to hang on with one hand while he worked with the other. After the job, he was exhausted. He broke out a cold beer and spread out on the fish hold hatch cover to breathe hard. I grabbed a root beer and joined him.

"I'm thinking that we'll run into albacore off of *San Geronimo* Island," Papa told me as we lay on the hatch cover. San Geronimo was still a couple hundred miles south of us.

"The Sacramento Reef is just south of *San Geronimo*. It's one of the nastiest places on the Pacific Coast.

"During a blow, one time, Mama and I sheltered behind *San Geronimo*. I decided to take a day off and go ashore and explore the island. Because of the Sacramento Reef, not many boats visit San Geronimo, but if you approach it from the north, it's no problem. There's a good beach on the east side of the island so we went ashore there. This time, we made a smooth landing in the skiff."

I wondered how Papa ever convinced Mama to get in the skiff again. Mama is the most stubborn person I ever met. When she makes up her mind, not even God can change it.

"San Geronimo is a worthless piece of rock. There's no water on the island so there isn't much vegetation. It has some scrubby sage brush and a few spindly pine trees. Mostly it's covered with birds.

"We hadn't been ashore a few minutes when a little Mexican man who looked like Robinson Crusoe came running up to us. He was short, thin and tanned, with long dirty dark hair and a long Zapata mustache. He wore tattered pants, sandals with rubber tire tread for soles and went bare chested.

"'*Buenos Días*,' he said. 'Welcome to *San Geronimo* Island. My name is *Rojillo* (Roger), the governor of *San Geronimo*.'"

Of course Mama had to translate everything that Roger said for Papa.

"Good old Roger probably had the loneliest job in the Mexican government. He was the lighthouse keeper on a God-forsaken, dry chunk of rock. *San Geronimo* Island was designated by the Mexican government as a bird sanctuary. He also had the responsibility of keeping the fishermen and yachties who anchored there from coming ashore. Not that there was anything of interest to see on that worthless rock.

"Once a month a supply ship from the mainland landed supplies for him. But, you know, Mexico runs on *mañana* time. Sometimes the ship would be a week or two late, sometimes it didn't come at all. Then Roger had to make do by eating from the sea and collecting rainwater to drink. He got a month off every year to return to the mainland, but the previous year, the ship hadn't come to pick him up. When his month of vacation was over, the authorities expected him to be back on the job, even though he had never left.

"He fell head over heels in love with Mama and invited us to dinner. He hadn't had any supplies from the mainland for weeks. I rowed back out to the *Cuantos* and brought a case of beer ashore for him. Roger caught three huge lobsters. Mama brought butter and potatoes and canned green beans. Roger hadn't eaten that well in ages.

"When we were getting ready to row back to the *Cuantos*, Roger asks, 'You will come back in the morning? Then I will show you my great treasure.'

"Mama wasn't really impressed and wanted to be on our way, but I had to see this hidden treasure. The next day I coaxed Mama into going ashore. Roger'd been hunting seals since he was on the island. He had a cave crammed with seal skins that he was going to take with him and sell when he returned to the mainland. He thought he would be a rich man.

"He didn't have any other means of tanning the pelts, so he tanned them with his urine. The caved reeked to high heaven. Mama couldn't wait to get out.

"As we prepared to launch the skiff and return to the *Cuantos*, Roger came running up the beach loaded with pelts. 'These are for you, Senora,' he said. 'I would like to make a gift of them to you.' Mama didn't know what to say. The last thing she wanted was to spend the rest of the trip with a bunch of smelly seal skins on the boat. I finally got her off the hook.

"'Tell him,' I said, 'that we don't have room on the boat for the seal skins. Tell him that we'll stop on the way home and pick them up.' Neither of us had any intention of stopping there again."

The afternoon melted into evening. Papa kept up a

constant stream of stories as he worked. The evening sun set the ocean on fire as it dipped ever lower.

"We'll need to get started on dinner soon," Papa said. "You know, when Mama first came with me on the *Cuantos* there was an old propane stove." He said as he handed me two potatoes to peel.

"When I first met her, she wasn't much of a cook. She'd learned to make the Mexican dishes that Grandma served every day, but she didn't know anything about American cooking." Remembering her southern fried chicken and biscuits made my mouth water. I had a hard time buying this.

"Aunt Gussie took Mama under her wing." Aunt Gussie, Papa's oldest sister, was a great cook. "She taught Mama, who was a quick learner, all of her tricks.

"By the time we built the *Aventura*, your mother became the queen of the galley. She was turning out her Mexican specialties, but she was also making my favorites like fried chicken with mashed potatoes and gravy. She cooked pot roasts or baked ham and even took to baking in her new propane oven. Mama was a first class pie maker. Aunt Gussie taught her to make light, flaky crusts. She even tried baking cakes at sea.

"I'll never forget the cake that Mama made with the starboard list."

"How could a cake have a starboard list?" When a boat had a list, it meant that it was leaning to one side.

"Mama was in the deck house, running the boat on August seventh of 1945."

"How do you remember the exact day she baked a cake?"

"Actually, the cake didn't come for several days, but August seventh, 1945 is one of those days that you never forget, as long as you live. I'll always remember what I was doing that day."

President Kennedy was still a young PT boat commander,

the *Challenger* had not blown up and the World Trade Towers had not even been built, so I had no frame of reference.

"I was on deck cleaning up after a day of fishing. " Papa continued. "I was just finishing up stowing the last of the fish in the hold and icing them down. Mama was running the boat in the deck house and had the radio tuned to a San Diego station that played big band music.

"This guy breaks into the show and says that we've just dropped an atomic bomb on Hiroshima.

"'Sharles,' Mama yelled at me, 'Quick, get in here.'

"I came charging into the deck house. The announcer was still taking about the bomb. One bomb vaporized a city the size of Omaha, Nebraska in a heartbeat.

"'What could it be?' Mama asked. She looked white and was having a hard time breathing. We were used to getting war news by then but something struck her different about this. Maybe it was the idea that one bomb could destroy an entire city.

"'I don't know Vicki, but it will sure set the Japs back on their heels.'

"'What if the Japanese have one of these bombs? They might use it on the West Coast. Los Angeles or even Costa Mesa?'

"'I wouldn't worry about that,' I told her. 'They couldn't get a bomber close enough to the West Coast to drop a bomb.'

"'How about a submarine? They got close enough to bomb Oregon.'

"'The Coast Guard would never allow a Jap submarine that close.'

"'Sharles,' she says, 'just last year they did. Remember, off Laguna Beach? They had airplanes, blimps and Coast Guard cutters, everything they could send out hunting it. They never caught it. What if it had one of these bombs?'

"Your Mama didn't sleep well that night. She tossed

and turned for the next couple of nights as the big news story unfolded. She couldn't get rid of the feeling that the Japs might have an A-bomb too."

Atomic bombs were just a fact of life for me. In school we practiced drop and cover drills in case the Soviets decided to drop a bomb on us. I had a re-occurring nightmare about fleets of Russian bombers flying over us and dropping strings of bombs. Having read several post-holocaust science-fiction books, I worried what it would be like after a nuclear war. I couldn't imagine what it must have been like to live in a world without atomic weapons.

"Two days later," Papa continued, "the War Department announced that a second bomb had been dropped on a city called Nagasaki and that it had been destroyed too. Two days after that the word came that Japan had had enough. The war was over.

"We were out at sea when we heard the announcement. The radios in the fishing fleet buzzed with the news. We were far from the rest of the country, but Mama wanted to celebrate. She decided to bake a Victory Cake.

"Everyone was in a festive mood, the radio blared happy, patriotic music. It was like a giant Fourth of July party.

"Mama was busy baking a chocolate cake in her oven, happily making the frosting on the stove top to cover it. She put two round pans with the cake batter in the oven and turned to melting the chocolate bar to make frosting.

"As the boat rolled to the swell, the oven rolled back and forth too. In the oven the cake sloshed from side to side in its pan. As the cake set, the boat rolled to starboard. That was it, the batter sloshed to the starboard side of the pan and set.

"When Mama took her cake out of the oven, it was thick on the starboard side and thin on the port side. She was besides herself. Aunt Gussie hadn't told her what to do in a case like that. She put the two halves together and frosted them. With two halves together, it looked even worse.

"She walked over to the two-way radio and picked up the handset.

"'Fishing vessel *Cuantos Pescados* calling the *Danny Boy*. This is Whiskey, Roger, Charlie, two, four, five, seven, are you there Faith? Over,' she says.

"'Roger, *Cuantos*, this is *Danny Boy*, October, Bravo, X-ray, niner two six three, come in Vicki.'

"'Faith, I need your help,' Mama says. 'I was baking a cake to celebrate VJ-Day. When the boat rolled it set and my cake is thick on one side and thin on the other.'

"'Is it a flat cake Vicki?' asks Faith.

"'No, it's a round cake. I made two layers that I frosted together.'

"'Well, that shouldn't be a problem then, honey. Just put the thin side on one layer on top of the thick side of the other layer. It should even itself out.'

"I'd been listening in on their conversation from the speaker on the after deck. I rushed to the cabin and grabbed the handset from Mama.

"'Now Faith, leave it alone,' I said 'This is the first cake I ever saw that had a starboard list. I'll always remember VJ-Day because of it.'"

The years following the war were a golden age for the Southern California fishing fleet. Papa and Mama made a great team and prospered in the post-war boom.

Chapter 10

Mama and the *Aventura*

The evening sky faded to darkness. After I cleaned up the dinner dishes, Papa and I moved to the foredeck to sit in the coils of anchor line.

"You're always talking about fishing on the *Aventura*. When did you get her?" I asked

Papa looked up at the stars. He was quiet for a minute, then answered. "The *Cuantos* had been good enough for me, but I decided that the leaky old stinkpot wasn't good enough for your mother. A lady needs certain amenities, even at sea. After she fished with me a couple of years, we built the *Aventura*.

"I spent the summer talking to the captains of all the best boats in the fleet. The one thing I heard, over and over again was 'I wish I'd built her three feet longer.' So I found a set of plans for a beautiful thirty eight foot Newport Beach style fishing boat, took them to a naval architect and said 'I want you to extend this boat by three feet.'"

I knew all about the Newport Beach fishing boats. They were designed for the conditions in Southern California. I had seen pictures of the *Aventura*. She, like others of her class, was broad and long with a deep round bottom, a raised deck forward and a sharp bow. Her deck house had big glass windows, a galley, mess table, head and steering station. She had a flying bridge on top of the deck house with a green glass windscreen and another steering station. Papa built a crow's nest for a spotter to stand and look for fish at the top of the mast. Her sheer dipped at the front of the deck house, sweeping aft to create a low freeboard at the stern to make pulling fish easy.

"When I built the *Aventura* I built her for Mama. She had the only head (that's a toilet in landlubber talk) in the fishing fleet. We built a shower on the aft side of the deck house and a big galley Mama could cook in.

"Whenever we anchored in a quiet cove in Mexico, the other boats rafted up with us. We were always the party boat because *Aventura* was the most comfortable boat in the fleet. She was practically a damned yacht.

"We laid her keel down in Hans Dickman's Boat Yard in the early fall. I had enough money in the bank that I didn't have to take a job ashore that winter. Little Mama got a job waiting tables on the dinner shift. I spent the winter building the new boat. Every day, Mama got up with me and went to the boatyard. She'd work with me all day then she'd knock off in the afternoon clean up and get ready for work. She'd put on her uniform and ride her bicycle the two miles to work. At ten o'clock, when she got off, I waited for her with the car to take her and the bicycle home."

Papa told me that he shaped the keel and every rib by hand. He went through the laborious process of steaming and bending the planks.

"The planks had to bend around the curved hull, so I put them into a long, sealed chamber and pumped steam in under pressure to soften them up. When the planks hardened again, they permanently took on the shape of the hull." By the time he was done, Papa was intimately acquainted with every plank and screw in the *Aventura's* hull, every nut and bolt in her machinery.

"Mama's job was to fill in the holes in the planks where the screws were counter sunk with wood plugs and sand them smooth. When the planking was finished, she started painting.

"I went to the bank to borrow money to buy the machinery for *Aventura*.

"'The tuna fishing industry has been good business for us,' the banker says. 'Prices keep going up and the equipment keeps getting better and better. We don't see any end in sight.' A lot he knew.

"I bought the best diesel engine money could buy, a Jimmy 6-71. We found a freezer unit to refrigerate the fish hold and a top-class shortwave radio. I put a propane stove with an oven in the galley and installed hot and cold running water.

"When the planking was done, I insulated and planked the insides of the fish hold."

Everything was perfect on the *Aventura*. It was a labor of love. Papa built the ideal tuna boat for his beautiful bride.

"I built a double berth in the fo'c'sle. It was just right for a tall man and a short wife. The berth was built athwart ship. The side on the forward end of the boat was shorter, so it was Mama's side since she's only five-one on a good day." Mama always said that she was five foot one and a quarter inch tall; I don't know why that quarter inch was so important to her. "Further aft on my side, the bunk got longer.

"In the spring, *Aventura* was ready and Mama smashed a bottle of Bud across her bow as she slid down the ways. I told Art Hill that this was a working boat and I wasn't going to use any damn champagne on her.

"'I christen thee *Aventura* and commit thee to the sea,' Mama said in time honored nautical fashion. You know that *Aventura* means adventuress in English don't you?" I nodded. Over the years Papa had built the *Aventura* up to almost mythical standards. I could picture a great Viking ship being committed to the sea.

"When I built the *Aventura* I installed the finest galley in the fleet for Mama. She hadn't been accustomed to such luxury growing up. The kitchen in *Abuelita's* house had a hand pump for coldwater and a wood-fired stove in those days. There was no hot water, electricity or refrigeration. To get hot water,

Abuelita kept a kettle on the back of the stove. They had an ice box in the corner and the ice man came around every couple of days to restock the ice.

"Mama had a gimbaled propane range. It was set on fittings that allowed it to swing fore and aft and from side to side as the boat rolled and dipped. This allowed the pots on the stove to stay fairly level despite the boat's motion. There was plenty of counter space and a stainless steel double sink. The galley had a refrigerator and the fish hold served as a twenty-two ton freezer. The cabinet space in the galley was enormous. Mama couldn't imagine having enough pots and pans to fill it all."

The night wore on. We steamed across an endless expanse of ocean with nothing to break the monotony in any direction. We took turns sleeping on deck that night.

"Papa, wake up. There's a light," I shook Papa's shoulder as the dawn began to break. Far ahead of us on the ocean I could see a red and a green light.

"That's another boat. You're seeing her running lights," Papa told me. We watched her progress as we steamed along on a reciprocal course. Papa got up and started a pot of coffee. As he was cooking breakfast the other boat came close enough for us to get a good look at her. She had a long plank that stuck out over the bow. I could picture Long John Silver forcing helpless captives to walk the plank. Was this a pirate ship?

"What's that long plank for?"

"That's a swordfish plank, PC. I added a swordfish plank to the *Aventura* after we fished her for a year." Swordfish are a very expensive fish and bringing a few home on top of a load of tuna made a great pay day. The Pacific swordfish won't take a hook so the only way to catch them is to use a harpoon. The boat has a plank thirty or so feet long, extending out over the bow. "When you sight a swordfish sunning itself on the surface, the boat has to creep up on it and position the plank over the fish. The harpooner walks out to the end of the plank and throws the harpoon." Papa talked with his hands. He made a throwing motion to illustrate his point.

"It takes steel nerves, a good eye and a steady hand to harpoon a swordfish," Papa said while he puffed out his chest. "With her sharp eyes Mama always spotted the swordfish on the surface. By this time she'd developed a knack for working the boat, ever so slowly, into position. I'd ignore the tuna lines and clamber forward and out onto the swordfish plank.

"The harpoon's about ten feet long and was stowed on the plank. It had a long line attached to it, stowed in tubs on the foredeck, attached on its other end to a brightly painted beer keg with a flag on a pole that we used as a float. When I harpooned a fish, I hurried back to the foredeck and threw the keg over board. All day long we'd circle the keg and fish for tuna. At the end of the day, we'd pick up the keg and haul in the fish."

"How come you had to wait all day?"

"We needed to be sure the fish was dead. The Pacific swordfish is a huge fish. It can weigh several hundred pounds and be over ten feet long. It could cut a man in half with its bill. We didn't want to haul a live fish on board"

"How could you get such a big fish on board?"

"Mama ran the boat alongside the keg and I'd grab the line with a boat hook, then we'd haul the fish close enough to the boat to get a loop of line around its tail. The mast had a heavy cargo boom attached to it so we'd swing the boom out over the water. At the end of the boom was a block; I'd reeve the line through the block and around the fish's tail then take a couple of bights (loops) around the windlass and haul in the swordfish. It hung in the air from the boom and we'd lower it to the deck. We cut off the sword, removed the head, opened the body cavity and gutted it, then we lowered the fish into the hold and filled the body cavity with ice to preserve it.

"One time I'd harpooned the biggest swordfish I ever saw. It towed the keg all day long trying to dislodge the harpoon. Late in the day, it gave up and floated to the surface. I hauled the huge beast aboard

"About the time that we got the fish's tail hauled up to the boom and swung the boom in over the fish hold, the swordfish came back to life and started fighting. I dropped down into the cockpit and Mama jumped through the companionway into the deck house.

"For more than an hour the great fish hung there and fought the lines that held it out of the water until it finally died. In the meantime, it cut the skiff, which was stowed on the deck, into kindling."

"This is the *Jessie L.* calling the *Poor* Boy, come in *Poor Boy.*" The metallic voice crackled over our little Mickey Mouse radio.

"This is *Poor* Boy, go ahead Tommy."

"Hey Sam, how you doin' today?"

"We're over the hump Tommy-boy. We hauled in a hundred sixty-four today."

"You still down off *Abreojos*?"

"Yeah, we're about forty miles north, northwest. It's been hot down here. Everyone's in fish."

"*Abreojos*," Papa muttered as he jumped to the radio direction finder to get a fix on the *Poor Boy*. "It sounds like that's where the fish are."

"Where's *Abreojos*?"

"It's just above Magdalena Bay." Papa marked the new course on the chart in pencil. "It'll be about a three day run from here. *Abreojos* it is."

Our second day at sea continued to unfold. We had

made almost two hundred and fifty nautical miles since we cleared Newport Beach, but we still had a ways to go. Punta *Abreojos* was almost six hundred miles south of us.

After breakfast, I cleaned up the galley. Papa checked the water temperature, then dropped down into the engine room to check on the engine and machinery. Oil pressure fine, oil level OK, reduction gear oil OK, the drive line belts all looked good. While he checked the machinery, I did a visual inspection on deck. The mast and rigging all looked fine; no obvious signs of any damage had shown up during the night. I climbed down into the fish hold and checked the sump; no water accumulating, the temperature still near zero. In the foc's'le I pulled up the floor boards and checked for water, there was only a splash.

As we made the remaining repairs and prepared the fishing lines we continued to steam south to the fishing grounds. By early afternoon we ran out of things to do. Hour after hour we steamed on. Boredom soon set in so I crawled into the coils of anchor line of the foredeck to read Edgar Rice Boroughs' *Under the Moons of Mars* and was soon lulled to sleep by the sun and the boat's motion.

It was a warm clear day, but I was awakened by rain. I jumped up and looked at the sky, there were no clouds anywhere. Then I heard a loud blowing sound and was drenched again.

"Whoa!"

A whale breached(surfaced) next to our boat and blew. I got showered in the spray from its surfacing and the moisture from its breath. The whale was so close that I could see its giant nostrils opening to blow and then closing again to keep out the water. Mesmerizing. I couldn't move or shout out. I had never seen an animal that large, that close. It rolled over to one side and looked at me with an eye that showed much more intelligence than I was used to seeing in a dog or cat. I felt as if it was deciding if *I* was an intelligent life form. If the whale surfaced a few feet closer to us, it would have capsized our boat.

I saw many whales that summer, but never again that close. Watching the whales play is a sight never to be forgotten. These huge creatures were larger than our boat. They moved through the water with the grace and precision of ballerinas. When they sounded(dove) they gently humped their backs and slid under the surface, waving their flukes (tail fins) high in the air; then, all of a sudden, they breached. They were very playful. Many times when they breached, they leaped entirely out of the water. These mammoth creatures went airborne, standing on their tails for an instant, then crashed down into the water sending a wall of spray in the air and creating a massive tidal wave. It looked like a gigantic belly-flop contest. Seeing the tidal wave they created reminded me of one of the stories Mama told me about when she was fishing with Papa on the *Aventura*.

Mama always had the sharpest eyes on the boat. She was on the flying bridge steering the boat when she saw something strange on the horizon. Papa was in the fo'c'sle taking a nap. (She says that he was always in the fo'c'sle taking a nap when anything exciting happened.)

Off in the distance, far away, she saw something strange in the water. At first she was attracted by the white water. They were far out to sea, in deep water, there should be no breaking water, no shoals for a hundred miles. The sea began to boil, then the surface of the sea lifted. Suddenly a wall of water higher than the boat moved their way.

"Sharles, get up here quick. Something's wrong."

Papa ran to the ladder and climbed to the bridge deck. Off in the distance he saw the dark disturbance in the sea. It was coming their way.

They watched as it came closer and closer. It was a wall of dark water rushing across the sea.

"It's a tidal wave," Papa said. (In those days they called them tidal waves, now they're known as tsunamis.) Papa turned the boat and headed straight for it. "Our only chance is to take it head on and hope we can ride it out." Mama dropped down on deck and began securing all the hatches and doors.

The wave got closer and closer, it grew in height. Finally, it loomed over the boat. As the *Aventura* approached the wave, the wave split open and passed around them.

It wasn't a wave at all. It was an endless pod of dolphins migrating across the ocean together. They were jumping out of the water as they traveled making what looked like a wave from horizon to horizon. As the *Aventura* moved through the wall of dolphins, it closed in behind them. They were surrounded by a seemingly infinite sea of dolphins. The gray mammals continued to part to let the boat pass. For ten minutes the *Aventura* plowed forward at nine knots as the dolphins, who could swim at twenty knots, leapt past them, then they were through. The dolphins swam into the distance and began to sink back into the ocean. Mama thought to grab her Brownie camera and snap off a shot.

•

We continued to steam southward. As darkness fell on our second night, Papa moved towards the galley.

"I think we'll have hamburger Spanish for dinner tonight." That was fine by me. It was one of my favorite one-pan meals.

Papa formed a couple of big hamburger patties and fried them in the cast iron skillet.

"PC, peel and slice an onion and chop up a bell pepper while I fry the hamburger".

When the patties were almost done, Papa added onions and bell pepper to the skillet. He added a can of stewed tomatoes, garlic powder, salt, Italian seasoning and black pepper when the vegetables were soft.

"Get some potatoes peeled and boiling," he instructed me.

We served the hamburgers on our plates with the sauce smothering them and covering the boiled potatoes. It was the best.

All the time we cooked, he kept talking about his adventures with Mama on the *Aventura*.

"You know, PC, we used to have some great parties on the *Aventura*. I need to find a way to work one of those parties into my book. I think it would really show the reader what our lives were like."

Papa and his friends kept in touch all day long on their two-way radios. When Papa's fishing partner, Stu, announced that he was running into *Todos Santos* Island for the night to work on his refrigeration plant, Papa decided to meet him there.

The little bay at *Todos Santos* Island is ringed by high hills, with a crescent shaped white sand beach in the middle. The *Aventura* was the first boat into the bay and Papa made his way to the lee of the hills. He climbed down from the bridge deck to let Mama run the boat while he went forward to clear away the anchor.

Mama guided the boat into the anchorage and cut the power. The boat glided to a stop. Papa tossed the big anchor over the bow. Mama eased the *Aventura* into reverse and took up the slack in the anchor line. The anchor bit in the sandy bottom and dug in. Papa let out more line as Mama continued to back down, then pulled his fingers across his throat in a cutting motion and Mama shut off the big diesel.

Papa went to work cleaning up the topsides and clearing away the gear that had accumulated after several days' worth of fishing. Mama headed for the galley and started a tray of lasagna. Before long the *He-Crab* lumbered into the bay.

"Hey Charlie," Jim Trammel, alone on the rickety old

He-Crab called out as he tossed Papa a line, 'How's fishin' today?' Papa held up seven fingers.

"Only got seventy fishes today, Jim. We decided to knock off early and come in for the night. Stu and Faith are on their way in too."

As Papa and Jim got the lines straightened away and hung old car tires over the sides of their boats to act as fenders, the *Danny Boy* steamed around the point. No sooner had Stu and Faith rafted up on the other side of them than they heard the unmistakable chug-a-chug-chug of the big old Buddha Diesel in the *Aphrodite* with Bob and Daisy Poole aboard. You could always tell it was Bob, just by the sound of his boat. Bob rafted up outside of the *He-Crab*.

"Hey Jim. Charlie, we heard you and Stu were coming in," Bob yelled as he made his lines fast.

When Hap on the *Happy Days,* who always fished alone, made the bay, he decided not to raft up. He dropped his hook and launched his skiff to row over. While he rowed over to the *Aventura*, Art Hill and the *Zola* rafted up to the *Happy Days.* Art's wife refused to go on a boat so he fished alone too.

In the galley of the *Aventura,* Mama took charge. She had already put her lasagna in the oven. Faith brought a casserole across from the *Danny Boy.* Daisy, who towered over the other two women, sliced a couple of loaves of French bread lengthwise and started building sandwiches from salami, ham and roast beef. When Art arrived, he brought fresh lettuce and tomatoes, having just come back from a run into San Diego. Stu brought the beer and Hap could always be counted on to break loose with a bottle or two of Canadian whiskey.

"Hey Blue Water, sing the one about the moon and the mountain," Stu shouted over the crowd. Papa, never one to miss a chance to show off his fine baritone, started singing.

"*The pale moon was rising above the green mountain,*
"*The sun was declining beneath the blue sea,*

"I walked with my love to yon clear crystal fountain,
"My love was named Mary, the Rose of Tralee. . ."
Everyone laughed and cheered when Papa was done.

"Here's one I picked up from some swabs on a limey destroyer that helped us escort a convoy from Delhi to Rangoon." Hap, who was just back from the war, said as he broke out his concertina. Bob pulled a harmonica from his hip pocket.

"The Irish are a hell of a race, parlez vous,
"The Irish are a hell of a race, parlez vous,"
The whole crowd chimed in.

"The Irish are a hell of a race, they'll kick your shins and spit in your face,
"Rinky dinky, parlez vous. . ."

When Hap was done, Stu grabbed a black comb. Nobody knew where it came from because God knows he never used it. He wrapped it in his big right hand until only a small portion showed, then held it under his nose, mimicking Hitler's mustache. He raised his left arm in a Nazi salute and started goose stepping around the deck.

"Ven der Furher says, ve are der master race,
"Ve say, Heil, Thwtt, Heil, Thwtt, right in der Furher's face.
. ."

As Stu completed his parody, the group broke out laughing.

"Vicki," Hap shouted, "sing us one of your Mess-a-can songs."

"Yeah," Stu chimed in, "sing a real seen-yor-ita song."

"No," Mama said. "Oh, no, I couldn't." I pictured Mama, never wanting to be the center of attention, trying to get out of singing.

"Oh come on," Daisy pleaded. "C'mon, let's sing *Adelita.* I'll sing with you." Mama was trapped.

Daisy graduated from UCLA, courtesy of a track

scholarship, where she won the women's PAC-8 shot put and discus championships. She majored in art history, but minored in Spanish. Daisy was the tallest person on any of the boats and stood more than a head taller than Mama. Putting her big arm around Mama's shoulder she pulled Mama to her side.

"Oh, all right. Hap, do you know *Adelita*?"

"Vicki, I been sailing in and around Mexico for thirty years, how could I not know it?" Hap grabbed his squeeze box and started playing the tune.

"*Adelita, se llama la joven*," Mama and Daisy sang.

"*a quien yo queiro y no puedo olvidar*," by this time Daisy had muffed the words and dropped out.

"*en   el   mundo   no   tengo   una   otra*
"*y con el tiempo me voy a cortar. . .* "

When she was done everybody broke into applause.

Come 'n get it boys, Faith shouted from the galley as she set out her casserole.

Mama brought her lasagna to the table. Daisy produced a potato salad to go with her hero sandwiches. Faith passed around silverware and glasses. The galley table filled to overflowing. Everyone loaded up their plates and found a place to balance them on their laps. Faith and Stu's boys took their food to the fo'c'sle. Papa, Stu, and Hap climbed up to the bridge.

"It doesn't get better than this," Papa said between pulls on a Lucky Lager bottle.

"I tell ya Charlie,"' Stu chipped in, "There's no finer life. Just look around. The sky ain't got a cloud, the water's so clean and clear ya can see the bottom."

"During the war I seen a lot of the South Pacific," Hap said. "And in the first war I was in the Med for mosta two years. There ain't no place better 'n this. No life better than pulling tuny."

They ate, drank and shot the breeze. The women huddled in the galley and talked girl talk.

It was getting late, but they were all feeling so good that they didn't want to go back to their own boats. Stu started fidgeting on the bench seat on the bridge.

'Hey Charlie," Stu leaned over and whispered. "I gotta go. Can I use your head?"

That was an unusual question on a fishing boat, because the *Aventura* was the only boat in the fleet with a marine toilet. Under normal circumstances, the men just walked over to the lee rail and let go. However, there were ladies aboard and Stu didn't want to embarrass anyone, least of all himself.

"Sure Stu, you know where it is. Do you have to do one or two?" Papa asked

"Does it make a difference?"

"Hell yeah, Stu. If you're doing number two then I need to give you water to flush with."

"Well, you better turn on the water then."

Stu climbed down the ladder and made a dash into the deck house. Papa took another long pull on his beer, then the devil touched him.

Being the thrifty Scotsman that he was, when he built the *Aventura* he didn't want to waste a drop of all that good hot water that was used to cool the diesel engine. He routed the water to a shower head on the aft deck so that Mama could take a warm shower while they were out fishing. He also routed the water into the head to flush the toilet overboard.

Papa waited until he was sure that Stu was good and settled and had done his business, then he reached over and hit the start button for the big Jimmy diesel.

He counted to ten to make sure that Stu had adequate time to finish up, then he jammed the throttle forward to full speed. The big diesel roared and a cloud of black smoke poured from the smoke stack.

"Oh-hoo, Oh-hoo, Oh-hoo." Stu cried from the head. Moments later, he came out of the deck house, soaking wet.

"Charlie, this is the God damnedest boat I ever seen," he said. "Not only do you got a head, but you don't even need no toilet paper. The damned head washes you automatically when you're done."

As the night wore on, the revelers eventually drifted back to their own boats. Before long they were all snuggled into their bunks getting rested to face the challenges of the next day.

Chapter 11

The End of an Era

We always kept the radio on while we were at sea. When we weren't listening to some other boat's conversations, we were tuned to the emergency band. To talk with another boat you called on the emergency band and arranged to move to another channel. If anyone got into trouble, they put out a call on channel 16 and the US Coast Guard responded.

"Help, help! Can someone please help us?" we heard a female voice over the speaker early in the morning of our third day at sea.

"Honey, put down the microphone," a male voice said

"No, we need help. I'm not going to sit out here and flop around anymore." This argument was happening somewhere out in the Pacific. The woman holding the microphone held the key down and we heard everything.

"Honey, the Coast Guard isn't going to come and pick us up just because the engine died, we're a sailboat."

"Well, were not sailing. I want to go home."

Papa flipped on the radio direction-finder and got a bearing on the broadcast.

"They're not far away. I reckon we should swing by and see if they're in trouble." At sea it didn't matter what you were doing, if another boat was in trouble, you dropped everything and went to their aid

Within half an hour, we saw a sailboat on the horizon. She was sitting dead in the water, laying in the trough and rolling violently to one side, then the other every time a sea passed under her.

"There's something wrong," Papa said. "Why don't they have any sails up?"

I was in love with the romance of sailboats. I had a dozen or so sailing magazines under my mattress in the fo'c'sle and read any book I could find on the subject.

She was a beautiful ketch, about a forty footer. I read a book about classic designs that spring. With a graceful spoon bow and a counter stern she looked like a John Alden design to me.

Papa hailed her. "Ahoy there, you folks in trouble?"

"No," the man answered.

"Yes," the woman shouted.

"Well, our engine died on us. I can't get it started again," the man said

"Where are you bound?" Papa shouted

"We're taking the boat back to San Diego. We just bought her in La Paz and we're taking her home."

"Why aren't you sailing? There's a stiff breeze." There was a long pause.

"Because we don't know how to sail," the woman yelled. The man glared at her.

"We were going to motor her back to San Diego and take sailing lessons there," the man admitted.

Over four hundred miles down the Mexican coast, we weren't about to tow a yachtie all the way back to San Diego.

"Well, we'll put a line on you and tow you as far as *Rosario*," Papa said.

He heaved a long length of half inch line across to the man who made it fast to their tow bit. Papa put the Ford diesel in gear and we started on a new course to tow the sailboat into *Rosario*.

"Damned yachties," Papa muttered as he took up the tension on the tow line. "It's a miracle they don't all drown themselves."

It took us the rest of the day to tow the sailboat into *Rosario*. I watched the beautiful white ketch in our wake and day dreamed about sailing someday. I fanaticized about flying the Jolly Roger and capturing rich Spanish galleons. When we pulled into the harbor at *Rosario* we found a San Diego Yacht Club outstation dock where we deposited our tow.

"I can't thank you enough," the man said as he cast off the tow line. "Would you like to come aboard for dinner and drinks?"

"No thanks," Papa grumbled back to him. "We've got a living to make."

"At least let me pay you for the tow," said the man as he reached for his wallet.

"Keep your damned money." With that, Papa coiled the line and headed the *Marine View* back towards open water.

"It's just not fair, PC," Papa mused while we made our way back to sea. "Rich people like that who don't know a thing about the sea can afford a boat to play with and I can't even make a living on a boat anymore."

Papa mused silently for a moment.

"It all started when the damned Japs started bringing their tuna over here," he told me. "We sank most of the Jap merchant and fishing fleets during the war, then our government sent an army of business and construction experts to Japan after the war was over to help rebuild them.

"We outdid ourselves. We rebuilt the Jap fishing fleet so well that they saturated the Japanese market."

In 1949 the American fishing industry was at its peak. With the European and Asian fleets all but destroyed during the war, American fishermen fed the world. Demand was never greater and prices never higher.

In early June that year, Portagee John on the *Lucky Strike* hit the first school of the year off of *Cedros* Island half-way down Baja. They were in fish in a big way. They couldn't pull them aboard fast enough for a day or two, then the fish disappeared without a trace. By that time, the fleet mobilized and a thousand boats combed the waters off of *Cedros* Island looking for tuna.

A week or so later the fish surfaced again. This time there was a massive school, the largest ever seen, from a hundred miles west of *Cedros* Island and all through the Gulf of *Sebastian Viscaino* almost to the coast of Baja. These weren't small early season albacore, they were big late season fish. Every boat on the fishing grounds filled their holds and ran for San Diego.

Word of the strike spread and every derelict afloat headed for the fishing grounds. Albacore were being caught in record numbers so close to shore that they were within easy reach for boats that normally couldn't go after them. The canneries sent buying ships to anchor off of Baja and wait for the fishermen to bring them fish. These buyers sold the fishermen ice, fuel, water and groceries to extend their trips. Of course, they bought the fish for a discount and sold their goods for a premium. Sport fishermen and boats without fish holds took loads of ice on their decks and covered them with wet burlap sacks to keep it from melting. They picked up all the fish they could carry, then ran to the buying stations.

My sister, Quita, was born in January that year. With a small baby to care for, Mama's priorities changed, she didn't want to go fishing anymore. Suddenly, she got the nesting instinct. It became more important to her to build a home and care for her baby than it was to go and take care of Papa.

Papa took my Uncle Santos with him as a deck hand; he was just about my age then. It didn't take long to fill the *Aventura's* hold. They steamed back into San Diego with twenty-two tons of tuna on board. At seven hundred fifty dollars a ton, that was worth over sixteen thousand dollars.

Several of Papa's cronies made port at the same time.

They tied up next to each other at the cannery dock and waited to have the cannery workers unload their catches. When they finally got their fish sold and had cash in hand, they retired to the Red Sails to celebrate.

The Red Sails was an upscale restaurant and bar on the wharf in San Diego. It started out life as a warehouse for the old sailing ships that used to unload cargo there. When more modern facilities were built it was sold and converted into a pricy seafood restaurant for the tourist.

The restaurant had a salty theme. The tables were built out of hatch covers rescued from old wooden ships. A skiff with a hole in the bottom leaned against the wall outside on one side of the front door; on the other side was a rusty old kedge anchor. The walls inside were finished with rough planks and covered with old nets, Japanese glass floats and paintings of sailing ships.

The lounge was separated into a lower area with the bar and a few tables and an elegant upper area with velvet covered booths. The tourist trade naturally took over the upper lounge. The fishermen, considered part of the atmosphere, were relegated to the lower bar.

Papa waited for Mama to pick him up, then they dropped Santos off to watch Quita. By the time they made it to the bar the celebration was already in full swing. Beer was flowing and the fishermen were spending money like drunken sailors.

"Hey Blue Water, I got a couple a stools over here," Stu shouted over the roar of the crowed bar. Papa sat and ordered a beer. Mama ordered a soft drink. She did not approve of drinking.

"Wow, that was some haul, huh Stu?" Papa said.

"Yeah, fishin's so good that I'm thinking about buying a second boat for my boys. Bob up 'ta bank says he can get me a loan, no problem,' Stu replied.

The party lasted all night. Never in the history of the Pacific fishing fleet had so many fishermen made so much money so quickly.

At two o'clock in the morning the bar closed. Most of the crowd returned to their boats to sleep a couple of hours. They all agreed to sail together on the ebb tide at six o'clock that morning. Mama was the only sober person in the bar.

A few of the revelers never made it to bed. Stu, Slim and Ole staggered back towards their boats that were rafted up together along the cannery dock.

"Hey boyzish," Slim said, "I got me a quart of Four Roszish in my cabin. Why don't you stop in for a quick drink?"

Stu and Ole couldn't think of anything that they'd rather do than to relieve Slim of his whiskey.

The tide changed and the sun rose, finding the three intrepid adventurers just polishing off the last of Slim's Four Roses.

"I guesh it's time to shove off," stammered Stu. "Faith'll be waiting for me."

None of the three caballeros were in any shape to run a boat, but all of them were too proud to let anyone else take their boats out of the harbor. Their judgment was impaired by massive quantities of alcohol.

At six o'clock the fleet cast off their lines and formed a parade down the channel and out of San Diego's harbor, horns and whistles blaring. Some of the boats were actually well handled

Stu, Ole and Slim wove their boats back and forth through the parade. Soon everyone knew that they had problems and were on the lookout to avoid a collision. They were especially worried about being skewered by the swordfish plank on Slim's *Sally J*. They need not have worried. The three party boys soon put themselves out of commission.

Stu was first. The *Danny Boy* lead the trio as he wandered

from the channel and ran up on the mud. Immediately after him, Ole on the *Norse Wind* ran aground. Slim, seeing the impending disaster swerved to avoid ramming the *Norse Wind*. Unfortunately his whiskey-pickled brain chose the wrong direction. Instead of swerving back into the channel, he turned directly into the jetty and ran the *Sally J* up on the rocks.

All three boats were in big trouble. The falling tide left them high and dry. Santos and Papa and two other boats stayed in the harbor to assist their partners. They waited until afternoon when the tide turned and flooded back in to float the stranded boats.

Papa put a tow line aboard the *Danny Boy* and revved up the big Jimmy diesel. The *Aventura* struggled and struggled and, as the tide flowed in, finally broke the *Danny Boy* free. By this time Stu was sobered up enough to work his way out of the channel.

The *Norse Wind* was pulled free too, but the poor *Sally J* was holed and sank. She was a total loss, but there were no injuries other than to the egos and pocketbooks.

A few days later Papa and Santos were at sea looking for albacore. They had a small load on board, but the *Aventura* was a big strong boat and had room for many more tons of fish.

Every day at noon the fishermen held a meeting over the two-way radio called the silent hour. That day horrible news broke: "The Japs have landed a freighter in Astoria with thirty thousand tons of albacore, all cleaned and ready to can. They're selling them for two hundred fifty dollars a ton." The canneries had been paying the American fisherman seven hundred fifty dollars a ton.

Papa knew what he had to do. They pulled in their lines and headed back into Newport Beach as fast the *Aventura* could carry them. After an all day run they tied up at the West Coast Packers cannery. Papa headed for Newport Beach instead of

San Diego because he was on good terms with the cannery owner in Newport.

"I'm sorry Charlie, I'm not buying any tuna," the cannery owner said. "The Japs have just dumped so many fish on the market for so cheap that I can't sell what I have in my storerooms. I'd have to sell my fish for less than they cost me to can 'em. I can't even afford to buy your fish for cat food."

They tried to sell their fish to the public from off of their boats. They sold them for ten cents a pound and couldn't get rid of them. Finally, they put to sea and dumped tons of dead tuna back into the ocean.

So it went up and down the coast. The Pacific tuna fleet died that day. They didn't know it then, but America joined the global economy in 1949. This was one of the first cases of American jobs being outsourced. The Japanese fisherman worked for so much less than the American fisherman and the American housewife didn't care where her tuna came from. The price of the little green and white cans on the grocery store shelves went down and she was happy. No matter that thousands of American families were without a way to make a living.

At first, the government didn't pay attention to the plight of the American fisherman. Then the fishermen's wives organized protest marches and sit-ins until someone in Washington finally took notice. A hearing was scheduled in San Pedro to investigate the situation. Papa led the fisherman's mission to discuss the problem with the California Congressional Delegation. I pictured the congressmen dressed in togas like a movie I had seen of the Roman senate.

"Congressman, we need some protection from the Jap tuna," Papa started off the meeting. "They're bringing in fish and dumping them on the market for less than it costs us to catch them. At two hundred and fifty dollars a ton, we couldn't make expenses, even if we could sell our fish."

"Mr. Wallace, I'm very sorry to hear of your plight," replied the congressman. "We'll take your situation into consideration."

"What're you going to do Congressman?"

"We'll hold some more fact finding meetings, then make a report to the Finance Committee."

"That's not good enough, Congressman. We need action and we need it now. You need to commit to us that you'll get a protective tariff passed."

"I can't do that Mr. Wallace. If we pass a tariff on Japan's fish, they'll retaliate and pass a tariff on our machinery. Then it'll be an all out trade war."

"Hell," Hap spoke up. "I just come back from fightin' them little sons-a-bitches. If we can whip 'em in a shootin' war, I reckon we can whip 'em in a trade war."

"It isn't that simple."

"Congressman, we need your commitment. You have to promise us some help," Papa pleded.

"Mr. Wallace, I can't do that. I have to balance the well-being of a handful of illiterate fishermen in California against the well-being of the entire country."

"I would think that what was in our best interest would be in the best interest of the whole country," Papa said. "During the war the government said that fishing was a strategic industry. It was so important to feed the country that if a man was an illiterate fisherman, he was exempt from the draft."

"Times change, Mr. Wallace," the Congressman said. "Japan is our ally now. They're our first line of defense against the Bolsheviks in Red Russia. If their economy collapses, the Commies could take over there too. Look at what's happening in China. We have to keep the Japanese economy strong.

"The cannery owners tell me that if they don't accept and can the Japanese tuna, then the Japanese will just can the tuna themselves and sell it directly to our markets. We have a multi-million dollar investment in the canning industry. The only way to protect the American fish canning industry is to take the Japanese fish. In the big picture, your little fishing boats just don't matter that much."

There was no relief from the federal government. In the end, the big money behind the canneries prevailed. Those who owed money on their boats lost them. Those who owned their boats put them up for sale for pennies on the dollar. You couldn't give a tuna boat away.

At the peak of the boom, Stu played big shot and took his Kettenburg Thirty-Eight into the Kettenburg yard in San Diego and told the yard manager "fix it." The bill came to over thirty thousand dollars. Stu had to borrow money from the bank to pay it off. When the bottom fell out of the albacore market, Stu lost the *Danny Boy.*

The Fisherman's Union had signed exclusive contracts with the canneries so that the canneries wouldn't buy fish from any boats that weren't part of the Union. The agreement didn't cover the Japanese tuna though. The Union required the boat owners to pay the skippers and crews at a certain rate. With the price of fish dropping so low, the boat owners couldn't pay their expenses, pay the crew, and make any money.

The only exception to this were the guys that owned their own boats and fished alone. They didn't have to pay out crew shares and they were just barely scraping by.

John McCready was the president of the Fisherman's Union in 1949. He had a forty-foot troller called the *Sunshine II.* John took to fishing by himself in order to make ends meet.

Ed Montgomery on the *King Fisher* had a different idea. The *King Fisher* was a big new steel boat and Jim still had to make payments to the bank. He figured that he could leave San Pedro by himself, stop in Ensenada and pick up a crew of Mexicans. He paid the Mexicans peanuts, they were glad to have the work and they worked hard. Then at the end of the trip he dropped them off in Ensenada and brought in his catch by himself. He convinced the cannery that he was fishing by himself and no one gave him any trouble.

Word got to John that Ed was cheating. John was determined to catch him. If John could prove that Ed was fishing with a non-Union crew, the canneries would have to stop buying his fish. John made it his business to be in port when the *King Fisher* came in. Then when Ed left, John sailed with him.

The problem was that the *King Fisher* was a much faster boat than the *Sunshine II*. John couldn't keep up with Ed and catch him taking on a Mexican crew. Ed was cagey, when he had his outlaw crew aboard, he never broadcast on the radio. That way no one knew where he was.

John put out a call on the Silent Hour to all fishermen to report it if they spotted the *King Fisher*. He wanted to catch Ed in the act. This put a lot of pressure on Ed.

At the end of the trip, Ed was in Ensenada dropping off his crew when the *Sunshine II* came steaming into the harbor. Ed knew that the jig was up. When Ed loaded his crew into the skiff to take them ashore, John took pictures with his Kodak. Ed pulled up anchor and headed for San Diego. John sailed alongside of him. Ed knew that when he hit San Diego the canneries had to refuse to buy his fish.

John, who fished alone, came out on deck to shout across at Ed and let him know that he'd been caught. Ed ran down to the fo'c'sle and grabbed his rifle. He drew a bead on John and fired. He hit John in the chest and John collapsed on deck. Then Ed rammed the King Fisher with the Sunshine II. He backed off and rammed her again and again until he was sure that she'd sink.

In the meantime, John managed to crawl into the deck house and get to his radio.

"Boys," he said, "I just been shot by Ed on the *King*

Fisher, he's rammed me and I'm goin' down. So long boys, it's been a good life."

The Coast Guard picked up the broadcast and sent Catalina Flying Boat to find them. The Catalina got there in time to see the *Sunshine II* go down. A Coast Guard cutter intercepted Ed on his way into San Diego and arrested him. They took the *King Fisher* in tow. During the night, Ed asked his guards to let him take a pee. He went to the lee rail, and slipped over the side.

With the collapse of the fishing industry, Papa couldn't make a living. He had the expenses of the boat to pay for and no income. He and Mama got jobs on shore, but he was never happy. Mama turned to her family for support. "Poor Sharles" *Abuelita* said. Papa couldn't stand the pity. He couldn't sell the *Aventura,* so he traded her for a farm on San Juan Island in Washington State. He thought that if they left the state on a new adventure he could turn things around. His fishing days were over, for the first time.

Chapter 12

Papa Gives Up

The ocean stretched on forever on every side of us. As the *Marine View* sliced through the water she threw a white bow wave. The old sailors called this running with a bone in her teeth. I often wandered back to the cockpit to watch our wake trail out behind us. We created a flat V on the surface of the waves where we passed. The incessant roar of the little diesel engine became background noise. Even though the sun blazed in the sky, the gentle breeze made the day bearable.

Late that afternoon Papa pulled up a bucket of water and took its temperature. He really didn't need to. It was obvious that we had crossed the line between the dark green northern sea and the warm, blue tropical water. We were now four days and some eight hundred miles southwest of Newport Beach. We were in albacore territory.

After several days at sea, I had my sea legs. Papa unfastened the halyards that controlled the jig poles and lowered the poles into place. I danced back to the cockpit and started to uncoil the fishing lines. Papa selected the appropriate weights for each one. One by one, the lines went over the side and trailed happily behind our little boat.

"Fish on," Papa yelled and pointed to the starboard jig pole. The parachute shock cord stretched out and the little loop of nylon line that hung below it went bar taut. Papa rushed aft to the cockpit and grabbed the leader that attached the fishing line to a two by two post at the aft end of the bulwark. He pulled the light line in until he could grab the nylon fishing line, then he pulled the fishing line in, hand over hand. I watched the muscles ripple in his arms as he pulled the big fish in.

There was a rainbow flash of colors in the water as Papa pulled the fish alongside the boat.

"She's a beauty," he said. I was too excited to speak. Our first albacore.

Papa grabbed the gaff hook and hooked the fish in the gills.

"Pescado," he yelled as he flipped the fish over his left shoulder onto the deck.

On deck, the fish flopped around. Papa grabbed the line again and shook the hook loose from the fish's mouth, then returned the jig to the water.

"Not bad for our first fish," Papa said, holding the thirty-inch long fish high for me to see. "Maybe twenty pounds or so."

I couldn't standstill. I wanted to run and jump. Now I understood the excitement of catching these big fish. After weeks of work, hundreds of miles of steaming, we were finally here, we were finally fishing.

"Fish on," I cried. The parachute shock cord stretched tight on the outer line on the port side. Papa moved across the cockpit and grabbed the line on the other side of the boat. Once again he pulled the line in, hand over hand, and gaffed the fish with a gaff hook. He turned and pulled the fish over the rail and into the cockpit, then he flipped it up onto the deck.

The albacore tuna is a dark, torpedo-shaped fish with long thin fins. One of the fastest fish in the ocean, it was built for speed. It has indentations on its sides for its long side fins to lay streamlined along its body when it puts on a burst of speed. The fins look like wings and allow the fish to glide effortlessly through the water at cruising speed. Out of the water it appears black, but pulling it up to the boat, it looks like a rainbow moving through the water. A medium sized fish in the tuna family, the albacore is about three feet long weighing twenty to thirty pounds; however a really big fish might weigh as much as sixty pounds. It is highly prized because it is all white meat. Van Kamp's markets it as the "Chicken of the Sea."

A migratory animal, the albacore spends its life swimming against the Humboldt Current that circles the North Pacific Ocean. On the American side, these fish swim near the surface and are caught by trollers. They cross the ocean south of the Aleutian Island chain in Alaska and dive to deep depths before being spotted again off the coast of Japan. The Japanese catch them on long lines. Some marine scientists believe that the albacore spawn off the coast of Hawaii in the spring. The albacore season starts in early June when the first tuna are found far down the coast of Baja California. They work their way north during the summer until in late August or early September they push north of the Washington coast and repeat their eternal journey.

Like the other fish in the sea, the albacore makes its living by eating smaller fish. One of its favorite meals is squid. Because it is a fast fish and can over take its prey we trolled for albacore at much faster speeds than you would troll for most fish.

Since the albacore tend to run in schools, when we got a hit on our lines, we wanted to stay in the school. We adjusted the boat's speed to match the speed of the school of fish. If it was a good school, we circled the boat to keep in the center of the school.

We hadn't hit a good school of fish yet, these were just stragglers. The afternoon passed with Papa watching the lines and occasionally pulling a fish. I spent most of the day in the deck house making sure that we were still on our course for his chosen fishing grounds off of *Punta Abreojos*.

I reflected back on our conversation about the good years and how the fishing industry collapsed. It was a different world today. We would be lucky to get two hundred and

fifty dollars a ton for our catch, nothing compared with what
Papa made thirteen years earlier. Still, we could pack nearly
twenty tons of tuna in our hold. A good trip could bring us five
thousand dollars, that was still a lot of money. Papa could earn
more in a good tuna season that he did all year long swinging
his hammer.

When Papa traded the *Aventura* for the farm on San
Juan Island, he and Mama were off on a new adventure. He was
returning to his roots, having grown up on a farm in frontier
Texas. Mama lived on a farm for most of her life, so it was
nothing new for her.

During their years on the Island, I was born.

The Island didn't live up to expectations. There was
never enough money to pay for all the things they needed. Papa
always had to take jobs off of the farm, leaving Mama to milk
two hundred cows, run the farm and raise two small children.

There were good times, but the winter weather wore
away at Mama's soul. She was used to the warm sub-tropical
climate of Southern California. She wasn't prepared for the
short winter days, the long, cold nights and the incessant rain.

Then there was nothing to do. Mama grew up in
Southern California, surrounded by family and friends. There
was always something going on, a fiesta, a wedding, a baby
shower, picnics and trips to the beach. On the island, she didn't
know anybody. Social life consisted of sitting around the
kitchen table with a cup of coffee discussing farm prices.

And Mama missed her mother. In her twenty-four years
of life she had never been away from *Abuelita*. When she went
fishing with Papa, the first thing she did when they got home
was to run up to Costa Mesa to see *Abuelita*. Now *Abuelita* was
thirteen hundred miles away.

Mama and Papa told me stories about life on the island.
Papa took a series of jobs to try to earn cash. He supplemented

his income with working on the salmon boats out of Puget Sound, but didn't make squat. He took construction jobs, he tried logging and building docks and barns, he did odd jobs on other peoples farms. He even worked in the lime kiln at Roche Harbor.

Roche Harbor is now a quaint little tourist town on the north end of San Juan Island. In the fifties, it was hell on earth.

The lime kiln made bricks. These bricks were used for construction in Seattle, Vancouver and Victoria. They were even sent as far away as Alaska and Hawaii. It was a going concern. The family that owned it grew rich and built a mansion and formal English gardens in Roche Harbor. The poor, dumb sons-a-bitches who made the bricks suffered.

The bricks baked in a series of furnaces. The lime was mixed with other ingredients and formed into bricks, then fed into the oven to be cured. When baked hard, they were removed, put on pallets and shipped out to build the cities.

"Charlie, you'll be on the furnace," the foreman told Papa on his first day on the job. "You stoke them furnaces to keep the temperature up. Then put the bricks into the furnace and take 'em out when they're done."

Hard, demanding physical work was nothing new to Papa. The furnaces were several hundred degrees hot. All morning long Papa stoked the furnace, put bricks in and pulled bricks out. Finally, after an eternity, the whistle blew and the foreman called 'Lunch.'

Papa sat with the other workers but didn't even open his lunch pail. He was too tired to move, too exhausted to eat. This job was just beyond human endurance.

"How long have you worked here?" Papa asked the old man sitting next to him.

"I been here twenty years," he said

The man was old and bent. His skin was splotchy. He looked totally used up.

"How old are you?" Papa asked him.

"I'll be forty-six next month."

Papa was fifty years old at that time. He knew he didn't want to end up like the old man. He got up, picked up his lunch pail and headed for the truck.

"Where you goin'?" the old man asked

"Home," Papa replied.

"But if you don't finish out the whole day, they won't pay you for this mornin's work."

"I don't need the money that badly," Papa said as he got into the truck and drove off.

Finally, the island defeated him. He couldn't make a go of it and he and Mama decided to go back to California and get jobs.

He put the farm up for sale, but had the same problem as the previous owner. No one was willing to pay cash for a failing dairy farm in the middle of nowhere.

Demoralized and defeated, he traded the farm for a big steel fishing boat, the *Amy D*, and moved his family back to Southern California.

I was only three years old at the time, but I remember the trip back from Washington.

The fish stopped biting and Papa retired to the fo'c'sle to catch a nap. I was on wheel watch and there wasn't another boat in sight, just the empty ocean. I reminisced about our move from Washington back to California.

Mama drove Packie, a giant Packard touring sedan, down the coast with my big sister, Quita, who was five years old by then, and me climbing all over her. Papa loaded all of our possessions in the hold of his big steel boat. We spent the whole trip looking out to sea to try to see Papa and Santos, who had become part of our family, on the *Amy D* as they brought the boat down the coast.

"Look, Mama," Quita squealed. "I see a boat." Mama pulled the Packard over in a view point.

"Where is it sweetie?"

"Right there, see?"

Mama strained to look. She couldn't see anything. Quita and I spent a thousand miles looking out to sea. Every smudge and dot we saw had to be Papa on the *Amy D.*

When we arrived in California, Mama drove directly to *Abuelita's* house. By this time, *don Teodoro* had died and *Abuelita* canonized him. She only remembered the good things about him as she lived by herself in the shack, surrounded by family, on the tomato farm.

Over the years, the shack had been built into a regular little house with electricity and indoor plumbing. Anna, Mama's oldest sister, and her family lived across the driveway; Mellie married a Marine named Paul (another gringo) and they built a house on the farm behind *Abuelita's* house. Mama's other sister, Ester, married Carlos and they built a house behind Anna and across the driveway from Mellie and Paul. In a few years, Santos married an American girl, Bev, whom he met in college in Washington, and they built a house between *Abuelita's* and Paul and Mellie's.

"Mama, where are the beds?" Quita asked.

"They aren't here yet, honey. Papa has them with him in the boat."

"When will Papa be here?"

"I don't know honey. Boats are very slow." Mama tucked Quita and me into our sheets. We shared a mattress on the living room floor.

"Where are we going to live? Are we going to live with *Abuelita*?"

"No, sweet heart, we'll find our own house."

"Everybody lives here, can't we build a house here too?"

"We'll see *mija*." Mama kissed us both and slowly

walked into the kitchen. I could hear her talking quietly with *Abuelita*.

"So Vicki," *Abuelita* said, "things didn't work out for you in Washington? Good, I'm glad you're home where you belong."

"Mama, I don't know what we're going to do. We didn't get any money for the farm. We don't have jobs. I don't know how we're going to live."

"You can stay here with us. There's always lots of food. We'll put in a crop of tomatoes in the spring."

"Charles will never do that. He can't live here. He's too proud for that. I'm so afraid that he's going to take that damned boat and try to go fishing again. Why can't he just get a normal job like everyone else?"

Papa did arrive a few days later. He spent the next few weeks looking for work and finding us a house. Mama immediately found a job at a Mexican restaurant in Santa Ana called "La Fonda." Finally one day, Papa came home with a big smile on his face.

"I found a house today. It's a little two bedroom on Liberty Street in Costa Mesa. It needs some fixing up, but we can Wallaceize it and it'll do just fine."

The Hill-Cunningham automatic pilot steered the *Marine View* for me. I just had to make sure that everything kept running and that the fickle auto-pilot kept us on course. I jumped down from my favorite perch on the counter top next to the galley windows and made myself a sandwich. *Marine View* was so different from Papa's last boat, the *Amy D*.

The *Amy D* was a big steel northern-style fishing boat that Papa used as the model for the *Betty B* in his novel. She was sixty-five feet long with a high bow, big deck house and broad, flat afterdeck. A big Caterpillar diesel engine gobbled diesel fuel and her fish hold held forty tons of fish.

"Just think about it," Papa told a skeptical Mama, "Even at two hundred fifty dollars a ton, that's a ten thousand dollar payday."

The problem was filling the hold. Papa and Santos made trip after trip and couldn't catch any fish. Finally he realized what was missing. During his big money days he had Mama as his deck hand. She had extraordinary vision. From the flying bridge or the crow's nest, she could see a school of fish that no one else saw. As long as she fished with him, he always came home with a full hold.

"Mama, I'd like you to go fishing with me again on the next trip," he said

"Sharles, I can't do that. We can't take the kids out to sea on a boat."

"No, I'm thinking you could leave them here. They could stay with your mother or Gussie."

"No. I don't want to go back. I don't want to leave the children."

"Look, Vicki, when you fished with me, we always caught fish. You were my good luck charm. I'm not doing anything now. We only need one good trip to make the season."

"Sharles, it's just not a good idea. I would lose my job at La Fonda. Francis wouldn't hold it open for me."

"If we have a good season, you won't need the job anymore."

Mama objected, but Papa was the boss. How different things were from today. Finally it was decided that she would leave her two small children, Quita and me, with Aunt Gussie and go fishing with him again.

A heavy, even sea was running, it was overcast and unusually cold for a California July day. The *Amy D* rose and fell to the rhythmic motion of the sea. Mama was on the flying bridge running the boat, Papa and Santos were in the cockpit tending to the lines. Actually, they were sitting around waiting to tend the lines, they hadn't had a bite all day.

"When you graduate from college," Papa told Santos, "You'll come back down to California and get a job teaching. Then you'll have the summers free to fish with me."

"Sharles, get up here quick," Mama yelled.

Papa raced for the ladder to the bridge deck. Mama's face was quickly turning from her usual lovely tan to pale to light green to darker green.

"Take the wheel, I'm going to be sick." Mama made a dash for the ladder and quickly dropped down to the deck. She rushed to the lee rail, leaned over the side and heaved. She didn't have anything in her stomach to vomit up, she hadn't been able to hold down any food in three days. She had always had a tender stomach, but after giving birth to two children, she was perpetually sea sick.

"It's OK, Mama," Papa assured her. "You just need to get your sea-legs under you."

"I don't want to get my sea-legs under me. I just want to go home."

"Don't worry, even Admiral Nelson was sea sick for the first three days out every trip."

"I don't care about Admiral Nelson or anybody else, I want to be home with my babies." With that, Mama started for the deckhouse door.

"Stay on deck, Mama. It helps to see the horizon. If you go below, you will just get sicker."

"I can stay on deck and be cold and miserable, or I can go below and be warm and miserable," Mama said. As she passed through the galley she grabbed a big pot to take with her to her berth in the fo'c'sle.

On day seven, Mama was still seasick and the *Amy D's* hold was still empty. Finally Papa succumbed to Mama's tears and complaining. He didn't bring home any more fish with

Mama than he had before.

Papa decided that the problem was the *Amy D*. The previous owner had practically given her away when he traded her for the farm. There was a reason why, she wouldn't fish. We never really knew why, but Papa suspected that she gave off some kind of electric current through the water that shocked the fish and chased them away. Even when they were in the middle of a school of fish, they couldn't catch any.

She was a failure as a tuna boat. Papa spent the entire first summer we were back in California trying to make a go of it fishing for albacore. He spent more money on fuel and supplies than he made for the few fish he caught. Mama's tips and wages from La Fonda not only had to pay for our house and food, but she was subsidizing a losing fishing endeavor.

The following summer, the year I turned five, Papa met Joe Gallo, who had a sardine net. The sardine industry had built a large fleet around Monterey and San Francisco. Then they fished out the area and the fleet was tied up, rusting at their moorings.

"Charlie, I know where to find sardines. Since there are so few sardines on the Pacific Coast anymore, they'd fetch a premium price. Just think what a forty-ton hold full of sardines would bring," Joe pleaded.

"I don't know, Joe. I'm a troller man. I don't want any damn net on my boat." For a troller fisherman, the ultimate indignity was to put a net on his boat.

"So, how you doin' trolling this year?" Joe asked.

Papa went to the bank and borrowed money against the *Amy D* to buy the equipment, to put the net on her and go after sardines.

It was a dismal failure. All summer long they went out, each time buying stores, diesel fuel and ice. Each time they came back, the hold was empty. They never found a single school of sardine that summer.

"You have to stop this." Mama implored. "You're spending more and more money and making nothing."

"But Mama," Papa replied, "I gave Joe my word. I made a commitment to fish the season with him and I have to honor it."

"A commitment," she shouted. "What about your commitment to me, to your family?"

And so it went. Trip after trip he came home with an empty hold. Every night Mama went to work waiting on tables at La Fonda where Francis welcomed her back after her abortive trip on the *Amy D*. We lived on her tips, they bought bread and milk. Her paycheck just covered the house payment. We lived on next to nothing.

Finally, Mama had enough. When Papa returned from another fruitless trip, she cornered him.

"You have to stop. We can't go on like this."

"Mama, I can't quit, I gave my word to Joe."

"You gave your word to me."

"I have to go, just one more trip."

"Then you are no longer the head of this family." she shouted at him. "Until you can start supporting the family, I'll be making all the decisions. My first decision is that you are not going back. If you leave on another fishing trip, we won't be here when you get back."

Papa lost his first family during the Depression. His first wife took their two daughters and walked out on him. He searched his soul and realized that he would do anything not to lose this family. Of course, all of this happened behind closed doors. Children weren't allowed to be part of serious family decisions. I would only learn of this discussion years later. I pieced the story together from accounts both Papa and Mama told me as a teenager.

The *Amy D* sat at her mooring in San Pedro and rusted

away. Most of what Papa made on shore went to pay off the loan he had taken to convert her to a sardine boat. Finally, when I was six years old, he agreed to sell the boat. He packed his tools and me into Ragamuffin, his work car, and we drove up to San Pedro to live on the boat, fix it up and get it ready to sell.

Ragamuffin was an old Dodge coupe from the Thirties that Papa used as a work car. He removed the back seat so that he could put all of his tools behind the front seat and have access to them from the trunk. When I rode with him, I rode in the front seat.

The front seat would only seat three people though. When we had to carry extra passengers, I climbed over the front seat back and across the tools to lie in the ledge under the rear window. I climbed up and hung on because below, piles of Papa's tools lurked. Various sized saws, sharp chisels, wrecking bars and blades for his big electrical saws waited for a boy to land in them. I was in mortal fear of falling off of the ledge into the death trap below me.

I remember scraping the rust off the *Amy D,* sanding and painting. I was so proud and happy that Papa allowed me to go with him. I followed him around like a love-struck puppy dog, living for any signs of his approval. At the end of the first week Papa called Mama to let her know how we were doing.

"We're doing fine. We'll be done here in a couple of weeks. Penny's doing great. Today he painted the handrails. He got more paint on himself than he did on the boat, but it looks good."

We cleaned up the *Amy D* and put her on the market. I loved that boat. She was so big I could get lost in her. She had a huge deckhouse and galley and many ladders that I ran up and down pretending I was fighting Captain Hook. She had giant living quarters below deck. Her engine room with its big Cat diesel was at once thrilling in its power and complication and frightening because it had so many ways to get hurt.

There was no market for tuna trollers or sardine boats. Papa had the *Amy D* for sale for a long time before he finally found a buyer.

"He's going to turn her into a Goddamn purse seiner," Papa told us at dinner. The combination of Japanese tuna and advances in purse seiner technology put Papa out of business, now his beloved big steel boat was going over to the enemy. But he sold her and Papa did not have a boat. It was one of the saddest days of his life. He had been fishing for sixteen years when he tied the *Amy D* up, said goodbye to the fishing life forever (again) and got a job on shore that he hated every day.

The sun dipped below the western horizon, the cloudless evening sky turned bright red. It was time to rouse Papa from his nap. He needed to get dinner started and always did a thorough walkthrough of the boat before it turned dark. As he climbed up into the deckhouse I told him what I had been thinking about.

"I was just remembering the *Amy D*. Do you remember when we sold her?"

"Oh God, PC. That was a terrible time in my life. That was when I had to get a job ashore. I went down to the Carpenters Union hall to try to join the union."

By this time he was fifty-five years old. The maximum age for a carpenter's apprentice was twenty-six. The only way you could get into the union was to go through the apprenticeship program.

"I worked construction with my brother, Bob, in the Bay Area after I left the Army between the wars," Papa told me as we started his nightly rounds. "It was good work and the construction business was booming. I thought that if I could get on, I could support the family.

"Since I couldn't join the apprenticeship program, I petitioned the union to let me in as a special case. They told me

I'd have to present my case to the board of governors.

"I showed up to the meeting prepared to beg for admittance. The board members were seated at tables in a semi-circle around me. They shot questions at me about carpentry. I answered as best as I could, but I knew I wasn't doing well. Finally, one of the board members had an epiphany.

"'Are you the Charles Wallace who organized the dockworkers in San Francisco in the Thirties?' he asked me.

"'Yes I am. I've been a union man all of my life. After San Francisco, I organized the Fisherman's Union in San Pedro.'

"'Hey guys, Charlie's a good union man. What do you say we let him in?'

"The board voted and it was unanimous. I was now a union carpenter."

After dinner it was my turn for a watch below. I crawled into my bunk and turned off the light. The steady hum of the little diesel engine, the soft gurgle of the water passing by as the bow cut through the waves and the gentle motion of the boat soon had me in a near hypnotic state. I fell asleep remembering the years when Papa was a carpenter.

Papa was never a good employee. He hated authority. He was often smarter and more experienced than his bosses and was not afraid of letting them know that. He went down to the union hall and put his name on the list. When a contractor needed carpenters they took them from the top of the list. When his turn came, he went out on the job. The contractor had to take him.

Papa learned his trade on the job. He got fired from many jobs before he became competent. He hated working for someone else. His best days were the days he got fired. Then he could draw unemployment insurance and work on his own projects.

Papa came home with a big smile on his face.

"I got fired today," he announced.

There were some holes on his pants where he had spilled battery acid from the car. I thought that they literally put a torch to him when they fired him.

"Papa, they burned you," I said.

He laughed. It wasn't until years later that I realized that they had not burned his pants at all.

When he used up his unemployment insurance, he went back to work. He worked long enough to max out his unemployment benefits, then got himself fired again.

Papa hated the work he was doing, building a tract of houses in an orange grove. The seller made a deal with the contractor to harvest his crop before leaving the property. The contractor was building over two hundred houses on the orchard and had a huge crew. The property owner hired a crew of Mexicans to pick his last crop of oranges.

After several months Papa was thoroughly bored with his job. He knew he had worked long enough to be able to draw unemployment again. Framing the roof of one of the houses was a hot, miserable chore. Papa put down his hammer and walked over to the water jug. Taking a big gulp of the iced water he stood on the roof's crown so that everyone could see him.

"*Aye, aye, aye.*" He let out a big "grito," then he started in on the words to "Jalisco".

"*Jalisco, Jalisco, Jalisco, tu tienes tus novia que es mi Guadalajara.*"

The Mexicans in the orange grove stopped what they were doing and stared at this strange gringo on the roof top singing one of their most exciting songs. Soon a voice joined him from the orange grove.

"*y una morena hechar mucha bala y baja del luna cantar en Chapala.*"

Then all of the Mexicans joined in. The song built to an exciting crescendo. When it was done, someone in the orange grove started singing "Guadalajara."

Every worker on the construction project stopped to witness the spectacle. The orange grove was alive with song and merriment. Soon a fancy new pickup truck came bouncing up the road and the supervisor jumped out.

"Charlie, what in the hell are you doing? Do realize this job is costing me eight hundred bucks an hour and you just cost me over thirty hours. I've got more than two hundred men on this job and they're all just standing around watching you sing."

When Papa pulled into the driveway that evening he had a grin on his face that would shine in the dark. He was very proud of getting fired in such a creative way. He told us the story at dinner and we laughed our heads off. Papa had imbued us with a sense of wanting to beat the system.

After dinner he took me out to the driveway where he reached into the back of Ragamuffin, and pulled out several boxes of oranges. The Mexicans had loaded his car with boxes of oranges while he was getting fired.

The next day I filled my little red wagon with oranges and started out door to door to sell them. In those days, the lady of the house was always home during the day. When she answered the door I told her "I'm selling oranges. My Papa got fired yesterday and brought home all of these oranges for me to sell." I sold every orange I could get my hands on. That was the first Christmas I had my own money for gifts.

Every evening, after he put us to bed, Papa stepped out onto the back patio and watched the sun set. He looked past the other tract houses, the downtown, the harbor. In his mind's eye, he looked far out to sea. He dreamt of life on the open ocean, the challenges, the joys, the freedom. Then he finished his beer, came inside, picked up the newspaper and resigned himself to his new life.

While Papa was in misery, Mama was happy. In spite of

her husband's off again, on again work record, at least she had a
stable home, a husband who was not running off adventuring,
and a steady income. We weren't well off, but she could pay the
bills every month.

Chapter 13

Building the *Marine View*

In warm southern waters there are flying fish. The flying fish that we saw in Mexico were about ten to twelve inches long and with gray bodies and yellow fins. They traveled in schools and when larger fish attacked, they broke the surface like a flight of the Blue Angels in their star burst formation and dispersed in all directions.

The flying fish doesn't really fly. It has long side fins that look like wings. Swimming at a breakneck speed through the water, it breaks the surface, leaps into the air and spreads its "wings." It can glide over the surface for a hundred yards or more. The fish chasing it can't tell where it is going to come down and loses interest.

Now that we reached our fishing grounds, we hove to for the night and drifted on the peaceful sea. The sea anchor was out and the flopper stoppers over the side. I finished cleaning up the galley after dinner and headed down to my bunk. After reading for a short time, I turned off the light and went to sleep.

Sometime, late in the night I heard a thump on deck. Then I heard a second thump, then a flopping sound. I sat up in my bunk and listened. Papa was sound asleep, his snoring shaking the *Marine View's* wooden planking.

I quietly slipped from my bunk and tiptoed up the companion way ladder to the deck house. In the deck house, I grabbed a flash light and went on deck to see what was making the noise. Several flying fish were flopping around on our afterdeck. I flipped them back into the water and returned to bed.

The next morning I awoke to the smell of coffee. The little Ford diesel hummed in the background, the sound of the water whooshed past my head and daylight poured in through the companionway to the deckhouse. I slipped into my shorts and tennis shoes and climbed up to the deck house.

"Mornin' *Mijo*. I was just about to rouse you out."

"Good mornin'. Where are we?"

"We're about forty miles off of *Punta Abreojos*. We'll be in fish soon. Look what Father Neptune brought us last night." Papa had several flying fish lying on the cutting board

"The flying fish can't see any better at night than anyone else," Papa said. "They were chased by bigger fish, took to the air without seeing where they were going and landed on deck."

"Fish for breakfast? Yuck," I protested

"This is what we're having. Either eat it or go hungry," was Papa's standard reply.

I scraped off the scales, gutted and cleaned the fish while Papa fried up a pan full of potatoes. He breaded the fish in corn meal, fried them in bacon fat and set them aside. Finally, he fried some eggs and put them on top of the potatoes.

I quickly learned to love flying fish for breakfast. The fish was sweet and didn't taste too "fishy." It went well with the potatoes and eggs. I couldn't imagine a better breakfast.

We took our plates out onto the fish hold hatch cover and watched the early morning sun reflect off of the deep blue sea.

"Could you have ever imagined a morning like this when we were building the *Marine View*?" Papa asked. We had come down a long road since the first time we saw her bare hull.

Three years after Papa gave up the sea he was down to his last few unemployment checks and needed to get his name on the hiring list at the Union Hall. He walked into the hall and up to the window where he registered for work.

"Hey, Charlie, how you doin'?" asked the bleached blonde behind the window.

"OK, Betty. It's time for me to go back to work."

"Say Charlie, you know something about boats don't you?"

"Yeah sure, I fished for sixteen years. I've built boats from scratch, from the keel up. Why?"

"Well we got a call this morning. Some jamoke is looking for a carpenter to help him build a boat."

"My God, Betty, don't let him hire a carpenter to build a boat. Carpenters and shipwrights are two different things. There's not a straight line on a boat, a carpenter will screw it all up."

"Well, Charlie, you're number one hundred forty-five on the hire list, but let me talk to Jack. Maybe we can send you out on the job."

Fate stepped in and Papa was back in the boating business. The job was for a man in Newport Beach named Bill Skinner. Papa knew Bill in the old days and he'd been a good fisherman. What in the hell was he doing building a new boat?

"I know times have been tough, but I've got a new angle, Charlie," Bill told Papa. "I got this here thirty-six foot shore boat offa some goddamn Navy cruiser or something. She's small enough that one or two men can work her, but big enough to bring home a good catch. I got this new fangled Ford diesel lined up for her. This is a Brit engine. Ford saw it and wanted the engine so bad that they bought the whole damned company.

"This little engine will push her along at hull speed, but only burns three-quarters of a gallon a hour. We won't even need a auxiliary to run the refrigeration plant. A damn auxiliary will burn more fuel than our main engine. This boat'll be so cheap to run that we can make money at two hundred dollars a ton. I worked it all out."

"OK, Bill. It's your money. Anyway, I need a job and I'd sure as hell'd rather be building a boat than working on a bunch of fucking tract houses."

On Monday morning, Papa was a happy man. He put on his work clothes, loaded his tools in the back of Ragamuffin and set off on a new adventure. When he came home that evening he was beaming.

"Vicki, you've got to see this little boat. She's so beautiful. Fine lines, good capacity, a beautiful wine glass transom. Bill is going to have himself a fine little package." Papa was so excited he talked about nothing else during dinner. Mama didn't say a word. She just silently picked at her food and glared at him. She knew.

Papa went to work on the boat. Bill's backyard became a boatyard. Papa set up his tools and ordered the materials he needed. Soon stacks of lumber surrounded the wooden hull. Papa used an unpaved alley lined with eucalyptus trees that ran between Bill's back yard and his neighbors for access to the makeshift boatyard.

The boat's keel was on big wooden blocks and huge timbers wedged between her gunwales and the ground to kept her upright. The *Marine View* was a converted Navy lifeboat. Thirty-six feet long and twelve feet wide at her widest point, she had a flat bottom that was designed to make her easy to beach. Being a launch, she was used during the war as a shore boat on a cruiser or battleship to ferry the crew back and forth between the ship and shore. After the war, the fleet was put into mothballs and she was declared surplus. Bill picked her up for a song.

Papa started by adding the deck beams, then plywood decks. Next came a tiny deck house made out of plywood and living quarters in the fo'c'sle. The Ford diesel was installed and tested. He found a refrigeration plant off of a tractor-trailer rig

and built a Rube Goldberg drive line off of the Ford to run it
and all of the other accessories needed on a working boat. Days
passed and he came home later and later each night.

Then one Friday afternoon, Bill came to him. "Charlie,
we've got a problem."

"What is it, Bill."

"I'm out a money. It's costing a lot more than I thought
to build the boat and I've run dry. I can't finish the boat myself
and I can't pay you to do it."

"God, Bill, that's awful. What're you going to do?"

"Well I had a idea. I've talked this over with my wife
and she agrees. Charlie, what I'd like to do is to have you finish
the boat, but I can't pay you for it. You finish the boat and we'll
be partners; fifty-fifty."

The fish was nibbling at the hook and Bill just had to set
it to reel him in.

"I know we can get the boat in the water in time for the
albacore run this year," Bill continued. "If we work real hard,
we can be making money by June. We can pack about twenty
tons aboard. That's five thousand dollars a trip. We're both
great fishermen. I figure we can fill her hold in a week, maybe
two at the most. That's twenty five hundred dollars you'll be
taking home every two weeks. Wouldn't the little woman like
that?"

There was never really any question what Papa would
do. "Well, Bill, it's an interesting offer. Let me go home and talk
it over with Vicki. I'll let you know on Monday."

Mama went out of her mind.

"What are you thinking? Don't you remember the *Amy
D?* We're still paying for that fiasco. How can you even think
about owning another boat? And how are we going to live? It
will take you a year to finish that boat. You won't have any
income. You can't do it and that's that."

The pull of the sea was too strong. In spite of Mama,

Papa called Bill that night and signed on. Bill officially fired him the next day and Papa drew unemployment insurance while he worked on the boat.

On Monday morning Papa was back on the job, eagerly planning the upcoming fishing season with Bill.

Then he found out about Bill's problem.

Late one night the telephone rang. Papa got up, went to the kitchen and answered the black wall phone.

"Hello?" It had to be an emergency. No one in their right mind would call at this ungodly hour.

"I don' know Charlie, I don' know," slurred Bill.

"Bill? What is it, what's wrong?"

"I'm not shure that we can do thish. I don' know if there's any money is fisssh anymore."

What had Papa gotten himself into?

Papa always saw the best in people. He didn't tell Mama about Bill being a drunk, but she knew the minute she saw him. His nose was bright red, he reeked of cheap whiskey. Mama's father had been an alcoholic and she hated anything to do with liquor.

Every cell in her body told her that her husband needed to walk away from this mess. She knew that a tuna boat could not support the family. She talked to him, she pleaded with him, she threatened him, but she couldn't convince him of the troubles that were coming.

Things did not go well. Bill and Papa spent too much time armchair fishing. Bill made too many mistakes that Papa had to redo. The time was getting away and the money was gone. Papa had to start putting his own money into the boat to get it finished.

Fall slipped into winter; winter into spring. Summer came and the albacore started running. Big commercial boats made record catches. Papa fought Bill to get the boat done.

I was in the second grade that year. As soon as school

was out, Papa decided that I would go to work with him every day. From that summer on, as long as I lived with him, when school let out, I was off to work on whatever job, whatever adventure he was working on.

My major job was run and fetch. "Penny, bring me a three-eighths inch bit for the brace and bit." Or "Penny, I need a two by four, four feet long." I was also good at pulling nails from used lumber so that we could recycle it. I was delighted to have him all to myself and proud that I was helping build his dream.

The best time of the day was lunch. There was a little grocery store about a block away, around the corner. At noon everyday he gave me two dimes and sent me to the store to buy two bottles of Hires Root Beer. They kept the bottles in a big orange and brown ice-filled chest on the worn wooded floor and the root beer was dripping wet, but ice cold.

When I returned, we sat down on a pile of fresh lumber or on the hatch cover, in the warm California sun and opened his big metal lunch pail. He took out the sandwiches that Mama packed for us and while we ate our lunch he told me stories about his past adventures. I learned about his growing up on the cotton farm, about his years in the Army and especially about his fishing adventures. He also told me about the books he was reading. He was a great reader of history. I learned all about the Ancient Greeks and the Roman Empire. He recited poetry and Shakespeare from memory. But mostly we dreamed about finishing the boat and all the adventures we would have when she was swimming.

The *Marine View* was built on a shoestring. First Bill ran out of money, then Papa ran out of money. Eventually, Papa took out a second mortgage on our house to raise the money to finish the boat. Everything on the *Marine View* was bargain basement priced. If he couldn't find a deal, then Papa made it himself. The two-way radio we bought for the boat was a used thirty-five watt set. This was what was referred to in the fishing industry as a "Mickey Mouse" radio. It could listen in to nearby conversations, but you had to be practically within shouting distance to talk to someone.

A muffler for the little diesel was expensive. To solve this problem, Papa took a piece of two inch pipe about four feet long and cut it in half lengthwise. He welded baffles into the pipe, then welded the two pieces back together. It was totally ineffective. When we got the boat in the water and fired the engine up, you couldn't tell that there was any muffler on it at all. Then he got creative and welded a long piece of copper tubing to the end of the "muffler." He ran the tubing all the way to the top of the mast and let the sound from the exhaust exit there. At the top of the mast, thirty or so feet away, the roar of the exhaust wasn't too bad and we made do.

By this time Bill had all but dropped out of the picture. I almost never saw him. My jobs included sanding, scraping and painting. I held the long boards that Papa cut with his power saw. Papa let me help install the glass in the deck house and the radio antenna on the mast. I painted the mast a buff color and installed the spreaders, the cross-wise pieces that held the jig poles in place when not in use. However, I had problems using a screwdriver. I never seemed to be able to get the screw to go in the last few turns. To solve this problem, I screwed the screw as far in as I could, then I took a hammer and pounded it in the rest of the way. Papa never caught me taking this short cut. This would have an impact on us later when we rammed the *Munashima Maru* and lost the radio antenna.

It was an exciting day when the cement truck arrived.

"We're going to put a ton of concrete in her bilge for ballast," Papa told me. "For every pound above the water line, you need ten pounds below the water line." We were putting very little weight on deck. The deck house was light and the mast and rigging didn't amount to much either.

The big truck backed up to the boat. The driver got out and put a series of troughs on the back of the rotating mixer to pour the concrete down into the boat. As the gray cement flowed into the bilge, Papa and I took trowels with long handles and smoothed it out.

After the cement dried, we put ceiling planks on the inside of the ribs to keep the weight of the cargo from pushing down on the hull planking and weakening the boat. Between the ribs and the ceiling planking, we installed fiber glass insulation to keep the fish hold cold.

After we finished in the fish hold, we moved on to the engine room. Headroom in the engine room was only about four and a half feet except for under the hatch combing where you could stand up. Actually, I could stand up anywhere in the boat, but Papa had to move around on his hands and knees in the engine room.

The central feature of the engine room was the little Ford diesel. Bill purchased the engine from a dealer and it was still new in its crate. Papa rigged up a tripod over the boat and attached a block and tackle to lift the heavy engine off of the ground and over the side of the boat. While he hauled it up, I pulled on guide ropes to keep it from smashing into the hull's planking.

"Get my half inch drill with a three-eighths inch bit," Papa instructed as we prepared to anchor the engine to heavy timbers in the boat's bilge. Papa pulled on the ropes to lift the engine off its bed and I moved it from side to side until it lined up perfectly, then we drilled holes though the attachment fittings and into the engine bed. Papa screwed big lag screws into the bed to hold the engine in place.

With the engine in place, Papa installed two large, stainless steel fuel tanks, one on each side of the boat, aft of the engine. We worried and fought these tanks in place, then strapped them down with heavy steel straps. The tanks gave the *Marine View* the ability to stay at sea for over thirty days at a time.

"Now that the engine's in place, we need to build a line shaft," Papa told me.

"What's the line shaft for?"

"It'll run the refrigeration plant, the bilge pumps, the generators and some other equipment." We installed the line shaft to the left of the engine. A V-belt from the engine drove the shaft; the shaft had a series of pulleys and V-belts that drove the other equipment. Papa built a lever that could shift the shaft into or out of gear. Of course, the whole system was designed and built with minimum cost in mind. It worked better in theory than in practice. It was always throwing belts and systems went down, necessitating a trip to the engine room to repair the problem. This usually happened during a storm or while we were docking.

The glory hole always reeked of chemical smells. There was diesel fuel, paint, varnish, paint remover, lubricating oil and, when the engine was running (which was all the time at sea), exhaust fumes. In a tossing sea this potent mixture of chemical fumes was enough to make the strongest stomach queasy.

After we completed the work in the engine room, we moved forward to the fo'c'sle. A companion way (stairs) just to the port of the steering station in the deck house led down into the fo'clse. The fo'clse was a snug, cozy little home. On each side a bunk sat fairly high up the sides of the boat because in the bow of the boat, the bottom narrows and down at seat level, there isn't enough room to put the bunks. Underneath the bunks were drawers and storage space. I had to climb up the drawers to get into the bunks. Forward of the bunks was a level area about four and a half feet wide at the aft end and three feet wide at the forward end. Papa cut a mattress down to fit this area. It was to be my berth.

We built the decks of the *Marine View* out of plywood and covered them in fiberglass. In the final coat, we mixed in clean, beach sand. (We made a midnight raid on the beach in Newport Beach to requisition the materials.) This made the decks rough and provided traction in the wet seas and when the decks were running with fish blood. You couldn't go barefoot on this deck; it tore up your feet.

The fiberglass came in big rolls. Papa cut a piece of half inch plywood in half lengthwise and fastened it together, over some saw horses, to make a table on which to cut the cloth.

"After we cut the fiberglass cloth to size, we need to impregnate it in resin," Papa told me. "We mix the resin with a catalyst to make it harden. If we don't get the mix right it will either never harden or be too brittle. Once we add the catalyst, we have to move fast, it only has a pot-life of about a half hour before it starts to set up."

We mixed the resin from five gallon buckets and saturated the fiberglass, then we laid down the saturated fiberglass over the deck much like hanging wall paper. When it cured, it created a strong, hard, waterproof surface. The problem with working with fiberglass was that the millions of tiny little glass particles got all over your skin and itched. Every night we came home and raced for the shower. By the time we finished the fiberglass work, my skin was a mass of red welts.

The summer was waning, the albacore season all but gone. We were nearing completion on the boat and Bill still owned half of it, but the situation got worse and worse.

Every night, when the bars closed down Papa got another "I don' know, Charlie" call. Bill was less and less a factor in the life of the boat.

"Mama, we're just about ready to launch the boat," Papa said cheerfully as he returned home from work one day. "We have to come up with a name for her."

"Name it anything you want. I don't want to be part of

it."

"Now Vicki, you know that I need you to christen her. It's bad luck if we just dump her in the water. You need to introduce her to Lord Neptune."

"Won't you ever get tired of these childish games? Can't you see that we have a family to take care of? When are you going to start supporting your children?"

"Well, at least help me with the name." Papa was sure that he could convince Mama to christen the boat when the time came.

"I don't want to play that game."

"Well, we've always talked about having a house with a marine view. This is probably as close as we'll ever come. We should name her the *Marine View*."

Now he had a name, but he still needed to convince Mama to christen the boat.

"We're going to launch the boat on Monday," he reported. "I'd like you to break a bottle of Bud over her and christen her."

"I can't. I have to take care of Jonny and Jimmy."

"Bring them along. I'll hold them while you christen her."

"I won't have my babies drug around a boat yard"

"Leave them with your mother then."

"Mama told me that this would happen. When you started working on that boat, she warned me. Charles, can't you just sell it and go back to work?"

She saw only trouble and despair in her future. She knew that the boat would soak up money. Money she went to work every night and earned in dimes and quarters.

I don't remember the launching of the *Marine View*. It was a non-event in our house. Mama refused to participate and I don't think Papa wanted to give her another excuse to get mad at him. Ignoring the traditions of the sea, when the boat was ready to be launched, Papa and Bill just had her hauled down to the harbor and dumped her in the water. I worried that without a proper christening, they were condemning the *Marine View* to a life as a hard luck boat.

I do remember her maiden voyage though. We made a big family event out of it. Because Papa invited all of our friends, Mama relented, agreed to be a good *soldadera* and packed a picnic lunch. We went down to the boat and cast off the lines. It was a warm sunny day and we cruised Newport Harbor. Papa hooked up a fishing pole for me and I sat in the cockpit trolling. I actually caught a couple of mackerel that day. My young mind ran wild with fantasies. I couldn't imagine what commercial fishing would be like, so I had images of pirate ships and Captain Hook playing though my mind.

The fishing didn't go well though. It was too late in the year to go after albacore, so Papa took the boat out fishing for mackerel or squid at night. These fish were bought by the canneries to make cat food. The canneries paid next to nothing for them.

Papa liked brailing mackerel. He almost always found a school of fish and seeing them pile up on deck, then filling the fish hold was instant gratification. He could go out all night, be at the cannery dock by day break and spend the day at home with his family.

Papa didn't get rich with the mackerel and squid. He made enough money to pay for expenses and make the payments to the bank. We lived on Mama's tip money.

By this time Bill was a real problem. He drank heavily and couldn't be relied upon. He was not paying his share of the way. Bill was dead drunk and getting ready to take the boat out squid fishing when he dropped the outboard motor that they used to maintain steerage way when fishing over the side.

Papa had had enough; he had it out with Bill.

"Vicki," Mama was in the kitchen preparing dinner

when Papa returned home, "I've got to do something about Bill. He's dragging us down."

"Why don't you just sell him your share of the boat?" Mama asked.

"I tried. He's out of money. He can't afford to buy us out."

"What are you going to do?" Mama put down her knife and stared at Papa. She already knew the answer.

"We're going to have to buy him out."

"Charles, you can't do that. We don't have any money." There was fire in Mama's eyes.

"I have to do something. Today he lost the outboard motor. If he keeps taking the boat out when he's drunk, he's going to sink her and kill himself."

"Good, that will get him out of our hair."

"You don't mean that. We've got too much invested in the boat to just walk away from it."

"What else can we do? Where are you going to get the money?" Mama's voice was rising.

"Well, we're going to have to take out another loan. I've already talked to the bank and they're willing to add on to our second mortgage."

"What are you thinking? We can't make the house payments and second mortgage now."

"It'll all work out, Vicki. You'll see. With Bill out of the way, I'll bring home all the money we make from fishing. We'll be able to pay off the loan in no time."

"No, I won't do it. I'm co-owner of the house, you need my signature to get the loan. I won't sign the papers. You can't do this to the family."

But he did. Mama refused to sign the loan papers, so Papa forged her signature.

It was winter time, or what passes for winter in Southern California.

"Just wait 'til summer, Mama," he told her. "We'll take the *Marine View* out after albacore and make a boat load of money." She didn't talk to Papa for weeks.

Chapter 14

Wolf Larsen

In 1958 I wasn't old enough to go fishing with Papa yet, but I was old enough to remember what happened. Papa tried a string of cheap deck hands that summer. At the end of each trip he paid them off and put them on the beach. They were totally useless on the boat.

In early July a big kid showed up, newspaper in hand.

"Hi, my name is Jim Spencer. I'm answering your ad"

"You ever fished before?" Papa asked.

"No sir. I'm a creative writing major at UC Berkley," Jim looked down at his shoes. "I'm looking for adventure. My writing professor told me that I have talent, but I don't have anything to write about. He wants me to go out and get experience in life so that I can have some tales to tell."

No one in their right mind would have hired Jim for a job that was physically demanding, required quick thinking, calm nerves, steady hands and where there was an element of risk that put both his life and theirs in his hands. But Jim had two great attractions to Papa: he worked cheap and he was a creative writing major.

It was a match made in heaven. Jim read all of the great works. Papa read everything. They talked long into the night about *Lord Jim* or Gibbon. They discussed Tolstoy and Dickens. For an added benefit, Jim was going to Berkley, that radical hotbed. This opened the door for them to talk politics as well. But it always came back to Jack London's *The Sea Wolf.* Jim was fascinated by the title character and it was Papa's favorite book.

The Sea Wolf is the story of a spoiled rich man who falls off a ferry boat in San Francisco Bay and is picked up by the outlaw sealing schooner *Ghost*. The tyrannical captain, Wolf Larsen, puts the rich guy to work as a cabin boy and terrorizes him though out the book. It is a dark psychological study of an abhorrent mind. Papa and Jim spent hours discussing Jack London and his characters.

Papa fascinated Jim. He had led the life that Jim dreamed about. A real Texas cowboy as a youth, Papa had been in the Army between the wars. He was a union organizer and a political activist. Jim drank him in. He was awake late into the night every night writing down the stories Papa told him. He filled writing pad after writing pad with his impressions of that fishing trip.

As the summer flashed by, the albacore worked their way up the coast of California to the Big Sur area.

Late July is usually a calm, peaceful time on the Pacific Coast. The summer of 1958 was an exception. The weather worsened as they fished their way north. An early storm swept down out of the Gulf of Alaska whipping up the seas; blowing like the devil. As the day wore on, the seas mounted until they were higher than the deck house. A cold, wicked wind blew the tops off of the seas; an icy rain hit the boat with the force of a shotgun blast.

The faithful little Ford diesel kept on turning, never missing a beat. The *Marine View* bobbled around like a cork in a maelstrom, everything on the boat in motion. One of the coffee mugs jumped from its hook in the ceiling above the galley sink and crashed to the deck. Jim nearly jumped out of his pants at the sound. He looked like a long-tailed cat in a room full of rockers, waiting for the next catastrophe.

The seas continued to grow. As the *Marine View* climbed each wave and the sea passed under her, she surfed down the back side of the wave into the next trough.

Everything was wet. Heavy green seas broke over the bow and rushed aft along the decks. The *Marine View* shuddered, then rose and tossed the sea aside. The water worked its way through the door on the aft side of the deck house.

Papa didn't trust the Hill-Cunningham automatic pilot to hold the course in heavy weather. The auto-pilot used two little bowls full of mercury to establish equilibrium and keep the boat on course. Papa carried a vial of mercury in the medicine chest to refill the bowls. When the boat was jumping around like a snake-bit stallion, the mercury splashed out of the bowls and the auto-pilot became useless. Little balls of mercury jumped around on the steering console and all over the deck as more and more of it sloshed out in the heavy seas.

Papa stood at the helm for hours guiding the boat through the wild seas because he couldn't trust Jim to hold a straight course. Jim probably figured that he was facing his death.

"Charlie," he whined, "we've got to run for cover. We can't survive out here."

"Goddamn it, Jim," Papa said, "the big Northern boats are still out here. This storm is going to blow over in a few hours and they'll be sitting on top of the biggest school of albacore we've seen since '49."

"*Marine View,* this is the *Misty,* come in Charlie." A metallic voice sounded over the two-way radio's speaker.

"*Misty, Marine View.* Go ahead, Al."

"Charlie, you running for cover? This blow looks like it's going to be a bad one."

"No, I think we'll ride this one out. The Norskies are all still out here fishing."

The big Northern boats almost never dodged a blow. The halibut schooners and purse seiners that came down out of Seattle were crewed by big tough Scandinavians. In the winter time they sailed into the Gulf of Alaska looking for halibut and cod. If they could survive in those harsh conditions, a little Southern California storm was nothing to them. The radio waves were alive with skippers named Ole and Sven and Gunner still talking about their catches.

It was an article of faith with Papa that his was always the last boat to leave the fishing grounds in bad weather. He knew that the first boat into the cannery got the highest price for their fish so he never ran for cover unless the Norskies went off the air. Papa made it his business to know who the skippers on the Northern boats were and what they sounded like. When they went off the air, he knew that the weather was so bad that they were running for shelter. Then and only then, would he condescend to abandon the fishing grounds.

All day long and through the night it continued to blow. The *Marine View* did a good job riding out the storm but Jim was terrified out of his mind. He climbed into his bunk and left Papa at the helm.

I pictured Papa as he stood rock solid fighting the storm hour after hour. When a wave came at him from an odd angle and rolled the boat on its side he shouted a stream of abuse at the storm as the boat shuddered, sloughed the water off and righted herself. When a wave was so high that the *Marine View* couldn't climb it, it came roaring aboard over the bow and Papa held on for dear life and cursed the storm at the top of his lungs. All night he fought the storm. It took on a personal nature. It was as if the gods threw a challenge at his feet and he, in the tradition of Jason or Odysseus, accepted it.

He was engaged in a fight to the death. Like a punch-weary boxer, he answered the bell round after round.

"Jim, get up here and take the helm." Papa called down to the fo'c'sle early on the second morning. "I hear a new sound" There was a constant thump-thump-thump coming from aft.

"I can't Charlie, I just can't," Jim said

"Damn it, Jim," Papa yelled, "you can either take the

helm or I'll throw your sorry ass overboard." Reluctantly, Jim crawled out of his bunk and climbed up into the pilot house.

"Just keep her heading into the swells," Papa told Jim. "She'll ride up them, then slide down the back side. Whatever you do, don't let her slough sideways. If one of those waves hits us on the beam, we're done for." He motioned with his hands to show how the boat would fall off sideways to the huge seas.

With that, he opened the cabin door and slipped out on deck. As Papa moved from behind the deck house, the full force of the gale hit him. He grabbed the rail and worked his way aft towards the engine room. Spray lashed at his face and the wind threatened to toss him overboard.

The boat was in constant motion. Papa stumbled around like a drunk as she rose and fell on the waves. There was a constant fore and aft bucking, but the boat rolled side to side giving the deck a corkscrew motion. It was like trying to walk on a moving roller coaster. Papa slowly pulled his way aft along the handrail.

In the deck house, the noise had been a steady thump-thump-thump. It was noticeable, but not loud. Out there on deck, in the teeth of a howling gale, Papa didn't hear the noise at all. He slid the engine room hatch cover open, the thump-thump-thump got louder. He eased himself over the hatch combing and worked his way down the companion ladder. His feet touched the deck; it sounded like he was inside a bass drum.

The steady little Ford diesel continued to purr but the thump-thump-thump drowned out the diesel's roar; made it seem like background noise. Down here the sounds of the machinery obliterated the wail of the storm. Papa reached over and turned on an electric light. He held on to the ladder to keep himself from being thrown onto the moving machinery.

He got quiet and listened. Papa had an almost Zen-like ability to filter out all of the other, normal boat noises and focus only on the out-of-place sound.

He listened carefully. The sound was coming from the reduction gear. If the engine or the drive system failed now, it could be fatal. If the engine stopped, the boat would immediately payoff and lie in the trough between the giant seas. They would capsize and sink.

Papa throttled back on the diesel and the noise immediately became softer. He finally located the source. It came from the flange that connected the propeller shaft to the reduction gear.

He needed to take a closer look at it so he grabbed a drop cord and bent over the flange. Sure enough, one of the nuts on the bolts that held the flanges together worked its way off and the bolt was backing out. Every time the bolt came to the top of its revolution, it banged against the reduction gear housing making the thump-thump-thump.

The whole world turned upside down. The boat rolled over onto her side. The deck wasn't under his feet anymore, but at his side. The hull he was leaning against was underneath him. That damn fool Jim allowed a wave to hit the boat on the beam and roll her over. Papa knew that boat would right herself, if that idiot Jim would just let her come up on her own.

There was a tearing sound and Papa felt an explosion of pain in his shoulder and left arm. The wool sweater he wore had a loose thread hanging from the sleeve. As the boat tossed on its side, the thread snagged the loose bolt on the flange. In a heartbeat, the thread pulled tight to the propeller shaft and Papa's left arm wrapped around the revolving shaft. the diesel yanked his arm from its socket. Every time the propeller shaft rotated, the loose bolt in the flange dug into the soft tissue of Papa's arm. In an instant he was a bloody mess.

He grabbed for the on/off switch on the engine to shut it down but it was out of reach. He tried to reach the fuel line; he figured that if he could pull it loose, the engine would die of fuel starvation. He yanked and yanked but it wouldn't budge.

Then, the sleeve tore loose from his sweater and he was free.

He grabbed for the companion way ladder and straightened himself up. He took quick stock of his situation. His left arm was hanging completely useless. His knuckles reached down to his knee. He was bleeding, but it wasn't arterial. The blood was flowing, not spurting out. He knew that his only chance was to make it back to the deck house.

Papa dragged himself up the companion way ladder using only his right hand. He timed each step with the roll of the boat so that he wasn't thrown from the ladder onto the engine as he released a rung to reach for the next higher one.

After an eternity, his head cleared the hatch combing and he got a lungful of clean air. The engine room reeked of exhaust fumes, diesel oil, cleaning solution, paint, and other chemicals. The clean ocean air felt like heaven.

His next problem was to get back to the wheel house. With only one hand to grip the rail he had to work his way forward, past the fish hold to the safety of the deck house. He grabbed the hatch combing with his good hand and inched his feet up and over the hatch unto the tossing deck. He managed to slide the hatch cover closed and secure it with his good hand.

Then he timed his lunge with the roll of the boat and grabbed for the handrail. He knew that if he missed, he would keep going over the rail. He also knew that Jim wouldn't be able to rescue him, that he wouldn't even know Papa was gone. He lunged for the rail and caught it with his right hand.

When the boat lurched forward, he let go and grabbed the rail a couple of feet further forward. He pulled himself uphill against the seas with the gale roaring in his face.

Papa finally made it to the deck house, wet from head to foot. His sweater's arm was torn away, his left arm dangled uselessly at his side and his shoulder looked like a chunk of meat in the butcher's case. Jim just stared at him with his mouth open.

"Jim, get the first aid kit from the fo'c'sle,' Papa said. "I need you to bandage my shoulder and make a sling for my arm."

"But Charlie, I've never taken first aid," Jim whined, "I don't know what to do."

"Goddamn it, Jim, get the fucking gauze out of the first aid kit and cover the bleeding. Then take the loose bandages and wrap it for me," Papa said.

Papa took over steering the boat as Jim fumbled around with his shoulder. Finally, Jim managed to wrap his shoulder with the bandage and make a sling for his arm.

"Jim, listen to me," Papa said. "There's a nut that's worked loose on the propeller shaft flange. You're going to have to go down into the engine room and fix it."

"Oh no, Charlie" Jim cried. "I can't go out there on deck. I can't go out there in this storm."

"Listen to me, you son of a bitch. If you don't fix it, the propeller shaft is going to come loose. If that happens we'll lose control of the boat, we'll fall off into the trough and the next big wave will roll us over."

"I can't Charlie. I just can't."

"If you don't do it we're going to die."

"I'd rather die up here on deck than trapped in that god-forsaken hole."

Papa paused and thought. "OK, Jim, go down in the fo'c's'le. On the shelf next to my bunk there's a pint of Scotch. You can get that for me can't you?"

Jim started down the companion way ladder like he was in a trance.

"While you're down there," Papa shouted after him, "there's an oar handle under my bunk. Bring that up too."

Jim stumbled down the companion way ladder and

found the whiskey and oar handle. Returning to the deck house, he handed Papa the whiskey. Papa up ended it and downed about half of the bottle, then gave the bottle back to Jim and grabbed the oar handle.

"I understand the whiskey, Charlie," Jim said. "But what do you want the oar handle for?"

"I'm going to use it to bash in your brains, you worthless son of a bitch, if you don't get your goddamn ass out of the deck house and down to the engine room and fix the flange."

Jim was dumbstruck. He knew that Papa meant it. He was more scared of Papa than he was of the storm or dying. He backed out of the deck house and onto the deck.

Jim somehow managed to work his way back to the engine room and put a new nut on the propeller shaft flange. In the meantime, Papa called the Coast Guard and declared an emergency.

"I need medical attention immediately and I can't leave my jack ass deck hand in charge of the boat," Papa said into the radio's handset.

"What's going on?" Jim asked as he came back into the deck house.

"I can't hold the boat through this storm," Papa told him. "I need to get to a hospital and you can't bring in the boat by yourself. I've called the Coast Guard to tow us in."

Within an hour, they heard the helicopter through the howling wind.

"Fishing vessel *Marine View*, this is US Coast Guard helicopter 2247, over."

"2247, *Marine View*."

"*Marine View*, we're going to lower a basket for the injured crewman. Put him in the basket and belt him in. We'll lift him off the boat and fly him to the cutter."

The helicopter dove down over the boat and dropped what looked like a bomb into the water. When the bomb hit the water it erupted into a column of red smoke. The chopper hovered over the boat and lowered a steel mesh basket about the size of a bath tub from a steel cable. With the howling wind, the chopper had a hell of a time trying to maintain its position over the boat. The basket swang in, smashed against the deck house, then flew out of reach.

"Jim, I need for you to go out on deck and grab the basket when it swings by," Papa said.

"Charlie, what am I going to do when they take you away? I can't keep this boat going."

"There's a hundred fifty-two foot cutter on its way," Papa told him. "They'll take you in tow back to Morro Bay. You keep this boat afloat until they get here. They're professionals; they'll know how to get her in. And Jim, one more thing, if you manage to sink my boat before they get here, I swear that I'll hunt you down and kill you if you survive."

Jim managed to grab the swinging basket and Papa climbed in. Jim couldn't hold the basket and fasten the safety belt. Papa couldn't fasten it with one hand so he just pushed his feet hard against the end of the basket and wedged himself in.

He didn't have time to think. The helicopter climbed and pulled away from the boat. It rose to about two-thousand feet before the crew started to reel in the basket. Papa dangled at the end of the steel cable in the raging storm. After what seemed like a lifetime, the basket came to rest against the metal beam that protruded from the top of the helicopter's door. Two grinning Coasties in helmets and life vests grabbed the basket and pulled it into the chopper.

"Welcome aboard, sir," a young Guardsman said. "Looks like you made it."

"That was one hell of a ride," Papa replied. "Tell me something. Before you lowered the basket, you dropped a smoke bomb. What was that for?"

"That was in case we dropped you, sir. It would give us

a location to go back and start looking for you."

"That bomb must have weighed two hundred pounds. What if you'd hit my boat? You'd have sunk her."

"Well, sir, then we would've been very sorry."

We were on summer vacation, so we were home that morning when the phone rang. Mama answered it. In a moment she went pale. Fire lit her dark eyes and she noticeably shook with anger.

"Yes, yes, we'll be there in the morning to pick him," she told the mysterious caller. Then she called work and told them she wouldn't be coming in.

"Get in the car. Now," she snapped at us. She was so angry that we obeyed her instantly.

There were four of us kids; my big sister, Quita, two years older than me and my little brothers Jon and Jim. They were four and five years younger and babies as far as I was concerned. I was seven years old

"We're going to Morro Bay to pick up your father."

It was a long drive to Morro Bay. We stopped at a restaurant for lunch. We got a motel room when we got there and ate at another restaurant for dinner. We never ate out and we never stayed in motels. Something was not right. Mama, who was every bit as frugal as Papa, was not the least concerned with money. Since we were all staying in the same room, that night I could hear Mama softly crying.

In the morning she got us up and dressed with a stern look on her face. We knew better than to cause any trouble.

"Now that your father has gone and hurt himself,' Mama told my older sister, she always talked to Quita like an adult. "I don't know how we'll get along. He went and spent all that money getting the boat ready, now he can't even take it out fishing." This was in the days before medical insurance and fishermen were independent businessmen anyway, they had no workman's compensation insurance. Not only was he not going to be producing any income for the family for months, but he was running up astronomical medical bills from his stay in the hospital.

Green lawns surrounded the modern looking hospital. Through the big glass doors we saw an admitting desk.

"Wallace?" the nurse behind the desk asked. "Charles Wallace, room 316. I'm sorry Mrs. Wallace, you are Mrs. Wallace aren't you?" I could tell that the nurse couldn't reconcile the way we looked with our Anglo name. "We don't allow children under thirteen above the first floor."

"Quita, you watch the boys while I go up," Mama said to my sister. "There's lots of grass and trees to play in."

"Can I go with you, Mama?" I asked. "I want to see Papa."

She assented and no one stopped me as we found the elevator. We rode to the third floor. We walked down long, gray corridors looking for Papa's room. The antiseptic smell of the hospital assailed my nostrils. The image I had in my mind of my father was of a fierce hero from Greek mythology, able to fight and win any struggle. I was stunned to see him helpless in a hospital bed.

He lay semi-conscious. A shaggy growth of red and gray beard covered his face, but he was pale beneath his heavy tan. Something was very wrong. I noticed the cast on his shoulder and arm. It seemed to encase his whole upper body. Cords attached to a frame above the bed suspended his left arm above his head.

When we came in he turned to us. It took a minute for him to recognize us, then he said "Vicki" weakly. He didn't even notice that I was there. She smiled through her tears.

"*Aye Dios mió*, Charles, what happened?"

"I got my arm . . . pulled out of its socket . . . by the engine."

"I knew that no good would come from that boat. I knew . . ." then her voice trailed off.

"But Mama," I said, "You never christened the boat. Papa told me that a boat that isn't properly christened is doomed"

"Shut up! Keep out of this."

I recoiled at the harshness of her response. I took a step back and let out an audible sob.

"Maybe we could still christen her." I said softly. "Maybe if we hauled her out and christened her all the bad luck would go away."

"Oh, *Mijo*, I'm sorry," she said as she put her arms around me. Tears filled her eyes. She turned back to Papa.

"How could you do this to us?" she snapped. "How am I supposed to support the family by myself?" Papa just looked up at her with his dull, blue eyes. Mama paced the room. "Mama warned me about this. She said you were never going to settle down."

Papa didn't respond. He just lay there in the bed, his eyes following her movements.

"You have to stop this. You have responsibilities now. You can't keep going off on these wild adventures."

Papa winced in pain as he tried to reach out for her hand.

"Oh, Charles," she said as she tenderly cupped his head in her hands. "We've got to get you home." She took a deep breath. "It'll be alright. We'll get you home where we can take care of you. We always manage to get by somehow."

She softly stroked his hair. She took his hand and tears ran down her cheeks.

We sat around the hospital room all day while the staff went through their routine of releasing a patient. While I was bored, Mama paced the room like a caged tigress. Late in the afternoon, the nurse came in to tell us that we could go. After she left there was a soft knock on the door.

The door opened gently and the large, soft figure of Jim

filled the space. Dressed in blue canvas deck shoes, the light colored blue dungarees, pleated in front, that we called "Balboa Blues," a fisherman's sweater and pea coat he looked every inch the mariner. He wore a Greek fisherman's cap on his head. Unruly red curls protruded from under the cap. You couldn't call him tanned. He was a mass of freckles. It was more like the freckles had grown and merged into one giant freckle that covered his face. Over his shoulder was his sea bag, in his other hand he held a leather bound book.

"Charlie, I just came to say goodbye."

Papa looked at him with dull eyes. He gave no sign of recognition.

"The boat's moored in the marina." Jim told him. "I sold the fish; the cannery will send you the check. Everything is put away, real ship-shape like."

Still no recognition from Papa.

"Charlie, I wanted to ask you to do something for me. Could you to write something about this adventure in my book? I'm going to write about this and when I tell my friends, I want to show them your comments to prove it really happened" With that, he handed Papa the beautiful leather bound book.

Silently, Papa turned the book over in his hand.

"Jack London's my hero." There was an awkward pause, then Jim continued, explaining himself to Mama rather than Papa. "All of my life I wanted to be Jack London when I grew up. When I was thirteen years old I discovered him and decided I wanted to be a writer. I wanted to roam the world having great adventures and write novels about them. I wanted to be rich and famous."

Papa took the book, opened the cover and stared at it for a long time. I could read the words embossed in gold on the cover: *The Sea Wolf* by Jack London.

Jack London's infamous Captain Wolf Larsen was a renegade schooner captain with a blood feud with his brother,

Captain Blood Larsen. They were both sworn to kill the other if ever they should meet again.

Papa closed the book and the fire returned to his eyes. He threw the book at Jim.

"You get out of here you worthless son of a bitch." I'd never heard him swear in front of Mama before.

Jim choked up. Tears came to his eyes. He sobbed audibly. He slowly stooped and picked up his precious volume.

"Before I met you," Jim stammered, "I thought that Wolf Larsen was the toughest son of a bitch that ever lived." There was a long pause.

"I was wrong."

Part 3

Chapter 15

Life on the Boat

The following summer, Papa took me fishing with him and we had our encounter with the *Munashima Maru*. After that, Papa quit fishing and we moved to Oregon, then the old itch for adventure got the better of him and we were again at sea, following the call of the running tide.

Our routine settled into breakfast, fishing, dinner, then quiet time. Papa was always up at the crack of dawn. I awoke to the smell of coffee perking and bacon frying. I pulled on my jeans or shorts and deck shoes and made my way up to the galley. The weather was uniformly beautiful. By the time the sun broke the horizon, it was usually seventy degrees.

After breakfast, I cleaned up the galley while Papa got the fishing lines ready to go into the water. Then for the rest of the day, we fished. Sometimes we got lucky and hit a school of fish. Then Papa pulled the fish and I steered to keep us in the school. Sometimes there were long periods of time between strikes and we only found one or two fish at a time. There were always interesting things happening in the water and we talked and talked to while away the time.

I loved it when a pod of dolphins came to play with us. I watched for hours as they paced the boat and took turns diving under the keel and in front of the bow. They never seemed to move their bodies; they just flowed along easily keeping pace with the boat. They were actually much faster than the boat and could take off and leave us whenever they wanted.

"When I die, I want to come back as a dolphin." Papa

said. "The old sailors believed that the dolphins were the spirits of sailors who died and were buried at sea."

That summer I saw sharks and swordfish basking on the surface. On the way into Santa Barbara Island one night we saw a whale shark, a strange animal. It was basking on the surface and was at least as long as our boat.

The whale shark is a gentle creature with no teeth. Like a baleen whale, it has baleen, or whale bone, in its mouth. It cruises along in the ocean sucking in water and plankton. Then it uses its tongue to push the water out of its mouth. The baleen acts like a strainer and keeps the plankton and small sea creatures from escaping. It then swallows its catch and starts all over again. We have a lot in common. Its whole life is dedicated to eating.

This shark was light brown on its back with white spots, much like a fawn. It had a high, humped back with a normal shark fin on it. Its tail was vertical, rather than horizontal like a whale's tail. On its underside, it was white. It sunned on the surface and paid not the least bit of attention to our boat. It was so large that it had no natural predators and felt very comfortable around us.

Occasionally we came across a sea turtle. These giant turtles were about five or six feet long and about four feet across. They were green and had barnacles and seaweed growing on their shells. They pretty much stayed away from us, but from time to time, when we dropped scraps overboard, they surfaced to eat them. Papa said that he would catch one for me and we could have turtle soup. I was horrified at the idea of eating one of these graceful creatures and begged him not to.

The sunsets were spectacular. The whole western horizon came alive with oranges and reds. It looked like the world was on fire. As the sun sank lower on the horizon, the sea lost its blue color and took on a darker tone. When the sun set, the sky was ablaze and the ocean turned first burgundy, then a dark black. As the sun dipped into the water, there was an instant, really only a second or two, when the color changed from orange to green. It flashed through several shades of bright green light, then was gone. Then the long slow swells undulated towards us in an almost hypnotic manner.

Evenings were the best time of the day. We pulled in the fishing lines, and if we were far off shore, we put out the flopper stoppers. The flopper stoppers were stabilizers that kept the rolling motion of the boat to a minimum. They were made out of galvanized steel and looked like little airplanes with a lead weight in the nose where the cockpit would be.

These stabilizers were attached to the outermost part of our jig poles on long lines. They were about two feet long and weighed about thirty or forty pounds with broad, delta-shaped wings like a jet fighter. When the boat rolled towards the side where the stabilizer was, the pressure on the line attaching it to the jig pole was released and the heavy weight in the nose caused the stabilizer to dive. When the boat rolled back the other way, the line pulled on the stabilizer and the wing offered resistance to the water and made the roll back slower. There was a stabilizer on each jig pole, so the rolling motion was dampened whenever a sea passed under us.

Off shore, at night we just shut down the engine and lay to. To keep the boat pointing into the wind we put out the sea anchor. A sea anchor is a large funnel shaped piece of canvas with floats on the top and weights on the bottom that is put in the ocean to create drag on the boat. Papa always used a war surplus parachute for a sea anchor. When the wind blew on the boat, the sea anchor held the bow into the wind so that it met the swells head on.

In the evening the wind died down and, with the flopper stoppers and the sea anchor, the boat took on a gentle motion riding over the seas.

After the fish had been iced down and the decks washed off, we cleaned up in a bucket of sea water, then started cooking dinner. Papa was the head chef, but I helped where ever I could. I peeled potatoes or chopped onions or other vegetables. I wanted to help and was eager to please Papa.

When dinner was ready, we took our plates and pots and spread them out on the fish hold hatch cover. Papa grabbed a beer and I grabbed a root beer and we sat on the hatch cover and feasted. Papa loved this freedom. It was the happiest I ever saw him in his life.

During dinner we discussed everything. He made plans for my brothers and me.

"You're going to go to college at the University of Oregon and get a degree," he told me. "Then you'll get a job and help pay for your brothers as they go to college. We'll help you, then you'll help them. You have to be careful to stay on course though. You can't let yourself get led astray by the first skirt that comes along."

There was never any doubt that we would get college degrees and have a better, easier life than Mama and Papa. Interestingly enough, these plans didn't include my sister. Quita was the brains in the family, she always got straight A's, but she was just a girl.

We planned many new adventures.

"When we sell the boat, we'll take a rafting trip down the Willamette River to Portland, then down the Columbia to the ocean. It'll be just like Huck Finn. We'll pull up on little islands in the rivers at night and camp and cook our meals over open fires." He was already off on the next great adventure.

Papa often talked about his book. He told me stories that were to become chapters in his book. We argued about how it should unfold. He promised me that when his book was published we would have so much money that he would buy me a little car. We discussed the best kind of car for a teenage driver.

Papa was very observant. He noticed that when teenagers got into car wrecks, there were usually a bunch of kids in the car. The kids got to playing and the driver was distracted, he reasoned, causing the wreck. Therefore, he decided that I should have a two-seat car. That way I couldn't have a bunch of kids in the car with me to distract me.

With this knowledge of his future plans, I used some of my fishing money to buy a couple of car magazines while we were on shore. I lay in my berth at night reading the magazines and dreaming about cars while Papa read another chapter of Gibbon. We started to discuss what kind of two-seat car I should have.

"The Triumph TR-3 is beautiful; I'd really love to drive one. And the Jaguar XKE; that's the best car in the whole world."

"Those are great cars PC. Austin-Healy makes a nice little roadster too, but my favorite has always been the MG TD" And so it went. We finally settled on the MG. It was a two-seat roadster built back in the early Fifties. It had big wire wheels, detached bullet shaped head lamps, the gas tank mounted on the trunk lid and a spare tire mounted on top of the gas tank. It had a convertible roof and the doors were cut way down so that your arm easily rode on the door while you were driving. It had all of the class and funkiness of a British sports car. Now all we had to do was sell his book.

Papa's book never got published and needless to say, I never got the little sports car.

After dinner I cleaned up the galley and we moved to the foredeck. Two huge coils of line that we used for anchor rode just forward of the deck house made big easy chairs. We rested our backs against the deck house, gazed at the stars and talked. He took a beer, a glass of wine or a glass of Scotch and I took bottle of root beer.

After the sun set, the sky darkened, the moon rose on

the eastern horizon and marched in its arch across the sky with Venus trailing close behind. The best time to watch the night sky was under a full moon. When it approached the western horizon it sent a long trail of light across the water. As the moon set, the light was a path from the far horizon, across the undulating waves right up to our boat. At times it was so mesmerizing that I thought I could get out and walk across it. Many nights we spent the whole night on the foredeck watching the moon and stars and occasionally grabbing a little nap.

The sky was clear and, far from shore, there were no city lights or pollution to mar our view. Papa knew all about the stars. He studied the stars to use them for navigation and could tell where we were by the position of the stars. He also knew all of the constellations and the stories behind them. He pointed them out to me, then told me the story about how they got their names. Mostly the names came from Greek mythology.

He showed me the Big Dipper and the Little Dipper, Orion's Belt and many more constellations, but he had a special spot in his heart for Cassiopeia's Chair.

"See that one? It's called Vicki's Chair."

"Vicki's Chair?"

"Yes, it used to be Cassiopeia's Chair, but I gave it to your Mother. Now it's Vicki's Chair."

"Look. what's that in the water?" I asked, seeing a soft, green glow that looked like neon under the water.

"It's phosphorescence. The ocean is alive with tiny organisms that we don't see. On a dark night, when something moves through the water and disturbs them, they give off light."

A large fish swam near the boat and we saw its trail in the water. We saw the long, lazy trail of blue sharks, the quick darting movements of barracuda. I loved watching the long trail made by the flying fish being pursued by larger fish which exploded into a starburst of glowing green as they broke the surface and went airborne.

"Can I put *Corky* in the water and row around to see the phosphorescence?" I asked.

"Sure, go ahead"

We untied the skiff from the cabin top and lowered her over the side. I fastened the painter (that's the line that is attached to the skiff's bow) to a cleat on the foredeck, being careful not to let it float back and get wrapped around the propeller. Grabbing the oars from the fo'c'sle, I lowered myself over the rail and into the skiff. As I rowed away from the *Marine View,* I suddenly became aware that I was all alone in a tiny boat, leagues from shore. If I lost sight of our boat, I was in real trouble.

Fortunately, it was a calm night and the lights of the *Marine View* were visible for miles. As I rowed around, leaving a glowing trail in my wake, I wondered if Mama had ever seen the phosphorescence. What would my friends think if they could see me now?

As I think back on all the time I spent with my father, the best hours of our time together were sitting in the coils of anchor line on the bow of the *Marine View.* Papa told his yarns and the boat climbed over one wave, then slid down the backside into the trough before climbing the next wave. Each time we slid to the bottom of the trough, a shower of warm sea water broke over the deck, cooling us down. It was a magical time for an eleven-year old boy.

Chapter 16

Papa's Book

The morning was warm and sunny. With our lines in the water, we both constantly scanned the tops of the jig poles to see if we had a hit.

"Fish on," I cried. I liked to be the first one to spot a strike.

"You called it, you pull it," Papa told me.

I dashed to the cockpit and grabbed the little leader line that attached to the fishing line. I pulled it in and grabbed the fishing line.

"It's a big one," I said as I strained to pull the line in, handover hand. There was the familiar rainbow streak in the water. When it got it close to the boat, Papa reached down and gaffed it.

"*Pescado*," was his familiar cry as he tossed the fish aboard. He winced as his left shoulder took the weight of the fish. He never fully recovered from his accident.

It was a slow day. We pulled a fish or two from time to time, but mostly we sat in the cockpit or on the hatch cover. I got impatient with the waiting, I wanted to be pulling fish non-stop. Papa was more accustomed to this leisurely pace. He was silent for the longest time, staring out to the horizon.

"I've been thinking about the book," Papa said after a while. When he was quiet for long periods of time, I knew he was working on his story.

"I've been thinking about Stu. He's such a great character he has to be in the book,"

"What will Mr. Stewart think about being in your book?"

"Oh, I can't call him Stu. I think his character should be a composite of several fishermen that I knew. I'm thinking I'll mix him in with a little Bob Poole and a little Ceece Kettle."

"Can you just make up people like that?"

"Sure, that's what books are all about. There were so many colorful characters in the old days that I have to work them all into the story somehow. Chips was the most interesting character I ever met. I have to find a way to get Chips in the book.

"Then there's Mac and Art. They were always getting into trouble. Did I ever tell you about the time that Mac and Art Hill came over to Gussie's for dinner?"

Aunt Gussie was Papa's oldest sister; she was sixteen when Papa was born. Gussie used to say that she thought their mother had Papa just for her. By the time Papa came around, their mother had eleven other children and the novelty of babies had worn off. For Gussie, Papa was a pet or a doll. She couldn't get enough of him. Whenever he got into trouble, Gussie was there to bail him out.

Gussie married a railroad man when Papa was still quite young and she followed him all over the country. By the time Papa moved to Southern California, Aunt Gussie's husband died and all of her children had grown up and moved away. With her brother, Charlie, and sister, Jewel, both living in Southern California, she decided to come west.

"Gussie sold her house in Texas and bought a big old house in Newport Beach, that she turned into a boarding house," Papa began. "This was during the war and her clientele was almost exclusively young Navy officers going through training at the nearby Navy bases.

"Before I got married, when I wasn't fishing, I stayed with Aunt Gussie in her boarding house and was her handyman.

I repaired anything that got broken and helped her fix up the place.

"Dinner was always an occasion. Aunt Gussie enjoyed the reputation as one of the finest cooks in Newport Beach and she laid it on for her young boarders. The boarders caught on to the game quickly.

"'Miz Carta,' they said, 'I recon that's one of the finest meals I've ever eaten,' or, 'I don't think I've ever eaten biscuits that light and fluffy.' Most of her boarders were Southerners and her Southern cooking reminded them of home.

"They learned that the more they complemented her cooking, the more she went all out on the next meal.

"Most of her boarders were college men. They were officers in the Navy and graduated from college before enlisting. They were educated, well spoken and without exception, polite. I loved to put on this tough old fisherman act and play with them." With his radical politics, near photographic memory and disdain for the military, I could picture him stirring up trouble.

"The Navy base in Long Beach ran its classes for young officers on two week cycles. Every two weeks, Gussie had a fresh batch of boarders and I had a fresh batch of victims.

"'You know,' I'd tell them at dinner, 'it's a good thing your classes don't run longer than two weeks. I have enough stories to last exactly two weeks, after that, I have to start repeating myself.'

"To make matters worse, I often invited friends to dinner. They all wanted to eat Gussie's cooking and with a boarding house, there was always enough for one or two more at the table. One night I invited Art Hill and Mac over. To spice things up and get the evening started, I told a story about a young Navy lieutenant who was testing fishermen on navigation.

"'The government decided that all us fishermen should be tested and licensed,' I told the boarders. 'I guess they thought that the Navy knew a lot more about the sea than we did.'

"At this point, Mac took his cue and joined in the fun.

"'I were there that day. This here young pup axed me 'How would you chart a course from Newport jetty to Avalon?'

"'I told him, 'I don't know nothin' about them charts. I ain't got none on my boat.''

"'What?' says he, 'what good is your compass without charts?''

"'I ain't got no compass neither,' I tells him.

"'Well, then how in the blazes do you know what direction to steer?' he says.

"'That's easy for me,' says I."

"The young officers were hanging on Mac's every word.

"'Ya see, I was borned and raised in the Ozark Mountains. Me ol' pappy taught me how ta tell directions by the side o' the tree that the moss grows on. All I have to do is look at me mast for the moss and I can tell what direction I'm goin'.'

"'So this young pup says 'You fishermen are the damnedest lot I ever seen. You drift around on the open ocean, out of the sight of land for weeks at a time without a clue where you are, but just as soon as you fills your fish holds, you makes a bee-line to the nearest cannery."

"'I was at that same exam,' Art chimes in. 'Now, Mr. Hill,' says that young feller, 'If you saw a boat coming head on, what would you do?'

"'I'd get the Hell out a his way,' I says.

"'No, no,' says the lieutenant, 'I mean, what signal would you give?'

"'None, at all,' I tell him. 'I ain't got no horn on my boat.''

"'Mr. Hill, you are supposed to give one blast on your horn or whistle,' says the young pup.

"'No, not me,' I says, 'I ain't going to do none of that whistle stuff. You see, I had to leave San Pedro on account of hootin' on my whistle. When I first started fishin' back in '30

I got me a cute little cabin cruiser and one of them books on the rules of the road. I memorized all that stuff about whistles. Every fishin' boat that I passed I gave two hoots on the whistle. The boys didn't take too kindly to it. They started callin' me "Hoot Hoot Hill." I had to leave Pedro 'cuz I couldn't take their ribbin' no more. I can't afford to have the boys down here find out about it. You ain't going to get me to blow on no whistle."

"After everybody left, while Gussie and I were cleaning up the kitchen, Gussie stopped in mid-dish with a deep look on her face.

"'You know, Charles, that Art Hill, he's a real character,' she said

"So I said, 'Why yes, Gussie, I suppose he is.'

"We washed dishes in silence for a few minutes, then Gussie started in again.

"'And your friend Howard Magruder, he's quite a character too.'

"'Yes, Mac's a genuine character all right.'

"Once again, we returned to the dishes. After a few more plates, Gussie stopped again with that strange look on her face.

"'And Martin Stewart, and Ceece Kittle, and Bob Poole, they're all characters. Why, Charles, all of your friends are characters.'

"'Gussie,' I said, 'I guess that's true. Fisherman tend to be colorful characters.'

"We went back to a comfortable silence as we finished up in the kitchen. Then Gussie had a horrified look on her face.

"'Charles, you too. You're a character too,' she gasped."

"Aunt Gussie is right," I said. "All of your friends are a little weird"

"That's what makes them such good characters for my book. They're interesting."

"Take Bill Bacchus," Papa said. "I've got to find a place

for him in my book."

"Bill Bacchus? I don't remember you talking about him."

"That's because he was a worthless so and so. Before I bought the *Cuantos,* I shipped out as a sea cook on a purse seiner called the *Albatross.*

"The *Albatross* was a fine ship and had a good crew, but her skipper, Bacchus, was a bully, a brute of a man. Bacchus had a voice that was more of a growl than a voice. It was low and threatening. His voice sounded more like the fog horn on the Golden Gate Bridge than the fog horn on the Golden Gate Bridge."

Papa never did well with authority and his experience on the *Albatross* did nothing to endear him to it.

"Bacchus made the lives of every man on board miserable," Papa continued. "He never told anyone fully what he wanted, then he berated them for not doing it right. He was quick to criticize and had no qualms about chewing a man out in front of the whole crew. He was a big man and didn't hesitate to use his size to intimidate people. On more than one occasion, when a crewman displeased him, he hit them in the jaw and knocked them off of their feet.

"According to maritime law, the crewman couldn't strike back and Bacchus knew it. To attack a superior officer on any vessel was considered an act of mutiny punishable by a sentence up to death. No one in their right mind would strike a superior officer, but Bacchus had no problem meting out punishment.

"We were making a set on a school of fish."

A purse seiner has a huge net on a steel drum on the aft deck of the boat. These are big boats. They have a skiff, usually made out of aluminum, roughly triangular in shape that is about twenty feet long and ten feet wide. When the crew sights a school of fish, one end of the net is tied to the skiff. The skiff then encircles the school with the net. The end of the net is taken back on board the boat and a line in the bottom of the net is pulled in closing the net, like a purse. Hence the name, purse seine. (Seine is French for net.)

"On this particular day, a greenhorn on his first trip had the responsibility of accepting the line from the skiff. He took the line and passed it up to the big wench, but failed to close the block the line ran over. When the man next to him stooped to close the block he was hit in the back of the head with a blow from the handle of a gaff hook.

"Bacchus happened to be there watching. 'Leave it be, Goddamn it.' He growled. 'That young son of a bitch needs to learn to close that block hisself. If you do it for him, he'll never learn. Then one day, you won't be standing there, he won't close the block and he'll pull the ass end off a my goddamn boat.'

"The crewman had to be carried to the galley for medical attention. The sea cook doubles as the ship's doctor on fishing boats, so I had to dress the wound and get the seaman in bed.

"My first voyage on the *Albatross* was my last. There is an old rule, 'you don't mess with the people who cook your food.' Apparently Bacchus paid attention to the rule. He more or less left me alone except for a few mumbled grunts and growls. That is, until the *Albatross* was heading back into San Diego.

"I was on wheel watch and was bringing the big seiner into the dock. Apparently, I did something Bacchus didn't like. He growled at me and called me some names, then violently shoved me aside and took the wheel himself. I grabbed Bacchus by the shoulder and spun him around. Then I landed a haymaker that crumpled him to the deck.

"I took the wheel back and brought the *Albatross* into the dock. By this time, Bacchus was recovered.

"'Goddamn you, Wallace,' he says, 'I'll see you in prison for this.'

"'No man grabs the wheel out of my hand without

telling me what he's doing first,' I told him.

"For obvious reasons, I didn't sleep on the *Albatross* that night. Usually, when the boats come in, the crew spends the night on them, then unloads the cargo in the morning and is paid off. Bacchus wouldn't have me on his boat for one more night and I couldn't wait to get free of Bacchus.

"I went ashore with no money and no place to stay. I wandered into the Travelers' Aid Society office and told them about my situation. The lady at the Travelers' Aid Society was very sympathetic and gave me five dollars to buy dinner and a room for the night.

"I was dressed in my Balboa Blues, canvas deck shoes, red and white stripped T-shirt, pea coat and watch cap. I looked every bit the old salt. I hadn't shaved for days. I was standing on the wharf contemplating what to do next when I felt an arm wrap around my shoulder.

"'*He lolled on a bollard, a sun burned son of the sea,*

With earrings of brass and a jumper of dungaree,' says a burly voice.

"I turned to see a Marine Corps gunny sergeant in dress blues.

"'*N' many a queer lash up I have seen,*' says he." I replied, '*But the toughest hooray o' the racket,*' he says, '*I'll be sworn,*

'N' the roughest traverse I worked since the day I was born,

Was a packet o' Sailors Delight as I scoffed in the seas o' the Horn.*"

(From Salt Water Poems and Ballads by John Masefield, The Macmillan Company, 1912)

"He was a kindred soul; a Marine who knew Masefield. The Marine repeated the next stanza of "Sing a Song of Shipwreck," then I said the next. We worked our way all the way through the poem.

"We introduced ourselves and headed for the nearest tavern. Soon we were long lost friends. I spent my five dollars on beer that night and slept on a bench down by the waterfront. I never shipped out on another man's boat again."

"Now I remember. You told me a story about Mr. Stewart and Bacchus."

"That's right. That's where I first met Martin Stewart. His boys Danny and Junior were getting old enough to go fishing with him. He owned a miserable little double ender with a gasoline powered Ford Interceptor V8 engine that never ran. His boat was so old she was full of rot and leaked up a storm.

"Stu shipped out on the *Albatross* that summer to make enough money to put a down payment on a Kettenburg Thirty-Eight. He was going to take Faith and the boys fishing with him.

"He was a good man, but Bacchus made his life miserable. Of course Stu got back at him. He never let a grudge go unanswered.

"A couple of years after his summer fishing with Bacchus, when Stu had the *Danny Boy,* Bacchus had been fired from his job as skipper of the *Albatross.* He couldn't find another job on the West Coast, so he bought a decrepit old cabin cruiser named the *Tondelaya* and converted it into a fishing boat.

"We were rafted up along side of the *Danny Boy* in the old *Cuantos* inside of San Martin Island. Hap and Bob Poole came over and we had quite a party going. Then the *Tondelaya* pulls into the bay.

"'It's that God damned Baccus,' Stu says.

"'Now Martin, you watch your tongue around the young ones,' says Faith.

"'Well, he's not welcome on my boat.'

"Sure enough, Baccus put his skiff in the water and he and his crew rowed over to the *Danny Boy.* He climbed aboard and acted like Stu was his long lost friend.

"'Hey, Stu, how you doin' ol' shipmate?" he croaks. Stu ignores him.

"By this time, we were breaking out the beer. Faith

hands a bottle to Moose and the little guy that were Bacchus' crew.

"'You got one a dem brews for me?" Bacchus asks.

"Faith reaches down into the ice bucket and grabs another bottle.

"'No beer for Bacchus,' Stu yelled. The party stopped. Everyone went silent.

"'What's the matter, ol' buddy?' Bacchus asked.

"'You made my life a living hell on the old *Albatross*, I'll be damned if I'll welcome you on my boat with a cold beer,' Stu says.

"Bacchus just melted. He slunk back to his skiff and rowed back to the *Tondelaya* without another word. After that, he never tried to join in on anyone's party again."

"It was a whole different world then," Papa told me. "It wasn't just the fishermen, it was the times. They're gone forever now. I really want to give my readers a sense of what it was like back then. Take the *Gray Ghost*, every fisherman on the Mexican coast feared the *Gray Ghost*."

"The *Gray Ghost*? I've never heard you talk about the *Gray Ghost* before."

Papa spent the afternoon filling me in on the legend.

During the war, the U.S. government gave Mexico a bunch of our old, outdated patrol boats to help patrol for German and Japanese subs. They were worn out when the Mexican Navy got them and the Mexicans were not too good at maintaining them. By the time the war was over, there could not have been more than ten of them still in service.

The *Grey Ghost* was the *Durango*, a ninety foot patrol boat with a forty millimeter Bofors gun on her foredeck. She was painted a light gray with white numbers on her bow and dark gray trim. The *Durango* was the only boat that the Mexican Navy had to patrol the entire Baja coastline, nearly two thousand miles.

After the war, Mexico decided that they wanted to build their own fishing industry. They passed a law declaring a twelve mile limit and forbid foreign boats from fishing in Mexican waters. If they caught an American boat in Mexican waters, they impounded it and fined the captain. The fine was usually more than the boat was worth.

"Elliot Burr got caught," Papa told me.

I had known Mr. Burr all of my life.

"It was during a big fiesta week and the local jail was full so they just threw him in the state penitentiary to hold him until they could arraign him. Then they forgot that he was there."

"The Mexican prison system is nothing like the US prisons," he went on. "They just throw you in and let you fend for yourself. The inmates run the prison.

"Elliot was a biker. When they took him in he grabbed his leather jacket and engineer's boots because he was afraid that if he left them on his boat, he'd never see them again. His first day there the inmates took him before a kangaroo court and tried him for his crime."

"I thought you said they just threw him in prison to hold him. He hadn't really committed any crime had he?" I asked. I couldn't imagine Mr. Burr as a criminal.

"It really didn't matter," Papa said. "There was a lifer, a convicted murderer, who ran the prison; they called him the 'governor.' The warden told the 'governor' what he wanted and the 'governor' and his gang of toughs made it happen. They all had homemade knives and the 'governor' even had a gun."

"On his first day, the toughs grabbed Elliot and took him before the 'governor.'

"'You will now be tried for your crimes," the 'governor' says.

"'What crime have I committed?' Elliot asked.

"'It doesn't matter, you will be found guilty,' the

'governor' replied.

    "'What happens if I'm found guilty?'

    "'Oh, you will be,' says the 'governor. 'We will fine you all of your fine gringo clothes.'

    "So they held the trial and found him guilty."

    "Of what?" I asked.

    "It didn't matter. They just wanted his leather jacket," Papa told me.

    They took his jacket, boots, jeans and shirt. Then they took him over to a clothes line and let him find some white wrap around pants like the peasants wear to cover himself.

    One night a group of thugs tried to kill the 'governor' and take over the prison. There was a full scale riot. The thugs were armed with knives and clubs. One of them only had an open safety pin. When the fight got going, the warden called in the Army. The Mexican troops went in with their guns blazing, not bothering to ask any questions. They put down the riot like no one in the U.S. ever saw. After all, who cared if a bunch of convicted criminals got killed?

    "What happened to Mr. Burr?" I asked.

    "He was in the prison for over a year while his wife, Nicki, and his lawyer tried to get him and his boat released. She had to sell their house to raise the money to get him out. To add insult to injury, when he was released, he had to pay for his room and board for the year he was a guest of the state."

    Getting caught by the *Gray Ghost* was no laughing matter. You could get a permit from the Mexican consulate in San Diego to use the Mexican harbors and anchorages, but it was not cheap. Papa always made sure he had a permit because he was not going to get into the same situation that Elliot got in.

    Even with a permit you did not want to get caught with fish in your hold. You couldn't prove that you caught them outside of the twelve mile limit. The Mexican Navy just might decide that you caught them inshore and take you in.

Papa's best friend Hap got stopped by the *Gray Ghost*. He had been offshore for a couple of weeks and the weather was kicking up, so he decided to run for cover. Every day during the Silent Hour whoever was hosting it asked if anyone had seen the *Gray Ghost*. You didn't want to take a chance getting too close inshore if she was around. The last report anyone had of her was up by *Ensenada*, so Hap thought he was safe. He had just come inside of San Quentin when there was the *Gray Ghost* as big as life.

Hap had his papers in order and kept a log to show how many fish he caught and where he caught them, but he had a gun on board. The Mexicans did not take kindly to carrying firearms. Not only was he carrying a gun, it was a BAR.

A BAR is a Browning Automatic Rifle, a light machine gun used by American forces during the war. Hap brought it back with him from the South Pacific where he won it from a Marine Corps sergeant in a poker game. He carried it with him to shoot sharks and seals and, fishing alone, it always made him feel more secure to have a firearm on board

The *Ghost* pulled alongside of the *Happy Days* so fast that Hap didn't have time to dump the gun overboard. The Mexicans dropped their boat in the water and came on over.

"'Permission to board, *Capitán*?" the Mexican captain said.

Hap couldn't say no, so the captain came aboard with three barefooted sailors that looked more like pirates than navy men. They wore short white peasant pants and sleeveless T-shirts, but they were packing Colt .45s on their belts and carrying M-1's. Hap was not about to make any trouble. When the boarding party came aboard, not one of them came up to Hap's chin. They were like miniature pirates.

The captain looked over Hap's papers and his men searched the boat. Hap kept the BAR under his bunk in the fo'c'sle wrapped in watertight oil cloth. He hoped they wouldn't find it.

One of the sailors comes on deck with the package in his arms. He said something to the captain in Spanish and Hap knew that he was in trouble.

"*Capitán*," the captain said, "this is a most serious matter. You know that you are not allowed to bring any firearms into Mexican waters."

"Captain Gomez," Hap replied, "I been carrying that old thing around since Pearl Harbor. I got so used to having it around. I plum forgot it was on board"

"You were at Pearl Harbor?"

"Yeah," Hap said, stretching the truth a little bit. "That ol' gun's been with me from Pearl to Okinawa."

The captain unwrapped the package and held the BAR in his hands. He handled it like an expert. The first thing he did was to check to see if there was a shell in the chamber, then he removed the magazine and sighted down the barrel.

"This is a truly fine piece, *Capitán*," he said. "It would be a shame if something happened to it. You know, there is a two year prison term for bringing automatic weapons into Mexico?" Hap just stared at him. He was caught red-handed and didn't know what to say.

"I too fought the Japanese," the captain said. "I have covered thousands of miles in the *Durango* hunting for their submarines. I would hate to have a valiant comrade in arms get into any trouble." Then he juggled the gun in his hands and it flew loose, over the rail. Hap's heart sank when it hit the water.

"A shame, *Capitán*. It seems in my clumsiness, I have just lost the evidence. We will go now. Good luck to you, Capitán."

"Mama and I had a run in with the *Gray Ghost* too," Papa said.

"Really, where'd you meet him?"

"We were down the coast, off of *Abreojos* on the *Aventura*. We were having some problems with the Jimmy overheating and I was fiddling with the heat exchanger.

"We were too far offshore to run in to do the work, so we just lay to and I climbed down into the glory hole to see if I could get it going again.

"Vicki was in the deck house, then I guess she went down to the fo'c'sle. Anyway, neither of us was on deck.

"I was working on the engine, up to my elbows in motor oil, when all of a sudden there was a different motion to the boat. We had a gentle swell running, but suddenly, it was flat calm. I cleaned my hands off and climbed up the ladder to poke my head above the hatch combing and there she was, the *Gray Ghost*."

"What'd they do to you?" I asked.

"Nothing. Mama gets on deck before I do. She's wearing shorts and a blouse tied up around her mid-riff and a bright red bandana tying down her hair. She starts shouting over to the *Gray Ghost* in Spanish.

"'Good afternoon,' she tells them. 'What are you doing here?'

"'Well, *señora*,' says the captain, 'we saw you lying to and thought we better see if you have problems. We thought that this was an American boat.'

"'This is my husband's boat,' she tells him. Then she invites them over for coffee.

"The captain and his mate came aboard and Vicki made a pot of coffee and brought out a pineapple upside down cake that she'd baked. We sat around in the galley drinking coffee and she talked with them a mile a minute in Spanish. I asked her later what they were talking about and she says she told them about her father and mother and how they came to America during the Mexican Revolution. When they were ready to leave she gives them some cans of creamed style corn and peaches.

They never even asked to see our papers."

Mama was like that. She could charm the skin off of a snake.

"So that was it? That was all that happened?" I asked. I expected some great tale of narrow escapes and daring-do.

"Well, I couldn't get the engine running right and decided to change the heat exchanger. I had a spare on board, so we ran for the coast and anchored in *Balenas* Bay. The next day, while I was working on the engine the *Ghost* comes along side again. This time they brought Vicki some huge lobsters, then took off on their business. From then on, I knew that we didn't have anything to fear from them."

"Hap wasn't finished with the *Ghost*. He ran into him again a few years later in Forty-nine. The tuna industry had crashed and we were all scraping to make a living. Like most of the boys, he couldn't afford to buy the permit to go into Mexican waters. He made sure he stayed outside of the twelve mile limit. He didn't want to have another run-in with the *Gray Ghost*.

"He was outside of *Cedros* Island and the weather started getting mighty strange. All of a sudden, the wind just stopped. The seas flattened out and the ocean was like a mill pond. He'd never seen anything like it.

"Then, in the afternoon, the seas began to build. They were getting four, six, eight foot swells without a breath of air. Hap checked the barometer and it was falling like he'd never seen before. He knew they were in for a blow.

"The San Diego Coast Guard station started broadcasting storm warnings. It seems that a *chubasco* was whipping up out of the South Pacific."

"What's a *chubasco*?" I asked.

"It's what the Mexicans call a Pacific hurricane. It came ashore at *Mazatlán*. There were hundreds of American boats in the area. They were in big trouble.

"The next morning, they're all running for cover. It was a matter of survival. They didn't care where the *Gray Ghost* was, they had to find a hurricane hole to get in out of the storm. All morning long the chatter on the radio was 'Where is the *Gray Ghost?*' or 'Have you seen the *Gray Ghost?*' During the Silent Hour there was a big debate on whether it was safe to run for cover or not. Then there comes this loud broadcast:

"'Senores of the American fishing fleet, this is *Teniente-Capitán Don Sebastian Luis Gomez Gonzales de Salamanca y Perdido*, better known to you as the *Gray Ghost*. I would like to extend the hospitality of the Mexican government to you all due to the inclement conditions. I give you my word of honor that no American boat seeking shelter in a Mexican port will be stopped or searched.'

"He didn't have to tell them twice. Most of them were already high tailing it for cover. Then Hap ran into a little bit of bad luck. His old Cat diesel broke down.

"He put out a call to the Coast Guard in San Diego, but they were so far away he was going to have to wait at least a day for them to come give him a tow. In the building weather, with a full hurricane on its way, Hap was scared. Then, just before dark, he saw a gray shape coming out of the wall of black weather coming at him. Be damned if it wasn't the *Gray Ghost*. He puts a line on the *Happy Days* and tows them into the lee of *Cedros* Island. Hap invited the captain aboard for a glass of Canadian Club, but he just drops them and says he has to get back out to his patrol area in case any other boats are in trouble."

The afternoon dragged on. We hadn't had a strike since Papa started taking. We both scanned the horizon, looking for the tell-tale sign of sea birds. When we saw nothing, we went back to talking about what should go in his book, but he never seemed to listen to my opinion. No matter what I said, he went ahead and did what he wanted anyway. I think he was just looking for an audience to sound off to.

"Fish on" I screamed. Finally, we had a bite. Papa jumped to the cockpit and pulled it in.

"Junk," Papa said with disdain as he shook the small shark off of the hook.

Throughout the summer, Papa discussed his book with me. I learned of his plans for Barney, the crusty old fisherman, Elizabeth, his twenty-something daughter, and all of the friends and acquaintances who populated his make believe world.

Chapter 17

Fishing

The sea birds were our friends. There were, of course, the sea gulls, but they tended to stick close to shore. I loved watching them soar. I also discovered *frigatas*, or frigate birds as the Americans called them. The frigate had an enormous wingspan and soared at heights above the ocean.

With long tapered wings and a two-pronged tail that was at least as long as its body, the *frigatas* soared elegantly above us. I thought that the *frigata* had total freedom. It could go anywhere it wanted.

I loved the albatross. These were big black birds with a huge wingspan. They followed the boat for days on end, hardly moving a muscle, waiting for us to throw some galley scraps overboard. The old sailors believed that the albatross was a harbinger of bad luck.

Then there were the pelicans. Papa taught me a rhyme about the pelicans.

> A queer old bird is the Pelican,
> His bill holds more than his belly can,
> He can hold in his beak,
> Enough food for a week,
> But I'm damned if I see how the hell he can!

The pelican, the Mexicans called them *pelícanos* (pronounced pel-**ee**-cahn-ohs with the accent on the "ee"), has a fleshy pouch under its long beak. It flies along the surface of the water looking for fish. When it spies a fish, it drops down and scoops it up in its bill. The water that comes in with the fish fills the pouch and the pelican has a large distended sack hanging from his bill. He uses his tongue to squeeze the water out and swallows the fish.

Papa told me about his experience with pelicans when he and his friend Stu on the *Danny Boy* were fishing off the coast of Mexico. They both had live bait tanks on their boats.

Live bait fishing was an art in itself. A large plywood tank on the afterdeck, with pumps to circulate the water, held the bait fish. The boat went in close to shore to find a school of small fish like smelt or anchovies. When they found the small fish, they dropped the skiff in the water and encircled the school with a net. The net had weights on the bottom to hold it down and floats on the top to keep it from sinking. Then they put the net on the winch and hauled it in close to the boat. When the bait was close to the boat, they used nets with long handles to dip the fish out of the water and throw them into the bait tank.

They didn't use jigs and lines off of their jig poles like the trollers. When they spotted a school of albacore, they dipped their nets into the bait tank and dumped a few scoops in the water. The albacore came to eat the bait fish and schooled around the boat. The fishermen then lowered jigs on short, stout poles into the water and jigged with an up and down motion. The tuna took the jig and the fisherman flipped it up on deck. When they were in a big school of fish this was a much faster, more economical method of catching albacore than trolling.

If the fishing was slow, the fishermen used large hooks onto which they threaded the small fish. The small fish took off like wounded fish when they were dropped in the water and the albacore took them.

It seemed to me like a whole lot of trouble to go through to catch the same fish that we were catching with a rubber squid or chicken feathers.

"Mama spotted a school of bait fish close into shore," Papa told me. "I took the *Aventura* in to get them. We dropped the skiff over the side and circled the school. By the time I was back on board and ready to start scooping the fish, the float line was filled with pelicans. Each of the damned birds landed on the net and scooped up a mouth full of bait fish. Their bills were so heavy that they couldn't lift their heads to swallow the fish. I had to take the boat hook and go around the net in the skiff and reach out and lift each of their heads so that they could swallow. As they swallowed the fish, they flew away and left me with the leftovers."

The birds lead us to fish. If there was a school of fish nearby, the birds formed large, swirling flocks in the sky. When they started diving on the water, we knew that they found small fish.

The key to finding a school of albacore was to watch the surface of the water for a "meatball." When the tuna found a school of smaller fish to feed upon, they attacked them from the bottom. The smaller fish rushed to the surface to escape their predators. They leapt out of the water in the hope of getting away. From the surface, it looked as if the water was boiling. As we grew closer to the "meatball" we saw it was composed of small fish, but from a distance, it was just a boiling motion on the water. A "meatball" always meant a school of hungry albacore. As Papa taught me to watch for "meatballs" he illustrated his lesson with a story.

His fishing partner Stu on the *Danny Boy* was trolling for tuna when his wife Faith spotted a "meatball" in the water. It was one of the biggest, most tightly packed balls of bait fish that Stu had ever seen. Stu put the *Danny Boy* in a tight circle around the "meatball" and immediately started pulling albacore. He and his sons pulled fish as fast as they could, pulling the lines in hand over hand. Within a few minutes Stu looked up to see that another boat joined the party, it was Ole on the *Norse Wind.* Soon another, then another boat joined the merry-go-round in ever bigger circles around the "meatball."

Fishing was good and none of the fishermen paid any attention to the big live bait boat that joined the fracas. The bait boat had a different goal though. They pulled up alongside of the "meatball" and started scooping up the anchovies into their bait tank. Stu saw what was going on and started yelling.

"Get the hell away from our meatball, you stupid bastards."

The bait fishermen just laughed and kept brailing. Soon other boats started protesting, but before the disagreement could escalate further, a huge blue shape surfaced in the middle of all the boats and opened its gigantic maw. A blue whale gobbled up the entire "meatball" in one bite and disappeared under the surface. With the bait fish gone, the albacore soon dissipated and there was nothing left for the fisherman to fight over.

Our days consisted of trolling the boat back and forth across the empty ocean. Papa dropped a deck bucket over the side frequently and pulled it up full of sea water. He put a thermometer in it to check the temperature.

"Sixty five degrees, too cold," he said. If it wasn't at least sixty-eight degrees, we headed elsewhere.

The Albacore are a warm water fish that won't swim into cooler water. The Humboldt current is coming up from the tropics at this point and is a minimum of sixty-eight degrees. If the water wasn't that warm, then we had wandered out of the current.

We could also tell if we were in the current by the color of the water. In our part of the world, the water is a deep green. As we headed off-shore suddenly we found blue water. There is a sharp dividing line between the green and the blue. It doesn't fade from one to another, it just instantly changes color. When we entered the blue water, we knew we had the Humboldt Current.

We dragged our fishing lines behind us all day. Papa rigged a ninth line from the top of the mast that he called the "whiskey line." Any fish pulled in on the whiskey line were used to pay for buying whiskey for the crew. The minors in the crew had to settle for root beer.

I was a full-fledged crew member that summer. Although Papa didn't pay me on shares, he did pay me ten cents for each fish we caught. I went back to school that fall with my pockets full of money.

"Fish on," Papa shouted as the bungee cord on the outboard starboard line went taunt. He dropped into the cockpit and grabbed the line with his bare hands and pulled it in, hand over hand. As the fish approached the boat, it was beautiful.

"I hate killing anything so beautiful," I said.

"That's how we make a living," Papa replied. "Everything in the world is part of the food chain. The big fish eat the little fish. We are just the biggest fish."

"It's a big one," Papa said as he pulled the fish up to the boat. Now he needed to get it aboard. It was at least a forty pounder.

To get the fish aboard Papa had a long gaff hook. This was a steel hook about four inches across with a sharp point on the end of a wooden handle about three feet long. He hooked the fish in its gills and waited for the boat to roll. As the stern of the boat lifted, he gave a mighty jerk. The momentum of the lifting boat, along with his muscle power pulled the fish from the water and over his shoulder to the deck behind him.

When Papa got a smaller fish on the line he called me back from the deck house.

"It's about time you learned how to pull fish," he said.

I took the line and pulled it in, hand over hand. The line was about one hundred feet long so I had a long pull. As the fish came close to the boat, the water exploded in color. There was a trail of gold in the water that looked like a neon light. This was the most beautiful fish I had ever seen.

I pulled the fish up and gaffed it. I waited for the stern to rise, then quickly flipped it aboard. It was not a tuna.

It was about four feet long with a flat, slender body. It had a square shaped head. Out of the water it looked gray and yellow. It must have weighed about ten or fifteen pounds.

"Hey, hey, you caught a *dorado*," Papa said. "They're good eating. We'll have *dorado* steaks tonight."

I had been in love with the sea since before I could remember. In school I read every book about fish, whales, sharks and boats that I could get my hands on.

"Papa," I corrected, "This is a male dolphin."

"The Mexicans call them *dorados* because they look like they're gilded with gold in the water. The Hawaiians call them *mahi mahi*. They're a fresh market fish and you get good money for them in San Diego."

That night we dined like kings. I never remember a fish tasting so good. Papa breaded it with corn meal and fried it in his cast iron skillet in bacon grease. It was firm and sweet with no fishy taste. I was learning to like seafood.

"*Pescado*," he cried out as the fish came aboard, a throwback to his days of fishing with Mama. He unhooked the jig from the fish's mouth and left the fish to flop around on the deck as he dropped the jig back into the water and grabbed the next line to pull in the next fish. It was a small school and Papa pulled the fish in, one after the other in a leisurely fashion.

Afternoon faded into evening. We always fished the morning and evening bites. The fish fed first thing in the morning and just at sunset.

"Goddamn it." Papa pulled in a line with the head of a fish on it.

"What happened, where's the rest of the fish?"

"Either a shark or a sea lion got it."

As Papa pulled in the next line, I saw a dark shape in the *Marine View's* wake.

"Papa, look. . ."

"Sea lion. I'll get the thieving bastard" Papa dropped the line and ran forward to the deck house. He emerged a minute later with an ancient doubled barreled shotgun in his hands. The stock was so old and worn that the wood looked black. Intricately tooled hammers were outside the end of each barrel.

"Take the line, start pulling it in slowly." Papa commanded as he broke the gun down and inserted a shell full of double aught buckshot into each barrel. I was terrified.

"Don't hurt the seal."

"It's not a seal. It's a Goddamn sea lion. If we don't kill him, he'll eat most of our school of fish and chase off the rest. We'll have nothing to show for our day."

"Can't you just scare him off?"

"Pull in that line."

I slowly pulled the line with the fish on it to the boat. The sea lion broke the surface in our wake. He blew out, took a deep breath and dived after the fish I was hauling in.

"Papa, don't hurt him. He looks like a puppy."

"Keep pulling."

The fish came closer and closer. Tears ran down my cheeks. As the rainbow flash of color got within a hands reach of the boat, the sea lion struck. He came from out of the turbulence in our wake, grabbed the fish and arched his head above the water.

I was shocked by the loud explosion. The muzzle flash from the shot gun reached almost all the way to the water in the fading light. The sea lions' head disintegrated in a bloody mess as two loads of buckshot destroyed his beautiful body. The water turned pink as the remains of the magnificent animal slipped slowly below the surface. I was stunned. I stood holding the fishing line with the albacore's head in my hand, crying.

Without another word, Papa returned the shotgun to the fo'c'sle and resumed pulling fish. I wandered forward to the cabin, took the helm and kept the boat in the school of fish. My eyes wouldn't dry; I couldn't see where we were going. I hated my father for what he had done.

"C'mon, PC. Help me put the fish away," Papa said as the fish stopped biting. For the first time in my life I didn't want to help him. I felt that those fish were somehow tainted with the blood of the sea lion. Dragging my feet, I reluctantly joined him as we dropped the catch on our deck into the fish hold. When all the fish were below, we went down into the fish hold and arranged the fish neatly in the bins and covered them with ice. We worked in silence. I worked sullenly at Papa's side. In my anger, I kept a meticulous tally of how many fish we caught each day so that I could claim my ten cents per fish when we sold them at the cannery. I felt that by taking my share of the money I would somehow hurt Papa, pay him back for this incident.

One of the major truths about commercial fishing is that you don't stop for anything while you are in a school of fish. When Papa was a sea cook on an tuna clipper, he said that he was the only man allowed to leave the fishing baskets when the fish were biting. Even then, he didn't get to leave the baskets until the end of the day when it was getting dark and the skipper knew that they would soon have to stop pulling fish. Then and only then, was he allowed to leave the baskets and prepare a hot meal for the tired fishermen to eat when the skipper finally released them.

I made one of my greatest blunders in a hot school of

fish. We hit a big school, but so did several other boats. There was a litter of trollers on the sea that day, all circling within this big school. I was at the helm and Papa was in the cockpit pulling fish. I saw another boat cutting through our circle. I learned my lesson from the *Munashima Maru*, I didn't want to hit him.

I straightened the boat out to let him pass.

"What in the hell are you doing?" Papa yelled at me.

"There's another boat cutting through our circle."

"Well ram the son of a bitch. He's trying to steal our fish."

The fishing industry was nothing if not competitive. If you found a hot school of fish you could count on the other boats trying to horn in on it. In this particular case, I broke off of our circle and lost our school. The boat that cut across us settled into a circle and began pulling our fish. Papa was furious.

"I'm going to run right through that bastard." he shouted and came forward to take the helm. He put the boat on a collision course with the other boat.

"Dive down to the fo'c'sle and bring up my shotgun," he commanded.

I ran for the fo'c'sle, fearful of what was about to happen. No matter how scared I was, Papa had trained me to follow his orders first and ask questions later. After the experience with the sea lion, I didn't know of what my father was capable.

We approached the other boat, Papa stepped out of the deck house, cupped his hands to his lips and shouted across the water.

"Standoff, you're in my school of fish."

The young man standing on the deck of the other boat replied, "Fuck off, old timer. Finders keepers."

Papa reached around the corner and produced the shotgun. "Standoff or I'll open fire, you goddamn poachers." The other boat ignored him and kept pulling fish.

Papa cocked both barrels on the old shot gun and aimed

for their bow. He pulled both triggers and there was a roar that split the afternoon and deafened me. By this point I was terrified. I watched enough television to know what a gunfight in the Old West was like.

We were far enough away from the other boat, Papa knew, that the buck shot in his shotgun would not have much effect. The shot hit the side of the boat with all of the effect of a handful of pebbles tossed against a wall.

"You crazy old son of a bitch." Shouted the young man on the other boat. The boat veered away and we resumed our circle in the school of fish.

"Papa," I cried, "Aren't they going to call the sheriff?"

He laughed. "There is no sheriff. We're on the high seas, in international waters. There's no one for him to call. Besides, if he did complain, he was trying to steal our fish. You don't go into court with dirty hands."

He handed me the shotgun and returned to the cockpit to pull fish. I stood, holding the hot-barreled gun, feeling the smoothness of the wooden handle, examining the scroll work on the hammers and barrel. The acrid smell of cordite assaulted my nose. My knees shook, my breath came in short gasps. I realized that Papa had won. He backed down the young man on the other boat. I didn't know whether to fear my father for his unpredictable action, or feel a sense of pride because he stood up to the other fisherman.

We never knew what our lines might pull in. We brought up lots of tuna, but we also pulled in barracuda, which are a nasty fish, wahoo, sea bass, dorado and an occasional shark. The sharks were worse poachers than the sea lions, but harder to deal with. Because they didn't come to the surface where he could shoot them, Papa had to take other measures.

When we brought a shark in on a line, Papa either cut the line, or just let the line go and drag the shark behind the boat all day. After we were done fishing for the day, he pulled in that line and the shark was dead. It suffocated because it couldn't sustain its breathing at the speeds at which we fished. Just to be sure, Papa always stabbed the shark with his sheath knife before he tried to remove the hook.

One of Papa's old fishing buddies had a run in with a shark. Jim Trammel was one of Papa's oldest friends. Jim had been an old timer when Papa moved to Southern California during the war. Jim took Papa under his wing and taught him most of what he knew about tuna fishing.

Jim's boat, the *He-Crab* scared me. A converted World War II landing craft, it had a flat bow that had once been used to drop onto the beaches to allow Marines to charge ashore into Japanese machine gun fire. Somehow the boat survived the war and was declared surplus.

Jim, who had lost his boat to the bank after the tuna industry crash, bought the old landing craft and made a fishing boat out of her. I knew that she had a flat bottom and was not designed to navigate on the open ocean. Worse than that, the *He-Crab* had no bulwarks or life lines. When I was aboard her, I was always afraid that I might slip and fall over the side.

Jim was out fishing when he brought a shark up to the boat on one of his lines. We caught mostly what the Mexican's called bonito sharks. Jim pulled this ten foot beast that must have weighed one thousand pounds up to his boat. When he realized it was a shark, he let it drop back and dragged it around all day.

At the end of the day, he went to retrieve his fishing lines and pulled the shark in. It looked helpless enough at the end of his line, lying motionless in the water.

"Careful with the thing, Jim," his deck hand said.

"I cain't bear to lose a good lure," Jim replied as he reached into the shark's mouth to retrieve his jig. The shark came to life and chomped down on his arm, taking his hand off at the wrist.

Jim's helper put a tourniquet on his wrist and called the Coast Guard

"Mayday, mayday, mayday. This is the fishing vessel *He-Crab* with a medical emergency."

"*He-Crab*, this is the US Coast Guard, San Diego. Please state the nature of your emergency."

"My skipper just got his hand bit off by a shark."

"Have you applied first aid?"

"Yeah, I got a tourniquet on it, but he's a mess."

"Very good, *He-Crab*, I'll dispatch a Catalina Flying Boat down to pick him up and get him to a hospital." This was before they used helicopters. "Please state your position."

"We's about fifteen miles southwest of South Coronado Island"

"Roger that, *He-Crab,* rendezvous with the Catalina in the lee of Coronado Island."

The *He-Crab* took off for Coronado, as fast as her big Jimmy diesel would push her. Just as the deck hand got the anchor over her bow, the big twin engine flying boat swept in out of the north, circled the island and gracefully settled onto the waves.

It was a huge airplane and loomed over Jim's little boat. A hatch opened in the side of the flying boat and two Coast Guardsmen dropped a inflatable life raft into the water. The raft immediately inflated and the crewmen hopped in and paddled over to Jim's boat.

They came aboard and applied emergency first aid.

"Here, sir, let me give you something for the pain," the Coastie said, brandishing a hypodermic needle.

"T' hell with that," Jim retorted, "get me some whiskey."

They lowered Jim into the life raft and paddled him back over to the flying boat. Other crew members pulled Jim up through the hatch and the paddlers followed. They deflated their raft and pulled it aboard.

With the hatch secured, the big airplane turned into the wind. It revved up its engines and spray flew everywhere. The flying boat sailed down the lee of the island, popped up onto the step and gained speed. Finally, it slowly, elegantly, lifted off of the waves and was airborne. The whole operation hadn't taken more than half an hour.

They flew Jim to San Diego where he was treated and eventually fitted with a hook to replace his hand. When I met Jim, he had the hook as a horrible reminder of the power and danger of sharks.

"Hey, PC, come out here and look at this," Papa yelled to me early in the day.

We hooked a *bonita* shark on our outboard starboard line. Papa pulled it up close enough to the boat for us to see that it was about six or eight feet long, then he let it go. It had taken the tuna that we had on the line and the hook caught in its mouth. We dragged it behind us all day and left that line alone. As the sun set, we decided to call it a day. Papa pulled in all of the lines and coiled them down, saving the line with the shark for last.

When he pulled the shark up to the boat it was dead. Before he cut the shark loose, Papa took his sheath knife and sliced a couple of large fillets from its body. Then he shook the hook loose and let the shark sink into the boat's wake.

"I'm going to make a cioppino out of these," he declared.

I wasn't too enthusiastic about adding a new dish to my repertoire. However, I had discovered prawns, perch, flying fish, dorado and a bunch of other new fish that I liked, so I didn't make too much noise over the idea of a shark cioppino. Besides, if I complained, I knew he would just tell me "You can eat it or go to bed hungry."

That night we were close in to shore so we ran for

Todos Santos (All Saints) Island. We pulled in behind the island and dropped our hook in a little anchorage with a white sand bottom. Papa went to work at once in the galley.

I peeled onions, chopped peppers and cleaned the shark fillets. The shark does not have scales like other fish. Instead it has a tough, leathery skin. I sliced off the skin, washed the fillets and cut them into two-inch cubes as instructed. Meanwhile, Papa worked his magic with spices, vegetables and broth. He started some plain white rice to go with the meal. He dug out a big loaf of French bread and slathered the slices with butter and garlic, to be grilled later when a burner was free. And of course the dago red. I don't know how much wine went into the *cioppino*, but in keeping with his training, at least a half gallon went into Papa.

He belted out song after song in his beautiful baritone voice as he cooked. We usually started with "Anchors Aweigh," the official song of the US Navy. Papa often sang old songs that were popular in the Twenties and Thirties. As he drank more, there was always a chorus of "Danny Boy."

As our singing reached a crescendo, the *cioppino* was ready. We took the pan of *cioppino*, the pan of rice, the garlic French bread and our drinks out to the hatch cover. By then it was quite dark. There were no lights to be seen on the shore. There were one or two other boats in the anchorage showing their anchor lights and with lights still on in their cabins. It was a comforting feeling to see the other boats doing the same thing we were.

There was a big motor yacht, what Papa called "a floating gin palace," at anchor too. Papa and all of the other fishermen looked down on the "yachties." They were not seamen.

We scooped ladles full of the *cioppino* out into our big, all purpose bowls. The bowls, like all of the table-ware on the boat, were plain light yellow in color and made of heavy ceramic with USN and a fouled kedge anchor in large blue letters on the bottom. Broad and flat, with about a two inch deep rim they were used for all of our meals. Even if we were eating something that wasn't soupy, the edges kept the food on our plates when the boat was rolling.

I dove into the *cioppino*. It was warm and steaming in the cool night air. It smelled a little funny though. I hesitated, then took a bite. I immediately choked on it and spit it out all over the deck.

"It's awful." I cried, "It tastes like pee." Papa was not happy at my reaction to his cooking. He took great pride in his cooking ability, especially his *cioppino*.

"Well, you better eat it, because that's all we are having for dinner. If you don't eat this, you'll go to bed hungry."

"Then I'm going to be hungry. I'm not eating that."

Papa tried to convince me that it was OK. Then he took a bite himself. He had a little more control. He spit his back into his bowl. Papa's famed *cioppino* tasted like ammonia.

We didn't know what went wrong with his recipe. Maybe there was still some soap left in the pan from when I washed it the night before?

That was the only time in my life I ever saw Papa throw food away. He quietly took both bowls and dumped them into the pot, then walked over to the rail and emptied the pot of *cioppino* into the bay. We warmed up a can of pork and beans for dinner that night.

Years later, when I was in high school, I learned what the problem was. Shark is regularly sold and eaten as a fresh market fish. In the old days, before truth in advertising laws, restaurants bought blue shark and served it to their customers as swordfish.

The shark is an ancient animal. It was swimming in the oceans when the dinosaurs ruled the earth. Fossilized sharks from sixty million years ago are not significantly different from the sharks swimming in our oceans today.

It is a primitive animal. It does not have bones. Instead it has a skeleton made from tough cartilage, like your nose. The shark has a primitive nervous system. There are recorded cases of shark attacks where the swimmer guts the shark with a knife and the shark's nervous system is so primitive that it doesn't feel the pain and goes on ahead with its attack. The shark also does not have a urinary system as we know it. The waste products collect in its flesh and it "sweats" the urine out through its pores.

To serve shark, you need to soak it in fresh water for twenty four hours before you cook it to get the urine out. You do not eat it as it comes from the sea. Our *cioppino* was liberally seasoned with shark urine because we didn't know this basic fact.

We stayed at sea for weeks at a time. Our goal was to fill our twenty ton fish hold. We never did bring in a full catch; our time offshore was limited by our fuel and water supplies. We carried a couple of fifty gallon drums of diesel fuel on deck, but when we transferred the diesel oil into our main tanks, it was time to run for home.

If we were in Mexico, home was San Diego, but when we worked our way north, home meant Newport Beach. It was Papa's home base, where all of his friends lived and fished.

Mac was a mackerel fisherman. He still had an old stink pot called the *Aurelie*. She was old and worn out when Papa met Mac many years before. She was so decrepit that Mac wouldn't take her out of the sight of land. Because of this, he couldn't go out after albacore. Sometimes he crewed on other boats, but he preferred to fish on his own boat and sleep in his bed ashore, so he settled for the smaller paydays of a mackerel fisherman.

We just came in from a trip and were tied to the cannery dock in Newport Beach waiting to be unloaded when we saw what appeared to be a pile of driftwood floating into the harbor.

As it got closer, we saw that it was the *Aurelie*. Something was wrong. She was listing heavily to port and was riding very low in the water; her stern was virtually awash.

Papa was the first one on the dock to accept Mac's line when he pulled alongside. He and a couple of other men tied up the *Aurelie* and Papa jumped on board to find Mac. Mac was slumped down on the cabin floor mumbling incoherently. A look of horror was frozen on his face and his eyes stared blankly into space, like eyes that had seen something too terrible to acknowledge.

"Whiskey, whiskey," Mac croaked. Papa stuck his head out of the pilot house and called over to the dock workers.

"Whiskey, somebody, get Mac a bottle. Quick."

One of the cannery workers dashed into the building and soon emerged with a bottle of Canadian Club. Papa took the bottle and propped Mac's head up as he forced a slug between his lips. Mac swallowed with a gurgle and began to mutter.

"Mackerel, mackerel as big as porpoises, as big as whales."

"Everything's OK now Mac," Papa cooed. "Take it easy, man."

"It's a fact," Mac continued. "I been fishin' for thirty years, man and boy, and never seen such a thing. I never seen such big mackerel." He grabbed at the bottle and took a couple more swigs.

"All night long I been workin', tryin' to get up a school. I tried everything. I moved me light, I shifted me anchor line to the stern. I sang to 'em, I cussed 'em. I stood in the rack on my head. I turned the rack upside down but nothin' worked.

"Finally, me light went out and I give up. I'm gettin' ready to come in when I hear fish breakin' astern, big fish. Just for the hell of it, I throws in a handful of chum and holds me brail down in the water. There was a rush of fish that sounded like a school of whales blowin' all at once. They hit me brail an' went right through it an' leave me stand in' there holdin' a brail in me hands that's got no net on it." Mac became more and more animated. He downed more whiskey. Papa and the others looked at each other with rolling eyes. They had all heard fish stories before. I just stared in awe.

"I reach for another brail and throw in some more chum. There's another rush an' they take the brail right out a me hands and leave me standin' there bare handed.

"I lashes a line onto another brail sos this time I can recover me brailer if they jerk it outa me hand. I get three fishes in me brailer and I can't lift 'em aboard. I have to rig up the boom and gurdy to haul 'em in. The most I could ever get aboard by hand was two fishes.

"They leaped outta the water so high that some of 'em landed on the deck and some of 'em went clean over the boat." At this point Mac's audience was becoming skeptical. One of the cannery workers looked skyward and rolled his forefinger around his ear showing that he thought Mac was crazy.

"You see that broken glass in the deck house? A big one leaped though that glass and I beat him with a gaff and couldn't kill him. I finally had to shoot him with two loads of buckshot to get him outta the pilot house before he did anymore damage." This was getting out of hand. Even I started to recognize it for a fish story.

"Since midnight I been fightin' them big mackerels. I'm all brailed under. Me side hurts where one a 'em hit me with his tail." Papa felt Mac's side. He looked up at the cannery workers.

"Somebody better go for a doc. He's got three broken ribs."

"They got outta control," Mac continued after another snort of whiskey. "I had to get outta there before they sunk me boat. I dropped 'em down the hold and high-tailed it for home."

By this time, the cannery workers had lifted the hatch cover off of the *Aurelie's* fish hold.

"Holy shit," someone shouted out. "Them ain't mackerel, they's albacore."

Early in the morning, Papa was still sipping his coffee and I was hard at work on my hot chocolate. I looked out the deckhouse windows at the empty sea all around us. Then we heard a call on the radio that froze the blood in the veins of every fisherman in the fleet. The one word that can suspend all work and focus the entire fleet as if it were a single entity.

"Mayday, Mayday, Mayday. This is the *Sea King*, we've been rammed by the *Olympus* just aft of the deck house. We're all stove in amidships and we're taking on water." It was Bob. We knew Bob and his boat. The *Sea King* was a big old, wooden troller, probably sixty feet long. The *Olympus* was a big steel boat down from Seattle. She was even bigger than the *Sea King*.

We sipped our coffee and listened to the radio.

The US Coast Guard responded out of San Diego. They were dispatching a cutter and sending out a helicopter.

"A damned helicopter isn't going to help them," Papa said. "They're taking on water. They need to stop the leak." I knew that Papa could save them, he could do anything.

Papa flipped on the radio direction finder (RDF) and as it warmed up, he paced the small deckhouse. Finally, the RDF was humming and he got a fix on the *Sea King*.

"I know that we can't get there in time to do any good, but we've got to try to help." Papa set the new course into the crotchety Hill-Cunningham automatic pilot. As he moved the throttle forward to full speed he knew we could never make it, it was a hopeless gesture.

No one in the fleet fished that day. Everyone was glued to their radios all day long. As the day progressed, we got more of the story.

"Last night we shut down for the night and lay to," Bob told one of his friends. "The *Olympus* was just coming onto the fishing grounds and had been steaming south all night. Early this mornin' her hand on wheel watch was tired and sleepy and not keeping a very good eye out. He didn't see our riding lights."

The *Olympus* T-boned the *Sea King*. She rammed her just abaft of the deck house. The big steel boat going full speed smashed into the wooden boat and split her open. Water poured in.

Boat after boat pulled alongside the *Sea King* and either put pumps aboard, or ran long hoses from their pumps into the *Sea King* to stem the flow of the sea. But the sea kept pouring in and the *Sea King* kept sinking lower and lower in the water.

"*Sea King*, this is the *Marine View*," Papa said into our handset. "Bob, can you read me?" There was no response. Our damned little "Mickey-Mouse" two-way radio was so weak that they couldn't hear our signal.

"Damn, I know how to save that boat. If I could just get someone to pick me up, I can tell them what to do."

"Papa, why don't you call the *Cromale*?" Molly had the strongest radio in the fleet. "Maybe she can hear you and pass it along."

"*Cromale*, this is the *Marine View*, come in." Again no response.

Papa became more and more frustrated. "I know how to help them. They need to fother something over the hole."

"What's fathering?"

"Not fathering, fothering. It's an ancient technique that Chips taught me. It was first used by Fotherus in the Roman navy. Fotherus was a ship's carpenter. His ship was holed and to save the ship, Fotherus took a sail and worked it over the bow of the ship. Then he moved it down the ship until it was over the hole. The pressure from the water on the outside of the hull pushed the sail into the hole in the ship and sealed it off. It was such an effective technique that they named it after

Fotherus.

"We have a couple of pieces of plywood on board that we could push down over the hole, but anything would work. They could use a mattress or something. The water pressure would push it against the hull and seal the leak. If I could only get someone to respond."

All day long we ran towards the *Sea King*. All day long we heard the progress of the rescue effort. We heard the Coast Guard cutter's progress; they would never make it there in time. The Coast Guard helicopter dropped gasoline powered pumps and survival equipment. The *Olympus* stood alongside and rendered assistance. Other boats in the fleet kept coming on line saying that they were approaching the site of the accident.

Papa got more and more frustrated. He was like a caged animal. He paced back and forth, he went out on deck, he fiddled in the engine room. Every half hour or so, he went back to our radio and tried to raise somebody. He never got a response.

Things were getting worse on the *Sea King*. She was taking on more water and the pumps couldn't keep up. The Coast Guard helicopter took off the injured crew members, but Bob, who had a broken arm, wouldn't leave his boat. The *Olympus* apparently suffered no damage.

A fleet of boats gathered around the *Sea King*. Nothing anyone tried could help. Papa yelled into the radio, but no one heard.

The radio was alive with voices, everyone wanting to know what was happening or to tell their version of the story. Every now and then Bob or the Coast Guard came on the air and everyone else went quiet. The tension mounted. It was a losing cause.

Papa knew he could save the *Sea King* if only he could get close enough to raise someone on the radio.

I made us some sandwiches for lunch. Papa hardly

touched his. A couple of hours later, we heard what we dreaded.

"Well, boys, this is Bob. We lost her. The *Sea King* just went down. I'm broadcasting from the *Olympus*. Thank you all for helping."

We got to the scene a half hour later. There were hundreds of boats milling around on the sea, doing nothing. The Coast Guard cutter arrived and took Bob and the remainder of his crew off the *Olympus*. There was an air of sadness. A noble lady just died and no one knew what to do next.

"I could have saved her," Papa's voice cracked, his eyes were moist. "I could have saved her if I could have reached someone at the scene."

The next day life resumed. We went back to our regular routines, dropping our lines and pulling fish. Papa and all of his friends stoically accepted the loss of the *Sea King*. Part of the fishing life was the loss of boats and friends. You took a moment to remember them, then you went on with life, but you always honored their memory.

The *Marine View* was not a good fishing boat. We never had any record catches or big days. The most I ever remember catching in one day was about thirty fish. We listened to the two-way radio at night and the other skippers talked about being "over the hump." They pulled in more than one hundred fish that day. Still, a thirty fish day was a big day for me. That was three dollars in my pocket. More money than I knew what to do with.

We didn't make big money that summer. We covered expenses and made equivalent to what Papa would have made if he had been working at a job or pulling unemployment insurance, but we didn't get rich. The goal, after all, was just to bring the boat north where Papa could sell it to some dumb landlubber that wanted to go fishing.

Chapter 18

Fish Stories

I not only learned about seamanship and fishing that summer, but I got an education about the people who populated this strange world. They were a mix of educated romantics, ethnic types following in their fathers' footsteps and displaced people struggling to make a living. It was on this canvas that Papa hoped to paint his epic novel. He spent much of the summer trying out his stories on me. I made a good audience; I listened hour after hour in total awe of these bigger than life heroes. He told his stories, honed them, changed them and then retold them. I don't know how much truth was left after the third or fourth iteration, but they got better each time he told them.

It was a slow day. There hadn't been much of a morning bite and the mid-day heat sapped our energy. We retreated to the shade of the deck house, keeping a sharp eye on the jig poles for signs of a strike. Occasionally, we caught a fish, but they only came in ones and twos. The fish seemed to be wilting in the Mexican sun too.

"*Beverly J*, this is *Provider*, come in Whitey."

Papa paid particular attention to the metallic voice coming from the Babel of the squawk box. "I haven't heard from Wes and Whitey in years."

"*Provider* here, go ahead Wes."

"Whitey, did you hear about Joe on the *Svetac*?"

"No, what happened?"

"He died last night. I guess his cancer finally got him."

"Joe Petrovich, now there's a name I haven't heard in a long time," Papa said. "I remember him from when he came south after the war."

"I don't remember you ever talking about a Joe Petro, Petro. . ."

"Petrovich. We used to call him Joe Son of a Bitch. No, I guess never did talk about him. It's important that a man learn to keep a secret. I guess I can talk about him now that he's gone."

"Who was he?"

"Joe, Yosef Petrovich, was a Slav, down from Anacortes, Washington. He grew up on his father's boat. His family came to America after World War I when their country was in ruins. They settled in Anacortes because there was a large Slavic fishing community already there.

"When the war broke out, Joe volunteered for the Army, even though he could get a deferment as a fisherman. He left his father and went off to fight Hitler. He ended up in the field artillery. When we met after the war, we had something in common. We spent many an hour quaffing beer and talking about the big guns." I remembered that Papa had been an officer in the field artillery.

"While Joe was off at the war, his father had an accident. He fell off of a slippery ladder climbing down to his boat on from the dock in Anacortes and landed on his back on the hatch cover. He broke his back in three places. When he healed up, he looked more like a question mark than a man. That was the end of his fishing career.

"When Joe got back, he took over the boat and supported the family. After the war the prices for albacore were so high that he started coming down here in the summer. His father was so messed up that Joe thought that the warm California winters would be better for him that the cold, wet Washington winters so he moved them all down here.

"For some reason, Joe never hit it off with the Italian fishermen. He had a feud with Rico Carelli on the *Bella Donna*. The *Bella Donna* was a big, new seiner. Joe's *Svetac* was an old wooded troller. If Joe hit a school of fish and Rico was anywhere near him, Rico made it his business to set on Joe's school. One time, they ran into each other at the Red Sails and got into a fight. Joe was getting the better of Rico when Rico's crew stepped in and beat the tar out of Joe.

"Joe fished with his nephew Johnny. Johnny's dad ran a machine shop and foundry up in Anacortes, but Johnny wanted to be a fisherman.

"Joe was in a hot school when the *Bella Donna* showed up. Joe knew that they're going to steal his fish, so he ran down to the fo'c'sle and grabbed his rifle. He fired a couple of shots over their deck to warn them off, but Rico was ready for him. His crew was all armed and they opened fire on Joe. They shot out all the windows in his deck house and filled his hull full of holes. One shot even hit Johnny in the shoulder.

"Joe got out of there and ran back to San Diego to get Johnny to a doctor. Of course, Joe didn't report anything to the Coast Guard. He was from the old country and didn't trust the authorities.

"When Joe got back to San Diego he called his brother up in Anacortes for help.

"I was walking down the dock when I saw Joe building something on the foredeck of the *Svetac*.

"'Joe, what're you building?' I asked.

"'Oh, nothing. Just a locker.'

"'That's a peculiar place to build a locker,' I said as I climbed aboard. 'That's a funny looking locker . . . What the hell?' The 'locker' was a cover over a small cannon.

"'Joe, what in the hell are you doing with that? You know that if the Coast Guard catches you, they'll have you up on charges of piracy?'

"'Charlie, you have to keep quiet. That bastard Carelli, he shot up my boat, shot my nephew. I can't let him get away with it. You can't tell anybody about this.'

"His brother cast a small brass cannon from plans they found in the library. It was a three pounder that used black powder to fire three pound round iron balls. It looked like something out of Horatio Hornblower.

"Sure enough, on his next trip out the *Bella Donna* found him. Rico started to set his net around Joe's fish. Joe's yells out a warning to Rico and Rico says 'What's a matter, you haven't had enough yet?'

"Joe and his brother ran to the foredeck and cleared away the little locker, exposing the brass gun. Joe loads it and aims for the *Bella Donna's* mast. His first shot took out their radio antennas. His second shot holed them. In a few minutes the *Bella Donna* was taking on water and going down.

"It wasn't unusual for a boat to just disappear without a trace. Joe dropped his cannon over the side and sailed on. The *Bella Donna* became one of the mysteries of the sea. No one ever learned what happened to her."

I grappled with this story for most of the afternoon. Finally, I had to talk to Papa about it.

"What ever happened to Joe? Did the police catch him?"

"No, nobody ever knew what happened. They just assumed that the *Bella Donna* was lost at sea."

"But Papa, you knew what happened. Did you tell the police?"

"No, *Mijo*. You don't go to the police with something like that."

"But I don't understand. You always told me that I have to be honest, that if I see something happening and don't do something about it, then I'm part of the problem. How could you not tell someone? Joe killed those men."

Papa was silent for a long time. When he finally spoke

again, it was in a low soft voice.

"*Mijo*, you know that I grew up in the West Texas. In my day, if a man insulted you, or threatened your family, you strapped on a six gun and settled it in the street.

"Joe was an honorable man. He was protecting his family and his livelihood. Sometimes a man has to do what's best to take care of his family. You don't interfere with something like that."

"But you didn't say anything for all of these years. Does anybody know what really happened?"

"No, Joe's brother's dead, now Joe's dead. That just leaves you and me. That's the way it should be. You don't talk with anyone about this either. Let it die with Joe."

I didn't know what to think. This seemed to contradict everything Papa taught me about being a good citizen. I pondered on the story for days before my mind was finally caught up in other events.

"Wow! Look at that boat." I was staring at a little white fishing boat with red and green trim as she worked her way into the harbor. She was so different and distinctive from the rest of the boats on the float that she stood out.

"That's the *Virginia*," Papa told me, "she's a Monterrey from up in San Francisco. I haven't seen Giuseppe for years."

"C'mon you miserable old bitch," Giuseppe cussed as he fought to bring the *Virginia* in to the dock; he was always talking to the *Virginia*. The *Virginia* was a cranky old thing. Papa caught Giuseppe's lines and made the *Virginia* fast to the float.

Giuseppe was one of the Italian fishermen who designed and built a style of boats known as the Monterey. It is very Mediterranean looking with a clipper bow, low freeboard, a fan-tail stern, sweeping sheer and a raised trunk cabin on the foredeck that ends in a little pilot house. They were originally sailboats, but as the centuries changed, became motor driven.

They were named Montereys because they were first developed around Monterey, California. Many of these boats were still around and were quite old. Giuseppe's was ancient.

The *Virginia* had come to life at the turn of the Twentieth Century. She was originally propelled by sails, but sometime in the 1920's her owner converted her to a big old single cylinder gasoline engine. The engine had a strange rhythm, it went chu-chu-chunk-chunk-chunk, chu-chu-chunk-chunk-chunk. Joe said it was saying "She catcha de fish, she catcha de fish." This ancient, rusted piece of machinery seemed to be broken more often that it was working. Actually, nothing really worked very well on the *Virginia*.

"Giuiseppe, how long have you owned the *Virginia*?" Papa asked.

"Sheet, Charlie, it seem like all a my life. She was my old man's boat. I took her over when he retired."

Giuseppe came down out of San Francisco every year to join the fleet off the coast of Mexico and fished his way north with the tuna.

"She's not very big for a tuna boat. What is she, thirty feet long?"

"Hey, she's from a long line of seaworthy boats. She got no problem on the high seas."

"Well, you never seem to be out there very long."

"I got no refrigeration. The ice only lasts about a week or so, but that's OK cause the fish hold don't hold that much and my fuel tanks only let me stay out a week anyway."

Giuseppe was strictly old-school; he had no radio on his boat. He joined the tuna fleet in late July as the fish moved up the California coast so that he could constantly run out to the fishing grounds, fill his small hold, and run back in. It wasn't that bad, really, because Montereys were fast little boats.

"Well, she's a beauty anyway," Papa said.

"She's a cranky old bitch. Sorry kid." Giuseppe always

complained about the *Virginia*. I couldn't understand why he would keep her if she was that bad, but it was a love-hate affair. "She got beautiful lines and great sea-keeping abilities, but all her equipments, they is old. She not like any of the modern boats with refrigeration and comfortable quarters. One of these days, I'm gonna sell her and buy me a modern boat."

Most of all he hated her keel.

"When they built the *Virginia*, the sons of a bitches laid down her keel out a green timber. When the timber cures, it warped. The *Virginia* has a wow in her keel; she always steer to starboard. You gotta be on top a her all the time to keep her on course. I couldn't use a automatic pilot if I had one."

Because the *Virginia* was such a small boat, Giuseppe fished alone. He liked it that way. He loved the solitude and the freedom. He had a second set of controls in the cockpit so he could pull fish and steer at the same time.

"OK, you cranky old bitch, we got this school to ourselves," Giuseppe told the *Virginia*. They were on the open ocean without another boat in sight. "We're gonna have a pretty good day."

"Whoa, this is one big son of a bitch." A huge albacore struck one of his lines. "Come to Papa," he said as he pulled it up to the boat and hooked it with his gaff hook, but he couldn't lift it aboard. He waited for the stern to lift and heaved, but the big fish wouldn't come.

"OK, we'll try something else," he said as he timed the next wave to come under the boat and stepped out of the cockpit onto the bulwark to give himself better leverage. He grasped the gaff hook with both hands and readied himself to pull in the big fish on the next wave.

"Yoww," The next wave didn't come. At least not from the direction Giuseppe expected. He leaned down to start heaving his fish aboard and the boat took an unexpected lurch.

Giuseppe lost his balance and tumbled head over heels into the water.

He plunged into the middle of the Pacific Ocean. As he went down, he kicked off his sea-boots, he knew that if his sea-boots filled with water, they'd drag him down, then he kicked for the surface. As his head broke the surface he saw the old *Virginia* steaming away.

There were no other boats anywhere in the vicinity, Giuseppe knew he was a dead man. He treaded water and stayed afloat for a long time. He watched as the *Virginia* got further and further away, then finally disappeared over the horizon. He said his prayers and goodbyes to his loved ones. He only hoped that someone would find the *Virginia* floating without a crew and learn what happened to him. That would give his wife and kids some closure.

He had no idea how long he was in the water.

"Damn, what's that?" After what seemed like hours he heard the grumble of a boat's engine coming towards him. Maybe someone in the boat's crew would see him and he'd be saved.

He turned towards the distant sound and waited for the boat to appear. Sure enough, chugging over the horizon he saw first the smoke from its exhaust stack, then a dark smudge, then finally he was able to recognize a boat coming towards him.

"Hey, over here," he shouted, waving his arms over his head, but there was no one to hear him. It was the *Virginia*.

Because of the wow in her keel, the *Virginia* steamed off in a giant circle. She would have gone around and around until someone touched her rudder or she ran out of gas. Now she was coming back to pick him up. Giuseppe knew he had only one chance. He gauged the course of his boat and swam to meet her. The *Virginia* serenely steamed past him. As she went by, he reached out and grabbed her fishing lines. Using the lines, he pulled himself up to the boat. Because she had such low freeboard (the distance between the water and the top of the bulwark) he was able to pull himself back aboard.

"You miserable old bitch, you came back for me," he said as he lay exhausted on deck. Except for his wet clothes and losing his sea-boots, he was none the worse for the wear.

From that day on, Giuseppe could not say enough good things about the old *Virginia*. "I'll never have another boat without a wow in her keel."

There were always chores do be done on the boat. In the evening, after we iced down the day's catch or in the afternoon when the fish weren't biting, we took care of the boat's needs.

"Take care of your boat and your boat'll take care of you," Papa told me.

A wooden boat twists and flexes as it rides over the seas. Things chafe and wear out. We were constantly on the lookout for worn lines, loose screws and the myriad of other things that could go wrong. Included in the regular routine was engine maintenance.

Our little Ford diesel ran virtually the entire time we were away from the dock. Since our main engine ran the refrigeration plant, we left it running in idle when we hove to for the night or when we were anchored close to shore. Over the course of a two week trip, the engine ran for over three hundred hours. Occasionally Papa needed to clean the filters and injectors or change the oil.

While we were in the engine room changing the oil, Papa started remembering his old friend Bob Poole. Papa loved to talk about Bob. Much to Papa's chagrin, Mama gave up fishing and stayed ashore when she had children. Bob's wife, Daisy, was another matter. Somewhere deep inside Papa, there was a streak of envy I saw when he told me the stories about Bob and his wife.

Bob was one of Papa's more colorful friends. He fished

alone on the old *Aphrodite* for years. The *Aphrodite* was a big wooden double ender with an ancient Buddha Diesel engine and a personality all her own. Bob, an educated man, loved to play the part of the crusty old fisherman.

Bob moored the *Aphrodite* in the harbor at Newport Beach. Newport Beach became something of a tourist attraction in the late Forties. After the war, hundreds of thousands of veterans and their families poured into Southern California from the cold eastern states after having been stationed in California during the war. These newcomers and their eastern relatives were eager for recreational activities. To take advantage of this new tourist boom, a tour company gave bus tours of various attractions. The quaint fishing village of Newport Beach was one of the attractions on the itinerary.

While Bob worked in the cockpit of his boat, he noticed the open "rubber-necker" (tour) bus coming down the street. The tour guide pointed out interesting sights to his gawking customers. As they came opposite the docks the guide swept his hand toward the boats.

"On your right, ladies and gentlemen, you will see the home of the Southern California tuna fleet. These treacherous little boats are taken far out into the Pacific by the brave fishermen you see before you. Often uneducated and illiterate, these brave souls pilot their frail craft far off-shore and back again without the aid of modern navigational equipment that they wouldn't understand, in search of the elusive albacore tuna."

Bob took exception to this spiel.

"That's damn right, you long-winded son of a bitch," he screamed up at the bus. "Nothing I learned at USC prepared me for the rigors of off shore fishing. Now, you get your damned ass outta here and don't let me ever catch you back on my docks, or so help me I'll break your God damned neck."

The bus driver took his cue and sped away as Bob

grabbed a gaff hook and rose out of the cockpit.

Bob told Papa and Art Hill about his encounter as they quaffed a brew that afternoon. After a couple of beers, he began to bemoan the loneliness of spending weeks at a time alone on the open ocean.

"Well Bob," suggested Art Hill, "you ought to get yourself a sea-cook."

"A sea-cook?"

"Yeah, find yourself some young girl that's dying to go to sea. Sign her on as your cook and you can have some companionship."

The idea sounded good to Bob. He put an ad in the local newspaper for a sea-cook and sure enough, several young women applied. He interviewed all of them and settled on Daisy.

Daisy was a big girl. She was over six feet tall and, though she wasn't fat, she was built like a line backer. Bob topped out at about five foot nine and weighed one hundred-sixty pounds. Daisy towered over him and outweighed him by about sixty pounds. She went to sea as his cook and before the season was over, they were getting married.

"Boys," Bob's voice boomed over the radio on the Silent Hour, "Daisy's decided that we oughta get married."

"Congratulations Bob," Art Hill replied. "It's about time you made Daisy an honest woman."

"As soon as we get back to Dago, we're gonna find a preacher."

"Why wait to get back?" another voice chimed in. "Hap's a licensed preacher. Aren't you Hap?"

There was a long silence. Then a quiet voice replied, "Yep. I guess my license is still good"

"You'll do it then," Art said. "Tomorrow at noon. A special Silent Hour. It'll be our first wedding at sea."

The next day, Bob and Daisy knocked off fishing early

and took sponge baths with sea water on the afterdeck of the *Aphrodite*. Bob put on fresh Balboa Blues and a white shirt. Daisy had a shore-going dress aboard. In her heels, she looked down at the top of Bob's head

"A veil. I have to have a veil." Daisy worried

"I got some fresh cotton netting." Bob said. "It don't even smell like fish yet."

Daisy used the silk rose she kept in the fo'c'sle as her bouquet.

At noon, they stood together, hand in hand, in front of their VHF radio.

"Ladies and gentlemen of the Southern California fish' fleet," Hap said, "we're gathered here today, or at least on the radio, to witness the union of Bob and Daisy.

"Hey Bob," Stu's voice cut in, "you got a ring?"

"No, I hadn't thought about a ring. I usually don't carry a selection of wedding rings aboard."

"Bob, and hi to you to Daisy, congratulations," Faith's voice broke in. "You have those little brass rings that we use to rig the leaders don't you?"

"Yeah, I have a bunch in my tackle box. Hold on Hap, let me go see if one'll fit."

A few moments later, Bob was back on the air. "Thanks, Faith. I got one that'll do the trick."

"OK, let's get on with this." Hap said. "Bob, do you take this woman, Daisy to be your lawfully wedded wife?"

They fished together for many years.

Daisy was tough as nails. Her brother was an all-state defensive end in high school, then an All-American at UCLA. After college he went on to a long career with the Los Angeles Rams in the NFL. All through his school years, Daisy was his tackling dummy. All year long, in any kind of weather, you could find Daisy and her brother practicing football in their back yard. Daisy was probably a better offensive lineman than most of the players on the UCLA team. She had to be to keep up with her brother.

Because of her big brother's athletic career at UCLA, Daisy was offered a track scholarship. She was the three time PAC-8 champion female shot putter and discuss hurler. When she graduated from college, she had no desire to stay at home and be a good little wife. She wanted adventure. She was made for the fishing life.

After the fishing season ended, Papa and his buddies were sitting around drinking beer.

"I've been having a hell of a time figuring out what to get Daisy for her birthday present," Bob offered, "but I finally figured it out."

"Well, what are you going to get her, Bob?" Papa asked.

"Daisy always wanted a Colt .45 automatic. I'm getting her one."

"Bob are you crazy?" shouted Art Hill. "If you give that crazy woman a Colt .45, she'll kill you with it."

"Art," Bob replied, "She don't need no Colt .45 to kill me. If she wanted to kill me, she could do it with her bare hands."

After a couple of years of wedded bliss, Daisy decided she wanted a baby. They had a strapping son. Daisy wanted her baby to grow up tough so she never dressed him in anything but diapers because she wanted him to be used to the cold.

"Bob, have you seen Junior anywhere?" Daisy asked. The toddler disappeared while they were at sea.

"No, Hon, I thought you were watching him."

They started looking for junior in all of the usual places.

"He isn't in the cabinet under the galley or hiding in the fo'c'sle," Daisy said. "I've already looked on deck."

"Let's look in the fish hold"

Finally, Bob and Daisy went down in the engine room.

"Bob, look." A pair of blue eyes looked out at them from behind the external flywheel on the ancient Buddha Marine

Diesel engine. Every time the flat portion of the flywheel came around they saw Junior smiling out. "Quick, shut the engine off."

Bob shut the engine down and reached under the flywheel to grab the baby. The bilge under the engine is where all the water that leaks into the boat collects. It also is filled with spilled diesel fuel and lubrication oil. Junior was coated in slippery goo.

"I can't get a hold of the little bastard" Bob said as he struggled with Junior. "Goddamn." He managed to get his hands on the diaper and pulled it out, minus the baby. Eventually, he was able to grab enough hair to jerk the young gentleman free.

"Look at him; he's coated in diesel fuel and lubricating oil from head to foot."

To clean him up, Daisy filled a sea bucket with clean diesel oil, set him in it and scrubbed him down. Then she drew another deck bucket of sea water from over the side and rinsed him off. A fresh diaper and the baby was on his way to causing new terror and chaos on board the rickety old boat.

We just had one of our better days. We were close to shore, so as I iced down the catch Papa took us into the anchorage at *Todos Santos* for the night. As we sat on the hatch cover eating dinner in the lee of *Todos Santos* Island, Papa told me the story of Sandy on the *Monterey*.

Everyone always waited for the big pay-day, Papa told me. There was a sort of gold rush mentality to fishing and fables abounded about boats that hit the Mother Lode. The fisherman's lore said that there was a mother school of albacore where the fish were so thick that you could walk across them. If only you could find that school, you could fill your fish hold in a day.

Sandy, he went on, fished with his brother Jack and young son, Tony on the *Monterey*. On a sunny Southern

California morning Sandy was the first one awake as usual. He put on a pot of coffee and stepped out onto the deck to relieve himself and take in the morning. As usual, he put the fishing lines over before he did anything else. As he stepped to the lee rail he already had a fish on the line.

A fish on the line was much more important than taking a leak. That fish was worth ten or fifteen dollars. Sandy ran to the cockpit to pull the fish. As the first fish of the day came aboard the sun broke the horizon. It was another glorious day on the gentle Pacific. Swells carefully lifted the boat, a light breeze played in Sandy's hair. The rays of the sun promised a warm day.

As soon as the first fish was aboard another hit the next line, then another, then another. In an instant Sandy had fish on all six lines.

"Hey Jack, get your lazy ass out here. We have fish on the lines."

And so the day began. Jack climbed down into the steel baskets that hung over the side of the *Monterey* and joined Sandy pulling fish. Tony took his place at the wheel and steered the old boat in a circle to keep it within the school they stumbled into.

Hour after hour passed. As each fish was brought aboard and the line hit the water, another took the jig. Fish began to pile up on deck. Sandy and Jack couldn't pull them in fast enough.

"Hey Tony," Sandy shouted over his shoulder as he pulled in a line. "Get out here. I need you to start stowing the fish in the hold."

Tony dogged down the wheel to keep the boat moving in a circle and went on deck to begin dumping the fish into the hold. An albacore is a good sized fish. Little Tony, who was about twelve years old, wasn't a big kid. After he fought the load of fish down the hold, he climbed down and dragged the fish to the bins, then shoveled a layer of ice over them. By the time he completed this task, he returned to the deck to find it over flowing with fish again.

"Goddamn, Sandy, when are we gonna get a break?" Jack asked.

"Don't even think about it, just keep pullin'."

Sandy and Jack pulled fish until they ached. Sandy never had the chance to take a leak, so he just went in his pants. They never had the chance to drink the coffee that boiled dry on the stove. They didn't eat breakfast and they didn't eat lunch.

"Tony, grab us a slice of that bread, huh," Jack called back. Tony dashed into the deck house and sliced a couple of thick slices off a loaf of French bread. He buttered them and took them out to the cockpit. Sandy and Jack opened their mouths and Tony stuffed in the bread. Sandy and Jack gagged and chewed and never stopped their rhythm pulling fish.

Fish after fish came on board. Soon their whole world consisted of pulling the fish up to the boat, hooking its gills with a gaff hook and as the boat lifted on a wave, using the momentum built up to heave the heavy fish over their shoulders and onto the deck, then release the line, grab the next one and repeat the process. Hour after hour they continued until their very souls ached. Their backs cried out in pain, their shoulders felt like they would explode. They were in the middle of the biggest strike in history.

All day long they pulled fish and all day long Tony dropped them down the fish hold, stacked them away and iced them down.

"Hey Pop," Tony called from the hatch combing. "The bins are all filled."

"Start stacking fish in the walkway between the bins."

The walkway filled up and Tony started stacking fish in the hatch combing.

"Pop, I'm gonna toss the frozen food overboard, OK? I need the space to stack fish."

Finally the fish hold was completely full and Tony couldn't get another fish below decks. Sandy and Jack kept pulling them in. Huge tuna flopped around on the deck.

"Pop, the hold's full, what ya want me to do now?"

"Start stacking them on the deck. Shovel some ice over them when they're up to the gun'nels."

Tony filled the area between the deck house and the gun'nels; he filled the area between the deck house and the hatch combing. Then he filled the side decks and the afterdeck. And still the fish kept coming aboard.

"That's it. There's no more room on deck Pop."

"Stack'em in the fo'c'sle."

Then, mercifully, the sun began to set.

In the Pacific fishing fleet the radios are on all the time. Throughout the entire day there is a constant chatter as one skipper is checking on another. Just before noon somebody went on the air and asked. "Hey, has anybody heard from Sandy on the *Monterey*?" No one had.

Twelve noon was the Silent Hour. It was an hour when everyone got off the air to hold a meeting. At different times different captains chaired the meeting. One season it was Joe on the *Argo*, another it was Hap on the *Happy Days*. That day it was chaired by Skip on the *Good Times*. His first topic of discussion was "Has anybody heard from the *Monterey*?"

The *Monterey* disappeared from the face of the ocean. No one heard from them, no one had seen them. Everyone was worried. Every year the fleet lost a boat or two, often with the crews. Everyone knew the inherent danger of going to sea in small boats.

A pall came over the fleet, then later that evening Sandy came on the air.

"Eureka. We done it boys. We hit the Mother Lode. We're in the middle of the biggest goddamn school of albacore you've ever seen. We've been pulling fish since before dawn.

They're still striking, but we had to pull in our lines and head for home. We got every inch of space on this goddamn little stinkpot covered in fish. I reckon we have twenty tons aboard. At two hundred fifty dollars a ton, that's over five thousand dollars. Not bad for one day's work."

In those days five thousand dollars was a lot of money. The best house in the neighborhood sold for about twenty grand. Stan Musial of Saint Louis Cardinals was the highest paid player in baseball history; he made about ninety thousand dollars per year. Ten years later, Dan Blocker would sign a new contract that paid him twenty thousand dollars per episode for Bonanza and it scandalized the public that one man made so much money.

Five thousand dollars in one day. It was unheard of. It was the gold strike of all gold strikes.

Every radio direction finder in the fleet tuned in to Sandy's broadcast. Within minutes the skippers had a fix on him and boats were moving in his direction as fast as they could travel. Everyone wanted to get a chance at his school.

But everything comes at a cost. The poor old *Monterey* was so loaded down with fish that her decks were awash. Water began seeping into her hold and engine room. Soon the fo'c'sle was filling with water. Too late Sandy realized their mistake.

About nine o'clock that night he came back on the air.

"Boys, we're in trouble. We got water coming in over the rails. We're throwing fish overboard to save the boat."

Half an hour later he came on once again.

"Boys, we're going down. I was just too greedy."

Chapter 19

The Great Race

There was a natural segregation in the Pacific fishing fleet. The oldest group on the coast was the Portuguese fishermen. They came from places like the Azores or the Cape Verde Islands. Whaling and the moderate climate originally drew them to Southern California and they were mostly based out of San Diego. The Italians were based further north in Monterey or San Francisco. From the far north came other ethnic groups. From Anacortes, Washington a colony of Slavic fisherman came south each year searching for albacore. From Ballard, in Seattle, came the big tough Scandinavian fishermen. The group out of Newport Beach were mainly "Americans." They were from places like the Ozark Mountains of Arkansas, the great plains of Oklahoma, East Coast locations like New Jersey, Brooklyn or Massachusetts.

The ethnic groups tended to stick together. When they wanted to talk, they hailed each other on channel sixteen in broken English, then transferred to their own bands and spoke their native tongues. As diverse as the fleet was, when someone was in trouble there was never any question of ethnicity. We all just helped one another.

Papa always carried most all the spare parts that we needed. We were usually the ones to help out other boats when they had problems.

"*Pices*, this is the *Marine View*." Papa was on the two-way radio. He had just overheard Big Bruce Johnson telling his friends that he was going to have to cut his trip short and return to port. He was running low on fuel.

"*Marine View, Pices*, go ahead"

"Yeah, Bruce, we're heading in tonight. You got enough fuel on board to last you four or five days?"

"Yeah, I figure we got about a week's worth left."

"We can pick up a couple of drums of diesel for you. That should be enough to get you home."

We ran into San Diego, sold our fish and re-provisioned. While we were at the fuel docks, we picked up two extra fifty-five gallon drums of diesel fuel which we lashed down on the afterdeck. Papa made arrangements to rendezvous with *Pices* off San Quentin Island.

When we met up with Bruce, we used our cargo boom to hoist the drums into the water. Since diesel is lighter than water the drums floated and Bruce pulled alongside of them. He wrestled them up to his boat with a boat hook, then picked them up with his cargo boom.

Sometimes the help came in the form of sharing knowledge. Many times I remember calls coming over the radio from a boat that was having engine problems. Some other captain, usually one of the old-timers, would give the calling boat instructions about how to make the repairs.

Many times a boat would need a spare part for something that had broken down. Being hundreds of miles down the coast of Mexico and often a hundred or more miles out to sea, getting spare parts was no easy matter. The drive line that drove our refrigeration plant had an insatiable thirst for V-belts. Because of this, Papa always carried several spares of each size on board. When Portagee John on the *Lucky Strike* lost his refrigeration, we were nearby and eager to lend a hand.

We met the *Lucky Strike* on the San Juan Sea Mount. Using the radio direction finder, Papa got a bearing on John and we rendezvoused with them late in the afternoon. On the open sea, with large seas running, we didn't want to raft up along side of the *Lucky Strike*. Papa brought the boat within hailing distance then let me throw a heaving line across to John.

The heaving line had a little iron ball that was about three inches in diameter and weighed about five pounds and on the end. The quarter inch hemp line was spliced around the ball to encase it in a monkey's fist. At the end of about fifty feet of quarter inch line Papa had spliced a fifty foot length of half inch line. I made the bitter end of the half inch line fast to one of the cleats on the after deck, then I coiled the remaining line in my left hand I took three loops of the line in my right hand, as Papa taught me, and whirled the iron ball and monkey's fist around my head. After several orbits, I let the line go and it flew across the water onto the deck of the *Lucky Strike*. John grabbed the line as it snaked across his deck so we had a link between the two boats.

"Hey Charlie," Portagee John yelled across the gap, "You got a pretty good deck hand there."

"He's about the best I've had, John." Papa replied. I nearly burst out of my shirt with pride.

Now Papa tied an oil skin package containing the V-belts to the bitter end of the half inch line and John pulled it across the water to his boat. When the exchange was completed, John heaved the line back to us and we were done. Another rescue completed.

No one ever expected to be paid back for exchanges such as this. We all knew that someday, we would be the ones needing the help. It didn't matter if you were Portuguese, Italian, Slav, Norskie or American, if you needed help, there was always someone to come to your rescue.

Because any of the ethnic groups were ready to come to your rescue didn't mean that they shared fishing information. When the Slavs hit a hot school of tuna, you could bet that they only told the other Slavs about it. That is what made it seem strange when Tryge Karlson started asking all the other skippers for sightings of schools of albacore.

Tryge (pronounced Trig) was a big Norskie based out of Fisherman's Terminal in Seattle. His boat, the *Freya III* was enormous. Papa and I were coming out of the harbor master's office in San Diego when we ran into a mountain of a man. Papa was a tall man but Tryge stood head and shoulders over him. He had enormous shoulders and thighs like tree trunks. His hands reminded me of catcher's mitts. Most of the Southern California fishermen were clean shaven, but long red hair and a fiery red beard gave him the wild look of his Viking ancestors. Unlike southern fishermen, he wore a plaid flannel shirt with the sleeves cut off over thermal underwear. How he could stand it in that heat I don't know.

"You Blue Water Charlie, ain't you?" Tryge asked Papa in his Norwegian sing-song accent.

"That's right, I'm Charles Wallace."

"I hear you a pretty damn good tuna man. My name is Tryge Karlson, I'm the skipper of the *Freya Tree*." Papa reached out to accept Tryge's enormous hand. "You like to see the *Freya?*"

"Can we?" I asked Papa. I was always interested in looking at other boats and the *Freya III* was easily three times the size of the trollers I was used to.

We walked along the dock in Tryge's shadow. He led us to a huge steel boat on the outer float. She had a blue painted hulled with gold trim and a big white deck house. Near the top of her mast was a crow's nest for a fish spotter with a huge pair of binoculars permanently fastened in place and triangular steel outriggers where jig poles would have been on a troller.

"She one hundred nineteen feet long," Tryge said as we climbed aboard. He saw me staring at the outriggers and explained. "We use the outriggers to lower the flopper stoppers. It make a more stable working platform."

He led us aft to the massive fish hold. I gaped in awe at the size of everything. As he climbed down Papa mumbled that it must hold over two hundred tons. Above the hold was a salt water ice machine. We had never heard of a boat that carried its own ice making machine. Forward of the fish hold, through a water-tight door, was the engine room. It reminded me of the engine room on the big Coast Guard cutter. Three GM diesels dominated the room, a huge main engine and two 80 hp auxiliaries.

"We carry enough fuel for a seven thousand mile range," Tryge bragged.

A ladder from the engine room led us up to the living quarters. There were a series of cabins for the crew. Each cabin held two men. I couldn't imagine having your own cabin on a fishing boat. The galley had a huge four burner electric range with two ovens, a double stainless steel sink, full sized refrigerator with freezer attached, fluorescent lighting, white paneling, and a work surface with built in cutting board. The sinks had hot and cold running water. There was a one hundred ten volt electric system throughout the vessel.

"We eat a lot of fish, har, har," Tryge laughed. "Cookie, he make Gravlax (a cured Norwegian salmon), salted herring, ludefisk, hallo fiskballer (fish balls), oysters, mussels, and smoked eel." It all sounded awful to me. The mess table was in what could only be described as a lounge, with books, magazines, a radio, and a phonograph. This boat had all the comforts of a luxury liner. Everywhere the walls were paneled with teak.

"Cookie, he got a private cabin. So does my engineer," said Tryge. "We got a desalination plant that makes fifty gallons of fresh water a day and a new flash hot water heater that warms the water as it passes thought it. We even got a shower in the head for the boys." That was unheard of.

Up another companion way ladder and we were in the

wheel house. At the aft end of the wheel house was the captain's cabin. Tryge had his bunk, his own head, a desk, book shelves and a dresser; all trimmed in teak and prettier than any yacht I had seen.

In the wheel house everywhere I looked there were new fangled electronic instruments. There was radar, a side band radio, VHF radios, a depth finder, a fish finder, and a radio direction finder. I hadn't seen this much electronic gear on the *Munashima Maru* or the Coast Guard Cutter.

The *Freya III* was a purse seiner. Papa always said "Our way of life is safe; they'll never build a net that can hold an albacore." Then in 1956 new materials started becoming available.

The old nets were made out of cotton twine. The nylon line used in the new nets was strong enough to hold blue fins, the huge three hundred pound tuna caught by the old tuna clippers. By the time I went fishing, tuna clippers were a thing of the past. They needed large crews and it took three men to haul in a single fish. With the new nylon nets, they could set around an entire school and haul them in with winches and machinery. Five men on a purse seiner could do a faster, more efficient job than twenty-five men on a tuna clipper of the same size. We heard of seiners that wrapped one hundred tons of albacore in a single set. Papa said that the new purse seiners were "damned fishing factories. They take all the skill out of fishing and make it a damned assembly line."

"I had her built at the Lake Union Dry Dock Company in Seattle," Tryge said. "It gonna take a hell of a lot of albacore to pay her off."

"How much does a vessel like this cost?" asked Papa.

"One hundred thirty thousand dollars," Tryge said without blinking an eye. Papa looked frozen. We couldn't even imagine how much money that was.

"Charlie, I need your help," Tryge said. "I'm new to the

tuna fishery. I'm used to halibut and salmon up north, but I hear there's a lot of money in tuna. I make you a deal. You spot a big school of albacore for me and I set on it. Then, I load your boat before I take a single fish for myself. You can get a full hold in a single day."

"Sounds interesting, Tryge," Papa said. "We'll keep an eye out."

Tryge invited us into the galley for a couple of beers (and a root beer), then we shook hands and wandered back to the *Marine View*. After we left Tryge, Papa poopooed the comfort and luxury of his ship.

"Air conditioning," Papa said. "Can you imagine air conditioning on a fishing boat? That barge isn't a fishing boat, it's a god damned yacht. Real fishermen don't need those things. Why doesn't that guy just dress his crew in dresses and put pigtails with little ribbons in their hair?"

"Are we going to help him, Papa?"

"It'll be a cold day in Hell before I give him the location of a fish," Papa said.

"Why? He seems like a nice guy, and he can fill us up in one day."

"You know the price of fish is based on supply and demand. Right now, the canneries are paying two hundred fifty dollars a ton. If that big barge of his lands two hundred tons of albacore, the canneries will be so filled up that they'll be working triple shifts. The price will drop to under two hundred dollars a ton for the next boat in."

The next morning we cleared Point Loma and headed back down to Mexico. I didn't give Tryge or the *Freya III* another thought for several days. It was getting late enough in the summer that the fish were working their way north. We had our lines in the water the first afternoon out and picked up a fish or two at a time. About three days out we started to hear Tryge's sing-song voice on the radio.

"*Lucky Strike*, this is the *Freya Tree*, come in John."

"*Freya*, this is *Lucky Strike*, go ahead"

"John, you see any damned albacore yet? I'm ready to start making sets."

Later that afternoon, Tryge was on the air calling Jim on the *He-Crab*, then it was Al on the *Misty*. From that point on, whenever we turned on the radio, Tryge was calling somebody, looking for a school of fish. When we anchored at Catalina Island, Papa talked to his friends about the situation.

"You know he needs a big school to make it worth his while to set his net?" Papa said to Hap. "It might take him all summer to find a school, but when he does, he can take the whole damn thing himself."

Five or six days later, we were in one of the best schools of fish we hit all summer. It was still before noon and we already pulled in over thirty big fish. That was over one hundred dollars worth of fish. As usual, Papa kept the radio on all day. Tryge had been on the air all morning, asking if anyone had found a good school. As usual, no one could help him, no matter how hot their school was.

Right about noon, Papa stopped what he was doing. He stood up straight and listened to the radio.

"PC, have you heard Tryge in the last hour?"

"No, I haven't heard him since he called the *Three Brothers*."

"Oh my God, he's found fish." Papa dropped what he was doing and ran to the deck house. As his hand closed over the throttle he shoved it all the way forward. "Pull in all the lines," he shouted over his shoulder as he pulled a chart from the rack.

I pulled in all the lines and coiled them down the way he taught me, then pulled in the jig poles. When I came forward to the deck house, he had the chart spread out on the galley counter and was plotting a course.

"What's wrong? Where are we going?" I asked.

"We're making a run for San Diego. That bastard is going to put a set around a school of albacore and fill his hold by nightfall. From his last position, I reckon he's about forty miles southwest of us. He can do twelve or fifteen knots in his big old barge. We can only do eight. We have to get to port before him. If we head in right now, at full speed and he heads in by eight o'clock tonight, he'll beat us in by an hour. We've got to beat him."

As we steamed northeast, Papa began to think about how he could make the boat go faster. We were bucking a swell, if he could run more east than north; we wouldn't have to fight the swell so much. That would be good too, because, when we hit the Mexican coast, we'd catch a slight north bound current to help us out. Once he had decided on our course, Papa started to think of other things. Our water tanks and fuel tanks were nearly full. We had almost two tons of water and fuel on board

"Get the emergency bilge pump out, PC," he commanded. "We're going to jettison our water." For the next hour I manually pumped all the water from our plywood water tanks in the fo'c'sle. When I was done, we were riding bow-high in the water because the fuel was stored aft.

"That's good, we must be getting almost an extra half a knot out of that," Papa said.

He stayed at the helm for the entire run into San Diego. He didn't trust the automatic pilot to keep us on the optimum course. The pilot steered by the compass, Papa was steering by the seat of his pants, judging each wave, making sure that we were always traveling at our maximum speed.

We ran though the rest of the day and into the night. As the night got later and later, Papa got more and more worried

"What if he passes us in the night?" Papa said. "If he gets by us in the dark, then there's no point in cutting our trip short. We might as well bite the bullet and keep fishing."

He knew that we would get a lower price when we came in, but we had already jettisoned our water; we would have to find more.

For his part, Tryge stayed off the air. He must have made his set and filled his hold. Then he turned his fast boat northeast and raced for San Diego. The sooner he got to port, the sooner he could get back out on the fishing grounds and start the hunt over again. He had massive payments to make to the bank and couldn't afford to have his boat to sit idle.

I cooked wienies and beanies because Papa wouldn't take his hands off the tiller. I ate while Papa cussed and swore at the boat, at himself, at Tryge and mostly at the fancy new equipment that put us in this position. After I cleaned up the kitchen, I headed down to the fo'c'sle to turn in. I lay in my bunk and tossed and turned. Sometime, late in the night I must have nodded off.

I woke with the morning light filtering down the companion way stairs. Quickly pulling on my shorts, I climbed up to the deck house. Papa was still steadfastly at the wheel.

"I don't know where the bastard is," he told me. "He still hasn't broadcast a word."

I started a pot of coffee for Papa and settled down to a bowl of raisin bran for breakfast. Shortly after seven am, we spotted the channel marker off of Point Loma. Papa steered the *Marine View* into the harbor and up the channel to the Bumble Bee Seafood cannery. As we cruised up the channel, we were both on the lookout for the *Freya III*. A boat of that size would be hard to miss. Papa let out a sign of relief, we didn't see her.

Along side the cannery dock, Papa wasted no time charging up to the manager's office to work out the price of our catch. He left me to supervise unloading our fish. I had never been in charge of unloading our catch before. Not knowing what I couldn't do, I went ahead and loaded the big steel buckets as they were lowered into our hold.

I was just climbing back up to the deck, when Papa came smiling down the pier.

"We beat the bastard. I got two fifty a ton. The cannery manager doesn't know about the *Freya* heading his way."

Papa joined me as we washed and sanitized the hold. When we climbed back on deck, there she was. The *Freya III* was just warping up to the cannery dock, low in the water with a full cargo of tuna. I was elated. I danced for joy as I felt like we cheated the hangman.

Chapter 20

The Summer Wanes

July melted into August. August quickly slipped away. The days shortened. The albacore worked their way north. We were fishing off the Channel Islands and albacore had been landed as far north as Astoria, Oregon.

"We're going to *Magdalena* Bay," Papa announced as we motored to the fuel dock in Newport Beach. *Magdalena* Bay was his favorite place on earth. "We're getting close to the end of the summer, and I want to see *Magdalena* one more time."

Baja California is a desolate, lonely place. It is one thousand miles of buff colored sand, dessert, tumble weed, cactus, scorpions and snakes. There are a few enclaves of human habitation, but mostly it belongs to the coyotes. There is too little water and too much sun, but along the coast, it has a beauty of its own. The ocean is a deep blue with clear warm water. Most of the time it gently laps on the rugged shore, but occasionally a storm blows in out of the northwest or, worse yet a Pacific hurricane, the dreaded *chubasco*, comes roaring out of the South Pacific.

Three quarters of the way down Baja California, about six hundred miles south of San Diego, the peninsula bulges to the west. Close to the mainland, around this bulge is a series of long, thin islands. *Isla Magdalena* is the longest of these islands and *Magdalena* Bay is in the lee of the island.

We'd been further south than *Magdalena* Bay earlier in the summer, but the fish were off shore and Papa wanted to make a big score. By the end of the summer, he was more concerned with an adventure than he was with the economics of fishing. It was a three day run to get there and a three day run back. We knew we would pick up very few fish on the way, but Papa's sense of romance and adventure were as strong as ever, so we topped off our tanks, iced down our hold and headed south.

"The entrance to the bay is through the channel between *Magdalena* Island and *Isla Santa Margarita*," Papa told me as we got close. "You have to be careful because there are reefs extending out from each island. We have to stay in the center of the channel."

As we entered the channel, I saw what Papa was talking about. At the southern tip of *Magdalena* Island is *Roca Vela* (Sail Rock). Just off of *Roca Vela* we saw the remains of a ship that had run aground on the reef while trying to cut the corner too close. In those days we didn't have depth finders, so Papa watched for kelp beds; the kelp always clung to the submerged rocks.

"After we clear the channel, we're going to turn north and make our way up the east coast of the island," Papa said.

The coast is Punta Belcher, a low triangle shaped piece of sand and dirt that extends out into the bay. To the south of the point we saw a few local fishermen's sad looking shacks.

"What are those things on the point?" I asked as we rounded Punta Belcher.

"They're iron pots, tanks, winches and the like that were left behind when the whalers left the bay."

"There were whales here?"

"Yes, from the 1850's up until the 1930's this was a favorite hunting ground for whalers, mostly Portagees from San Diego. In the winter, the gray whales made their way south from Alaska to breed in Magdalena Bay. In the early days, the whalers bragged that they could walk across the bay on the whales' backs."

Around the point, in a natural bight in the island, lies

Man-o-War Cove, the best anchorage in the bay. The water was clear and blue. We dropped our anchor in about thirty feet of water. I was surprised that I could see the bottom. The sea anemones and star fish stood out in bright contrast to the white sand. Crabs scurried along the bottom and fish swam under the boat. Dropping a fishing line over the side, I immediately caught two nice sea perch that we ate for dinner that night.

The weather was hot on our cruise down and I was sweating up a storm. I stripped off my clothes and dove in the water. Papa wasn't enthusiastic about going in the water so I swam alone. I felt like I was born in the water.

It was at least one hundred degrees on deck. The sea water was in the seventies. When I hit the water I had an immediate feeling of relief. I went in headfirst and sank deeper and deeper into the clear water. I always swim with my eyes open, so I could see the fish along side of me; they had no fear of humans.

The bottom of the sea looked like a forest, with all sorts of multi-colored plants and animals. The fish themselves were a rainbow of colors. Nothing in this magical wonderland was plain. Finally, my lungs ached and I broke the surface for breath. On the boat, Papa had his rifle on deck, watching for sharks.

I grew up swimming in the ocean off California. After spending a couple of years in Oregon, where you can't swim in the cold ocean, I was delighted at the buoyancy of the salt water. I felt as if I could float for days. In fact, there are many accounts of sailors who survived for several days in the ocean before they were miraculously picked up by another ship.

To my surprise and delight, a pod of dolphin swept through the bay. They leapt entirely out of the water, spinning in the air. They were in a playful mood, and cavorted around he bay, sweeping back and forth in a small group. At first I was a little scared as they came towards me, but they dove under me and I watched and followed.

The pod moved together as a single unit, then broke apart or cavorted on the surface, then reformed into a unit. I heard a high-pitched shrieking and a clicking in the water as they talked to each other. They flowed through the water without seeming to move their bodies. I was lucky enough to swim above them for a while, looking down onto their dark grey bodies. As they surfaced, I saw that their bodies were actually striped, dark grey on the top, a lighter, silver-gray on their sides and almost white on their bellies. They moved serenely along, letting me get within a few feet of them. They weren't large animals, not much longer than I was tall. I was used to seeing much larger dolphins in the open ocean.

Of all the sea life in the bay, the animals I found the most interesting were the big turtles. They were four to five feet long and about four feet across. They swam right along side of me or under me with no fear. They are air breathing creatures, so they surfaced at intervals to breathe, but spent most of their time feeding along the bottom.

Watching them swim was amazing. With their rear flippers together to form a tail; they do all of the work with their front flippers gliding through the water with the ease of an airplane flying though the air. When they found a tasty bite to eat, they dove on it headfirst, with their tails rising above them. Slow, lazy strokes kept them in position over the rocks where they grazed. Even close to the shore, in turbulent water, they managed to hold their positions over the rocks and eat. When they needed to come up for air, they made a few quick strokes and rocketed to the surface. They were truly in command of their environment.

A tiny run down and nearly abandoned fishing village sat sadly above the beach. The few fishermen took their *pangas* to sea from there.

The *panga* was an open wooden boat about twenty feet long with wide bows and rounded sterns. When the fishermen came home, they dried their catch on a series of wooden racks to prepare it for market. The village consisted mainly of men; I don't remember seeing any women. There were a few skinny, mangy looking dogs and some dirty boys though.

The fishermen in the village were poor and worn out. They all looked very old to me, with bent backs and missing teeth. Occasionally we talked with them as they took their *pangas* out or brought them in. They, of course spoke Spanish, and Papa was very limited in his Spanish. I, on the other hand, had to learn Spanish to talk with Grandma, even though English was spoken in our home. I was his translator, but I wasn't very good at it.

Each morning the *pangas* left for sea before daybreak, each evening they returned in the evening light. The fisherman steered their little boats up to the yachts in the anchorage and dickered with the yachties to sell their catch. Gringos always paid more than they could get from the fish buyer in San Carlos. Occasionally, a boat passed close to us and Papa yelled across to the fisherman.

"*Quantos Pescados hoy?*" (How many fish today?) Papa yelled.

The old fisherman in the boat cut his outboard and let the boat drift.

"*Fue un dia bueno. Tengo muchos pescados, y diez langustos.*"

Papa looked at me with a puzzled look on his face.

"He says it was a good day. He has a lot of fish and ten lobsters."

The old man held up a lobster in each hand.

"*Quieren langustos para tu cena?*"

Papa understood that he was trying to sell us lobsters.

"*No tengo dinero,*" Papa said and turned out his pockets. The fishermen in the bay knew that the American fishing boats rarely bought their catch.

The fisherman told us they had homes and families

somewhere else, mostly in San Carlos, a poor desolate village
further up the bay. They came to the fishing camp in season,
leaving their families behind

The land in Baja is so dry, desolate and worthless, that
it only seems natural that the people would make their living
from the sea. I couldn't imagine what made people want to live
there.

Papa decided to cruise up the bay to *Entrada de la Tortuga*
(Turtle Inlet) on the mainland side of the bay. A long spit of
sand protects this inlet and the water is shoal in the entrance.
We anchored outside the entrance and put *Corky* in the water.
As always, I took the oars and Papa sat on the stern seat giving
me directions. It was a long row through the entrance and up
the inlet. The eastern and northern shores were covered with a
mangrove swamp. To the west were wide sandy beaches.

We saw several black spots on the sand. The several
became dozens, then hundreds of moving black spots. As we
got closer, we saw that they were the giant sea turtles sunning
themselves on the sand

We came ashore on the sandy beach in the middle of
hundreds of the huge turtles. I ran up to the nearest turtle and
climbed on its back. The hard shell, covered with barnacles and
weed, made for an uncomfortable ride.

The turtle wasn't too happy to have a hitch hiker. At
first it turned its head and tried to bite me.

"Watch out for its mouth. Those turtles have a hell of a
bite," Papa shouted as he ran to catch up.

I pulled back my feet and grabbed a handhold on the
forward edge of its shell, behind its head. It turned and reached
back, then tried to dislodge me with a flipper, but I was out of
reach. It bolted for the safety of the sea. A turtle bolting on land
is an amusing thing to watch. It has all the speed and grace
of a garbage truck. I hung on and the turtle slowly worked its
way down the sand towards the water. On the land the turtle is

virtually helpless, in the water it is in its natural element. I was smart enough to jump off before the turtle was awash.

When we returned to Magdalena Island, we went ashore and walked up the beach. There was a terrible rucus around the point. It sounded like rush hour traffic back in LA. As we rounded the rocky point, we saw hundreds and hundreds of sea lions and sea elephants on the beach. They all seemed to be roaring at the top of their lungs, the sound was deafening.

These beasts grow to about twelve to fifteen feet long and weigh well over a thousand pounds. Their barking filled the air. When a big male happened into another's territory a fight ensured. They reared up on their hind ends and shouted at each other. I rarely saw them actually get physical, but they had great shouting matches.

As soon as the creatures saw us, they fled to the safety of the ocean, all of them, except for a half-dozen big bulls. The bulls, protecting their harems, charged us, or as close as a sea lion can come to a charge on dry land. Papa looked around for a safe way out and said "Quick, run for the rocks."

We ran to the rocks on the point and climbed up. Sea lions are not good climbers, so they sat at the foot of the rocks and roared at us for an hour or so before they lost interest and gave up. When the sea lions returned to the sea, Papa decided it was safe to come down out of the rocks and head back to the skiff.

To Papa, *Magdalena* Bay was the Garden of Eden. It was warm, with a constant sea breeze to cool it off in the evenings, the waters blue and clear. Sea life was abundant and civilization had not ruined it. In all the years after we sold the boat and he gave up the sea, he constantly talked about *Magdalena* Bay. He wanted to sell everything we owned and move down there. Another grand adventure.

After our vacation to *Magdalena* Bay, we settled back into fishing. We worked our way back north and soon were fishing off the coast of California. Most of the nights, we just laid to, but occasionally the weather was nasty and we ran for cover. The Channel Islands consist of a chain of eight islands running parallel to the California coast, roughly forty miles or so off shore. The only island that allows you to land is Santa Catalina. The others are either part of a national wildlife refuge or owned by the military. However, we could anchor in their coves and bays in bad weather.

On the southern end of Catalina, on the leeward side is a pretty little harbor with the island's only town, Avalon. Avalon exists solely for the purpose of grabbing tourist dollars. Since we didn't have any dollars to spend, we usually elected to anchor further up the coast in Catalina Harbor. Catalina Harbor was one of the favorite anchorages for the fishing fleet.

When the fish were close to shore we went into Catalina Harbor, more for the camaraderie than because we sought shelter. We always found friends at anchor there.

As we pulled into the harbor, Papa saw the *Aurelie* and motored over to her. Mac already had his hook down, so we tossed him a couple of lines and rafted up to him. I was excited because I loved listening to Mac's hillbilly accent.

"Hey Blue Water, good to see ya. C'mon aboard," Mac shouted over the roar of our little diesel. "How's fishin'?"

Papa held up both hands and extended all ten fingers, then he pulled them into a fist and extended them again. He repeated this once more.

"Thirty fish? Not a very good day, huh?"

"We haven't found a good school this whole trip," Papa replied. "Seems we just keep picking up stragglers."

It didn't take us long to tidy everything up and put the boat to bed for the night, then we climbed over the rail and onto the *Aurelie*. Mac was waiting with a cold beer for Papa. I had to bring my own root beer because he didn't have any soda pop aboard.

"Well, if the fishin' wasn't too good, how about I stand you to dinner?" Mac was known throughout the fleet as a good sea cook. He fed us fried chicken and fried potatoes that lived up to his reputation.

Mac and Papa talked late into the night. I curled up on the settee and fell asleep. When Papa shook me awake it was dark outside and the stars twinkled in the sky.

"Time to head for bed, PC," he said.

While we were getting ourselves together to leave, Mac got up, went down to the fo'c'sle, took one of the mattresses off of the berths and put it on the floor boards.

"Mac, what in the hell are you doing?" Papa asked.

"Well, Charlie," he replied, "this old stinkpot has already sunk on me twice. If I sleep down here I'll wake up when the water comes up over the mattress. I'll still have time to get up and pump her out, but if I sleep up here in the bunk, by the time the water gets up high enough to wake me up, it's too late."

I slept soundly in the *Marine View* that night, secure in the knowledge that our stout little boat wouldn't leak and sink in the night.

On another occasion the weather was kicking up, so we made a run for Catalina Island. It was a late summer weekend and the bay was full of pleasure craft. With the weather turning nasty, the rest of the fishing fleet was looking for cover too. The *Marine View* was nothing if not slow. We were one of the last boats to come into the anchorage.

The little boat basin was full. Everywhere we looked there were boats. We couldn't find a safe place to drop our anchor. Then Papa noticed a spot at the back of the anchorage that was wide open. There were no other boats around the spot at all. We didn't know why we were so lucky; maybe some big boat just pulled out. Whatever the reason we picked our way through the anchored boats to get to the spot.

Papa went out onto the foredeck to drop the thirty pound Danforth anchor. By this point in the summer, I was an old hand at handling the boat in general and anchoring in particular. Papa used hand signals since I couldn't hear him over the virtually unmuffled roar of the engine. When we approached our anchorage, he held both hands in front of him, palms down, to signal me to slow down. I took the boat out of gear and let her drift. She came to a complete stop and Papa dropped the anchor over the bow. When it hit the bottom he signaled me to reverse. I put the engine into reverse and eased back on the throttle. The anchor slid along the bottom for a few feet, then dug in. Soon the boat was standing still, even though I gunned the engine trying mightily to make it back up. The hook was down and we were secure.

We entered the bay at high tide. Exhausted from our day's work, we ate a quick dinner and dropped into our bunks for a goodnight's rest. I woke in the morning to hear Papa swearing.

"Jeee-sus Christ. Will you look at that."

I charged up to the deck house to see what was going on. The ribs of an ancient wooden ship rose all around us. The reason the other boats left this spot open was because they knew that there was a ship wreck here. We anchored inside the ship and when the tide dropped, we were surrounded by the ship's rotting ribs. Trapped in the wooden prison, there was no way out.

Papa was furious that we lost a whole day sitting in the stinking old ship waiting for the tide to rise. Sometime in late afternoon the tide was high enough that we could motor out of our jail and resume fishing. Our lesson here was to pay attention to local knowledge. If the locals aren't doing something, there's probably a pretty good reason why. Come to think of it, we didn't learn that lesson. We were to get another severe dose of lack of local knowledge later that summer.

Chapter 21

Point Sur

Days melted into weeks. The warm summer sun baked us and gave everything a lazy feel, but all things have to end. It was late August and I had to be back in Eugene in time for school to start the day after Labor Day. We had been off shore for thirty-one days and were running low on water and fuel. Papa knew that we had to go in, and that this would be our last stop. When we shipped out next, we would be starting the thousand mile trek north to Florence on the Oregon coast.

When we were at sea, we always navigated by dead reckoning. It's not as bad as it sounds. We knew where we were when we started. We knew how fast our boat could travel and we knew what our course was. Every day, every couple of hours, we checked our charts and marked our progress. The water conditions told Papa when we were over a sea mount or a bank. The temperature of the water told him whether we were in the Humboldt Current.

We had a general idea where we were, but we really didn't need to know our location anymore than we needed to know the time of day. If the sun was up and the water was warm, we fished. If we were in a school of fish, it really didn't matter where in the world we were.

At the end of the day, Papa said, "Well, PC, it's time for us to head in. I want you to chart a course for us to San Diego," then he went below and opened a beer.

I started by trying to figure out our current position. I watched Papa often enough that I knew what to do. I turned on the Radio Direction Finder and tuned in a station in San Diego, got a fix on them and plotted it on the chart. Then I tuned in a station in Newport Beach, got a fix on them and plotted that on the chart too. This is called 'triangulating." Our current position was where the two lines crossed.

Now I knew where we were. I drew a line from our position to San Diego. I used the parallel rules to walk across the chart from our position to the nearest compass rose on the chart and read the heading. Parallel rules are two clear plastic rulers fastened together with metal cross arms with little metal knobs on each ruler. The navigator can place the bottom ruler on his course line, them move the top ruler up the chart without losing the course. In this way, he "walks" the rulers across the chart to a compass rose where he can read the direction of his course.

After applying the correction for magnetic deviation, I wrote the course on the chart over the line marking our course. Then I took the dividers and measured off five nautical miles from the scale on the side of the chart. I placed one leg of the dividers on our current position and walked them along our course to San Diego. I counted the number of "steps" I took, multiplied by five and had our distance. I wrote this on the chart, then divided the distance by eight (eight knots was our cruising speed) to get the time it would take us to reach our destination.

"I have the course and time, Papa," I shouted down into the fo'c's'le.

"Put the course into the autopilot and take us home."

I pushed in the knob that activated the autopilot and turned the tiller until we were on our new course then I pulled out the knob and let the autopilot take over. Papa never checked my work or questioned my course. He had probably worked this out long in advance. It was a long run in. By my calculations, it would be early morning before we sighted land.

We had dinner as usual, then Papa told me to go below and get a few hours sleep. I would be on wheel watch at midnight. I climbed down to the fo'clse and snuggled into my bunk.

There are few things in this world as wonderful as sleeping in your warm, cozy bunk on a boat under way. You feel safe and comfortable. You hear the swoosh of the water as the bow cuts through the waves a few inches from your ear. There is the steady hum of the engine, far away on the other end of the boat. It is like being in the womb. I always slipped off to sleep in a matter of minutes.

It seemed like I just closed my eyes when I heard "Rise and shine. It's time for you to take the wheel watch." I reluctantly climbed out of my bunk and dressed. I climbed up the companion way ladder into a dark wheel house.

"Whatever you do don't turn on the lights, you'll ruin your night vision," Papa said. "Keep a sharp eye out. Remember, you won't be able to see other boats; you're looking for their riding lights. If you see a red or green light, then the boat is moving. If you see both a red and a green light, then the boat is coming straight at you. You learn to judge if you're on a collision course. If the relative position of the lights doesn't change, you're on a collision course, so come get me." With that, he went below and climbed in his bunk. With the lesson of the *Sea King* being rammed by a sleepy helmsman on the *Olympus* still fresh in my mind, I kept a sharp lookout.

I had the night to myself. I wandered out on deck and watched the stars. I stood or sat in the deck house and surveyed the empty sea. Nervous about my course, I must have re-checked my calculations a dozen times. On one or two occasions, I saw the white riding lights of other boats sleeping on the sea. Once I saw a green light moving off to our starboard side. Early in the morning I saw what looked like a floating city, an ocean liner passing by.

Sometime around three a.m. I picked up a flashing light, dead on our bow. "Papa," I called down to the fo'c'sle, "I see a flashing light."

Papa slowly got up and came up to the deck house. He gazed out of the windows at the flashing light.

"How long is the flash and how long is the pause?" he asked. I had no idea. I watched for the light. It flashed, I counted the seconds. Fifteen seconds between flashes.

Papa took me over to the chart and showed me the marking for Point Loma. It said "FL fifteen seconds."

"That's the light house on Point Loma," he told me. "We are on course to enter the channel at San Diego."

That was one of the proudest moments of my life. I charted a course from somewhere far out on the Pacific Ocean, out of sight of land, ran the boat all evening and night and arrived at our destination precisely when and where I predicted. We lined the boat up between the lights marking the channel and entered the harbor as the sun rose.

We motored directly to the cannery dock. As usual, we tied up and waited for the cannery workers to accept our fish. While we waited, Papa suggested that we walk up the block to a little diner for a real, on-shore breakfast.

I quickly brushed my teeth and made sure I was in presentable clothes. Then we climbed off the boat and up the ladder to the dock. I started to take a step and stumbled. I caught myself and tried to take another step. Again I lurched. I was staggering around like a drunk on Saturday night. Papa started laughing.

I wasn't amused. I couldn't walk. What was wrong with me? I tried again and nearly fell on my face. *It must be a brain tumor*, I thought.

Papa laughed. "You've been at sea for thirty-one days, "you need to get your equilibrium back. You're so used to the deck rising to meet your steps that you can't walk when the ground doesn't rise up to meet you."

This was the opposite of getting your sea legs. This is where the phrase "as tipsy as a drunken sailor," came from. I had to get my land legs back. Now Papa started to walk and he was stumbling around too. We staggered up the block and headed to breakfast. By the time we walked a couple of blocks, we were handling the land like old pros, you would have thought we were landlubbers.

When we finished breakfast and walked back to the boat, the cannery was ready to take our fish. They swayed the big steel buckets over our side and down into the fish hold. Papa and I dropped into the hold and started packing the albacore into the bucket. It was easier to handle the frozen fish than it had been when they were fresh. They were hard and not as slippery, but their eyes were dull and lacking color. It didn't take long to load a bucket. As soon as a bucket was filled, the man on the winch reeled it up and dropped us another. We soon emptied our load.

Papa went up on the dock and talked to the cannery men while I cleaned and closed up the fish hold. Then he came down and fired up the engine. My job was to cast off the lines, so I climbed up to the dock and untied the stern line, carefully coiled it and dropped it down onto the boat's deck. Then I untied the bow line and carried it with me to the ladder. I climbed down the ladder with line in hand so that the boat couldn't get away before I got on board and put one foot on the boat's rail. With my other foot I shoved off from the dock. We motored back over to the public floats.

We got tied up and walked back around to the cannery. Papa went up to the office and took care of business with the owner while I watched them unload and start processing our fish. Soon Papa came down with a wad of green bills in his pocket. They always paid cash.

"Well, PC," he said, "it's time for us to start heading

home. I don't think we'll have time to do much fishing on the way home, so let's get the boat ready."

The next day we steamed up the coast to Newport Beach, our base of operations all summer. We motored up to the public dock and rafted up alongside an old fishing boat that looked like it hadn't left the dock in decades.

Getting the boat ready was really not much of a task. We needed to clean her up, wash out the fish hold, and do routine maintenance on the engine and machinery. After fixing the little things that got broken on our last trip, we stowed our fishing gear and started packing for the trip home.

We brought a lot of stuff with us from Oregon that Papa stowed at Aunt Jewel's house when we went fishing. Now we had to retrieve the tools and equipment and stow it all in the boat's hold. While we were doing this, we said our goodbyes to Aunt Jewel. The next night, we drove up to Santa Ana to say our goodbyes to Mama's family.

We called Mama on the phone that night to tell her we were heading home. Long distance calls were expensive and we had only talked to her once or twice all summer. It was so good to hear her voice. I felt homesick just talking to her.

We still had the Ford wagon to deal with. We couldn't take it home on the boat so Papa put an ad in the newspaper and sold it to the first man who came to look at it. Now we were on foot. Anything that we needed, we had to get close to the marina so that we could walk back with it.

Finally we were ready. We sailed with the tide the next morning. As was our tradition, we had our last night ashore dinner at Len Yi's.

"Well, Mama Lee, this is our last time here. We're heading home in the morning," Papa told her.

"No, you no go. I like have you here. We like see boy. Here, you take best table tonight." All of the staff came by our table to say goodbye.

"Don't we get a menu?" Papa asked as she walked off.

"No, I order for you today."

Dish after dish kept coming to our table. I started the summer hating Chinese food and ended the summer eating all kinds of exotic dishes I had never seen or heard of before.

We rolled back to the boat so stuffed that we had trouble climbing across the old fishing boat to get to the *Marine View*. As was our normal pattern, we cast off from the old fishing boat and moved over to the Standard Oil dock where we filled our fuel and water tanks and got ready for sea.

"Before we hit our bunks we better make a quick check to see that everything is secure so that when we leave the harbor and start rolling around it won't go flying," Papa said. By this time, we were quite expert at this.

Early the next morning Papa brewed coffee and made hot chocolate. I rolled out of my bunk and got dressed. As the sun broke the horizon, we cast off from the fuel dock for our trip north. We motored up the harbor and past the stone jetty. It felt good to have the ocean rollers beneath our feet again.

A sense of sadness came over Papa. I knew it was because this was the beginning of the end. His agreement with Mama was that he would come south to get the boat and fish our way north. When he got home, he would sell the boat and use the money to start a business. He promised Mama that he would not go fishing again. This exceptional summer was his last hurrah.

We cruised northwest out of Newport Harbor for the last time and headed up the Santa Barbara channel towards Point Magu. As we rounded Point Magu, our course continued northwest between Santa Cruz Island and Oxnard on the mainland. The day went by and we chugged further and further from our fishing grounds. Late in the day we rounded Point Conception and adjusted our course to clear Point Arguella.

Our goal for that first leg of the trip was Morro Bay, the same Morro Bay where we picked Papa up from the hospital years before. Our boat was slow and we were steaming against the wind and waves. It was very late at night by the time we cleared Point Buchon and headed into Morro Bay. The huge haystack shaped black rock for which the bay gets its name stood guard as it has since time began.

We found the public dock in the dark and moored for the night. It was late and we were tired, so we dropped into our bunks without another word.

The morning dawned to beautiful late summer weather. The sun shone, there were no clouds in the sky. A light breeze wafted in from the sea relieving what would otherwise have been a hot day. Slowly the harbor came to life. Papa fixed breakfast and we decided to walk up to the marina to take showers. When you are traveling by boat, you never know when you will be able to take your next shower.

As we walked along the docks towards the shower with our towels and clean clothes in hand. Papa stopped dead in his tracks. He stared down at a beautiful, big gray fishing boat.

We stood and looked in silence for a long time. Tears formed in Papa's eyes. It was as if he stumbled upon a long lost child. I asked him if he wanted to go on board and meet the owners. This was something we did with many a good looking boat this summer.

"No, let's go take our showers," he replied.

As we walked away from the big gray troller, I looked back over my shoulder. Written proudly across her stern in gold script was the name *Aventura*.

We walked in silence to the showers. I knew that Papa was thinking about the *Aventura*. Finally, I broke the silence.

"Why don't you want to meet the *Aventura's* new owners? Don't you want to see her again?"

"No, I don't want to be reminded."

"Reminded of what?"

"Those were the best days of my life. I had everything then. Fishing was good, the canneries were paying high prices and you mother was different."

"Different? How?"

"In those days, she still looked up to me. She trusted me. I don't know . . . it's different now. Now she fights me every step of the way. I just want to make things better for the family, but she can't see that. She wants me tied down in some damned nine to five job, swinging my hammer every day. It's stifling me. It gets so closed in that I can't breathe."

While we showered his mood lightened and he began to talk again. I had heard most of his stories, but was always willing to listen again. He and Mama had high adventure aboard the *Aventura* and listening to him repeat his stories was like watching a favorite old movie again.

We returned to the *Marine View* by another route. When we got there I stood on the dock and looked long and hard at her. She had been my pirate ship, my Viking long ship, my fantasy vessel all summer long. I learned so much from her, how to steer a course, how to navigate, how to pull a fish, how to tie knots and bleed the air out of the fuel line on a diesel engine. But she was ugly, butt ugly, by comparison. I could see why Papa loved the *Aventura* so. She was not only functional and a treat to live on, she was beautiful. There are times in life when function and art merge and form a kind of beauty that was not intended but endures just the same. By comparison, the *Marine View* was a garbage scow.

Papa was quiet and sullen the rest of the morning. After lunch, when he walked up to the harbormaster's office to check on the weather, I decided to stay on the boat. As he sauntered off and I got out one of my sailing magazines and headed up to the foredeck to read curled up in the coiled anchor line. The sun was warm, the day quiet and pleasant. We had had a long day and a short night the day before and I was tired. Before I knew it, I was dozing.

I don't know how long I was asleep, but I awoke instantly as I felt coldwater closing over my head. I had rolled off of the deck of the boat in my sleep and fallen between the boat and the float. I hit the water on my back and as I looked up I could see the bottom of the boat closing against the dock as the wave action moved it back and forth. I was trapped under water.

I knew that if I didn't get out of the water on the next roll of the boat, I would drown. Righting myself into a vertical position, I held my breath and waited for the boat to start rolling away from the dock. As it started to move I kicked my feet to bring me to the surface, needing to time it just right. If I wasn't out of the water by the time the boat rolled back against the float I would be crushed by twenty tons of fishing boat.

Breaking the surface and grabbing the toe rail on the float, I pulled myself up and flipped onto the dry surface just before the boat rolled back against the float. I made it, I was still alive.

Back on the boat I went below to dry myself off and change my clothes, then hung the wet clothes over the rail to dry. When Papa returned to the boat he was so preoccupied that he never even asked me how my clothes got wet. I don't think he ever knew how close he came to losing his son that day.

Papa brought news from the harbormaster's office of a front moving in. We needed to get going to get around Point Sur, one of the nastiest spots on the Pacific Coast, before it hit. The folks at the harbormaster's office offered their opinions.

"I wouldn't go out there in this weather," the harbormaster told him.

"We're on a tight schedule," Papa replied. "We can't sit around here for a couple of days waiting for the weather to clear."

"Well, if you're gonna go, everybody stands out to sea goin' round Point Sur," he was advised

"Why's that?"

"Because there's a reef that runs out from the end of the point. There's shoal water for nearly a hundred miles."

"If we're going to beat this weather front, we don't have time to stand a hundred miles out to sea."

"Well, there's ten or twelve fathoms over most of the reef, but when the wind blows out of the northwest, the seas coming in from across the Pacific buildup there and it's a real mess."

Papa was in such a funk from seeing the *Aventura* and knowing he was about to give up the sea for the last time that he ignored the local knowledge like we had done at Catalina Island. We filled our fuel tanks, topped off the water tanks and headed back out to sea. It was a non-threatening afternoon, in spite of the ominous weather report. I couldn't believe that we were headed for foul weather; there wasn't a cloud to be seen.

We picked up a pod of dolphin as we rounded Point Estero. Dolphin always bring good luck to a ship. First there was a bubbling on the surface of the water; then I could make out their dark fins cutting the surface. As we got closer, a whole pod of dolphins exploded towards us. Coming at us from all angles, it looked like a fleet of submarines had launched their torpedoes at us. These friendly mammals bore down on our boat and at the last minute, split in many directions, some going starboard, some to port and some under the boat. Alongside the bow they jumped and frolicked in our bow wave. Easily keeping pace with the boat, they moved effortlessly through the water. The dolphin seemed to communicate with each other. They leapt out of the water, one on either side of the boat, at precisely the same time. It was a big game to them.

North of San Simeon, where Hearst's Castle is located, is

Point *Piedras Blancas* (White Rocks) and then Point San Martin. By the time we got to San Martin, it started to blow. A dark bank of clouds moved in out of the northwest and the seas built. The wind whistled through the rigging so loud that it drowned out the roar of the engine. The day got dark very early. Soon we had to turn on our running lights, but it didn't matter. We were not in danger of colliding with another vessel. No one else on earth would be dumb enough to try to cross the reef in that weather.

By six pm, Papa pronounced it a "blow." By nine pm it was a gale. Late in the evening, our little Mickey-mouse radio told us that winds had reached hurricane force. We were in trouble.

The seas built. Now, when we were in the trough, we looked out the deck house windows and couldn't see the top of the next sea. The wind was so nasty that the top of each sea was blown off and there was as much water around us in the air as there was under us in the ocean. The rain came down in sheets. It didn't fall, it blew in horizontally, like it had a will of its own, desperately wanting to turn us over. It pelted the deckhouse windows with the force of a shotgun blast. Everything was drenched.

A thunder cell moved over us. It started to hail. Our decks quickly were covered with a sheet of ice an inch thick. As the hail fell, it covered the deck house roof. Because of the curvature of the roof, designed to facilitate water runoff, sheets of ice flowed past our windows as they crashed to the deck.

The sky lit up with lightning. There was the smell of ozone in the air. The roar of the thunder overwhelmed us. It seemed to have a physical effect, knocking the breath out of our lungs. The hair on the back of my neck seemed to stand straight out.

The rigging started to glow an eerie green.

"Saint Elmo's Fire," Papa gasped. It is caused by massive

amounts of static electricity built up in the air. It glowed in the rigging, then started to trail behind the rigging like it was being torn apart by the ferocious wind. We looked like a ghost ship.

It was cold. The wind sliced to our bones. Even in the relative safety of the deck house we felt the affect of the wind and the cold. This monster storm swept down out of the Gulf of Alaska, bringing its frigid Arctic blast with it. Having spent the summer in the sub-tropics, we never wore more than a T-shirt and shorts or maybe jeans on a cool morning. Most of the time, I just wore a swim suit. Charred brown from the harsh Mexican sun, we weren't ready for this kind of cold.

We started putting on clothes. First, we added long-sleeve T-shirts, then flannel shirts over that, then sweaters. We put sweatshirts on over our sweaters. Then our heavy pea-coats and wool watch caps. I have never been so cold in my life.

With each new wave, the *Marine View* dutifully climbed the peak, and when we came out on top, she literally dropped into the trough. We were so high above the trough that when the wave moved out from under us we hung in mid-air. The boat dangled there for a heartbeat like in a Road Runner cartoon, then dropped ten or twenty feet and smashed into the trough, before it started to ascend the next wave. Each time we smashed down into the water, the *Marine View* shook to her ribs. Everything that wasn't nailed down went flying.

When the boat came out of the water, the propeller wound up to an incredible speed. As we crested the top of each wave, we heard the propeller whine as the engine cranked up, then we fell and at the bottom the boat impacted the water with a shattering blow. We learned the rhythm of the seas and managed to secure ourselves each time the boat dropped. As we climbed the next wave, I scrambled about the deck house and down into the fo'c'sle, securing whatever broke loose on the last drop.

We got the hell beat out of us. For hours on end, we

went through the cycle, climb a wave, come out on the crest, propeller howling, drop into the trough, slam into the water, then climb the next wave.

"Should we turn around, Papa?"

"We can't. The only safe course is to drive right over the waves. If we try to turn and don't turn fast enough, one of those waves will break over us and roll us over, then they'll swamp us and we'll sink. Even if we do manage to turn around, if a wave breaks over the stern it'll poop us and we'll go down. Our only option is to keep sailing into the waves and hope we can keep climbing over them."

For hour after hour, Papa stood at the helm. The Hill-Cunningham Automatic Pilot had long since become useless. Papa didn't trust me with this level of responsibility, so he manually steered the boat over each new wave. It took a great deal of skill to keep the boat on a course that allowed us to climb diagonally across each wave, then turn in mid-air and be ready to face the next wave when we hit the trough. We drove on through the night. All night long the horizon was lit up by flashes of lightning. Papa never flinched.

He sent me down to my bunk, more because I was less likely to be thrown around and hurt than because he wanted me to get any sleep. I didn't sleep, no one could. It was like being on the inside of a cement mixer.

Eventually night waned and dawn slowly broke. It was a cold, wet, limp dawn. In the daylight, the seas looked even scarier. The storm still raged about us. The sky was gray, the sea was gray, our world was reduced to the patches of gray that we could see from the deck house windows. The only break in the monotony of the gray were the white caps as the fierce wind tore the tops off of the waves. We dared not go on deck, with the wind and the waves; we would surely have been carried overboard. The decks were awash anyway, water burst over the bow each time we crashed down into the sea again and flowed like a river along the side decks and onto the aft deck before the *Marine View* finally shed it over her stern like a duck shedding water from its back.

There was no way to cook. Papa couldn't even have a cup of coffee. There was no hope of keeping any pot or pan on the stove for long. We had a box of Hostess donuts in the cupboard. I dug those out and we shared them. When they were gone, I found a box of saltine crackers. Any forays into the cupboards had to be well-timed and quick. I needed to get in and out as we climbed a wave, because if the cabinet door was open when we crashed down, the contents would be all over the deck in an instant.

The day dragged on and we continued to get pounded. Papa skillfully piloted us up each wave and down the next. Hour after hour the beating continued. The morning slowly drained away.

"I'm hungry," I told Papa around noon.

"There's not much we can do about it now. You'll have to do the best you can."

I managed to snatch a loaf of bread and slide out four slices between waves. After we crashed into the trough, I grabbed a jar of peanut butter from behind its rails on the shelf above the sink. Trying to spread the peanut butter on the bread in the tossing galley was a trial. Eventually I managed to cover two slices and dropped them into the sink where they would not fly away. Putting the peanut butter back, I had to wait for the right moment to open the refrigerator door to get out the raspberry jam. A small latch on the door kept it from flying open in the rough seas. I knew that as soon as I released the latch the contents of the refrigerator would spill all over the deck.

Somehow I was able to slide the jam out without making a mess. Spreading the jam on the bread in the tossing boat was another matter. I missed the bread and left a huge glob of jam on the counter, then I got it all over my hands. By the time I got the bread covered in jam and the sandwiches put together, I needed a bath.

Papa's eyes never left the windows. Early in the afternoon, I went down into the fo'c'sle and saw something that sent a cold shiver down my spine.

"Papa, we're taking on water."

"How deep is it?"

"It's up around the floor boards."

"OK, get up here and start the bilge pumps."

I climbed back up to the deck house and flipped the toggle switches to start the electric pumps going. I could barely hear the sucking sound over the wind noise, but to my satisfaction, the water in the fo'clse went down. I turned on the bilge pumps in each of the three water tight compartments and let them run for the remainder of the trip.

Still the storm raged on. The hours continued to pass. Afternoon melted into evening, then it got dark again. We began our second night in the teeth of that unholy gale.

"Fire up the Radio Direction Finder and plot our position again, PC," Papa said. Every few hours we triangulated our position and marked it on the chart.

I took two readings, and where the lines crossed on the chart I made an X and circled it. Then I wrote the time.

"Papa, we're five miles further south than we were last time." The wind and waves gained strength and we were actually going backwards over the bottom. If this kept up, we would eventually be blown back onto Point San Martin. That would surely mean a watery death on the rocks at its feet.

"Well, there's nothing we can do about it, we have to just keep on going," he said. All through the night we steamed on. Climbing one wave, then falling into the trough before we plowed into the next. Water came over our bow and ran back along the decks. The howl of the wind was a constant chorus.

Then the engine missed a beat.•
Our trusty little Ford diesel was the only thing keeping us alive. Without power, we would swing around into the trough and the waves would capsize us and swamp us. The engine hiccupped again. It had run for hundreds and hundreds of hours without ever missing a pulse. Now it was going to fail us?

Papa thought hard.

"It's either dirty fuel or air in the fuel line," he said. "If it's dirty fuel, we can switch tanks, if it's air in the fuel line, we have to bleed the line. We'll have to shut the engine down to bleed the line." Please, God, I thought, let it be dirty fuel.

The only way to switch fuel tanks was to go to the engine room. Papa wasn't going to let me go on deck, even though I kept telling him I could, and he couldn't let me steer the boat while he went back there.

Then the engine hiccupped again, and began to run rough.

"Take the helm. You have to steer diagonally up the swells. Don't let a wave catch you on the beam."

I knew exactly what to do. I grabbed the brass lever and took us over two or three waves while he watched. In the meantime, the engine sputtered like it was going to die. Papa opened the deck house door and slipped out onto the deck. He was gone for only a few minutes when the engine started to run smoothly again. It settled down into its normal cadence. Soon he was back at the deck house door.

"It was the fuel. This pounding we're taking must have stirred up the silt in the bottom of the tank. It seems to be running much smoother from tank number two."

By this time it was night again. Papa sent me down below to my bunk again. Once again I couldn't sleep. When I got up in the middle of the night to check on him, I stepped out of my bunk into seawater. With all three pumps running, the water was still rising. There was nothing else we could do.

Papa reached back and grabbed the handset of the radio.

"Mayday, Mayday, Mayday, this is the fishing vessel *Marine View*, over."

There was no response. We listened and listened and all we heard was static. In the storm, our little radio couldn't even raise the Coast Guard. He tried again and again but got no response. We couldn't even hear other boats talking on the radio.

"I guess we're in this by ourselves," he said as he hung up the handset.

On through the night we sailed. I wouldn't go down to the fo'c'sle again because I didn't want to get my feet wet.

Dawn broke on the second day. The seas seemed just a little smaller, the wind a little less violent. We trudged on. By early morning, we were making headway again. Finally, we rounded Point Lobos and headed into the relative calm of Monterey Bay. We had taken thirty-six hours to go thirty miles into hurricane force winds.

The *Marine View* rounded Point Lobos and Monterey Bay opened up before us. We steamed into the lee of the point battered and bruised. There wasn't a muscle in my body that didn't hurt. We had been tossed around so much in the storm that I stopped noticing when I slammed into a counter or bulkhead. Papa never complained about anything, so I kept my mouth shut. I had bruises all over my body, but in the early morning sunlight I could see that Papa had a large gash over his eyes. Something must have hit him when it flew through the air. He kept wiping the blood from his eyes, unaware that he was bleeding. We were leaking badly and riding low in the water. I was afraid that we would start taking water over our decks soon. The *Marine View* hurt as badly as I did.

Everything took place in slow motion. The sun broke

through and the clouds disappeared. Suddenly warm steam rose from our decks adding to the surreal atmosphere.

Looking for a place to tie up, we motored along cannery row. I was shocked. There were row upon row of sardine seiners moored in the bay, abandoned and rusting. The wooden boats had long red lines of rust running down their sides from iron fasteners that looked like trails of tears. The steel boats just had large patches of rust all over them. The fleet had fished the sardines out and the boats didn't even try to put to sea anymore. Old pots and modern seiners lay dying in the bay. There was an aura of sadness. It may not have been noticed by the shore dwellers, but for a seafaring man, it was tragedy.

We pulled into a public dock and asked where we could find a facility to haul our boat out of the water so we could repair the leaks.

"There ain't no boat yards around here no more. They've all gone out of business, unless you want to go to the yacht club and pay yachtie prices," an old salt told us. Finally, Papa met a man who said that there was a boat yard in Moss Landing, a few miles up the bay that was still in business.

We motored up to Moss Landing and made arrangements to have the *Marine View* hauled out immediately. She wallowed onto the marine railway car where we secured her and they hauled us out. I couldn't believe my eyes. As she came out of the bay, water poured out of her. Her bottom looked like a colander through which you drain a pot of spaghetti noodles. I couldn't count all the places she was leaking. How had we stayed afloat?

We were so tired that we didn't care. With the boat safe on dry land, we climbed into our bunks and slept. I don't know how long we slept, but it must have been the next day before either of us stirred. When we did wake, we had voracious appetites. Papa cooked everything he could get his hands on and we ate every bite.

It was a miracle we survived. There were over two hundred places in her bottom where the constant pounding had torn the planks loose or forced out the caulking and let in the cold sea. We spent the next few days replacing and refastening planks, caulking and painting. The month of August got away from us. We had not planned on having to pull the boat out and repair her.

We finally got her back in the water. Papa called Mama to let her know that we were all right.

"Hi Mama, we're in Monterey Bay at a little town called Moss Landing. . .

"No, we had some rough weather, but we made it OK. . . No, we're not in any trouble. . .

"The storm wasn't that bad. They exaggerate things on TV. . . I heard about it too, there were two boats that went down." Obviously, Mama heard about the storm and was worried.

"We had to haul the boat out of the water. . . Well, we took a pounding. We sprung some butt joints, we needed to refasten the bottom and re-caulk her. . ." Now Mama was starting to get the picture.

"I know that we're out of time. I could put Penny on a bus and send him home. . . No, Vicki, I can't just walk away from it. We came down here to bring her home. . ."

The conversation went on for a long time. Finally Papa said good-bye.

"Well, PC, I think we've had enough," he said as he hung up the phone. We're going to leave the boat here and head home."

Epilogue

Papa kept his promise. That fall he found a buyer for his boat. As he had hoped, he found an accountant who wanted a toy. Papa got five thousand dollars in cash and the second mortgages on two houses for the *Marine View*. He quit the sea again forever (for the third time) and devoted his energies to raising his family.

Mama used the cash to open the *El Sombrero* Mexican Restaurant across the street from the University of Oregon campus. It was an unqualified success. She followed *El Sombrero* up with five other Mexican restaurants in Eugene, all of which were as warmly received.

"At age sixty-two, I've finally learned how to make a living," Papa said as he retired from carpentering three years after our adventure. He turned the two second mortgages into a little real estate empire. Both borrowers defaulted on their payments and skipped town. Papa took over the principal position on both houses and he and I went in, cleaned the houses up and remodeled them. Papa rented them out and became a landlord. The business agreed with him. He built an apartment in the detached garage behind our big house, then divided our house into a duplex so that he had four rental units. Soon he traded his houses for larger properties. He ended up with two large apartment houses, several rental houses and duplexes, and a worm farm.

No, he never lost his taste for adventure. After the *Marine View*, Papa built the *Odysseus,* the *QE3,* the *Barbara,* all salmon boats, and finally, the forty-one foot ketch *Blue Water*. The *Blue Water* was Papa's brainstorm to make tuna fishing viable again. She was a ketch, a two masted sailing vessel with a huge fish hold. Papa planned on sailing her to and from the fishing grounds and only running the engine when he was docking in the harbor or to run the refrigeration plant. By saving on fuel costs, he would again make trolling for albacore profitable. This was when he was in his eighties. I have pictures of him at age eighty-five being hoisted to the top of the mast to repair a broken halyard. He was quite a guy.

May 15, 1993, Papa's ninetieth birthday. More than thirty summers had passed since our great adventure. It was a pleasant spring day in Eugene. Mama and Papa's cozy little house was full of friends and relatives. Paul and Mellie drove up from California. Santos flew in from South Carolina. I brought my family down from Seattle. Papa and I were on the patio, I was manning the grill, watching steaks cook, Papa sat nearby in a lawn chair.

"Here's the cake." Mama had aged well. Now sixty-eight, she could pass for fifty. Her long hair was still black, her dark skin smooth.

"Does it have a starboard list Mama?" Papa laughed loudly. The family joke was now a half a century old.

"Oh, Charles, doesn't that ever get old?"

"*Salud*," he said, raising his bottle of Budweiser. I grabbed my can of root beer (I still don't drink beer) and clinked his bottle.

"*Feliz cumpleaños*, Papa."

"*Mijo*, do you ever think about Point Sur?"

"All the time. It was one of the defining moments in my life." Before Point Sur, I was a little boy, always unsure of myself, always afraid. Since then I can honestly say I have never been afraid to do anything in my life. We talked of our adventure often; it created an unbreakable bond between my father and me.

"What were you thinking when we were caught in that storm? Were you afraid?" he asked

"No. Never. Not for a minute." I could see Papa's eyes, now clouded over with cataracts, moisten as he looked back over the years.

"Why? How could you have not been scared?"

"I looked up at you and you weren't scared. I figured that as long as you weren't afraid, I had nothing to worry about."

"I've never been so scared in my life," his voice cracked. "I cursed my soul that I had taken you out there to die with me. I never thought we would get out of that alive."

In all my life, I have never witnessed a more heroic act than my father standing at the helm hour after hour, with no rest, little food, little to drink, taking the beating of his life. And yet he hung on when many a lesser man would have just given in to the inevitable. He held our lives in the palm of his hand for thirty-six hours. He stared death in the eye and never blinked

CPSIA information can be obtained at www.ICGtesting.com
Printed in the USA
BVOW060822010512

288964BV00004B/1/P

9 781608 300723